THE LAST STONE CAST

THE GOLDEN MAGE BOOK THREE

C.G. GARCIA

I0525538

Fantastical Press

www.CGGarciaAuthor.com
Cover Design by C.G. Garcia
Model Stock Photography by Janna Prosvirina

ISBN-10: 0692529349
ISBN-13: 978-0692529348
Second Paperback Edition

For Max

ALSO BY C.G GARCIA

Fractured Multiverse
The Supreme Moment
Black Crimson (Blood Fire Chronicles Book One)
*coming soon

Old Souls Trilogy
Old Souls
The Ties That Bind the Soul
The Name Within His Soul *coming soon

The Golden Mage Trilogy
The Kingdom of Eternal Sorrow
The Man Within the Temple
The Last Stone Cast

CHAPTER ONE

A commotion outside his suite door interrupted King Diryan out of his troubled thoughts. The news of Domnae Eban's ascension to Ans-domnae following the death of Ans-domnae Raynor had been an unpleasant surprise that morning. Telling Aidric of it had been even more unpleasant, though necessary. He hadn't in the least bit liked the flash of barely contained rage in Aidric's eyes when he had learned of Eban's appointment.

The lad's deep-seeded contempt for the new Ans-domnae wasn't healthy, but there was nothing he could do for him if Aidric refused to speak of the reason behind the intolerable hatred between them. Until he did, the lad would continue to harbor that rage, allowing it to slowly eat away at his spirit until he either self-destructed or did something permanent about the

1

problem—likely something violent.

Diryan groaned as he rose from his chair to go investigate what was starting to sound like a shouting match. *Seni help me, the last thing I need is more trouble!*

However, Seni wasn't inclined to oblige him today. Before he could reach out a hand to the doorknob, the king was nearly bowled over by the door swinging open. Before he could growl out his outrage for the unannounced intrusion, his Seneschal marched into the study followed practically on his heels by a bedraggled man covered from head to toe in travel dust that quickly made the angry words die away forgotten on Diryan's tongue.

The travel-worn man was Valin, a mind-mage of considerable power, but more importantly, Lamia's Spymaster in Mihr. Only the direst of news would have made him risk blowing his cover to come to the palace to report in person instead of sending his message through various other means as was his usual protocol. That he had also felt that his news was too important to trust to relay properly through thought-speech was especially cause for alarm. Suddenly, Diryan knew only too well what was stirring in the wind.

"I think, Ion," Diryan said quietly, "that you should summon my councilors—and Aidric. I have a feeling that whatever news brings Valin here today will require a spell of silence before it can be revealed and would be best if it's initially heard by all of us. Tell them I shall meet them in the Council Room." Then, as an afterthought, he added, "Oh, and bespeak all members of the Circle, as well. Tell them to be prepared to come to the Council Room at a moment's notice."

Ion nodded briskly and immediately set about his task while Diryan motioned for Valin to follow him. To his surprise, as they entered the Council Room, Aidric was already casually leaning against the far wall beyond the long conference table and his designated seat as Mage-general.

"Did you fly down here?" Diryan asked him, shaking his head.

"If only I could," Aidric replied with a grin. "It would certainly make my life damned well easier! I was on my way back from Keldan's suite and just happened to be passing the Council Room when I received Lord Ion's summons." He glanced at Valin. "I take it Roderick is up to his old tricks again? Judging from the tone in Lord Ion's mind-voice, I wouldn't have been surprised to hear that someone had spotted Seni's hand coming down from the Thrones to destroy all of mankind."

"Seni forbid," Diryan said as he walked over to stand at his place at the head of the table while Valin headed for the foot where all informants of the crown reported. "We have plenty enough to worry about as it is if Valin has to report what I think he will."

Aidric nodded but said nothing as Diryan's councilors began to file in, all wearing nearly identical doomsday expressions as they took their assigned places. At Diryan's nod, Aidric proceeded to cast the required wards against magical attacks and prying eyes and ears. Once completed, Diryan motioned them all to take their seats save for Valin, who alone stared straight at the king across the table with dark, expressionless eyes.

"You may address this council, Valin," Diryan said formally into the following silence.

Wasting no time, Valin began, "I have come to report that Mihran soldiers are now, as we speak, on the march in Northern Mihr. From the bits and pieces I was able to overhear here and there, their goal is to besiege the Kemosian palace."

Seni help us all, so it begins!

There were several sharp intakes of breath, but Valin didn't seem to notice, the spy's eyes never flickering away from him. A couple of his councilors opened their mouths to speak, but Diryan held up his hand to silence them. He waved Valin to continue.

"It's a considerable force," Valin explained gravely, "consisting of at least two hundred thousand non-magical fighters, a third of those mounted cavalry and archers, and at the very least, one hundred adept mages, near as many mind-mages, and a handful of empaths. Every male within the Mihran borders that isn't in the cradle or a breath away from his journey to the Thrones due to old age was recruited."

Diryan's eyes hardened as several of his councilors cursed loudly.

Aidric merely nodded to himself as though he had expected no less. Of all the men present besides Valin, Aidric knew Roderick's mind the best. His councilors, however, looked as if they had suddenly been kicked in the teeth by a sleeping horse.

"Valin, how far away are Roderick's troops from the Mihran-Kemosian border?" Diryan demanded.

"About half a day," the Spymaster replied.

Diryan cursed creatively and then said grimly, "I was afraid of that. The troops we now have along the border could not possibly turn back an army of that magnitude! Even the whole Kemosian army could not match odds with such a monstrous force!"

"But *our* entire force combined with theirs can," Aidric added quietly.

As Diryan nodded reluctantly, understanding began to flash across his councilors' eyes as they began to realize the full enormity of Aidric's words. There was only one reason why Diryan would send out the whole of Lamia's magical and non-magical forces.

He rose from his seat. "Gentlemen, I do believe that the time has come when I can stall what is inevitable no longer. I had hoped for more time, but Roderick was never one to dally long." He turned to the Seneschal and commanded, "Ion, summon Horae Adorjan, the Circle, and several scribes to come here at once. Lamia's silent war with Mihr has come to an end—no, it *must* come to an end. If it's war Roderick desires, then by Seni, Lamia will give him one he will never forget!"

"But Your Majesty, shouldn't we discuss this more thoroughly?" Lord Talus surprised everyone by speaking up suddenly. Diryan couldn't remember the last time Talus had ventured his opinion before the other councilors had all spoken their piece. "Such an important decision should not be made in haste. Surely—"

"I am well aware of that, Lord Talus," Diryan cut him off, nodding at Ion to carry out his commands when Ion hesitated, halfway risen from his seat, "and I assure you, all of you, that this decision was not made hastily. It has been uppermost in my mind ever since my spies began to report the rising military activity in Mihr several moons ago. Roderick isn't a minor illness that will go away on its own accord given enough time. He is like a plague, a force which can be deterred for a while by a healer's ministrations, but will inevitably return to attempt to overwhelm the body until the healer intervenes again. Such a force will *never* be defeated until it is utterly destroyed! I, for one, would like to see the end of the plague which has ravished our lands for so long!"

Diryan's monologue was cut short by the arrival of the first member of the Circle.

"Why was I not informed of this meeting earlier?" Lady Gaelle demanded the moment she entered the room after Aidric had opened the shield.

Aidric openly rolled his eyes in annoyance, but Diryan was more diplomatic in his irritation of the intolerable woman. Never had he regretted his decision to approve the petition to promote her as the female representative of the mind-mages for the Circle as he did now. At a time like this, he just didn't need the added irritation of putting up with the woman's spiteful tongue.

"I ask that you take your seat, Lady Gaelle," Diryan said sternly, his eyes hard and full of warning. "All will be explained when *all* are present." There was no room for egos or personal vendettas today.

Her shoulders visibly tensing at the change in the king's demeanor, Gaelle wisely did as he directed without another word as the rest of the Circle members began to trickle in, all wearing similar looks of anxiety on their faces. Ion and Horae Adorjan were the last to arrive. Unable to thought-speak, Ion had been forced to fetch him from his chamber on the opposite side of the palace.

Horae Adorjan, a man of middle-age who still looked like a man in his twenties came adorned in his scarlet and gold robes of ceremony. The scarlet symbolized the blood that would inevitably be spilt during the war, and the gold represented Seni's light of judgment for all its participants. The symbol of the order of the Horae, a blood-red sword embedded into the seat of a golden throne, seemed to blaze on the breast of his robes with its own ethereal light.

In the Horae's right hand was the scroll which Diryan would have to sign in his own blood in order for his declaration of war to be noted and approved by these particular priests of Seni. In his left, he wielded the ceremonial dagger Diryan would use to bind his blood to his decision.

Diryan couldn't help feeling a little apprehensive when he took in the full effect of the Horae. *This is really happening*, he thought grimly as he rose from his seat to meet the Horae face-to-face at the foot of the table, proud that his stride exuded only confidence and none of the doubts within his heart. *I'm about to bind myself in a way that has not been done since my great-grandfather declared war on Rathtyan. All the lives lost in this war will be on my soul forever. Why, for the love of Seni, did this war have to occur during my reign?*

All those present immediately rose to their feet as Diryan greeted Horae Adorjan. Only the sound of everyone's anxious breathing could be heard as Diryan then proceeded to sink down onto one knee before the Horae, both hands positioned on top of his bent knee, to begin the *Kiai* Ceremony—the ceremony to declare war before the eyes of Seni.

Diryan gazed up at Horae Adorjan's expressionless face solemnly and began, "I, Diryan of the House of Lasha, King of Lamia, do hereby petition our divine lord, Seni, through the Order of the Horae, for permission to declare war against the evil that has the kingdom of Mihr within its grasp."

He continued to explain in great detail all the atrocities that King Roderick had committed during his reign and this last act against Kemos that he felt not only warranted his action to declare war, but also was his sworn duty to the kingdom by virtue of the treaty Lamia signed those many years ago.

Horae Adorjan listened attentively, although he knew, and everyone present to witness this exchange knew, that this formal petition was all just for the sake of ceremony. Horae Adorjan was well aware of the silent war between Mihr and Lamia, and he would have already put forth the question of war to Seni long before this summons. Therefore, when Diryan finished stating his case, Horae Adorjan was ready with an answer.

The Horae placed his hand firmly on Diryan's shoulder and said in a vibrant voice, "Your declaration, by the will of Seni, is granted, Diryan of House Lasha, king of Lamia. Rise."

As Diryan slowly rose to his feet to once again tower over the Horae, who was at least a handspan shorter, Horae Adorjan handed him the ceremonial dagger, its jeweled hilt covered with various symbols of warfare in the Ti'ar language. Diryan took the dagger delicately as though the lightest touch would shatter it, never once taking his eyes from the Horae.

Adorjan then held out the still-rolled contract of war between them, clenched within both hands and began to chant a strange incantation which Diryan had never heard before. The moment the last syllable left his lips, the Horae quickly released and pulled his hands away from the document, spreading his arms wide in presentation as the contract, now suspended in midair, unfurled in a flash of golden light.

Diryan flinched involuntarily away from the brilliant light, blinking his eyes rapidly in an effort to clear the little lights flashing across his vision. The chronicles of his great-grandfather, King Palles, had documented his own *Kiai* Ceremony, however the details of everything that had taken place were sketchy at best.

The chronicles had mentioned this mystical unrolling of the scroll, but failed to mention the whole theatrics of it. He could hear his councilors and the Circle muttering excitedly behind him in awed tones.

When his vision had cleared, he started as he looked at the suspended contract before him and saw that the words were glowing a brilliant, golden light. He suddenly felt like a child gazing in wonder at his first sight of magic.

"With your blood, you will bind your spirit to those who would serve your cause," Horae Adorjan abruptly said, dragging Diryan's attention away from the scroll back to the matter at hand.

He raised his eyes once again to the Horae, and drawing in a deep breath, he lifted his left hand, slashing his palm with a quick swipe of the dagger before he could think too hard about what he was doing. He was so numb that he hardly felt the sharp sting.

Then, as blood from the wound began to flow down his arm and drip onto the floor, he recited the ritual words, "With this, my life-blood, I bind my soul to my cause. I, Diryan Lasha, of my own free will, shed my blood as the first blood of many that will be shed in the coming war with Mihr."

Wondering at the steadiness of his hand, Diryan reached out and placed his bleeding palm onto the contract, his blood the only signature needed on the document. The moment his palm touched the parchment, he felt something akin to the shock felt when a healer thrusts a huge surge of healing energies into the body, only multiplied threefold. His back arched, and he opened his mouth reflexively to let loose a cry, but no sound emerged. Dimly, he realized that, like the words of the contract, he too was glowing with golden light.

Then suddenly, it was over, and Ion was at his side, grabbing ahold of his shoulders to stop him from collapsing to the ground. The contract had vanished from sight the moment he had removed his palm from the parchment. Bemusedly, Diryan realized that the wound on his palm had also disappeared, leaving behind only a thin, white scar as the only proof that it had been there at all. Not a trace of his spilled blood remained.

"A chair! Bring me a chair!" Ion shouted to no one in particular.

Several of Diryan's councilors jumped up and simultaneously reached for the king's chair. They all looked incredibly comical the way they practically fell over themselves trying to be the first to get him his chair. If Diryan's mind hadn't felt as if it had just been turned inside out, he might have laughed.

It was Aidric who finally shoved them all aside with a look of disgust and brought the chair to him.

Diryan sank into it gratefully with a smile for the lad, the room all the while trying its best to turn upside down and sideways at the same time. Diryan clutched the arm of the chair with one unsteady hand, and began rubbing his throbbing temple with the other.

"Seni help me that I'll never have to endure such a rite ever again…!" Diryan muttered under his breath.

"Majesty, are you well?" Ion asked anxiously, wringing his hands in his all too familiar sign of agitation. "Do you need a healer?"

"No need," Diryan replied gruffly, the effects of his ordeal thankfully beginning to diminish. "My wits are merely scattered. Just give me a moment to allow the effects of the magic to wear off, then I shall be myself."

Aidric patted him affectionately on the shoulder before returning to his seat. The Seneschal, however, continued to hover at Diryan's side, frowning and still looking unconvinced that his king was all right.

Diryan turned to the Horae. He was still standing in the same spot as passively as ever, his demeanor reminiscent of one of the statues of war heroes that lined Lamia's Temple of the Horae. He wondered if the ceremony had been completed—no hoped. He didn't think that his body would take another magical shock so well again so soon. He wasn't as young as he used to be!

As if reading his mind, Horae Adorjan nodded to him and then stated rather formally, "As is Seni's wills, I shall now take my place among the councilors of Lamia to offer my personal council during these dark times of war."

Voytek was instructed to bring one of the spare chairs to the head of the table where the Horae would sit—directly to the left of the king. However, before Horae Adorjan could take his assigned seat, a chair suddenly overturned and clattered to the ground with an appallingly loud crash as Aidric jumped to his feet and without a word, vaulted the table between Lord Talus and Lord Claudium, darting across the room towards the door as though he had suddenly been found guilty of treason and was desperate to escape the clutches of the headsman.

"What in Seni's name—" Diryan exclaimed as he rose unsteadily to his feet, staring after the Mage-general as though the lad had suddenly gone mad.

He cursed his disorientation as he proceeded to stumble after Aidric, stopping only long enough to command those from the Council that had started to follow to remain in their seats until he returned. Ignoring the protesting voices behind him, he hurried out of the Council Room in enough time to see Aidric skidding around the corner down the hall, heading towards the main courtyard.

14

Damn it all, what is it this time? he thought irritably as he staggered down the hall after Aidric, wondering why he had ever been born to wear a crown.

CHAPTER TWO

Aidius, Aidius, not again! Not again! Aidric thought anxiously as he ran in a full sprint across the courtyard towards the entrance to the Mage Hall. Several people lounging and soaking in the warmth of the suns or just strolling across the yard gazed at him curiously, but he ignored them. There would definitely be gossip tonight speculating why the Mage-general was racing through the courtyard as if someone had just told him that his suite was going up in flames, but that was something that he would have to worry about later. Right now, his main concern was reaching his suite and Allison, not squelching troublesome gossip.

In her frantic thought-sending, Raya had said that Allison was in the grips of another Foresight attack, and this one was three times worse than the one she had suffered that night on the Eve of the Birth of the

World. She had not been able to bring Allison out of the trance.

She is foreseeing the war, Aidric thought grimly as panting, he reached the door to his suite. *I'm certain of it!*

The first thing he saw when he flung his front door open was Raya struggling to hold Allison in a sitting position in the middle of his sitting room as Allison's body convulsed with small spasms. Allison's face was whiter than the marble floor she sat on, her jaw clenched as though she was in pain, and her eyes stared out vacantly at nothing. The prickling on his skin signaled that Raya was trying to magically bring Allison out of this latest attack.

Raya didn't spare him a glance as she said through clenched teeth, "My voice can't reach her! My mind-probes see nothing but illumination! She's aware of what's happened to her. I can sense that much. She's fighting, trying not to lose her sense of self, but I'm afraid that it's a losing battle!"

Aidric needed no further encouragement as he rushed over to them, unconsciously shoving Raya aside as he took Allison into his arms and immediately linked his channels to hers so that all the magical energy sent by Seni, Himself, would also flow through him. Hopefully it would relieve her overwhelmed mind and body and leave only the foreseen images, themselves, behind.

In the back of his mind, he wondered why Raya had not tried a similar tactic to reach Allison, but once their channels linked, he found his answer. A tremendous amount of magical energy instantly began to thunder through his body, and he frantically struggled to keep his mind from being overwhelmed as Allison's had been.

"Aidric, you fool!" he heard Raya's panicked voice say distantly somewhere within the illumination of power that threatened dangerously to consume his mind.

Then, there was no more room for anything but to fight the currents of energy as they crashed like rivers of fire throughout his body, considerably more than he had ever attempted to channel through both his body and mind. Somehow, he had to get rid of it, but he couldn't think straight.

Allison was far beyond helping him now. Aidric sensed that she was now using the last of her strength to cling to the tiny spark in her mind that was still *her* and not that blazing inferno of light and the images of a possible future. He knew that she couldn't possibly hold her mind together for much longer, sensing, through their mind-link, that she was weakening with every heartbeat.

Casting the energy forth to be absorbed by the air

was out of the question. Energy of that magnitude could very well level the palace and maybe even half the kingdom. Without a specific spell, the rogue energy would also eventually consume him and then backlash through Allison's channels and consume her as well. Even if he were able to get all of Lamia's mages to link channels with them to divide the flow of magical energy, the energy would still have to go *somewhere*.

At least a dozen implosion spells would have to be cast before the energy would be totally spent. However, the problem with that idea was that only he, the twins, and Allison knew how to cast such a spell, and at the moment, two out of the four couldn't spare the concentration needed for such a spell, and the other two were in the Council Room.

"THE MAGE-FIELD HAS NEED FOR SUCH ENERGY," an alien voice suddenly boomed in his mind, almost causing him to lose his grasp on what little reality he had managed to maintain.

The Mage-field? Whose voice had that been? It was a voice that Aidric had never heard, but at the same time, there was something uncannily familiar about it.

The voice was immediately followed by a powerful image of currents of energy abruptly switching course to flow in reverse up a series of corridors and through an opened door into a vast darkness until golden-illuminated hands reached out from what could only be the Mage-field as seen by Inner-sight and "caught" this flow of magical power, drawing it back deep within that chaos made of light. It was with this image that Aidric suddenly understood what must be done, although such a thing had never been attempted since no one outside the Providencen priests and until recently, four of the warriors mentioned within the Prophecy of the Six knew how a Mage-field was created.

What have I to lose that won't be lost anyway if I don't attempt to do this? was Aidric's last feeble thought before he opened up the "doors" in his mind that kept the flow of the Mage-field energy at bay, though he didn't reach for the energy of the Mage-field as was usual when he opened those doors in his channels. He used every ounce of his strength and concentration to direct the energy currents thundering throughout his body through those mental doors. Sure enough, he "saw" that the energy did indeed begin to flow into a vacuum of darkness as it had in the vision.

However, before he could even begin to feel relieved at this unexpected success, Aidric felt something begin to pull on the flow of energy that he was directing towards the Mage-field at an alarming rate with no signs of slowing down. In a panic, he slammed the "doors" shut in his channels even though some of the excess energy still remained. There was a tremendous explosion of light in his mind, and he suddenly realized that he was airborne a split-second before his back slammed into something solid and slid bonelessly to the floor.

Stunned, Aidric could only lie where he had fallen, wondering what had happened. His head felt as though it was about to explode, and the rest of his body throbbed as if it had been trampled by a herd of *antar and* crazed horses. Through ringing ears, he heard the sound of footsteps pounding on the marble floor and a cacophony of agitated voices.

A hand lightly touched his shoulder, and he forced his eyes open, startled when a pair of worried, smoky-blue eyes blurred into vision.

"Diryan?" he croaked out cleverly as the king breathed a huge sigh of relief.

"Lad, you certainly pick the worst times to try to earn yourself a few days bed rest," Diryan grumbled as a couple of healer's robes came into Aidric's line of sight.

Then, as Aidric hazily looked around at his surroundings and realized that he was lying near the marble column located at the southwestern corner of his sitting room, he remembered everything.

"Allison!" he cried as he tried to rise, ignoring all the muscles that instantly screamed with pain.

"—is in the same wretched condition as you are, although unconscious, but nothing that the healers say a little rest will not fix," Diryan said as the healers prevented him from rising with gentle, but insistent hands. "They say it's merely magical shock. Raya and a half dozen healers are attending her now, so relax. What I want to know is what in the name of Seni and the Thrones above happened just now? When I arrived here—it couldn't have been more than a couple of depths after you did—both your body and the Lady Allison's were glowing brilliantly to the point where neither I nor the Lady Raya could venture anywhere near!"

Aidric closed his eyes with a slight groan, resigning himself to the healer's ministrations, before answering, "I'm not certain. There, at the end, I may have lost control of my channels, but—I'm not certain. I linked channels with her in an attempt to relieve her of the great magical energies flowing within her mind and body, but they were more than my own body could channel safely. I tried to purge myself of this tremendous magical force by sending it to the Mage-field where it could do no harm."

"Whatever gave you such a foolish notion?" Diryan exclaimed, shaking his head as if to a very thick-headed child.

"A—voice," was all Aidric said, still unsure who

had spoken that solution into his mind. He opened his eyes and smiled at Diryan's expression. "Don't look at me like that, Diryan. It worked, however foolish, didn't it? Allison and I are still living and Lamia isn't leveled. What does it matter who it was that advised me?"

"Lad, if you were not already lying flat on your back, I would have felt inclined to knock you there myself!" Diryan growled. "Of course it matters! Alien voices whispering in your mind could cause all sorts of calamities! What if it was Roderick's still unrevealed spy that had discovered you in such a vulnerable state, and seeing his chance, strove to have you destroy yourself and the maiden?"

"You're beginning to sound as paranoid as me," Aidric replied with a weak smile.

Diryan merely snorted, but the lines of worry on his forehead didn't fade.

"Aidric!" Raya's voice suddenly interrupted, shouted from Allison's old room, he realized with a start. *How could I have not seen them carry her past me?* "Allison is conscious, and she refuses to allow the healers to give her something for her headache until she sees you! She's pretty agitated, so I think you had better come now even if you have to drag your arse down here!"

Despite the healer's protests that he shouldn't

move, Aidric stiffly rose to his feet with Diryan's aide, surprised that his body didn't hurt half as badly as he had expected once he had put some weight onto his legs.

"I'm certain that whatever it was that she has Foreseen has to do with our coming war with Mihr," Aidric explained to the king, leaning on Diryan's shoulder heavily as they hurried to Allison's room.

The moment Allison, lying pale in her bed surrounded by healers, caught sight of Aidric, she blurted out, "Aidric! Lamia has no time!"

She struggled to sit up, but as the healers had done to him earlier, they insistently pressed her back down onto her pillows. Still feeling somewhat trampled, Aidric shucked off Diryan's arm and limped to her side.

"You don't need to fuss over me," Allison insisted. "I'm *fine*—just a little shaken, but you have to *go*, Aidric! Roderick has a second, even larger army than the one heading for Kemos marching from another kingdom into Mihr across their eastern border!"

"But how does she know about the first—" Diryan began to ask but was silenced by a sharp look from Aidric. Several of the healers looked scandalized by Aidric's audacity despite the situation.

"How many?" Aidric demanded.

"I-I'm not sure," Allison replied uneasily. "In the

distance, the troops seemed to go from one end of the horizon to the other. I only *know* that there's considerably more men and women in this army than the one that you're already aware of, but not how many."

"No matter, milady," Diryan said, "but did you Foresee where this second army was heading?"

"No, Your Majesty," she said with a weary sigh. "I only know that they're marching into Mihr but got no sense at all of a final destination."

"But where did Roderick acquire such an enormous force?" Aidric wondered aloud.

Allison surprised them all by answering, "They aren't Roderick's troops. They're Mordant's. In one of my visions, I saw a man in shadow readying them to march. When he moved into the sunlight, I saw that it was the same mage that tried to kidnap me on the way to the Temple." She closed her eyes and shuddered. "I could never mistake that face."

When Allison opened them again, her gaze turned to the king. "I don't know if you know this or not, Your Majesty, but Mordant's crowned himself king, but of what land, I'm not sure. One of my visions showed Mordant assassinating a king, a short, rather plump brown-haired man, and holding whom I assume to be the crown prince—a boy around five years old—hostage."

"That could only be King Al'nar of Bar'taiver,"

Diryan stated, "but I didn't think that Bar'taiver had such a large military force!"

"They don't," Aidric said grimly. "Mordant is rumored to have some ties with the king of Rathtyen, so perhaps he recruited troops from him."

"We must return to the Council Room," Diryan said urgently, already heading for the door. "Aidric, I need—" Diryan hesitated, stopping in the threshold and eyeing Aidric with a worried frown.

"Diryan, I'm *fine*," Aidric assured him. "My channels may be a bit bruised, as is my flesh, but I'm no worse off than the last time I was on the front lines in Idona."

The king reluctantly nodded. "I want you to rally every mage, mind-mage, and empath in the kingdom and have them come to the courtyard," he instructed, no longer speaking friend to friend, but king to Magegeneral. "We need them on stand-by, ready to leave at a moment's notice until the final strategic decisions are made. Once that is completed, then return to the Council Room."

Aidric nodded curtly then turned back to Allison as the king left, took her hand that felt entirely too cold, and brought it to his lips for a light kiss. "Could I ask that you give us a moment of privacy?" Aidric directed at all the healers in the room without taking his eyes off Allison.

They all nodded and hurried out of the room, closing the door behind them.

"Don't you dare apologize, Aidric!" Allison said fiercely before Aidric could open his mouth. "I knew this day would come. We both knew. You serve your kingdom, and your kingdom needs you a hell of a lot more right now than I do. I'll be all right here. You know my healers'll make sure I don't lift so much as a finger without their say so."

Aidric smiled. "I believe it. And you're right. I'll not apologize for my duty. I spent the better part of my adult life apologizing for it." His expression turned serious. "I don't know whether I'll be able to see you before I depart with my troops, so I'll say my farewells now. I'll keep you informed on as much as I can through thought-speech, but you cannot bespeak me."

"I figured as much," Allison replied, clasping his hand in both of hers and bringing it down to hold against her chest. Aidric could faintly feel the beating of her heart. "I could accidentally call you in the middle of a battle and make you lose your concentration at a crucial moment."

He nodded. "As for now, I want you to rest. I don't know what Seni was thinking when he sent you a warning that your mind couldn't handle, but we all know he doesn't do anything for naught. Perhaps he intended for you to be too weak to leave the palace to join the battle, and for that, I'll be eternally grateful. Knowing that you are here at the palace safe from Roderick's clutches will be what I need to keep me going through the atrocities of this coming war. Remember that I love you, my little cat, and I pray to Seni that we'll see each other soon."

"I love you too, Aidric," Allison whispered hoarsely, tears shimmering bright in her eyes. "Take care of yourself, and may Seni bring you back to me safe."

Aidric felt his heart lurch painfully. That was the first time in all these long moons since she arrived in Lamia that she had ever called on Seni rather than her own god. Maybe that was a good omen.

He bent down and kissed her with so much passion that they both trembled.

"So little time to say goodbye," he whispered when they finally broke their kiss, "but I guess it will have to be enough."

She looked so beautiful, smiling up at him bravely through her tears. Aidric knew that he had to leave now before he started crying himself. It would not do very well for the psyche of his troops and the Council to see their Mage-general with tears streaming down his face! He straightened and released her hand reluctantly.

"I must go before Diryan begins to wonder if I'm

lying unconscious in some dark corner."

"Yes," Allison said. "I've kept you here long enough. Tell Raya, Selwyn, and the twins that I said 'bye since I probably won't get the chance."

Aidric couldn't resist bending down for one last all-to-brief kiss. "I'll do that. Until next time, little cat."

"Until next time." she echoed quietly, then more fiercely, "but I swear to you, Aidric Stanisnik, if you get yourself killed, I'll storm the Thrones themselves and drag you back by the scruff of your neck!"

Aidric had no doubt that she meant every word.

***

Aidric walked into the middle of a heated debate within the Council Room after completing his task. He only caught the end of what Lord Claudium was saying, but it was enough to tell him that the councilor and the Lord Commander were arguing over where the Lamian troops could be placed the most strategically.

Not surprising since Lord Commander Pyrs and Lord Claudium were, at best, grudgingly allies as neither one of them could stand the sight of the other. Word had it that they had slighted each other one too many times in the past, sparking the animosity between them, though they had done it so long and so often that no one, likely not even the men in question, themselves, knew who had insulted who first.

Lord Commander Pyrs also made no pretense of liking Aidric either since Aidric obviously always had the ear of the king where that was not always the case with him. Aidric suspected that the only reason Lord Claudium was civil to him was because it allowed him to indirectly thumb his nose at Lord Pyrs in a very public way. Aidric would have found the whole situation amusing if it hadn't caused him so many difficulties in the past.

Aidric quietly and as inconspicuously as he could made his way to his seat as the Lord Commander replied heatedly to Lord Claudium's previous remark, "That's preposterous! What need we place half our manpower at the Kemosian palace when the Kemosian army will be protection enough? That would only weaken the force of our initial charge! I believe a direct assault by the full force of both our magical and non-magical troops on the Mihran army the moment the first line of troops cross the Kemosian border will give us the upper hand from the start.

"Roderick won't be expecting an attack of such magnitude at the beginning. It's possible that such a vain creature as he believes that his army's movements have gone unnoticed by us. Perhaps we should even recruit half of the Kemosian troops for this surprise attack. A pity that we don't yet have the forces of Oleria, Sonon, or Sersia. However, in time—"

"It's not wise to already factor in help that has not been offered," Diryan warned. "Although our treaty with those kingdoms ensures them our help should they ever be invaded, remember that *they* don't necessarily have such a pact to aid each other."

Aidric had to bite his tongue to prevent himself from laughing at the man's astonished expression. Clearly, the Lord Commander *had* forgotten that fact, and from the equally stunned looks of everyone else, they had apparently forgotten as well. *Or perhaps they have always assumed that the treaty bound the six kingdoms to each other as they were bound to Lamia. A dangerous assumption, that.*

"There is also another variable you haven't considered, Lord Commander," Aidric said into the following silence, "the second, mysterious army that Roderick has secretly stashed away in Bar'taiver. We do not yet know what he intends to do with such a force."

Pyrs glared at him and gave Aidric his best "who asked you?" look, while Lord Claudium looked smug and the rest of Diryan's councilors and the Circle merely looked thoughtful.

"That is yet to be proven, Mage-general," Pyrs retorted darkly.

"It's been Foreseen by one with a powerful gift of

Foresight," Aidric replied calmly. "That is proof enough for me."

"Yes, Foreseen by *her*," Pyrs spat back. "How do we know that the Golden Mage won't ultimately cause our downfall by sending a large portion of our army chasing after phantom armies that so far only she has supposedly Foreseen?"

The moment the words left his lips, the Lord Commander suddenly seemed to realize to whom he was speaking since his eyes widened slightly, and he noticeably paled. Aidric merely raised an eyebrow, but for once in his life refrained from biting the man's head off. This wasn't the time for him to allow his personal feelings to control him, not when Roderick's first monstrous army was less than half a day's march from the Kemosian border.

It was General Caith, maybe the Lord Commander's strongest supporter, who surprisingly spoke instead. "Lord Aidric has a point, Lord Pyrs," he said quietly, his voice sounding alien to Aidric's ears since he seldom heard that voice at a level no lower than a shout. The Lord Commander suddenly looked dangerously close to bursting an artery in his head. "We have never discounted a Foreseeing in the past, so there's no reason to start now. I, for one, would rather have an army prepared for the appearance of a second army and it all be for naught than need an army to face a second enemy army and not have one prepared."

"Unfortunately, Roderick doesn't give us much time to prepare for either army," Aidric added. "I agree with the Lord Commander that a preemptive attack against the Mihran army the moment they step on Kemosian soil would prove to be the most effective, but I disagree that we should use our full force. There's just too many ways that battle could go wrong to gamble on leaving the palace with only the Kemosian army to protect it.

"At least a dozen of our mages, mind-mages, and empaths should be sent. Don't forget that Roderick has several mages, including Mordant, that can construct portals. The Lady Allison didn't Foresee that they will do so, but that doesn't mean that they won't or haven't done so already. Remember, Seni only reveals to us what he chooses.

"At least the distance won't be a problem, nor the different destinations of our troops. Remember, I have the power to construct and safely control more than one portal at a time."

Apparently, this was news to most of the Circle. Some of them, the dukes especially, looked started by this latest revelation. Their surprise made Aidric wonder if they really understood the extent of the power he was capable of wielding.

Aidric continued as though he hadn't noticed

their surprise, "I can have all our troops at the Kemosian palace *and* lined up on the Kemosian-Mihran border if King Diryan so chooses before Roderick's troops can even see Kemos beyond the horiz—"

As if on cue, Seer Penrith suddenly groaned and slumped over onto the table with a meaty *thunk* that echoed ominously throughout the room. Aidric was instantly on his feet and making his way down to the Providencen priest, while both Zenas and Aren, who were on either side of the Seer, were trying to decide whether to touch him or not. Across from Seer Penrith, Horae Adorjan's eyes glittered with interest. It wasn't often that any of the Horae were able to witness the magicks of their fellow Brothers.

With the help of Aren—the old linguist could only stare—Aidric eased Penrith away from the table into a more comfortable position in his chair. The Providencen priest's eyes stared vacantly off into whatever vision had him enraptured—an important one if Seni found it fit to send Penrith this Foresight while he was still among others that were not of his priestly sect.

Not a sound was heard while Penrith sat frozen in his visions. Even the Lord Commander had lost most of his earlier anger and was staring at Penrith with eyes full of wonder and anxiety. Diryan wore his infamous "why me?" expression as he, too, stared anxiously at the Seer.

Foresight delivered by a Providencen priest was seldom, if ever, good news. In fact, there was a popular saying in Lamia involving the Providencen priests and Foresight: "The earth will rain and the sky will bloom before a Providencen priest's Foresight will make a smile bloom."

A few depths later, or to Aidric, an eternity later, Penrith's eyes blinked and sense came flooding back into them. He didn't seem at all perturbed by his experience or by the fact that he was the object of every eye in the room. He did, however, have a slight smile on his face.

I believe we shall all be seeing flowers blooming in the sky next time we look up into the thrones, Aidric thought bemusedly and then brushed all further thoughts away as Seer Penrith opened his mouth to speak.

You would have thought that it was Seni, Himself, who now sat proudly in that chair ready to deliver a new revelation to the world the way everyone was eagerly staring at the Seer. Aidric could almost taste the anticipation in the air.

"Our divine lord, Seni, has spoken to me," Seer Penrith began in a clear, strong voice.

Aidric wondered why he hadn't been weakened or at the very shown signs that he had been affected by the experience, as Allison had, but he knew that the Seers would embrace the Dark God, Arioch, before they would reveal that secret.

"It is His will," Penrith continued, "that we, of this council, shall be granted the knowledge that indeed the blasphemer, King Roderick of Mihr, has a second army numbering in the hundreds of thousands preparing to leave Bar'taiver with the intention of capturing the palace of Na'ar."

There were many sharp intakes of breath as Penrith rose slowly and dramatically as though he was preparing to speak an even greater revelation. Aidric feared that it was the knowledge that Roderick had miraculously recruited the aid of a third army of the same enormous proportions as the first two, but his fear quickly turned to annoyance when Penrith spoke his next words.

"My task here is concluded," the Seer stated.

He then calmly walked out of the room, leaving behind a very flabbergasted group.

"Typical," Aidric said dryly before the room erupted into a cacophony of excited voices that didn't decrease in intensity for a long while.

CHAPTER THREE

From behind several bushes in the courtyard, Allison, cloaked from sight by the invisibility spell, secretly watched the last of the four portals Aidric had built using the combined channels of a dozen of the most powerful mages disappear in a flash of brilliant light. Earlier, Allison's skin had positively crawled with Mage-field energy when she had stepped into the courtyard. Now, as if somebody had closed a door, the magic suddenly vanished from the air around her, though she could still sense the residual magic from his spell if she concentrated hard enough.

Sighing, Allison stealthily made her way back to their suite—she had started thinking of Aidric's suite as "their" suite for some time now—careful not to bump into any of the other spectators and well-wishers. She had been forbidden by the healers to leave her room, but when Aidric had relayed to her through thought-speech that the troops were preparing to leave for Kemos and Na'ar, nothing short of death—and maybe not even then—would have kept her away from seeing Aidric and the rest of her friends off. No matter how much her mind wanted to shy away from thinking about it, she knew that it could very well be the last time she saw any of her friends, including Aidric, alive.

Before his departure, Aidric had hastily filled her in on everything that had happened within the Council Room. He told her of Seer Penrith's unexpected Fore-sight attack as well as an exciting turn of events soon after.

To everyone's surprise, a message had come from the Lamian ambassador of Oleria via thought-speech of King Chephalus's desire to offer the aid of his military forces to Lamia. They were, after all, western neighbors of Kemos, and they had just as much to lose as Lamia if Roderick gained control over Kemos. The fight, King Chephalus had said, was as much his as it was King Diryan's.

Apparently, having two neighboring kingdoms under Roderick's control didn't sit well with the Olerian king, especially one with a Mage-field as powerful as Lamia's. It would only be a matter of time before Oleria was under Roderick's control as well.

Thus, with this new non-magical force within La-mia's hands, after a fierce debate, Diryan had decided to split the whole of the Lamian army into two equally divided forces, one to contend with the Mihran army marching towards Kemos and the other to deal with Roderick's newly revealed secret army that was on the march towards Na'ar. The Olerian army was to aid Kemos.

Aidric hadn't been able to recount any more than those fleeting details since the time had come for him to begin building his four portals. However, the little that Aidric had been able to tell her about their military strategy had only left her hungry for more infor-mation.

Allison had another ten depths or so before a healer would return to the suite to check on her. Per-sonally, she thought their fussing was a bit excessive. After all, she had only felt weak and drained—nothing that a little sleep wouldn't cure, but the healers be-haved as though she was on her last dregs and would instantly die should she even try to sit up, much less get out of bed.

Although—to be fair, their wariness was probably born out of a desire to avoid having to face Aidric's wrath if, God forbid, she happened to worsen and die under their care. She had, after all, been at the receiv-ing end of Aidric's infamous temper once, and the consequence was that she had had freaked out and nearly killed him.

The suite seemed unusually desolate when she entered. The place just didn't seem the same when she knew that Aidric wouldn't be there tonight and maybe not for many nights, thereafter.

How in the hell will I ever stand being here all alone? Allison thought gloomily as she plopped down onto the couch, dirty boots and all, with no regard for the furniture.

She felt so useless. She had all of these strange and frightening abilities at her beckoned call, but she still wasn't allowed to step beyond Lamia's Shield. What good was having powers if she couldn't use them as they were meant to be used?

However, she didn't know whether to be relieved or annoyed at the restraint. She often felt like a dog held on an extremely long leash that gave the illusion of freedom, only to discover that her freedom did indeed end just short of the border when her neck was painfully jolted back. Yet, the thought of going out to war and using her powers to maim, to kill, all in the name of justice and a centuries-old treaty was truly frightening.

Allison sat brooding on the couch for a long moment before she sighed in frustration and said to the walls, "There must be *something* I can do to help. And to hell with all the healers and their bed rest! Let them all have conniption fits because I'm out of bed. All this idleness is going to drive me crazy!"

She jumped to her feet with more energy than she had felt all day, suddenly knowing just the person she had to see. It was time that she paid her a visit anyway.

***

"What is their position?" Aidric asked his head scout, a mind-mage named Faigen who had an incredibly long thought-speech range almost as infinite as the range Allison was capable of reaching.

Upon arriving at their rendezvous point just a few spans southeast of the Na'aran palace, Aidric had immediately sent out a party of his most skilled scouts across the border into Mihr composed of several mind-mages, empaths, and a single adept-mage to stake out the oncoming force from Bar'taiver. That had been well over three sand-marks ago, and Aidric had almost driven himself mad over the anticipation. Perhaps Seer Penrith had been mistaken? What if, at the last moment, this second army decided to switch course and head to Kemos to aid their comrades in their attempt to capture the Kemosian palace and he didn't learn of it until it was too late to send reinforcements?

However, when Faigen had finally thought-spoken him, the news he had delivered put Aidric's worst fears to rest—only to raise new ones. Faigen's scouts had at last located Roderick's second army.

"They're now a sand-mark's march away from Na'ar's southeastern border, Mage-general," Faigen reported, a note of awe creeping into his mind-voice, which spoke volumes since Faigen was seldom ever moved by anything. *"I've never seen the likes of it! It's monstrous! Their lines seem to stretch from horizon to horizon, and we are yet to see the end of their ranks!"*

Aidric swore under his breath as he saw the slightly distorted images Faigen sent into his mind. They were images from a general's worst nightmare. *"That they are so near to the border is unexpected,"* he sent. *"Aidius, either they travel with inhuman speed, or Roderick has somehow managed to find a rogue mage with more power than even Mordant wields to transport them all at once from Bar'taiver through a portal. Faigen, can you see who leads them?"*

Although a thought-speaker second to only Allison, Faigen's image projection abilities were mediocre at best, therefore the images Aidric received from him were only fleeting and didn't hold long enough for him to make out individual faces.

"There is one who rides in the center of the ranks, Mage-general," Faigen replied after a short pause, *"one cloaked*

in black with their face hidden within a hood. He or she is surrounded by a tight circle of similarly dressed men, minus the hood. Dervia says that they're mages, and that our hooded friend is a most powerful mage, indeed. Here's the image of him."

"Mordant," Aidric spat the moment he caught his first glimpse of the hooded figure. For just the shortest of moments, he had caught sight of a flash of silver cloth underneath the folds of his outer, black robe— the mage's house color. *The probability of Roderick leading the attack against the Kemosian palace has just multiplied exponentially.*

"Take care, Faigen. That bastard has an uncanny gift for sniffing out spies and scouts."

"We shall, milord," Faigen sent, sounding unconcerned. *"Do you wish for us to try to impede their progress?"*

Aidric paused for a moment to consult his maps. The terrain of central Mihr from the Na'aran border to the Bar'tain border was mostly hilly with a spattering of trees here and there, much like the land surrounding the Lamian palace—not a very good terrain to hide scouts.

But also not a very good terrain to hide an army of that magnitude, Aidric thought with a frown. *Is Roderick so confident of the secrecy of this second army that he would march them across land that is essentially wide open? That just doesn't seem like him, paranoid bastard that he is. Or is this essentially Mordant's move? Just what are those two snakes up to?*

Aidric chewed on those troubling thoughts for several depths before sending, *"Faigen, send a quarter of your party back towards the border with all haste. Have them befuddle the minds and senses of as many of the Mihran border battalions as they can into thinking that the approaching Bar'tain army wears the colors and crest of Lamia. Have the empaths induce them into a killing rage as well. Perhaps we can deplete this monstrous army enough to even the odds by sending Roderick's own men at each other's throats. As for your remaining party, do your best to try to thin out their ranks before they reach the border. Have Dervia cast those ghastly illusions she does so well, and see if we can't rattle their nerves a bit."*

"Yes, Mage-general," Faigen replied. *"I'll keep you informed should anything else develop."*

Aidric rubbed his temples, already feeling one of what was sure to be many headaches he would have in the long days to come and looked up just as Gwidon, General Caith's Second-in-Command, stepped into the tent. Aidric motioned for him to join him where he sat by the little make-shift table covered with maps, quills, and ink. They had much to discuss.

Gwidon, of an age with Aidric, was General Caith's protégé, a young man that showed considerable talent, so much that when Caith retired, it was his intention to pass on the flame of Arms-general to him. Brown-haired and bronze-skinned, at first glance, Gwidon was often mistaken as General Caith's son.

Gwidon could have been Caith twenty years ago. The only difference between the two was the piercing blue eyes Gwidon sported instead of Caith's hard brown. Now, those penetrating blue eyes stared down intently at Aidric, full of strain, but also alive with the fire that every professional soldier carried before the major battle.

"They are nearly upon us," Aidric informed him as the young man seated himself across from him. No need to explain who "they" were as they had just spent the last sand-mark discussing the Bar'tain army. "My scouts have spotted them on the march a mere sand-mark from Na'ar's southeastern border." He pointed to the approximate position on the map before him. "The force is considerably larger than you and I first thought, and that's just putting it mildly. I can't even give you an estimate, for I wouldn't even know where to begin."

Gwidon's mouth twitched slightly, but other than that, his expression didn't change. Aidric envied him his control. Yes, Gwidon could have very well been General Caith's son, for mentor and apprentice shared not only similar features, but also that same stoniness.

"A majority of battles have often been won in the past when odds were not favorable," Gwidon noted matter-of-factly. "It would be an ill omen, indeed, to begin this war by being one of the minority that were not so victorious, but I have faith in our troops."

"As do I," Aidric said, "and if Seni wills it, all will be well." He then quickly filled the Second in on the tasks he had assigned his scouts in Gwidon's absence as well as his discovery that the troops from Bar'taiver were indeed led by Mordant. "Are your troops in position?" Aidric asked when he had concluded.

"Yes," Second Gwidon replied crisply. "Three brigades now stand cloaked in invisibility a few hand-spans from the banks of the Shallows River and the Southeastern Road."

Aidric nodded. Earlier, he and Gwidon had discussed the best possible strategic position for Gwidon's troops. They agreed that the most likely point where Roderick's army would attempt to cross the border would be near the Southeastern Road where the river was its narrowest. If the army attempted to cross the Shallows River at its wider points, then they would run the risk of being ambushed while half of their army was in the process of crossing, which was precisely what Aidric and Gwidon planned to do despite the narrower width. The river near the South-eastern Road still had a width of several hundred handspans and would take a significant amount of time to cross.

Unless Roderick decided to have his mages build portals to transport his troops across, which they both doubted since it would be a wasted drain on his mages' reserves for such a negligible distance in the grand scheme of things, the mages would most likely build a bridge of solidified Mage-field energy in order for their troops to cross. Aidric reasoned that their crossing could be hampered easily enough by having his own mages disrupt their bridge spell. With a small portion of Mordant's hopefully reduced army—if the mind-mages Aidric sent were successful in their tasks—across the river, a large portion submerged and struggling against the river's strong current, and the rest still on the Mihran side, Lamia would definitely have the upper hand in the battle.

However, their plan had too many variables that could go wrong for Aidric to feel confident about their success. Nothing ever went exactly according to plan, after all, and nobody had ever accused Aidric of being an optimist.

"Based on Faigen's information, I believe we would do well to position at least twenty mages and a good mix of mind-mages and empaths across the river into light terrain to deal with Mordant and his bevy of mages," he informed Gwidon. "I believe I'll go with them, to deal with Mordant myself. Without Mordant's leadership, then we'll see how long this monstrous army can hold its ranks together."

At Gwidon's nod, Aidric began to roll his maps

and placed them into their map cases. He and Gwidon had done all they could to prepare their troops for the upcoming battle. Now, with all the majority of their troops in position, the Mage-general and Second readied themselves to ride out to join their troops for perhaps the hardest part of warfare, to await the approach of the enemy.

CHAPTER FOUR

"Are you sure the king won't mind the interruption?" Allison asked anxiously for at least the tenth time as she followed Ileanna to King Diryan's study.

Ileanna smiled and patted her arm reassuringly. "Of course he won't, my dear, so stop fretting. Our visit, after all, won't be just for idle gossip. I think your idea is a good one, and I believe my husband is not such a fool as to turn down a good offer when one falls unexpectedly into his lap!"

Reassured somewhat, Allison began to organize her thoughts as they reached the study and the queen knocked on the door. Much to Allison's relief, Ileanna had been sympathetic to her position and had insisted that they immediately speak with the king about it. Although nervous about actually presenting her proposition to King Diryan, especially if Lord Ion, with his all-seeing eyes and disapproving frown, happened to also be present, Allison was determined to make herself as useful as possible while Aidric was away fighting on the battlefields.

At King Diryan's muffled invitation, Ileanna swung open the door and quickly ushered Allison inside, probably so Allison wouldn't have a chance to suddenly change her mind at the last moment and bolt. The queen was well aware of how Allison hated to seek an audience with anyone.

To her immense relief, the king was working alone at his desk. Diryan's eyes narrowed when he looked up and saw who his latest visitor was. Allison had to fight her initial impulse to cringe under his stern eye.

"Should you not be in bed, Milady Allison?" the king demanded, frowning with disapproval.

Allison relaxed and had to bite her lip to keep from giggling inappropriately. The king sounded like a concerned father reprimanding his daughter.

"Oh, Diryan," Ileanna said with a laugh as she floated over to her husband and planted a light kiss on his cheek.

"I feel fine, Your Majesty," Allison assured him.

"Despite what the healers said to you, I don't feel as weak as I did at first."

"You are certain?" he pressed, eyeing her suspiciously.

"Positive, milord."

He nodded and his frown melted into a smile. "I wondered how long it would be before you appeared in my study. You wish news of Aidric, correct?"

"Of course—but that's not primarily why I'm here."

"Oh?" he said, raising an eyebrow. "What can I do for you?"

Allison hesitated, not really sure how to begin, but Ileanna saved her from her awkwardness by answering for her, "Dear, she wishes to offer her services to you."

Diryan nodded as if he had expected as much and said, "I appreciate the offer, milady, but you know that I cannot allow you to go beyond our borders. It's simply much too dangerous for us all to expose you like that, and even if it were not, I would never send anyone who has yet to finish their mage training to the battle lines, no matter how desperate the need."

"Oh, I'm aware of all that, Your Majesty," Allison replied shyly. "Actually, what I had in mind was offering my thought-speaking abilities for your use. Aidric says that my range is far greater than anyone else's, mind-mage and mage, alike. I would very much like to help in this war in any way that I can. I'm a Lamian citizen now, after all. Shouldn't it be my duty to offer to do all that I can for my kingdom, especially in times like this?"

Diryan chuckled and said, shaking his head, "Aidric was correct in calling you spirited, milady. I gladly accept your generous offer. I would be a fool not to!" Allison and the queen shared a smile. "As of now, information from both the Lord Commander in Kemos and Aidric in Na'ar has reached us through a series of relays between mind-mages at various points between the two nations and this palace. Tampering, as you well know, can occur anytime between those relays, but if there was only *one* sending instead of many, then the chance of vital information being lost or stolen would lessen dramatically, especially if the sending and receiving were to be strongly shielded. I know well the strength of your shielding capabilities. Indeed you are a gift sent straight from Seni!"

"Well, I don't know about that…" Allison said modestly, her cheeks flaming in embarrassment. "I'm just glad that there's something that I can do to help, although I understand that relaying the messages from the mind-mages to you is Lord Ion's job. I wouldn't want to intrude—"

"Nonsense," Diryan interrupted with a wave of

his hand. "I have use for Ion's abilities elsewhere. In fact, relieving him of this task would be a relief for him since he was just complaining to me a few depths ago that there are simply not enough sand-marks in the day to complete his many duties."

Oh, then he would definitely love Earth with its twenty-four hour days! Allison thought with amusement. She suddenly recalled how, several moons back, Aidric had asked her how anyone on Earth ever got anything done with such short days compared to Lamia's roughly forty-nine hour ones. Once again, Allison had to bite her lip to keep from chuckling. *Simple, we didn't and only thought we did.*

"I just sent Ion on ahead to the Council Room and was just about to join him and the rest of the Council when you knocked on my door," the king continued. "I have just received an offer of military aid from King Govannon of Sonon. Why not join me in this meeting, and we shall make your first assignment to inform both Aidric and the Lord Commander of this new development."

Suddenly, as she eagerly nodded her agreement, Allison didn't feel so worthless—or so alone as she locked eyes with both the king and queen and saw the kindness and care that lay within, something she very rarely had seen in the eyes of others from her own world.

***

As Allison sat quietly in the seat assigned to her while Diryan and his councilors argued over where the newly recruited Sononese troops could serve best, she couldn't help but sneak glances at the Sononese ambassador, a man whose skin was exotically nearly as dark as his straight, raven-colored, shoulder-length hair, but what really captivated her was his startlingly deep blue eyes that made his dark face all the more striking. He was dressed in layers of thick, woolen robes of midnight black that were only a shade darker than his skin, and his hands were covered in black gloves of the same material.

Curious as to why she had never seen a Sononese in Lamia, Allison had asked Lady Kiara, one of the mage representative for the Circle that was seated to her right, about their absence. Kiara had whispered back that there had not been a mageborn child in Sonon for centuries, so none had reason to send their children to Lamia.

In addition, since the Sononese terrain was ninety-nine percent desert, their heat-adapted skin could not tolerate the climes of any other kingdom, with the exception of Kal, for long. Even now, Allison could see him shivering underneath all those thick, black robes, though *she* thought it was a little too warm in the room.

Allison supposed she should be ashamed for gawking at him, even though she did so surreptitiously, but the Sononese ambassador was doing his own fair share of staring at her, especially when King Diryan and she had first arrived into the Council Room. Her blonde hair probably appeared as exotic to him as the whole of him did to her. He also seemed to be well informed on his Lamian prophecies. He kept casting nervous looks in her direction as though he expected her to attack him while his attention lay elsewhere.

A fresh face to gawk at the Golden Mage and wonder if she's going to eat your children tonight, Allison thought sardonically as she turned her attention away from the ambassador back to the Council.

As her roaming gaze fell on the scribe, Voytek, Allison noticed that instead of recording the ongoing conversation between the king and the others as was his duty, he was busy staring blatantly at the ambassador as she had been. But wait—were his eyes just a little *too* glazed? On closer inspection, Allison found that his eyes were indeed glazed over and distant, a look she often saw when people were thought-speaking.

But Voytek isn't supposed to have the thought-speaking

ability, Allison mused as she narrowed her eyes at the redheaded boy, beginning to feel a little concerned.

Maybe he was sick?

Rather than alert the others to the boy's condition and end up embarrassing herself and him should he prove to have only been daydreaming or falling asleep, she decided to gently probe the boy's mind using a combination of mind-magic and a healing technique Aidric had taught her to determine if the boy was feeling ill and too duty-bound or shy to speak up.

At the first touch of her probe into his mind, Allison's concern immediately changed to alarm when she determined that he actually *was* thought-speaking someone, and she heard a little of what was being said. Although she didn't recognize the voice that was bespeaking Voytek, she had a damned good idea who it must be by the direction of the conversation.

Not caring whether she was about to look stupid or not, Allison stood up abruptly, her eyes fixed on Voytek, who was so engrossed in his secret conversation that he didn't notice her sudden action at all, and demanded, "Who are you thought-speaking, Voytek?"

Diryan had been speaking when she had stood up, but stopped in mid-syllable at her words. All eyes immediately turned to first her, then to Voytek, who, against the weight of all of those eyes, finally realized that something had happened while he was off in his thought-speaking trance.

"Wh—what?" he stammered in confusion, his face flushing a shade of red to match his hair under all their scrutiny.

"You were thought-speaking somebody, weren't you?" Allison accused as everyone in the Council couldn't decide whether to gape at her or him.

"How did you kn—" Voytek started to say and then turned an interesting shade of purple when he realized just how far he had just crammed his foot down his throat.

Allison turned to Diryan, whose face was also turning an interesting shade. "I thought that he couldn't use thought-speech, Your Majesty," she said pointedly.

"Apparently we are all learning differently today," the king replied, his voice dangerously soft.

Before Diryan could say more, Voytek suddenly bolted for the door, pretty much confirming Allison's suspicions. Roderick's spy was at last identified. Clever, to plant a spy that was merely an awkward boy, a servant that would be ignored by the upper echelons.

But Roderick didn't count on me, someone who's part of those circles but does not hold their same views on the servants.

Voytek got the surprise of his life when his face suddenly slammed into something solid where there should have been nothing but the air of the door he had thrust open. He also found that he was quite paralyzed before his body hit the floor like a sack of grain.

"Roderick was clever to use him," Allison said into the confusion that followed after Voytek's attempt to flee, voicing her earlier thoughts, "but the boy is obviously not too bright to use thought-speech and then try to run away in a room full of mind-mages and mages."

Allison felt a sense of triumph as everyone suddenly looked at her with new respect and the Sononese ambassador actually bowed his head to her. Maybe now he wouldn't see her as a monster, and as a bonus, she was finally able to do something constructive with her mage powers.

"How did you know?" someone asked from the back of the room, and Allison started when she realized that it was Galen who had spoken. She still felt a sense of dread whenever she was in his presence.

Allison turned to face him, forcing her eyes to meet his, and replied more steadily than she felt, "His eyes were distant, and at first, I thought that he was just feeling sick or he was woolgathering. I probed him just to be sure, and I overheard him speaking to a man whose voice I had never heard, but it was pretty obvious who he was by what was being said."

"You were *not* supposed to be able to hear us, wench!" Voytek spat at her with considerable effort due to the restriction of the spell.

"Someone pick that piece of filth up and put him in a chair," Diryan ordered, his voice low and dangerous. "There are a few questions I wish to put to him."

"You'll never get any answers from me!" Voytek snarled as Allison eased the effects of the spell around his throat and Ion picked up his limp form and placed him into a chair. "No one can touch me! Not you—not even my m-master!" His harsh laugh was that of a madman. "Only death—only death—and I'll at long last be free of you all!"

Then, to Allison's horror, Voytek began to convulse violently despite her spell. He also began to foam at the mouth like a rabid beast, and blood began to ooze out of everywhere—through his eyes, nose, ears—and still he laughed maniacally, choking on the blood that was rising from his throat.

His laughter sent chills down her spine, and Allison resisted the urge to throw her hands over her ears, praying that the laughter would stop. Then as if a god, whether her God or Seni, had heard her silent plea, Voytek's laughter abruptly ceased, and his body stopped convulsing. She knew he was dead before Dallan, the healer representative for the Circle, pronounced him so.

"A death spell," Kiara said gravely into the uncomfortable silence that followed Dallan's announcement. "The boy knew he was going to die."

"Ion, bespeak a couple of guards to take him away," Diryan ordered, glancing over at the boy's body with contempt. "Dead or no, the boy still unknowingly answered one of my questions. It would be safe to say that Roderick knows of the army that we have sent to Na'ar to intercept his Bar'tain army. Perhaps he is even aware of every military move we plan to make thanks to that vile piece of filth in that chair."

He turned to Allison. "Milady, you must warn the Mage-general and the Lord Commander that Roderick is likely aware of our plans. I only hope we are not too late to prevent what could very well be the worst tragedy in Lamian history."

Allison nodded and immediately reached for Aidric's mind—only to discover that a wall of Mage-field energy blocked her from reaching him. Frantically, she battered at the barrier with everything she had in her, to no avail. With a sense of dread, she reached for the Lord Commander's chief mind-mage and met up with the same wall of energy.

When she came back to herself, she found that she was seated on the floor and everyone was staring down at her strangely—but standing at a distance from her, she was quick to note. So much for the triumph she had earned earlier.

"I can't reach them!" Allison said urgently as she picked herself off the ground, swaying a little with dizziness. It was Diryan who offered his arm to steady her. "There seems to be a barrier of Mage-field energy around both locations that I can't penetrate no matter how hard I pounded at them with my mind!"

It was times like this that she missed cell phones.

"But I thought only a Domnae has the knowledge to erect such a barrier!" Duke Alaric protested.

"You forget that Roderick was taught magecraft by a Domnae," the king said grimly, "and apparently he learned more than he should have been taught. He must have sensed Voytek's death. He knew we would try to warn them, and I have little doubt which of our two armies is going to suffer the most."

He turned to the Sononese ambassador, who had been the quiet observer throughout all of the excitement, and asked, "Ambassador Kalaron, in light of all that has happened here in this room today, would King Govannon still be willing to make his military force available to us?"

It was quite a while before Ambassador Kalaron gave his answer.

***

"They come," Keldan suddenly heard his twin say excitedly in his mind, followed immediately by the same thought that had been pestering him like a trapped bee in the back of his mind ever since General Caith and he had departed with their troops from the palace courtyard. *Why did I ever allow Aidric to talk me into this?*

Because you are the one best suited to lead in Aidric's absence, a little voice whispered logically in the back of his mind—much too logically.

Since not even His Mightiness, Aidric, could be in two places at once, the question of who would lead the magical troops in his place against the Mihran troops heading for the Kemosian palace was raised, and Aidric had immediately pointed a graceful finger at him. Skilled in military logistics, Keldan knew that Aidric had made the right decision, but that didn't stop him from feeling a little apprehensive about his new power position.

To lead was to have the burden of mistakes fall completely onto your shoulders, and Keldan wasn't sure that he was mentally ready to deal with the emotional responsibility of it all. He had, after all, seen what that same responsibility had done to Aidric over the years, and it was nothing to smile about. Yet, it was his duty, and he would see his troops through to the end and hope that his burden was not too heavy for his shoulders to carry when all was said and done.

Keldan strained to see over the legions of both Lamian and Olerian troops that were positioned in the open field before him. Although the troops were perfectly visible to him and his own magical troops, they were in fact cloaked entirely in the invisibility spell, set upon them by Aren and him using a method of bardic magic so unique that only three people would have known it had been done—himself, Aren, and Allison.

To those not gifted with bardic magic, the sound of the wind blowing gently over the grassy plain, whipping through the soldiers' hair, and batting at their uniforms was merely that, the sound of the wind, but most importantly, it was merely the sound and natural energy of the blowing wind to an enemy mage that might be probing for magical residue. To Keldan and Aren, a distinct melody could be heard through the light resonance of the blowing wind, a melody sung with Nature's breath that they had constructed themselves by melding the energy of the wind to their will.

As a final touch, several mages had constructed illusions of birds swooping down to the ground in search of food, as well as deer and other small animals occasionally running across the field where, in actuality, the troops stood. These illusions required such a small amount of energy that it was not necessary to draw from the Mage-field and risk one of Roderick's mages detecting it. The energy was drawn from the magical residue of nature that was ever-present in the air.

Against the horizon, Keldan could just discern the shadow of the approaching army. It would only be a few depths now before the Mihran troops advanced to their point of no return.

"Aren," Keldan sent, *"ready your squad for attack, and await my signal. This is it, little brother! May Seni guide and protect you!"*

"And you, big brother," was Aren's only reply, but Keldan barely registered it because he was already sending similar instructions to various squads of mages, mind-mages, and empaths that he had positioned throughout the ranks of the non-magical troops.

It seemed he waited for an eternity for the Mihran army to reach the point where Lord Commander Pyrs had planned for his troops to charge the unsuspecting enemy, his nerves wound up more tightly than a bowstring and his jaw clenched so tightly with tension that it ached.

However, just when the waiting was about to drive him mad, Keldan caught the signal from General Caith, and Keldan broadsent to every mind, both gifted and non-gifted, *"Now!"*

Keldan sincerely wished that he could have seen the effect that Roderick's troops saw of over fifty thousand men suddenly bearing down at them from what appeared to be the very fabric of the world when scant moments earlier, they had seen only an opened field with a couple of spooked deer bouncing across. It most assuredly must have been quite a sight!

Then he had no more time for such frivolous thoughts as the first Mihran mage attacked him, in the form of an all-out blast of power intended to shatter his shields. Keldan saw him coming soon enough to begin to softly hum a counter-spell of music that in essence, worked as a mirror to send the spell back to its caster.

The mage's eyes widened in sudden understanding and fear that the opponent he faced was not a mere mage a split-second before his own reflected power crashed into his shields in a flash of brilliant golden light and continued on through his body. When the flash of light cleared, only the charred remains of what vaguely resembled a human body lay in the grass.

Grimly, Keldan turned to the next couple of mages bearing down on him against the backdrop of clanging swords, the cursing and cries of men, and the dim melodies of his brother using bardic magic. Before either mage could lift a hand against him, he began to sing, weaving a spell that would entrap them in an airless barrier of music. Both mages hesitated in whatever spells they were about to cast forth at the sound of his first note and stared at him in confusion for a moment before resuming their spells. Had they not paused for those few crucial moments, then maybe they would have had a fighting chance against him.

Several heads around him turned as the melody Keldan had sung hung in the air, his voice caught in an infinite loop that sounded out across the field above the cacophony of battle, before the music circled around the two bewildered mages and entrapped them inside its barrier of power. Ironic, that the last sound either one of them would hear before they died was the beautiful melody sung by the bardic-mage that had killed them.

Keldan stumbled as several swords tried to hack at him and only met with his magical shields. He sang a short melody, and those attacking his shields began to drop down like flies, spelled to sleep. He did the same to those in his path as he suddenly caught a glimpse of a hooded, black- and gold-robed figure standing off to the side away from the fighting who was gathering energy into his body.

Roderick! he thought with a snarl of the blackest hate. So the bloody bastard had the courage to lead his own army, after all. Well, now that he had Roderick within his sight, Keldan didn't intend to leave him until either he or the bastard lay dead.

Catching sight of his brother fending off the attack of a rather ancient looking mage, Keldan sent, *"Aren! Come with me! I've spotted Roderick, and I don't intend to allow him to leave this battlefield alive!"*

CHAPTER FIVE

A idric felt them coming before he actually had a visual of them. The earth, itself, seemed to tremble with the force of the advancing army, sending its vibrations through the soles of his feet until he could feel their approach in every bone in his body. Around him, his battalion of mages, mind-mages, and empaths shifted uneasily. He could feel the fear, tension, and adrenaline emitting from them through his own empathic senses.

"Just remember to keep your heads," he warned them as the first line of troops became visible over the horizon. Indeed, their ranks did seem to stretch from horizon to horizon.

For many in his battalion, this was their first battle, and Aidric remembered well his first battle and the fear—too well for his own piece of mind as he had been forced to face Roderick. He had nearly died because of a stupid mistake caused by his inexperience, but Seni's own luck had been with him that day. He had managed to wound Roderick severely enough to send him running home yelping with his tail between his legs. He could only hope that these new mages were wiser and less reckless than he had been at seventeen.

Hastily, Aidric pushed those dire thoughts away. He was already in a grim enough mood as it was, caused by the not-so-good news Faigen had reported to him a few depths earlier. As Aidric had commanded, Faigen's scouts had done their best to thin out the enemy ranks, but they more often than not met with little or no success. All in all, they had only managed to spook and confuse only around a couple hundred men with Dervia's illusions and their mind tricks, the effect of removing a single grain of sand from the top of a towering dune.

At least the scouts Faigen had sent to wreak havoc with the Mihran battalions along the border had met with much better success. According to them, they had the Mihran soldiers jumping at their own shadows and seeing blue uniforms with the tear of Lamia practically radiating from their breasts everywhere they looked. Most of them were almost drooling at the anticipation of running their swords through a Lamian's chest. As far as Aidric was concerned, that was the only good news he had heard all day.

The restlessness of his battalion was suddenly painfully audible in the abrupt stillness in nature all around them that was caused by the approaching masses. Even the breeze seemed to have frozen in fear of Mordant's monstrous army.

You certainly have a knack for boasting your own morale, don't you? Aidric thought sardonically as he broadsent to his troops, *"Remember, not a sound when they march past, and I don't want any would-be heroes taking any cheap shots at the soldiers no matter how much you believe that you will get away with it. The only reward would-be heroes can claim after a battle is a funeral pyre conducted with all the honors of the kingdom. It may be an honor, but what good will it serve you if you are no longer around to appreciate it? Remember, attack only when the squad across the river dunks a huge chunk of their ranks into the river."*

To the squad that waited in ambush across the river, he sent, *"They are near and fast approaching. Expect them in only a few depths. Remember, don't be too hasty in disrupting their bridge spell. Several tens of thousands need to be across if we have any hope of claiming the edge we need."*

His last command before Mordant's army was too close in range to broadsend safely was to the mindmage positioned with Gwidon. *"Elrich, inform Second Gwidon that I have sighted the Mihran army and to prepare his men for attack within a few depths. Be steadfast, and may Seni guide and protect us all today!"*

From the moment that the first ranks of the enemy army began to march past his battalion, Aidric knew that something was wrong. Something in the air just didn't feel right to him, and at first, he dismissed those feelings as nerves. However, as his feelings of unease continued to intensify as line after line of soldiers passed him, he suddenly knew why.

The Mihran battalions along the river were making no move to attack the approaching ranks even though they should have seen them as Lamian soldiers. In fact, they seemed to not see them at all, continuing to mill around along the river's bank in obvious agitation, never once giving Mordant's troops a second glance.

Aidric's first thought was that his scouts were mistaken about their success with influencing the minds of the border battalions, but the more he pondered over it, the more that explanation just didn't hold water.

That still doesn't explain why these border guards don't seem to be reacting to the arrival of this monstrous army, he mused. *The army marches across the land in plain sight where any fool can see them, and yet, instead of falling back into their ranks as any seasoned soldier worth his pay would, they continue to mill around like undisciplined children without a care in the world. For all they know, this army could be Lamian soldiers wearing the uniform of Mihr! It just doesn't make sense!*

He watched with a sense of impending doom as a couple of mages fell out of the ranks and began to build a bridge of Mage-field energy as expected. Aidric immediately felt the familiar prickling on his skin caused by the casting of magic near one who was mageborn. It was a relief to feel something so familiar and normal in light of his anxieties, despite the fact that it was an enemy mage who was doing the spell-casting.

He rose on the balls of his feet, ready to draw energy from Lamia's Mage-field the moment the first bodies began to fall into the thundering waters of the river and his eyes intent on the golden illumination stretching from bank to bank that only those with inner-sight could see. Only a few more lines—

Without warning, the golden bridge vanished from beneath the soldiers' feet, and Aidric and every Lamian soldier within sight of the river got the shock of their lives. Instead of plunging into the chilly water, the lines of soldiers continued to march across the river as if they had suddenly developed the ability to walk on air.

An illusion! Aidric's mind screamed to him as he stared stupidly at a sight that he had never thought to see in his lifetime. *The whole thrice damned army is an illusion! But how—why—where in the six hells is the* real *army?*

As he and the rest of the Lamian army stared at the ghostly images, frozen in uncertainty, he received his answer. Behind the ranks of his and Gwidon's troops that were still cloaked from sight under the invisibility spell across the river, the whole of the Bar'tain army suddenly appeared in the blink of an eye, but this time Aidric was certain that this monstrous army was *not* an illusion!

"An ambush!" Aidric sent to Elrich, but he needn't have bothered since the enemy was already attacking.

However, before Aidric could command his troops to cross the river to aid their comrades, the border battalions no longer seemed like witless children and suddenly began to charge towards his own battalion. It was then that he realized why his scouts had failed in their mind tampering.

Mages—they are all mages! he thought in disbelief, feeling all of the blood suddenly drain from his face. A general's worst nightmare had suddenly come true. *Seni help us, we have been ambushed with a river at our backs!*

Just when Aidric thought things couldn't possibly get any worse, they did—much, much worse. The army that he had thought was totally illusion abruptly proved otherwise when they attacked. Only the first three-fourths of the army had been illusion. The last fourth, the two mages who had cast the bridge spell, and the hooded Mordant with his circle of mages were real. With a feeling akin to panic, Aidric realized that they were surrounded.

Frantically, as Mordant's mages began their magical attacks, Aidric reached for Allison's mind, hoping that the range was not farther than he was capable of reaching. A split-second later, he realized how futile his attempt was as his mind-probe immediately hit against a barrier of Mage-field energy. Having been a novice once in the Temple of Seni, he immediately recognized the obstacle and knew who had cast it, a man foolishly trained in magecraft by a Domnae.

"Damn you, Roderick!" Aidric shouted defiantly into the sounds of battle all around him and began to draw a huge amount of energy from the Mage-field. Allowing his fury to grow, he intended on finishing off Mordant once and for all with the implosion spell.

Unfortunately, a blast from behind that nearly knocked him off his feet broke his concentration, and Aidric was forced to cast the energy he had gathered away at the offending mage that attacked him, molding the energy into an enormous, green fireball that tore through the mage's pathetically constructed shields and instantly incinerated his body until only a few ashes remained to scatter in the breeze.

The huge quantity of magical energy Aidric had

used in the construction of that fireball unfortunately drew Mordant's attention to him, and the bastard probably realized just how slimly he had escaped a similar fate, suddenly ordering his circle of mages to attack Aidric simultaneously as Mordant turned his horse in the opposite direction from the fighting.

"Coward!" Aidric raged after him. "You fear to face me!"

Then the attacks came, seven all at once in the form of fireballs half the size of his, racing towards him from three different directions. With an oath, Aidric frantically flung a tornadic windstorm at them, snuffing out all but two of them that had been cast too rapidly to counter on contact.

This time he was bowled over as those two fireballs slammed against his outer shield almost simultaneously. A blinding light flashed before his eyes as two of his shields shattered under the force of impact, and hot tears of pain sprang to his eyes. He hastily wiped them away as he leapt to his feet, blinking his eyes rapidly to try to clear the white lights that flashed across them.

Luckily, his windstorm had also flattened Mordant's mages, and they were slow getting to their feet. Aidric promptly plowed them with the same fireballs that they had intended to send him to Aidius with.

None of the seven had time to utter even a little whimper before they were reduced to ash.

As the smoke from his fireballs cleared, Aidric saw Mordant in the distance building what could only be a portal. Cursing more profoundly than he had ever cursed before, Aidric broke into a sprint towards the Silver Mage, all the while praying to Seni that he would reach the portal in time to stop the bastard. A few dozen handspans just short of the portal, Aidric suddenly slammed into an invisible barrier of Mage-field energy.

The hooded figure never turned as he calmly led his horse into the portal.

With a howl of rage, Aidric blasted the magical barrier to shards with a dagger of power, sprinted towards the portal with his ears still ringing from the blast, and dove into the portal just as it winked out of sight in a flash of golden light.

***

Where in the six hells is the Mage-general? Gwidon thought anxiously as, for once in his life, he was at a loss of what to do.

He could plainly see that his troops were being butchered like so much livestock, and the bloodbath would only get worse. He was seriously considering surrender, but since Mage-general Aidric was the official leader of this portion of the Lamian army, he could not do so without first consulting with him. Unless of course he was dead, and Seni help them all if that was true.

Gwidon had last glimpsed the Mage-general being bombarded by dozens of fireballs, but after the smoke had cleared, he was simply *gone*, elsewhere, or the Thrones forbid, reduced to ash.

For the first time in his life, Gwidon resented not being gifted with any thought-speaking abilities. His mind-mage, Elrich, had been cut down almost at once, so he had no way of thought-speaking the Mage-general to determine whether he was still alive.

Men seemed to come at him from all directions, and his own men fought to protect him. However, Gwidon could see that they were all fighting a losing battle. It was only a matter of time before he was cut down, and if the Mage-general wasn't already dead, he would be forced to surrender or be killed himself, leaving his men with no clear command.

Hellsfire! I can't wait a moment longer! I must order our surrender and save what is left of my men! I only pray that General Caith and the king understand my decision.

As the swords continued to clash together all around him and blood continuously splashed across his uniform and face from those who were dying to keep him unscathed, Gwidon, acting Arms-general to an army fighting a losing battle, fished into the right breast pocket of his uniform for the square of silver cloth that bore the golden Natian symbol of surrender that both he and the Mage-general carried but had hoped to never use.

Then, before he could pull out the cloth, the sound of men charging reached his ears above the cacophony of the clashing swords and the dying like a miracle sent straight down to him by Seni. Second Gwidon looked up towards the northwestern horizon in bewilderment and nearly choked as he saw an army wearing the colors of Sonon charging towards them like Seni's avenging saints. An equally loud commotion behind him had him looking across the river in disbelief as more Sononese soldiers charged to their aid. Now, instead of the Lamian forces being surrounded, the Bar'tain forces were now caught in their own trap.

With a whoop of joy that was uncharacteristic of him, Gwidon shouted to his ranks, "For Lamia and Seni, fight to victory!"

***

Today was the happiest day of Keldan's life.

At his feet between his brother and him lay the

charred remains of Roderick. Keldan could hardly believe how easy it had been to cut the king of Mihr down. Between the two of them, they had sung a song of all-consuming flame, and the bastard and all his puny mage protectors had gone up in a wall of fire. Every cry from Roderick's lips was like sweet music to his ears, sweeter than any music that could ever have come from his own lips.

"I can't believe we finally defeated Lamia's greatest foe," Aren said in an echo of Keldan's thoughts, shaking his head in stunned disbelief, "who in the end turned out to be not so great."

At the sight of their fallen king, the Mihran troops had turned tail and run. They had been instantly pursued, and a good many of them had been captured and taken prisoner. They were now being prepared under the Lord Commander's guidance for transportation to Lamia's dungeons.

His scorched face still hidden within the folds of what was left of his hood, Keldan knelt down onto one knee to remove the scrap of burnt cloth for their first glimpse of the dead Mihran king's face. "I wonder what expression the filthy bastard took to his grave?" he remarked as Roderick's face was revealed.

Keldan did a double-take as he stared down at the face of a man that could have been a century old as Aren let out his breath in a low hiss.

"It's not him…"

Several heads turned with equal looks of anger and disbelief as the implications of Keldan's words sank in.

In the distance, Keldan could hear the familiar screams of the first victims of Roderick's death spell.

***

The first thing Aidric became aware of as he stumbled out of the portal and promptly landed flat on his face was the sound of someone laughing. Scrambling onto his feet, Aidric quickly scanned his surroundings for the source of that laugh, expecting a blast of power to hit him at any moment. That was Mordant's style.

With a jolt, he realized that he was in the Throne Room of the Na'aran palace. Both the king and queen sat bound and gagged on their thrones, their necks collared and chained to the snowcat carvings on the tops of the back rests of their throne seats above their heads, while the laughter continued in mockery of them all. Though his conscience ate at him, Aidric knew that there was nothing that he could do for them at the moment. To help them would be like inviting death with open arms.

Cautiously, Aidric's eyes roamed the room, daring not to move as he strained to see into every darkened corner, behind every column, and beneath every tapestry for the slightest hint of a human shape hiding behind the thick material. Finally, his eyes rested on the black-cloaked figure he had at first mistaken to be a shadow that stood against the far west wall next to a large tapestry of Na'ar's emblem, two fighting snow-cats against a backdrop of the kingdom's colors of silver and green.

"Are you such a coward, Mordant, that I had to chase you through your own portal to force a confrontation between us?" Aidric asked the figure darkly, every pore in his body alert and focused on the other man. "Shouldn't *I* be the one laughing?"

The figure pulled back the hood of his cloak until it rested on his shoulders before he turned to face Aidric. In the darkness of the room where only four mage-flames burned in the lanterns against the wall, Mordant's features were hidden in shadow. Then quite calmly, Mordant deliberately stepped into the light.

Aidric bit back an oath.

"Mordant—I think not," Roderick said as his lips stretched into a sadistic smile. "A clever lad such as yourself, I'm highly disappointed that my costume fooled even you. However, you *did* follow me into my portal, so at least in that you didn't disappoint."

"Together again," Aidric said coolly, refusing to show any emotion at this unexpected turn of events even though his mind was racing. "I still remember the last time we were in this position. If my memory serves me correctly, I last sent you home yelping for your mother's tit. I can't even begin to express how much pleasure it gives me to have the opportunity to do so again!"

"Ah, but my unfortunate lad, the tables are definitely turned in my favor this time," Roderick purred, reminding Aidric of a satisfied cat with a feather sticking halfway out of his mouth. "This time you will surrender yourself to me most willingly."

Aidric laughed in the fool's face. "And just what makes you believe that I'll do such an incredulous thing?" he demanded. "You'll be but ash and crumbling bones between my fingers before you can even blink again."

"I don't believe that a certain young lady will like the consequences of that at all," Roderick replied, his tone suddenly turning from narcissistic to dangerous.

"Just what is that supposed to mean?" Aidric spat back at him, the tension in the air between them suddenly thickening.

"Bring her," the Mihran king called to someone that was apparently hovering in the wings.

Aidric had experienced shock after shock today, but none had shaken him so severely as seeing Mordant step calmly into the room and roughly thrust a

shockingly familiar bound and gagged woman forward. Green eyes filled with fear and pain met his
briefly as she fell to the ground.

Allison.

All thought of caution was instantly driven to the
four winds and replaced with a white-hot rage beyond
reason.

"You bastards!" Aidric snarled, Mage-field energy
instantly flooding into his body.

However, just as he lifted a hand to blast Mordant
with all the energy he had gathered, his shields abruptly shattered in a flash of brilliant, white light, and
he felt something cold ram into his right shoulder.
Only when he felt the hot stickiness flowing down his
side and his cheek was slamming into the cold, marble
floor did he realize what he had just allowed to happen
to him.

Weakly, he pawed at his shoulder with his left
hand, and sure enough, his fingers touched the hilt of
a dagger. His skin tingled strongly with magic as he
struggled to wrap his hand around the hilt, confirming
his suspicions. The bloody thing was a spelled dagger!
It was no wonder that all his shields had shattered so
easily. He felt a sharp pain followed by a gush of wet
warmth as he wrenched the dagger free.

Thoroughly pissed off, Aidric tried to rise to his
knees, marveling that no one had attacked him again,

but the ceiling decided to pick that exact moment to become the floor, causing him to fall down onto his face again. A wound as minor as a shoulder wound should not have caused the amount of weakness and dizziness that he was now experiencing. Even the destruction of his shields wouldn't have affected him this severely!

Aidric forced his eyes to open wider, and through a blurry assault of bright colors, he struggled to focus on the blood-covered blade. Just as he feared, mingled with his blood was a hint of bright green fluid.

Tangel, was his last fleeting thought before his mind was overwhelmed by a rising darkness that he had no choice but to succumb to.

CHAPTER SIX

"What do you mean he has disappeared?" Diryan demanded sharply, sitting back into his chair in the Council Room that seemed to have become a permanent part of his body in the last few days and wishing he was free to see a healer to relieve his damned headache.

The previous buzzing of his councilors and the Circle suddenly ceased as though they all had been spell-silenced. If that was the case, Diryan silently thanked the soul that had done it, for the silence was *much* easier on his splitting headache.

Looking solemn, an expression that looked alien on the lad's face, Second Gwidon replied, "I mean just that, Your Majesty. The last I saw of the Mage-general, he was being attacked by at least a half dozen mages. Fireballs were being flung back and forth, and when the smoke cleared, he was just gone, as were Mordant's mages. In all the chaos, no one seems to have seen what became of him. We didn't find a body, but you know that doesn't say much when a mage battle is involved."

Diryan closed his eyes and began to rub his temples more furiously, hoping that everyone would interpret this action as him trying to soothe a rising headache and not see just how much this latest news affected him. *How am I ever going to tell Ileanna?* he thought, his heart aching, which was immediately followed by an even more troubling thought. *Seni help me, how shall I tell the Lady Allison?*

Allison was currently in the Healer's Hall helping with the wounded. Ileanna was also there to offer what comfort she could to both the wounded and their families. His wife's presence seemed to have an amazing soothing effect on people, and right now Diryan wished she were exerting that soothing effect on *him*.

Diryan slowly opened his eyes and forced himself to gather what little composure he had left after such a trying few days. "I want you to question every soldier again, magical and non-magical both, that fought in the battle in Na'ar, even the wounded," he ordered Gwidon. "I cannot believe that out of thousands of men and women, not one soul knows what became of the Mage-general. Report directly to me when your task has been completed."

"Yes, Your Majesty," Gwidon replied, bowing deeply before he turned on his heel and briskly left the room.

After waiting a very nerve-wracking quarter-moon for his troops to return from both Kemos and Na'ar, Diryan didn't think that his days could get any more hellish, but after Second Gwidon's report... Aidric missing—what else could possibly go wrong?

It had been bad enough not having any communication with any of his troops during the duration of the discovery of Voytek's betrayal to the return of his troops from Kemos eight days after the battle ended since Roderick's barriers around the two kingdom were still up, preventing either party from communicating through thought-speech. He would have to petition the Temple to send a Domnae to deal with the problem, but until then, he wouldn't waste time worrying about it. Too many other more pressing problems had arisen in the aftermath of the two battles for him to worry about something that didn't demand immediate attention.

For the life of him, Diryan still didn't know how they had pulled off the two victories, especially against such odds. When Second Gwidon had returned with his troops, Diryan learned just how impossible and utterly hopeless their situation had been down in Na'ar.

If King Govannon had not been willing to send his troops into the midst of such a devastating battle, Diryan knew that the Lamian forces would have been crushed, and Na'ar would now be in Roderick's hands.

As it was, Na'ar had already been in a precarious position. Roderick had managed to take the royal couple hostage before a combination of Sononese and Na'aran troops were able to retake the palace. In the chaos of that battle, Roderick had easily slipped through their fingers, taking the king and queen with him. It was only a matter of time before Roderick would demand his ransom, a ransom Diryan would not hand over without a fight. Although severely depleted, Lamia's army was still a powerful one, and he was prepared to send it full force against the Mihran palace if it came to that.

The only problem was that he needed Aidric, more so now than he ever had in the past. Just where on Seni's World was the lad? He refused to even *think* that Aidric was dead.

"Any word from Valin?" Diryan asked the Seneschal hopefully.

"No, Highness," Ion replied, a hint of weariness laced into his voice. These days, even the ever-vibrant Seneschal was looking haggard. "With the barrier surrounding Na'ar preventing him from getting any messages to his contacts, he would have to journey to La-mia afoot to deliver them, and we both know how impossible that is at the moment. He would be blasted straight to the Thrones before he could even set foot outside the Mihran palace."

"Damnation!" Diryan growled. It seemed as though he would have to deal with the Temple immediately after all.

Dealing with any sect of the Brothers in Divinity was always precarious. He only hoped that the High Priest would understand how essential it was for everyone it would affect, not just Lamia, to remove that damned barrier. If Casimer decided that the Brothers in Divinity couldn't become involved, then Diryan didn't know what he would do. He needed information from Mihr, and he needed it badly!

"Ion, summon Horae Adorjan," he ordered, "and also a healer. I fear my head will burst if I don't rid myself of this wretched headache soon!"

***

The sounds of agony and the smell of sickness were everywhere. Allison wrinkled her nose and tried not to think too much about all the wretched souls lying in cots all around her. Her sanity could only take so much, after all, and the sight of hundreds of mangled bodies would be enough to push her over the edge if she allowed it.

When Healer Dallan had asked for her assistance after all the wounded had been brought in—more than all the healers in the palace could possibly handle—Allison had been eager to help, not realizing just what she was getting herself into. Yet, when Dallan had led her into Healer's Hall, she had instantly paled and had to turn her head quickly and swallow hard to keep from vomiting when she had caught her first sight of the solders' ghastly injuries.

The soldier she now worked on, a woman that looked as if she had barely left puberty, had lost an arm to a sword. Though one of the field healers had tended to her on the battlefield, the work he had done was only enough to prevent her from bleeding to death or dying from the shock. Now it was Allison's job to completely heal and seal off the battered tissues, muscles, and nerves of the stump before infection set in.

Allison was so intent on her work that at first, she didn't notice the new presence in the room until her empathic senses suddenly picked up more than the usual agonies and pity of the Healer's Hall. The feeling was stronger, more complicated. Allison raised her head and instantly froze when she saw the king anxiously scanning the room. When his eyes finally picked her out and met her own, she instantly knew that something had happened to Aidric.

For a while, all they could do was stare at one another. Allison's mind had gone totally numb, and the sounds of the injured suddenly faded away into the distance. Diryan's expression was unreadable as he made his way over to her, but his feelings were completely clear, almost as if they spoke to her.

He was here to tell her that Aidric was missing.

Allison nearly shrieked when a hand suddenly tapped her on the shoulder—she was so intent on the king—but bit back her cry when a healer's robes came into view. "Allison, if you're finished here," the young woman said, "I could use your help with—" She cut off abruptly when she, too, caught sight of the king. "Oh—uh—never mind. I'll ask Clarine."

Allison hardly heard her as the healer scurried away.

"He isn't dead," Allison said when Diryan was within earshot.

The king blinked in surprise. "How can you be so certain?" he asked slowly. "Unless—" Alarm suddenly flashed in his eyes, and his gaze shot to her bloodied hands. "Do you wear his life-ring?"

"No," she replied, slowly rising to her feet, the blood staining her hands forgotten.

"Then how can you be so certain?" Diryan persisted.

"I just am," Allison said firmly, then, as the king stared hard at her, struggled to explain, "I don't understand how I know, but I think that it's because we are linked empathically somehow. It's kind of like the feeling you get when you know someone's just been in a room even though it's currently empty."

Diryan nodded, looking thoughtful. "I believe I agree. Such a link has been known to have formed in the past between lovers that share the empathic ability."

Allison blushed. She still couldn't quite get used to the matter-of-fact attitude of the Lamians towards sex as if they were merely speaking of eating or breathing.

"Perhaps you could use this link to locate him?" the king asked hopefully.

Allison shook her head. "It doesn't work that way. I think the link is only on an unconscious level, and all it tells me is that Aidric is still alive because his presence is still, well, *present*."

Diryan sighed. "I knew it couldn't be so simple."

"Majesty!" A voice suddenly called from across the room. Diryan and Allison turned as one and saw Second Gwidon hurrying over to them. It was clear from his demeanor that he was excited, though his face betrayed no emotion. He bowed before Diryan, sparing her only a sideways glance, before he said, "I have news of the Mage-general."

"You've found him?" Allison demanded before the Second could say another word.

Gwidon looked scandalized. Allison merely shot him a dark look. At the moment, she had no patience for proprieties.

"No, milady, only a hint of what's become of him," Gwidon replied neutrally. He was probably too much of a soldier to let any of his emotions creep into his voice. "One of the wounded mages that fought in his battalion just awakened from shock-sleep, and he reported last seeing the Mage-general racing towards a portal that had been opened in the distance by a black-cloaked figure, Mordant in all likelihood."

"Reckless fool!" Diryan muttered, and Allison readily agreed. "Unfortunately, that raises more questions than it has answered, but I believe we can safely assume that all did not go as Aidric intended else he would have reappeared by now. Perhaps Valin will know something of this—if it doesn't take that Domnae five years to arrive here to deal with that damned barrier! At any rate, you have done well, Gwidon."

Before Allison could ask who Valin was, Diryan dismissed Gwidon, turned to her, and asked, "Milady, would you be so kind as to bespeak the Seneschal and ask him to meet me in my study? If I hear any word on Aidric, then I'll send for you immediately."

Allison started to protest, but a stern look from the king quickly silenced her. She nodded reluctantly, and then to her surprise, and possibly to the surprise of all present in the room, he reached over and embraced her tightly, unmindful of her blood-spattered dress.

"I'm certain that all will be well in the end," he said as he released her, "but be damned that Aidric will give me a head of hair to match my wife's!"

Allison found that she couldn't concentrate on her patients after Diryan left the Hall, her mind shrieking with worry over Aidric. She knew that she was being totally selfish in light of all those currently worse off than she, but even those self-deprecating thoughts couldn't shake Aidric from her mind.

Where was he? Was he hurt? Did Mordant, heaven forbid, take him prisoner? As she struggled to concentrate on healing the nasty-looking burns on her latest patient's chest, those same question's kept whirling around in her mind until she thought they would drive her mad.

She lifted her hands from the man's chest. It was still red and a little swollen, but nevertheless healed of most of the damage. Allison swayed as a wave of exhaustion and dizziness washed over her, threatening to send her pitching to floor.

It seemed all the worry and stress on top of the personal energy she was expending with her healing that she was forcing her body to endure had at last caught up with her. The numbness she had been experiencing was at last crumbling beneath the strain of her emotions. However, before she could suffer the indignity of falling on her face, she suddenly felt hands steadying her from behind. Allison closed her eyes, infinitely grateful to her savior, who turned out to be Keldan.

"I believe you have done quite enough for today," the bardic-mage said firmly. "What good can you possibly do if you end up the patient instead of the healer?"

"I just didn't realize—" she started to say but he instantly cut her off.

"No, you did not," Keldan scolded, sweeping her up into his arms before she knew what was happening. "You need rest, little lady, and I'll make damned sure that you get it!"

"I can walk on my own two feet, thank you," Allison retorted, earning a snort from him.

"Sure you can, and that's why only a depth ago I had to hold you up before you ended up becoming better acquainted with the floor!"

That shut her up, at least until he had carried her

to her suite where she insisted that he instantly put her down on the couch. "You didn't come looking for me in that pit of hell just to save me from passing out," Allison said as she waved him to join her on the couch. "You've heard, haven't you?"

"Yes, but you are taking the news considerably better than I would have thought," he said, raising an eyebrow.

"Just give me a few moments until the numbness of the shock wears off, and I promise you, I won't disappoint," she said wearily. "I guess I just can't really believe that it's true. I knew that something like this could happen, and I tried to mentally prepare myself for the worst. Still, deep down, I really didn't think that—that this c-could hap-happen—"

Now, without the added distraction of the Healer's Hall and her patients, the tears came, and she shamelessly let them flow freely. Wordlessly, Keldan reached over and embraced her. It felt strange to be comforted by someone other than Aidric, especially a man that could be so intimidating at times, but she was glad for Keldan's presence. A friend's offered shoulder worked just as well as a beloved's.

"What could've happened to him?" she choked out between sobs. "What if he's hurt and lying in some ditch where no one could possibly find him?"

"Don't be so pessimistic," Keldan chided gently.

"He'll turn up eventually, or I don't know Aidric at all."

"And in the meantime, we do what?" Allison demanded, pulling away from him and wiping at her eyes furiously. "Sit on our rumps and *hope* that he comes back! Well, I won't!"

She stood up abruptly and began to pace. Keldan watched her anxiously, though he said nothing, sensing perhaps that what she needed was time to sort through her maelstrom of emotions and thoughts without his added opinions. Allison was grateful for his foresight.

What could she do? Roderick's barriers prevented any thought-speech from entering Na'ar and Mihr. She had told Diryan the truth about her empathic link with Aidric. It was practically useless other than as a point of reassurance. He wasn't dead, she knew, but how long would that be true? If Roderick had indeed captured him, then the hourglass had already been overturned, each falling grain of sand bringing Aidric closer to his death. She held no illusions about that.

Then almost on its own accord, the answer came to her. Yet, it was almost unthinkable.

"There *is* something that I can do to find him," Allison said determinably a few moments later, reaching a decision she had hoped to never make. She stopped pacing and looked down at Keldan, who still sat watching her with concern. "I can Soulwalk."

"But you can't even remember how it was done the last time you unconsciously invoked it," Keldan reasoned quietly. "*Can* you do it again?"

"We won't know until I try," she insisted, trying to sound more confident than she felt. "Despite the fact that I've refused to even try to Soulwalk in the past, that didn't mean that I never thought about it. To be honest, I thought about it every day. That day I walked on that Idonan battlefield in spirit form, Raya and Maldon told me that my body was completely saturated with Mage-field energy. I've thought and thought about that ever since, and I believe that the reason why I did that was to preserve the life in my body while my soul was elsewhere. The Mage-field is, after all, made up of both life and death energy, and isn't the soul supposed to be something like a person's life-force?"

"Makes sense, but casting the spell is altogether a different matter," Keldan pointed out. "It's dangerous to attempt spells without the proper incantations—or the proper mentor. My magic is bardic, worlds different than an adept-mage's, as you well know."

"But I'm pretty sure that this is a spell that needs no incantations," Allison insisted. "How else could I have cast it and in my sleep, no less? Keldan, please understand that this is something that I have to do.

With that barrier up, moving in spirit form is the only hope I have to find him right now. Please help me do this."

Keldan was silent for a long while before he sighed, sounding resigned, and said, "I suppose I would be wasting my breath by trying to convince you to forget doing something so utterly foolish. Aidric never listens to me, so why should I believe you will? You two are too similar for comfort. All right. I'll help you even though I'm going against my better judgment. I don't want you to try something so dangerous alone, but at least allow me to call in my brother and a couple of adepts to assist us."

"Fine," Allison said, relieved that he had caved so quickly, "but the mages must be Raya and Maldon. Remember, the fact that I can Soulwalk must be kept secret. Aidric—" She swallowed hard against the lump that instantly formed in her throat. "Aidric wanted it that way."

"I've already summoned them and explained all," Keldan admitted sheepishly. "They should be here any moment, but Allison, is it wise to keep what you are about to do from the king? Let's say that you succeed and locate Aidric. How then will you explain your sudden knowledge to him?"

"I'll just tell him I had another Foresight attack," she answered readily.

He frowned. "Lying to the king is considered an act of treason, Allison."

"Only if you get caught."

"Treason is still treason," he insisted firmly just as Aren, Raya, and Maldon came barging through the door without knocking.

"What's treason?" Aren asked with interest.

"Nothing, little brother," Keldan hedged.

"Where's Selwyn?" Allison asked anxiously.

Raya smiled knowingly. "Still aiding the injured in Healer's Hall, so you don't need to fear discovery, Allie."

"Then I guess we shouldn't waste any more time," Allison said more bravely than she felt. "I think the best place to try would be my old bedroom since it happened there the first time."

They all nodded and followed her lead. Once in the bedroom, she settled herself onto the bed, positioning herself flat on her back, and instructed the others to arrange themselves in a circle around the bed in order to better watch over her.

"Don't be alarmed if you see my body start to glow," Allison warned. "I'm going to be drawing an incredible amount of power from the Mage-field, and after that, the only thing I can do is follow my instincts and rely on everything Aidric has taught me. Try to rouse me if you think something's wrong."

"You mean, if your pretty face suddenly decides to turn blue," Aren said wryly.

"Exactly, and if I *do* manage to succeed, watch my vital signs closely. As I understand it, my soul can easily become lost in the spirit plane, or I can simply be away from my body so long that it dies. You, acting as my physical anchors, should be able to reach me through thought-speech easily enough."

"I don't know what the rest of you think," Maldon interjected uneasily, "but it all seems awfully risky to me. Are you certain you want to do this, Allison?"

"I would happily run myself through with a sword if I knew it would bring Aidric safely home," was her reply as she closed her eyes and began to draw energy from the Mage-field before she could freak herself out about it. Only then did she sheepishly realize that her reply wasn't a very reassuring one.

Allison allowed the power to run freely through her body, to intermingle with her own life-energy until her body was completely saturated. Only then did she allow the two energies to merge. What happened next was the most terrifying experience of her life, even more terrifying than her first journey through a portal.

The moment the two energies combined within her body, what felt like a sledgehammer suddenly slammed with a bone-crushing force into her chest, and for a few horrifying moments, she couldn't breathe, gasping after a breath that was no longer there. She struggled to open her eyes, to cry out in fear and pain, but it was as though she had lost all feeling and control of her body.

Then without warning, Allison violently lurched forward, and for an indeterminate time after, she felt nothing at all. Gradually, sensation began to return to her body, but she knew immediately that something was not quite right with the way she felt—too light-headed, too transparent. When at last she was able to open her eyes, she nearly shrieked when she found that she was staring into her own impassive face that glowed eerily with a golden-white radiance.

Dear God, I've actually done it! Allison thought with amazement and a little bit of fear as she realized that she was hovering only a few inches above her own body. Her first experience with Soulwalking had *not* been like this! However, she had thought she was dreaming then, and she had moved about unconsciously as if what she saw were the images of a dream.

Not sure how to move about while in spirit form, she willed herself to the ground, hoping that her soul would obey her. Sure enough, her "feet" instantly touched the ground near the foot of the bed where Aren stood watch over her body. The sensation was similar to that of moving through a portal.

She paused to examine herself in childlike wonder, amazed at what she saw. Although she no longer had a body, the image of her soul was still dressed in the blood-stained apprentice uniform she had been wearing, and when she held out her "arms," she could still see a dim image of her flesh. She glanced over at her body again and quickly looked away. With the blood that soaked her dress and her face so pale, she uncannily looked like a corpse brought in from the battlefields.

Experimentally, Allison reached out a hand to touch Aren's shoulder and quickly drew it back as if a snake had suddenly bitten her when her hand went straight through his shoulder and emerged through the other side. Aren unconsciously brushed at his shoulder as if at a fly that had landed there.

He feels it. He feels the energy of my soul! I wonder if you have to be a mage to sense my presence? That was something worth exploring later on, but for now, finding Aidric was her main priority.

"Hey, did it suddenly get cold in here?" Aren's said abruptly, breaking into her thoughts.

"Not that I've noticed," Keldan answered, turning to frown down at Allison's still form.

"Well, there's a distinctive chill at my back that wasn't there a depth ago," Aren insisted.

"Perhaps Allison's magic is causing it," Raya suggested, moving over to Aren and feeling the air behind him with her hand.

Allison experienced a slight tingle as Raya unknowingly passed a hand through her upper torso.

"Yes, I also feel it," Raya announced, stepping back in order for Maldon to inspect the area himself.

"Strange," Maldon muttered when his hand also passed through Allison's ethereal body. "Perhaps we should attempt to rouse her."

"No need," Allison said, knowing that her voice was heard only in their minds. She chuckled when they all flinched and cast their eyes onto her body in the bed. *"That cold,"* she continued, not bothering to keep the amusement out of her voice, *"behind Aren is me. My spell worked."*

Then to prove her point, she calmly walked through Aren, wanting to pay him back for all the times he had made her uncomfortable with his crude comments. To her immense satisfaction, Aren yelped and began to rub at his body furiously. It was worth the disorientation she experienced as a result of her life-energy intermingling momentarily with his to see the look on his face.

"She stepped *through* me!" Aren whined, turning to glare down at Allison's body since he couldn't see her spirit.

"Are you all right?" Keldan asked anxiously to the air, ignoring his brother's whining completely.

"That depends on whether or not my body is still breathing and my heart beating," Allison replied, suddenly feeling a little anxious herself. In the enchantment of this new experience, she had forgotten that the longer she stayed in spirit form, the more danger she brought to her body.

"Your body is still functioning normally," Keldan reported a moment later to her relief.

"Then I'm off to find Aidric," Allison said determinably and closed her "eyes" to begin her search.

CHAPTER SEVEN

*W*et—*hard surface—where in the six hells am I?*

Aidric awoke sluggishly to those confusing thoughts, his cheek digging painfully into a jagged, stone surface and his legs lying in a shallow puddle of freezing water that emitted a foul, indeterminable stench. His head ached dully as if he'd had a little too much wine. Aidius, he was thirsty!

Slowly, he lifted eyelids that suddenly felt as though they weighed more than a mountain and found that it didn't improve his situation at all. It only made his head throb more insistently. Wherever he was, not even a sliver of light was present. Had he gotten drunk the night before? He didn't think so.

With a groan, Aidric attempted to pull himself up into a sitting position, only to hiss in sudden pain when fire seemed to run engulf his shoulder. He fell back onto his face and then froze when he heard the unmistakable clank of chains hitting stone.

"What in the six hells—" he said or tried to say, finding that no words could get past his throat.

Someone had spell-silenced him! Suddenly the pain in his shoulder and head seemed like only minor discomforts.

He *remembered*.

Aidric now knew damned well where he was, and the thought made his blood begin to boil. He had allowed himself to be bested by his greatest enemy, and now he was a prisoner in Roderick's dungeons. How long had he been unconscious? A long time, he decided when he noted the dryness of his throat and the stiffness in his body from lying in such an uncomfortable position.

How could he let this happen? How could he have been so *stupid*? He knew damn well that he had left Allison safe within the Lamian Shield. There was no way Roderick could have penetrated it to abduct her.

Besides, even if by some strange twist of fate Roderick *had* managed to penetrate the Shield, Roderick wouldn't have bothered with Kemos and Na'ar. If he would've allowed himself to think rationally, Aidric would've known all this. Instead, he had allowed his rage to cloud his reason and had played right into Roderick's hands—just as Roderick knew he would.

But how did the bloody bastard manage to cast an illusion of Allison? It had never been possible before. He, himself, had attempted to cast an illusion of Allison several times in the past without success. He had never been able to give his illusion golden hair. It had always appeared white. Aidric had even had Allison attempt to cast an illusion of herself once. It too, had failed.

How did he do it? Aidric thought in frustration. *What has the viper discovered that we haven't? Or—does it have something to do with the Dark Powers?*

Aidric supposed he would never know, and he would be damned first before he ever gave the bastard the satisfaction by asking.

Ignoring the searing pain in his shoulder, Aidric carefully pulled himself to his knees and noticed that his hands and ankles were shackled. He had been too disoriented before to notice the hum of power against his skin, but they were definitely magically forged, making them essentially indestructible, even for a mage with his power. He expected no less from his oldest enemy.

"How I've longed to see this for many years," Roderick's unmistakable voice said somewhere in the darkness. "The mighty Aidric Stanisnik, on his knees before his new master."

Aidric squinted into the blackness before him, but couldn't see the Mihran king anywhere. He needed light. He would be damned before he faced Roderick blind. He reached for the power of the Mage-field and in the next instant, received the shock of his life. The power was not there! All of his channels were blocked! Had he not been spell-silenced, he would have howled in rage.

He hammered at the blocks with all the strength of his mind but to no avail. He didn't even manage a single crack in the blocks. Weak, and panting from his efforts, Aidric fell back against the wall of his cell in defeat.

"You only waste what little strength I have allowed you to maintain," Roderick's voice said, dripping with satisfaction and amusement. "You of all people should know that the blocks of a Domnae cannot be broken, and as you can see, my mentor taught me very well."

Aidric mentally groaned. Roderick's Domnae teacher again. Aidric thrice damned the wretched man for ever having been born. Would Roderick's past Domni tutelage ever cease to haunt them all?

In the darkness before him, a white light suddenly appeared in a bright flash, and he turned his face sharply away from the unexpected assault to his eyes.

When his vision cleared and his eyes adjusted to this new illumination, Aidric saw Roderick standing inside his cell in front of the door, a large ball of white light held out in his right hand.

The light eerily illuminated the bronze skin of Roderick's face, making him appear pale and ghostly, while his golden eyes sparkled maliciously. As if in mockery of Aidric's earlier mistake, he was dressed in the same silver robes and black-hooded cloak he had donned earlier to masquerade as Mordant.

"A pity," Roderick continued spitefully as he looked down his nose at Aidric, "that you who has always had something to say can't even grunt out a curse now. I would've enjoyed seeing you raging like a trapped animal. Perhaps I should dismiss my mute spell. I'm in the mood for a little amusement."

Roderick gestured between them, and Aidric immediately felt the bonds in his throat vanish. Once free, he resisted the urge to do just as Roderick wanted him to do and bit back the curses that had been ready at the tip of his tongue. Instead, he looked up at Roderick's smug face defiantly. Then his lips spread into a diabolical grin, and slowly, he began to chuckle.

The smug look immediately melted from Roderick's face, and a blazing anger flashed in his eyes. The ball of light instantly turned an angry red.

"You're so certain of your victory," Aidric said

between chuckles, his voice somewhat hoarse, but nevertheless strong. "I am only one man, and there are many more to take my place should you kill me. Lamia cannot be defeated so easily!"

"I wouldn't be so quick to laugh were I you," Roderick said darkly, visibly struggling to contain his rage.

Aidric's arms began to prickle as he felt Roderick draw a considerable amount of power from the Mihran Mage-field and a second, alien source until Roderick's entire form glowed with a clashing mixture of sickly yellow and white light. "Did you really believe that I would kill you so swiftly? Long have I waited to have you in this position, and should I choose, your torment will amuse me until I tire of you—and I don't tire so easily."

"If it's fear that you wish from me," Aidric said coldly, "then you'll be waiting until the hand of Seni delivers the just to the Thrones at the end of time."

Roderick's eyes narrowed. "We'll see," he said, stepping closer to Aidric.

"Remember this," Aidric warned. "As long as I still breathe, it's not finished between us!"

"And with my aid, you will breathe for a long time, yet—indeed long past the time when the relief of a death that, if I so choose, will be eternally from your reach is all you can think about."

Then before Aidric could wonder just what the bastard meant by that cryptic remark, Roderick cast forth the power he had gathered and began to chant an incantation that made his blood turn cold.

"*Aeon tier lansanie ta disanie, di tie parlan tarren ta calus sior!*"

As he felt the sickening wave of dark power encircle him, for the first time since his capture, Aidric wanted to scream in terror and dread.

CHAPTER EIGHT

Oblivious to everything but the task at hand, Allison concentrated on creating a clear mental picture of Aidric and opened her mind and empathic senses in search of any feelings or images of Aidric. For a long while, she sensed nothing of him, and that had her worried. Maybe he was unconscious, or someone had made sure he was heavily shielded from any outside probes.

Both scenarios filled her equally with horror. If true, then that would mean that the man she loved was now in the clutches of the worst piece of scum possible.

Trying not to panic, she had just decided to try something else when her senses suddenly detected a tendril of emotion, so faint that it was almost nonexistent, but it unmistakably had Aidric's "flavor." Instead of feeling overjoyed about finally locating him, Allison only felt a cold dread. The emotion she had picked up from him had been a sudden burst of terror, and it had come from beyond the magical barrier surrounding Mihr.

Aidric was *never* afraid.

Allison remembered that night so many moons ago when Aidric had been fighting in Idona when she had unwittingly Soulwalked and had found herself on that Idonan battlefield by merely wishing to be with Aidric. She now tried that same method again, hoping that it would work again when she was doing it consciously.

Almost instantly, she felt a strange sense of disorientation that she would've been hard pressed to describe. Although she *knew* that she hadn't moved, Allison nevertheless felt an overwhelming sense of movement, as though the world around her traveled past her, instead.

A breath later, she found herself "standing" at Aidric's side as if she had suddenly emerged from a portal. A quick glance around showed that she was now inside what looked like a rock-walled dungeon cell three times as horrifying as Lamia's own cells. Aidric, himself, was shackled like a common criminal, his back slumped against one of the filthy stone walls.

He looked more furious than she had ever seen him, even surpassing the rage she had sensed the time when he had barged into Diryan's study and learned that the man responsible for causing her to have one of her panic attacks was Domnae Eban. It distorted his face until he was almost unrecognizable. She felt a trickle of instinctual fear pass through her being but quickly shook it off. She couldn't afford to allow her emotions to distract her.

Allison drew her thoughts together, preparing to thought-speak with him, and froze when she suddenly sensed another presence in the dank cell. At first glance, she had mistaken the cloaked figure leaning casually against the wall opposite Aidric next to the cell door for a shadow in the semi-darkness, but now that her senses weren't so singularly focused on Aidric, she saw and felt exactly who the figure was even before he stepped into the illumination of the crimson ball of light that was held magically suspended in the air above the door.

Roderick.

The hate that instantly flooded her soul was jarring, so much that everything abruptly blurred around her, and she had to struggle for one terrifying moment to maintain her foothold on reality, focusing hard on Aidric and thoughts on how he had landed in such a wretched position. What kind of atrocity or treachery had Roderick committed in order for Aidric's guard to be down low enough for him to be captured?

The sound of Roderick's voice instantly turned her attention from Aidric to him. She realized with sudden alarm that the bastard was chanting an incantation, and before she could even think of how to stop him, the sound of chains rattling furiously beside her reached her ears. Allison whirled around in enough time to see Aidric levitate to a height of at least six feet, all four limbs stiff, and his arms hanging immobile at his sides.

Roderick chuckled nastily. "A living statue. That will be your sole purpose from now on."

"You'll have to try harder than this if you wish to humiliate me," Aidric spat down at him. "As I warned, things are far from finished between us. It would be wise to watch what lurks within the darkness of every corner. The time will come when one of those corners won't be empty."

"You are quite right, *Mage-general*," Roderick purred. "Your bones will ornament one of the corners in my study nicely when the sound of your wailing for death becomes tiresome."

Laughing, Roderick extinguished the light and strode out of the cell, the sound of the thick, iron door banging shut after him sounding so final, like the echo of a judge's mallet after passing his judgment.

"Bastard!" Aidric snarled after him.

Once she could no longer hear Roderick's footsteps, Allison wasted no time in thought-speaking him, *"Aidric, it's me, Allison. Are you all right?"*

To her surprise, he didn't reply. In fact, it seemed as though he hadn't heard her at all. Aidric had closed his eyes, his face appearing more drawn and weary than it had only seconds before, and he was muttering softly under his breath.

Allison willed her spirit up to him until they were eye to eye. Again, she attempted to thought-speak him, but it was no use. It was as if he didn't possess any thought-speaking abilities at all.

Roderick must have blocked all *his abilities*, she realized with a sinking feeling, *as Aidric once blocked mine.*

Concentrating more closely on his muttering, she was proven correct when she was able to pick out a few words, recognizing them as Ti'ar. From their meaning, it was clear that he was chanting an incantation to try to break through those magically-placed blocks.

Maybe I can help him break them, she thought determinably and immediately set to work.

Allison sent a mind-probe into his mind and immediately met up with a force she had not expected. It was a spell, of that she had no doubt from the powerful, condensed energy her probe encountered. However, the energy she touched was as alien to her as the magic of the Mage-field had been when she had first experienced it.

It was clear that the power didn't originate from a Mage-field—it didn't feel alive as the Mage-field did. There was nothing of the sense of nature in this power as was evident from her first touch of the Mage-field but something dark and threatening, decaying, as if the power was what gave spark to a plague's devouring force. And the plague in this instance was this ominous spell, a spell, she discovered after a little more careful prodding, that was securely intertwined and fused with Aidric's own life force. What in God's name could be its purpose?

By now Allison knew enough of mage-lore to know not to tamper with spells that exceeded her own understanding, but the urge to do so was almost overwhelming. Instinctually, she knew that the casting of this dark spell was the cause of the horror she had sensed in her search earlier. However, she could detect none of its effects on Aidric no matter how deeply she probed his mind and body.

Frustrated, Allison turned her attention instead to something she *did* understand and could possibly do something about—the first of a network of the many spell-blocks that Roderick had placed on him. Pulsating with Mage-field energy, the block was like a ten-foot-thick steel wall and her mind-probe the feather that brushed against it in the improbable hope of breaking through. It was the most powerful energy-block she had ever encountered.

After checking it for any points of weakness and unsurprisingly finding none, Allison decided to ram it with as much energy as she could safely channel and hope that it was enough to at least crack it. She reached for the Lamian Mage-field, feeling the by-now-familiar giddiness she experienced every time at her mind's initial touch, but instead of the energy flowing through her mind and into her channels as usual, it just flowed straight through her and dissipated into the air around her. Shocked, she frantically released the flow, and after stemming her panic, she tried again but met up with the same results.

What in God's name—

Then it suddenly dawned on her. Aidric had once explained to her that what allowed a mage to draw and channel power from a Mage-field was a combination of something physical, a part of the frontal lobe of the brain unique to the mageborn and in a sense, the doorway to the mage's channels and the mental ability to "touch" and manipulate the natural energies of the world. That was why she hadn't been able to contain the energy. She no longer had a physical body, a medium, to channel the energy through.

Cursing, Allison focused her attention on Aidric again. He was still muttering his incantations without any indication that he had even felt the Mage-field energy she had dispersed within the cell. Even blocked, he should've felt at least *something* of the magic! She was so far out of her depth that she would likely do more harm than good trying to rid him of the blocks.

I guess I'll have to get him out of here the hard way, she thought, frustrated to the point of screaming.

She needed to return to her body and tell King Diryan that she had found him. By Roderick's earlier words, he seemed to want to keep Aidric alive down here for quite some time. Hopefully that would buy the king enough time to send troops to storm the Mihran palace, or at the very least, stage a distraction for Roderick elsewhere in order for her to lead a group of mages into the bastard's dungeons to rescue Aidric.

Before she departed, Allison planted a kiss on his lips or tried to since she wasn't substantial. Her ghostly kiss caused him to abruptly stop his whispered incantations. Aidric's face became distressed.

"I must already be going mad," he said into the darkness, his voice thick with strain. "I could swear to Seni that I just felt Allison's lips press against my own."

No, not mad, she thought a little guiltily, wishing that he could hear her, and then fervently, *but I promise you that soon you'll feel my touch in the flesh!*

Then, before the anguish of having to leave him

behind in such a terrible place in the hands of such a vile man could break her, Allison forced herself to draw up a mental picture of her old bedroom where her physical body lay. A split-second later, she felt the same disorientation of what she now knew was her spirit rushing across the great distance between kingdoms. However, when her journey abruptly came to an end, she cried out in dismay when she saw that she wasn't "standing" in her old room with her friends but in a strange, misty and gray world of nothingness.

Cold fear began to sweep through her entire being as she glanced frantically around at her surroundings and encountered that same gray murkiness everywhere. Her sense of direction had also gone all to hell. If she'd been in her physical body, Allison was sure that her heart would have been beating to the point of exploding.

She looked down at the ground and immediately wished that she hadn't, an infinite abyss of grayness stretching below her, as well. It was as though she had suddenly been suspended within a physical version of pure madness.

Where in the hell *am I?* Allison thought wildly, wondering if she had indeed accidentally stumbled into one of the six hells of Ter-ob that Aidric often mentioned.

"Allison—"

She whirled around at the sound of her name, her entire being flooding with an overwhelming fear. What she saw behind her almost broke her mind.

"S-Soren?" Allison stuttered in utter disbelief, staring at the ethereal figure before her of the recently deceased Domnae in a kind of numbed shock. At his solemn nod, she continued to stammer, *"But how—why—dear God, am I dead?"*

Looking around at her gray, foggy surroundings, that last question made horribly too much sense. How else could she explain this impossible world around her? Had she stayed away from her body too long?

Soren shook his head, and Allison felt dizzy with relief. *"No Allison, you aren't dead,"* he confirmed, his tone still strangely grim, *"I have brought you here to this plane between worlds to give you a warning. Do not—"*

Suddenly, the misty-gray world, along with Soren, vanished and Allison was traveling at impossible speeds again. A few seconds later, her spirit violently slammed into something unforgivably solid in a great flash of golden light, knocking her senseless. It was some time before her muddled senses settled again, and the first thing she noticed was the screaming pain, a sure signal that she was once again in her body.

Her lungs began to burn as she instinctually drew a strangled breath. A scalding hand was pressed up against her forehead, and only then did she notice the icy chill that lay just beneath the pain. She moaned and began to shake violently.

"Allison!" she heard a deep voice say urgently, sounding miles away. Another scalding hand grabbed her throbbing hands and began to gently chaff them.

"Aidius! Keldan, her hands are like ice!" she heard a second voice exclaim, a feminine voice she felt she should know, but whose identity was just beyond the grasp of her muddled memory.

"What did you expect?" the same deep voice that had called her name said curtly. "How could she channel that much energy through her body for so long and *not* pay a heavy price? I must have been mad to have allowed her to attempt a spell that none of us knows anything about!"

"To the six hells with all this secrecy!" another voice interjected. "I'm going to fetch a healer."

"No—oo!" Allison managed to croak out, her eyes flying open as her memory suddenly came flooding back to her through the muddiness of her mind, recognizing the voices as those of Keldan, Raya, and Maldon. With considerable effort, she turned her head and focused her eyes on Keldan's strained face. "Keldan, d-don't let h-him!"

"Damn it, *no* secret is worth the cost of your life!" Keldan growled.

"Please," Allison pleaded hoarsely, "I-I'll be ffine."

"Fine my ass!" Raya exclaimed angrily. "I don't call turning blue and feeling like a block of ice *fine*! Hellsfire! Your body was starting to *dim*! The magic was consuming you! You were lucky that our Summons brought you back at all! Where in Seni's name did you go? To Aidius's gate?"

"So it was you—" Allison whispered, more to herself than them. "You drew me b-back before Soren could finish his w-warning."

"Soren?" Aren said, frowning. He turned to his brother. "Isn't that the Domnae who—she must be delirious."

"I'm not!" Allison hissed back as forcefully as she could with chattering teeth. "I s-saw him—somewhere—he said that it was a p-plane of existence between worlds. He b-brought my spirit there to give me a warning, but before he could—he c-could tell me, you yanked my spirit back here."

Then she closed her eyes as a wave of weakness and dizziness washed over her. Thankfully, the others remained silent, though it was probably because they were flabbergasted and didn't know how to react. Had anyone ever talked to the dead?

"I found Aidric," Allison whispered after a few moments of silence when she was able to think clearly again, "shackled in Roderick's dungeon. That bastard did s-something to him, but I'm not sure what. There's some sort of s-spell hovering around Aidric, a powerful one that wasn't f-fueled by Mage-field energy or even anything *resembling* the natural energies that exist all around us. I didn't think that was possible, but it exists a-all the same. All of his channels and mind-mage abilities have b-been blocked."

"Thank the Thrones above that he's still alive!" Raya said, her eyes mirroring her relief.

"Yes, but for how long?" Keldan said grimly. "Roderick has wished for Aidric's death from the moment Aidric sent him screaming back to Mihr with his ass on fire."

"I think that Roderick plans to—to t-torture him," Allison choked out. The tears she had been unable to shed in her spirit form suddenly spilled from her eyes. She was surprised at the magnitude of relief she felt once the dam had finally broken. "I arrived in the cell in enough t-time to hear the last of Roderick's threats. Judging from his words, I think he plans to draw it out as l-long as possible. If we act now, then there's still h-hope that we can get to him before Roderick has a chance to do anything! I need to see the k-king right now!"

Allison started to get up, but her body simply refused to obey her. Invoking her Soulwalking ability had left her more drained this time than it had the last.

Maybe she had been nearer to death than she wanted to think about, but that didn't matter. Aidric was her sole concern now.

"The only person *you're* going to see right now is a healer," Raya stated firmly. "We'll take care of reporting everything to the king—and I do mean *everything*, Allie."

Allison started to protest, but the look in all their eyes made it clear that any arguments would fall on deaf ears. Weak as she was, she definitely was in no condition to stop them. Instead, she decided to compromise.

"All right," Allison said slowly, reluctantly. "I'll see a healer, but I have conditions."

"Lady, you've been living with Aidric for far too long," Keldan said wryly, but he was smiling. "That infamous stubbornness has rubbed off on you."

"Not stubbornness—determination," she corrected. "As I said, I'll see a healer, but it has to be Dallan and only if my ability to Soulwalk is kept from him. I'll just tell Dallan that I tried to channel more energy than I could safely hold within my body. In a sense, that really is true. My second condition is that I want to speak with King Diryan, myself."

"You still intend to keep the fact that you can Soulwalk from the king?" Keldan asked flatly.

"Is that what you two were discussing earlier

when we first arrived?" Aren asked.

Keldan nodded, but that was the only acknowl-edgment he gave that he had heard his brother. He kept his eyes fixed sternly on Allison. His disapproval was plain for anyone to see.

Allison sighed and closed her eyes. "No, you're right, Keldan, and not because of any punishment. I suppose that His Majesty needs to know about the Soulwalking. He would've found out sooner or later, though *I* had hoped that it would be much later."

"In that case, I'll bring the king here, myself," Keldan said, his eyes softening. "Aren, go fetch Dallan if he can be spared. If not, Ardith will do just as well."

Allison began to protest, but the flash of warning in Keldan's eyes froze all of her protests in her throat. She might as well save her breath. Allison had learned long ago that Keldan could be as pigheaded as Aidric when he chose.

"Those two can be trusted to keep this behind their teeth," Keldan said pointedly to her. "Any other healer will gossip. I'll return shortly, I hope."

"God, I feel like someone tried to turn me inside out!" Allison said with a grimace the moment the twins had left the room.

"How did it feel?" Raya asked curiously.

"What? Leaving my body?" Allison asked. At Raya's nod, she did her best to explain what really couldn't be explained. "For one thing, it was scary. It was like someone had hit me hard in the chest with a club, and I couldn't breathe. Then I seemed to lurch forward, and for a long while, I knew nothing. I think that I blacked out or was in a state very similar to unconsciousness. When my wits came back, I suddenly realized that I was looking down at my own body. There are no words that could ever possibly describe what I felt at that moment. It was like being at your own funeral or something—but that's not quite right. As for moving around, I only needed to use my will."

"What did that feel like?" Maldon asked. "Aren said that it felt as if a cold wind had pierced his body when you walked through him."

"It's hard to explain—a feeling of transparency, of lightheadedness, like I was drunk, but I could still think straight. However, I found out the hard way that I can't perform anything except mind magic while in that state. I wanted to try to break the magical blocks placed in Aidric's mind, but when I drew energy from the Mage-field, it just passed right through me. If there's a way to use magecraft while in spirit form, then I don't know where to even start learning how."

"It must've been really frustrating," Raya said sympathetically.

"If only I would've been able to break those blocks in his mind!" Allison lamented. "What good is being able to Soulwalk when I can't do anything with it but observe and thought-speak?"

"And apparently, speak with the dead," Maldon added carefully, watching her reaction.

Raya shot him a troubled look. "*Can* you speak with any of the dead you wish while in your spirit state?" she asked tentatively.

Allison looked from one to the other. "I don't think so," she replied slowly. "Soren brought me to him. Meeting up with him was the last thing that I ever expected to happen. I think you both are misunderstanding me. When I invoke my ability to Soulwalk, nothing in the world around me changes with the exception of me. I think the plane I'm in while in spirit form is so close to the one we all live in that the only difference is that you can't see me, although *I* can see and hear everyone clearly without any of you having to thought-speak me. I can't even begin to understand how any of it works, so I can't be sure if that's even right.

"The place where Soren took me was different. It was a misty, gray world of nothingness where the only things that were remotely substantial were him and myself. There were no sounds, no smells, not even a sense of direction. Where that place was in the grand scheme of things, who knows? I didn't see Aidius's gates if that's what you're thinking."

"What do you suppose he wanted to warn you about?" Raya asked.

Her tone was still a bit skeptical, but Allison couldn't find it in her heart to take offense. How would she feel if the roles were reversed?

"I have no idea. All he said was 'do not' before I was pulled back to my body by your Summons. Maybe he didn't like the idea of me Soulwalking. After all, according to all of you, it almost killed me."

Before either Raya or Maldon could comment, the door to her room suddenly swung open, and Keldan entered with King Diryan fast on his heels.

"Keldan tells me you have found Aidric," Diryan said immediately, not bothering to waste any time with pleasantries.

Allison nodded, suddenly feeling nervous, and replied, "I have, Your Majesty. How much has Keldan told you?"

"Practically nothing," the king grumbled, glancing heatedly at the bardic-mage. Keldan winced involuntarily under that glare.

"I apologize, Your Majesty," she said quickly. "I assure you that it was at my request. I thought that it would be best if I would explain the situation myself."

"I presume you have used that empathic link we discussed earlier to locate him?" Diryan asked.

"No." Allison swallowed nervously. The next few

words wouldn't be easy to say. "Aidric and I—well, we haven't been entirely straight with you on the extent of my abilities."

"How so?" the king demanded, his eyes darkening.

The other three looked as though they suddenly wished to be elsewhere. There was no telling how Diryan was going to take the revelation of her ability to Soulwalk, in and of itself, but he would definitely be pissed that such a dangerous and momentous secret had been purposely kept from him. That, she thought, was the understatement of the year.

Allison gulped and forced herself to go on, "I have an ability that no other mage except, according to the Order of the Providence, the Natian Six possess, one which Aidric felt no one should know about." She paused, as if dramatically, but that wasn't her intention. There was no easy way to reveal it, so she just blurted it out. "I have the ability to—to Soulwalk."

To her disbelief, Diryan's dark look suddenly disappeared completely, and he began to chuckle. "Child," he said, shaking his head in amusement, "I know of your ability. Aidric, himself, told me."

"I had no idea…"

The king sighed and said. "Typical. He probably just assumed that you knew."

"The only thing I assumed was that he had kept it from you," Allison said dryly. "He was pretty adamant that *no one* should know. All this time, I was worried that you would fly into a rage because we had kept such a big secret from you!"

"Seeing you in this wretched condition, I assume it's from you having used this ability to locate him rather than from working in the Healer's Hall," the king noted. "I was under the impression that you didn't know how the spell was cast the first time."

She nodded. "I didn't. That was why I refused to even try to cast the spell before now. I was afraid that I would end up either killing myself or becoming lost in the spirit plane. I don't think that I have to tell you why I made the attempt today."

"No, you do not," Diryan agreed, "and from the anguish in your expression, I doubt that you have good news to report."

"He's in a cell in Roderick's dungeon," Allison said gravely, proud that her voice didn't warble.

Diryan didn't look in the least bit surprised. "I thought as much," he said with a sigh. He turned to the others. "Would you please leave us?" he said in a tone that made it an order and not a request.

Although looking reluctant, they quickly obeyed him. Allison thought it was odd that the king had asked them to leave. What was so secret about the matter that Diryan didn't want anyone but her to hear?

When the door had closed after Maldon, Allison said, "Your Majesty, I think that Roderick plans to torture Aidric to death. He's already cast some sort of spell over him. I can't even begin to guess its purpose. If we hurry, then maybe we can get him out of there before Roderick can hurt him."

Diryan silently regarded her with a peculiar expression on his face—was it pity? A feeling of dread instantly washed over her.

"Allison," he said quietly, "we cannot go to his aid."

"What do you mean?" she demanded sharply, not sure if she had heard him correctly.

"At the moment, we don't have the manpower to spare on what would have to be a direct assault on the Mihran palace," Diryan replied unhappily. "Our forces were depleted more severely than all expectations by the last two battles, and with all the wounded to boot, at the moment, we could not possibly win a battle against that palace. Remember that Roderick still has access to an ungodly amount of troops from his allies. Although he very well lost the equivalent of a whole army, he still has hundreds of thousands of men ready to lay down their lives for him at his signal."

"Surely you could send just a handful of men to sneak into the Mihran palace, at the very least," Allison insisted stubbornly. "A whole army isn't really necessary is it? I know that you still have several spies who could—"

She was cut short by a sharp look from the king. "Aidric speaks too freely with you, I fear," he muttered, then sighed as if resigned. "With the magical barrier still up around Mihr, I have no communication with any intelligence I have within the borders, and even if I did, I would not order them to attempt such a rescue. Roderick is not such a fool as to imprison Aidric where he could be easily reached. He is undoubtedly heavily guarded by both magical and physical means, and any tampering in either aspect would likely bring the bloody bastard running. I would be sending them to certain death. Aidric is the only man alive I believe would have even a remote chance of successfully executing such a rescue, and tragically for all of us, he is the man that needs rescuing."

"So what you're telling me is that we do *nothing?*" Allison asked shrilly, not quite believing her ears. "Don't you care about him at all? My God, he's practically your son, and you would sit here and do nothing while Roderick tortures him to death!"

Diryan flinched and then turned his head away from her sharply, his expression looking seconds away from crumbling. Allison immediately regretted her biting words. She didn't mean to hurt him, but once again she had spoken in anger what was better left unsaid. When he turned back to her, his face was indeed wet with tears.

"Do you not realize that having to make such a difficult decision has caused me an endless amount of pain?" he said quietly as two more tears fell shamelessly from his eyes. "I have suspected his fate long before I came to you with the news that Aidric was missing, and I have thought of little else since. By the Thrones above, child! He has replaced the son that my wife and I lost so many years ago!"

"I-I'm—sorry," Allison stammered, stricken, tears of her own starting to stream down her cheeks.

She felt like the worst piece of filth alive for brutally jamming the knife already stabbing him in the heart so much deeper. Allison doubted that anybody other than Ileanna and Aidric had seen the king cry. The she had forced him to show her this kind of vulnerability made her sin all the more worse.

"But Aidric—won't he be expecting—" Allison choked over a sob before she could complete the thought, hating herself for crying. After what she had just done, she didn't have the right to cry.

"No. As it's true for the royal couple of Na'ar, Aidric is well aware that if he ever hopes to escape Roderick's clutches, it will have to be done through his own power."

The king sat on the edge of her bed and, to her shock, embraced her gently like a father comforting a beloved daughter.

"With those blocks on his mind, I don't see that there's any hope at all," Allison said bitterly as her tears began to soak into the delicate *sholkie* material on Diryan's shoulder.

"You underestimate Aidric," the king assured her. "He is a man that has often proven that there is no such thing as a hopeless situation. Let us just pray to Seni that Aidric's time to face Aidius has not come."

For the first time in her life, Allison did send up a prayer to Seni.

CHAPTER NINE

I'm doing the right thing, Allison thought determinably as she wrapped her cloak around her shoulders. Despite the certainty of that thought, she couldn't quite shake a tiny tinge of doubt from her mind. *Aidric needs me. I don't care what King Diryan said. I can't just sit here on my ass and let Roderick torture him to death!*

She grabbed the pack of food and gear she had prepared for the journey, and with a few whispered Ti'ar words, it disappeared into her personal magical storage plane, which Aidric had helped her construct a moon ago. Silently, she slipped out the door, a ghost in the darkness.

The Mage Hall was thankfully empty as Allison silently made her way down the hall and to the south exit. Cautiously, before she opened the enormous door, she sent out a Probe of Inquiry into the night and detected only a half dozen presences on the grounds between the Mage Hall and the stables, none having the feel of mages or mind-mages. They were most likely servants or stablehands doing a few last minute duties before retiring for the night.

Allison had hoped to avoid meeting up with anyone she knew and having to explain why she intended to take such a late night ride. She never had been good at lying, and given what everyone knew of her relationship with Aidric and that he was now missing, they would more readily believe that the Temple had renounced Seni before they believed her story. She dreaded her encounter with Master Ahern. If he didn't believe her story, she ran the risk of him becoming suspicious and deciding to rat her out to the king.

She also didn't dare cast the invisibility spell over herself since any magic felt in her room would probably send half a dozen mages running to her suite to investigate. She still wasn't confident enough in her magecraft to shield her use of the Mage-field from detection. As it was, the twins, Raya, and Selwyn watched her like a hawk. It was a wonder that she had even made it out of her suite undetected.

As if she was a burglar in the night, Allison stealthily crept towards the stables, all the while feeling as though the eyes of the entire kingdom stared accusingly out of the surrounding darkness. Each careful step was more agonizing than the last, each footfall sure to betray her. Although she had not suffered a panic attack for many moons, she now walked a fine, sharp edge between reason and that suffocating, cold fear.

Almost angrily, Allison shoved that turmoil of emotions away. She had to be strong for Aidric. Anything less would be a far greater betrayal to their love than if she had simply chosen to listen to the king and do nothing. She was no longer that scared, insecure girl who would have rather died than to defy her stepfather. Even so, some part of her soul, buried deep within a steel determination, still bled from that old wound—would never completely heal, she knew.

Allison hastily melted into the shadows of the palace when two faint voices reached her ears from somewhere ahead of her, gradually getting louder until she finally caught sight of their shadowy outlines in the gloom heading towards her. She held her breath, her heart pounding in her ears so loudly that she feared the two figures walking past would hear it, and prayed that they wouldn't look her way. Although the shadows hid her from a casual glance, their meager cover wouldn't withstand a direct look, and as before, she didn't dare cast the invisibility spell in case they were mages.

She breathed a silent sigh of relief once the two

people, a young noble couple she instantly recognized, passed by without so much as a glance in her direction. Luckily, they were too absorbed in each other to notice anything else.

Even when the couple had turned the corner, Allison remained stock-still, not even daring to swat at the annoying insects that buzzed around her face until she was certain that no one else was in her vicinity. Only then did she step out of the shadows and hurry over to the stables. Thankfully, she met with no other close calls. As she suspected, Master Ahern was still up and overseeing his workers as they finished up their work for the night. At the sound of her approach, Ahern spun around and then blinked at her in surprise.

"M'lady Allison, what brings you here at such a sand-mark?" he asked, frowning slightly. "Are you planning on leaving for a journey *now*?" The tone of his voice said how much he disapproved.

"I wouldn't exactly call it a journey," Allison replied cautiously, doing her best to look pathetically depressed. "I couldn't sleep, and I thought a short ride would help—that is, if you don't mind—"

"I don't think you should be ridin' alone at this sand-mark," Ahern said, shifting his feet uncomfortably. "M'lord Aidric would have my hide if I let you go and something happens t' you."

God, he's not going to let me go! There must be something

I can—

"Please, I—I have to—get away—" she pleaded, surprising herself by producing a few tears. "All those pitying eyes—all the pain in the Healer's Hall—please Master Ahern, I need to get away from the palace! I promise not to be gone long. I just need some time to myself."

At the sight of her tears, the Stablemaster looked away awkwardly. "Well—" he said reluctantly. "I suppose it wouldn't hurt you t' go out for a couple 'o sand-marks, you being a mage and all—as long as you don't wander far."

"Thank you," Allison said sincerely, still sniffling, though inside she was doing cartwheels. The first hurdle had been cleared. "I really appreciate this. I just hope Destiny won't be too upset about having to leave her warm stable to go out into the chill."

Ahern waved over one of the stableboys and ordered him to bring Destiny's saddle and tack while he proceeded to fetch the mare himself. Within a matter of depths, horse and rider were ready to ride. A still uneasy Ahern bade her a good ride and promised to be waiting for her when she returned.

He's going to be waiting an awful long time, Allison thought guiltily as she urged Destiny into a gallop once they were a few yards away from the stables, all the while feeling Ahern's eyes boring into her back.

It was only after she had circled around the palace grounds and had ridden for a little over a sand-mark in the direction of the Lamian/Na'aran border that she noticed the sound of distant hoofbeats behind her. Her first reaction was to wonder who would be riding at such a late sand-mark; her second was to become alarmed. Had Ahern not believed the story she had fed him after all? Had he just pretended to go along with her and then had sent someone to trail her to see where she really was going?

Quickly, before the approaching, unknown rider came within visual distance of her, Allison cast the invisibility spell over herself and Destiny and hastily led the mount over to the side of the road to wait for the rider to pass.

She nearly lost her seat when a relatively cheerful voice said into her head, *"Nice try, Allie, but we already caught sight of you before you cast your spell."*

"Raya," Allison sent back dully, *"and Selwyn, I presume. I should've known."*

Dismissing the spell, Allison waited for them to catch up with her, knowing that trying to evade a mage and an empath was pointless.

"Just where in the six hells did you think you were running off to?" Raya demanded when she was within earshot.

"He needs me," Allison said stubbornly, meeting

the younger girl eye to eye as Raya rode up alongside her.

Selwyn, seeing the beginnings of a battle of wills between them, wisely kept to the background.

"You would go against the king's orders," Raya said pointedly, "defy him and all of Lamia by crossing the border—presuming you can even manage that. Do you really believe that the border guards will just happily open the Shield and bid you a good journey?"

"Do you think I would be that *stupid*?" Allison replied dryly. "I never planned on going through the border station. And don't look at me that way, Raya. You would do the same if it was Selwyn who was in Roderick's dungeon!"

"But *I* am not the *Golden Mage*," Raya challenged. "The kingdom can afford to lose a mid-level mage like me to such a foolhardy quest, but Lamia can't afford to lose *you*."

"The kingdom was doing just fine *without* me!" Allison growled, her horse beginning to dance in response to her agitation so that she wasn't able to say anything more for a while as she attempted to soothe the animal.

By the time Allison noticed the prickling on her arms, it was too late. A flash of golden light abruptly assaulted her eyes, but even before her vision cleared, she understood only too well her mistake. Her mage senses were eyes enough for her. Raya had taken advantage of her distraction and entrapped her within a barrier of sheer power. Allison had reflexively allowed her guard to be down around her friends, a habit she had never given a moment's thought to.

For a moment, Allison was too stunned to react, staring dumbly at her two friends with her mouth agape. Besides Aidric, only Raya would have dared such a thing.

"I'll remove the barrier when you're ready to come to your senses," Raya said calmly. "Until then, it stays up, even if it takes until next winter's end to convince you that what you're doing is damned foolish."

Anger quickly replaced surprise, and if looks could kill, then both Raya and Selwyn would have been dead a dozen times over. However, it wasn't with anger that Allison's face burned but humiliation. Like a sudden shock, it began to race through her body before she could think to stop it.

"Uh, Raya, I don't think doing that was such a good—" Selwyn began uneasily.

Allison began glowing an angry green as she effortlessly drew power from the Mage-field and allowed it to fill her body, a crashing wave of exhilaration as heady as a strong wine. Then with a blast that nearly rocked the young couple off their horses, she threw a dagger of pure power at her magical prison, shattering it as easily as if it had been a fragile eggshell. She didn't know which was louder—the screams of the horses or the cries of her friends.

Even after the horses had been calmed again, no one spoke, but both Raya and Selwyn conspicuously moved their mounts away from Allison. It made Allison sick to see the sudden fear in their eyes, the doubt, but she brutally shoved those feelings down. She couldn't afford to allow herself to be swayed by guilt and self-disgust.

"You can try to stop me from here to the border," Allison said slowly into the thick silence, "but it'll just be a waste of your time and mine."

Then she sighed, and the rest of her anger faded away. Only then did she start to feel the first effects of her channeling within her body in the form of flu-like body-aches. She had overdone it with the dagger of power, she knew, and would no doubt be cursing her rashness later on. Time enough for that later.

"I know you both mean well," Allison continued wearily, "but understand that I will *not* just sit in that suite while nothing is done to rescue Aidric from that bastard! All my life I've just meekly done what others wanted. Now I have a chance to do something for myself for once. Ride back and tell King Diryan what you must, even the truth. I know that I'll have to face his wrath when I return, but *anything* will be worth Aidric's freedom—even the loss of my own."

Not bothering to wait for their reply—maybe even afraid of hearing it—Allison turned away and urged Destiny into a trot, hoping that they would listen to her and return to the palace.

For a few moments, she thought they had done just that, until she heard the hoofbeats coming up behind her and Selwyn say, "Hey, you didn't really believe that we would allow you to go alone to face Roderick, foolish quest or not."

"I don't need your help," Allison said curtly as they caught up to her, each riding on either side of her as if they intended to be her jailers instead of her riding companions.

"Ha!" Raya snorted. "You *have* been living too long with Aidric. Stubborn, the both of you! Well, Lady Golden Mage, you'll have our help whether you wish it or not. What kind of friends would we be if we let you run off to face the very real perils of Mihr alone?"

"But—" Allison protested.

"No 'buts,'" Raya cut her off firmly. "If we can't persuade you to give up this foolhardiness, then we'll all be fools in this together. A fool to watch your back is better than having no one at all." She glanced over at Selwyn, who nodded vigorously with a grin.

Allison looked from one to the other suspiciously,

half believing that once she let her guard down that Raya would hit her with a sleep or paralysis spell—or maybe even just hit her physically to knock her out—but the look in their eyes and her own senses were telling her that their offer of help was sincere. Having them along *would* give her better odds of success, and besides, Raya was right. Having someone to guard your back while inside hostile territory was something she couldn't look sideways at.

"All right," Allison said slowly. "I'll accept your help and gladly." Then sheepishly, "I admit, when I rushed out here, I was letting my feelings do the thinking, but that still doesn't change the fact that I'll do whatever it takes to rescue Aidric."

"*We* shall," Raya corrected with a crooked smile.

"And now," Selwyn broke in, "that the two cats are no longer arching their backs and claws have been retracted into their proper places, may I ask just how milady proposes to cross the border without going through the border station?"

"Simple," Allison replied with a grin. "Instead of going through the border station, we head southeast of Biros, and *I* open the Shield."

As she suspected, both Raya and Sel were totally dumbfounded by this revelation. Only the four mages assigned to each border station as gatekeepers knew the spell that allowed the Shield to be opened the fraction needed for travelers to pass. The only copy of the spell lay in the vaults of the Temple of Seni under spell-lock, and only the High Priest held the magical "key." At least they were the mages who were *supposed* to know the spell. That didn't necessarily mean that they were the *only* ones, and Allison said as much.

"Aidric taught it to me," Allison replied to the questioning in their eyes.

"Why doesn't that surprise me?" Raya said dryly. "How did the beast manage to learn—no, don't tell me. I don't think that I want to know."

"Good," Allison said firmly, "because even if I wanted to tell you, I can't since I don't know how he learned the spell, myself. I'm not even sure *I* want to know how he did it! I have a feeling that it probably involved something shady. I never bothered to ask, and he never saw fit to tell me."

"Have you ever actually used the spell?" Selwyn asked anxiously. "Will the border guards or the mage be able to detect that the Shield is being opened?"

"To answer your first question, yes, I've opened the Shield once before. Aidric insisted that I at least attempt it, and I was successful. My tampering was never noticed, which answers your second question. Aidric devised a variation of the spell used to open the Shield that essentially doesn't open the Shield the way the mage at the border opens it."

"He would," Selwyn muttered.

Raya shot her husband an impatient look and waved Allison to continue.

"Instead of creating a hole in the Shield as the mage at the border does, Aidric transformed the very essence of a portion of the Shield. The spell causes a magical flutter in the Shield so small that it can be interpreted as merely the natural pulses of the Shield's energy. The opened portion of the Shield also looks no different to anyone's Inner-sight."

"So, what you're saying is that after you cast this spell, you can just walk right through the Shield as if it wasn't even there even though to a mage's Inner-sight, the Shield is still closed?" Selwyn asked skeptically, casting a dubious eye at his wife.

Raya merely looked at Allison expectantly.

Allison shook her head. "There's more to it than that. The energy of the spelled portion of the Shield is converted from a perfectly stable state to a very unstable one, but it's still as solid as the rest of the Shield— that is, solid to your normal physical state. A second spell must be cast before you can pass through the Shield. That spell draws a portion of your body's life-energy from within until it forms a circle around your entire body. The Shield around Lamia was created by that long ago Lamian king from his life-energy, so, when the circle of life-energy around you meets with the unstable life-energy that *is* the Shield, it melds with it a lot like the melding of two external shields by two mages. It's what allows you to pass without hindrance or detection. As long as that circle of life-energy encases your body, your physical body remains nonexistent to the Shield, itself."

"Whoa, whoa, back up!" Selwyn sputtered. "What is this about the Shield consisting of life-energy—"

"You mean, you don't know?" Allison asked, staring at him in disbelief. "Didn't Aidric tell you?"

"Apparently, there was much our pal, Aidric, forgot to mention," Raya answered flatly. "Lord Seni above, he could be a Providencen priest with all his secrets that he conveniently forgets to confide—" Raya paused suddenly and then looked from Allison to Selwyn with an expression of growing horror. "Aidius, do you know what this *means?*"

"What are you talking—" Selwyn began, but was immediately cut off.

"The Shield!" Raya exclaimed shrilly right over Selwyn. "Aidric holds the knowledge of how it can be opened, and he's in Roderick's hands! What if that bastard decides to probe Aidric's mind for any secrets? Seni help us all, he will have his armies of darkness swarming onto the palace grounds within a day!"

Before the girl's panic could reach a higher level,

Allison said hastily, "Not even *I* could break through Aidric's mind shields, and I'm far better at breaking shields than even he is. As far as I could tell in my spirit state, Roderick wasn't able to even scratch the shields around Aidric's mind. He was only able to place those weird shields beyond Aidric's own so that no energy could be channeled or any of his mind-mage abilities could pass them, and that, only because he was Domni-trained. Remember that Aidric is also Domni-trained, and his shields are likely constructed using Domni methods."

"Seni be praised," Raya said, relieved, "but unfortunately, Aidric's mind shields can't prevent that bastard from—"

Pain!

Allison felt the side of her body slam into the ground before she even realized she had fallen from Destiny. She hardly registered the sound of horses whinnying or the hands that tugged at her, lost in a terrible pain that felt as though her very soul was being torn to shreds with searing claws. She couldn't breathe, couldn't scream. She could barely even think with any kind of coherence. If not for the excruciating pain, she would have thought that she was having a panic attack.

Then as fast as it had begun, the pain stopped, and

Allison was left blinking up dazedly at a very fright-ened Raya and Selwyn, her chest hurting and gasping as if she had just completed a hundred mile marathon. Her skin didn't tingle at all with residual Mage-field energy, so she hadn't been attacked with magic. If not magic, then what in the world could have—

She sucked in a sharp breath. If not an external attack, then it had to be her empathic bond with Aidric! Worse, that kind of pain could only mean one thing. Allison tried to sit up and was stopped by a firm hand and the look of sheer panic on Raya's face.

"Don't move, Allie!" Raya ordered, "You took a hard fall, and you could've broken something—your back, your neck. Allow Selwyn to examine you first."

"There's no time for this!" Allison insisted ur-gently, pushing their hands away as she tried to rise again. "Nothing's broken. What I felt—it's Aidric! That bastard is torturing Aidric!"

Selwyn swore as Raya helped Allison to her feet without any more protests. A sharp pain abruptly shot through her side as both Raya and Selwyn helped her mount, but Allison barely noticed it. She had thoughts only for Aidric and reaching him.

As the three friends galloped as fast as their horses could carry them towards the border, Allison prayed to both God and Seni that she wouldn't arrive too late to save Aidric.

CHAPTER TEN

A idric hung suspended in the air, as limp and life-less as a ragdoll. His head lolled at an uncom-fortable angle against his shoulder, and he would no doubt have been screaming in agony if he had still been conscious. Roderick took in the sight of him as dispassionately as if he was merely looking out a win-dow at a bird perched on a tree limb and not at the half-dead body that he had just drawn more than half of the life-energy from.

The sense of his greatest enemy's life-energy flow-ing through his own body left Roderick feeling as giddy as a child attending his first festival—not to mention feeling more powerful than he ever had felt before.

Too bad the fool was too pure of heart to dabble in the Dark Powers, Roderick thought smugly, *else his power could have surpassed the combined powers of every mage through-out the lands. Unfortunately for him, I had no such qualms. Lord Arioch is a greater master than Seni ever could be! The Dark Powers have already allowed me this first triumph. Now let's see if they will give me my second.*

A door slammed in the distance, immediately drawing him out of his thoughts. His senses determined that Mordant's presence was near, and he rolled his eyes in impatience, turning away from his prize just as the door to Aidric's cell swung open with a bang that was loud enough to wake the dead clear into Hrefna. Roderick bit back the angry retort on his lips when he saw the look of barely contained excitement on Mordant's face.

"What is it now?" Roderick asked in a bored tone, looking down his nose at the newest mage-king of Bar'taiver. *...and soon to be the newest* dead *king of Bar'taiver, if all goes as I wish*, he thought with amusement.

Mordant ignored his tone. He was simply too excited to be offended.

"The Golden Mage has been spotted within our borders," he said, not able to keep the excitement from his voice.

Capturing her was as important to Mordant as it was for Roderick as Roderick had promised to use her to help Mordant lay siege to the Rathtyen palace. Like

Roderick, Mordant was not content with just one throne.

"Ah, so the little golden fish has taken the bait," Roderick said, gesturing at Aidric and smiling diabolically. "Does she travel alone?"

"No, she travels with a young man and woman. The woman, at least, is a mage of some power, but your guardsmen weren't able to determine the status of the man. They're within the Evrei Forest, nearing the Telek River."

"And how is it that a legendary mage is foolish enough to travel into enemy territory so openly?" Roderick wondered aloud. "Are my men certain that the three aren't an illusion?"

"Quite certain," Mordant assured him. "They had been traveling under the invisibility spell, but unfortunately for them, the sound of a horse whinnying where there was none revealed their position. However, from their behavior, your men were quite certain that the Golden Mage and her companions weren't aware that they were being observed."

"How absolutely delicious!" He walked closer to Aidric, reached up, and gave his leg a vicious yank. "Did you hear that, Your Mightiness?" Roderick demanded, his voice mocking. "Your lover has come to visit you. A pity that she'll get no farther than a hundred spans from the palace grounds. What say you about that?"

To his disappointment, the Mage-general didn't even twitch. Perhaps he had drained him a bit too much. No matter. His purpose had been served. Later on, when he had the leisure, Roderick could revive Aidric for his amusements. Until then, he had a much larger fish to reel in.

Roderick turned to the Silver Mage. "Come Mordant. It's time to set the next leg of our plan into motion. By the first rays of dawn, the Golden Mage will be ours."

***

When he could no longer hear the echo of footsteps, Aidric dropped his pretense of unconsciousness and lifted up his head, snarling with hatred into the devouring blackness that was his prison.

"Bastard, if you so much as get even a hundred spans of her, I'll make you regret the day you breathed your first breath!" he vowed furiously.

He had no time to lose. With Allison and her two companions—most likely Raya and Selwyn—so near the palace and their impending doom, every depth would count. Although Roderick had indeed drained him of a good portion of his life-force, the demonspawn hadn't taken as much as he had thought.

Aidric had made sure of that.

That was why the pain had been considerably more excruciating than it should have been. He had fought the perverse invasion with all his soul. He only prayed that what strength he had managed to prevent Roderick from stealing would be enough to break through the blocks in his channels.

Through the eternal sand-marks of his miserable imprisonment, he had been poking and prodding at the blocks, filthy concentrations of dark energy that Aidric had never had to deal with before. Even his training in the Temple and the knowledge he had concerning the darker magicks didn't prepare him for this tedious task. The energy in the blocks Roderick set in his mind fed hungrily on any life-energy he used in his attempts to crack them. In fact, the more energy he thrust against them, the more the blocks seemed to strengthen. So far, the only thing attacking the blocks had accomplished was to give him the most incredible headaches.

With his earlier failures, that left him with only one alternative, one that he disliked using no matter the circumstance. There were only two forces that gave a mage power that were not like that of life- or death-energy—love and anger. As he had done on that Idonan battlefield so many moons ago, Aidric planned to use anger in an attempt to build up enough power to blast through the blocks. He had been preparing himself to utilize that type of attack ever since Roderick had used the Dark Powers to drain his life-force, and this latest outrage of Roderick's plan to entrap Allison was the final nudge his turmoil of emotions needed to provide him with all the anger and hatred in his soul for such a destructive spell.

It was now or never. The battle that needed to be fought inside his mind required the deepest concentration, and Aidric was already beginning to feel the first serious pangs of hunger and thirst that Roderick's dark spell had condemned him to. That was a distraction he couldn't afford. One mistake and he could sear his own mind away to nothing, which he suspected, was precisely what the bloody bastard wanted him to do since Roderick had failed in his own attempts to get past any of his mental shields. Only Allison's rogue magic had been able to shatter them.

Focusing his mind inward, Aidric began to draw all the energy of his anger together until his body began to glow a brilliant white. He could barely feel the power gathering behind Roderick's blocks, but it was enough for him to take control of and begin to mold it into a dagger of power a hundred times more powerful than any he had ever constructed. Then with a purely mental cry, Aidric shot all the power of his anger simultaneously at every block in his mind like a loosed arrow.

Had he not been magically suspended in the air, the resulting blast caused by light and dark powers meeting would have knocked him off his feet. His mind was suddenly a blazing inferno, his senses driven into chaos. He tried to scream, but no sound emerged. His mind knew nothing but pain, and his entire being seemed to be filled with a consuming light.

"Aidric!" a vaguely familiar voice called through the haze of pain in his mind, and desperately, Aidric clung to that unexpected presence in his mind before the last shreds of his self could be seared away.

The presence instantly grasped his mind firmly and slowly brought his consciousness back from deep within the pain. Like an anchor, the presence prevented him from falling back down into that dark, agonizing abyss.

Then a feeling of warmth washed through Aidric's entire being, very similar to the experience of having healing energies sent into the body, but unlike a healer's energies, this energy felt vaguely of Magefield energy that had been interwoven within several other energies he couldn't even begin to identify. As abruptly as they had first appeared, the fire and pain inundating his mind vanished as the healing energies swiftly soothed his abused channels, leaving not even a hint of damage in their wake.

Aidric blinked heavy eyelids and stared dazedly out into the darkness, confused as to what had just happened to him. Then with a start, he realized that he was no longer paralyzed or floating in midair but lying sprawled out on the rough, cold surface of his cell. His back was also being thoroughly soaked by the filthy water seeping along the stone floor. Weakly, he raised himself to a sitting position.

That voice, he thought confusedly, *a male voice. I know it, but who? And more importantly, why did he help me?*

"Enough wit-wondering, Mage-general," the voice commanded sternly. *"Never mind the who, whats, and whys. You don't have the time! The Golden Mage cannot be allowed to fall into the hands of Roderick and his pet mage, or all hope will be lost for not only Lamia, but mankind. You must go to her before Roderick can entrap her."*

"But how!" Aidric cried within his mind in frustration, the rattling of his shackles echoing appallingly loud throughout the cell. *"These damned blocks—I can't break them! I've tried and tried, and as you know, have failed miserably! If you know of Allison and our plight, why then can you not go to her aid? Dammit, I've heard your voice before! Just who in the six hells are you?"*

Aidric climbed unsteadily to his feet, a hand leaning heavily on the jagged wall behind him, and scanned the area of his cell, but he couldn't locate anything resembling a figure in the darkness. Nevertheless, his empathic senses were maddeningly screaming out to him that a presence *was* physically near.

Then without warning, a blue, misty and shapeless glow appeared directly in front of him, so close that he scarcely had to extend his arm to touch it. At the same time, all the hair on his arms and at the nape of his neck began to stand on end, signaling that very powerful magic was being performed.

He suddenly found himself in a position he hadn't been in since he was a child—helpless to protect himself from a magical attack. He took an involuntary step away from the hazy manifestation, his shackles nearly sending him onto his backside as he eyed it warily.

The blue mist began to rapidly coalesce, taking the shape of a man, featureless at first, then with more defined detail that had Aidric wondering if he had gone mad after all. The ethereal man now standing before him, glowing with a blue light that was almost painful to look at, was none other than Domnae Soren—the very *dead* Domnae Soren. Aidric mouthed his name, but no sound made it past the huge knot that had suddenly formed in his throat.

"I do not go myself, Aidric Stanisnik, Soren said slowly, staring gravely with hollow, transparent eyes into Aidric's eyes, an experience that was uncanny enough to cause Aidric to cast his eyes away uncomfortably, *"because I can only do what is permitted me. I've been*

permitted to heal what you so foolishly did to yourself, and I can also lend you the use of the powers I now wield that you may break the magical blocks the blasphemer Roderick has bestowed upon you. That is all. The rest is your task, alone." He held his hand out to Aidric. *"Now, no more words, my friend. Take my hand, and my power will be at your disposal."*

Before he could even think about what he was doing, Aidric's hand shot out and "clasped" the Domnae's hand. Although there was no feeling of firm flesh within his hand, there was a feeling of substance, perhaps what air would feel like should it solidify and a person was suddenly able to hold it. Then Aidric had no more room for thought as a power unlike any he had ever experienced instantly began to flow into his body, leaving behind a feeling as heady as good wine in its wake.

The power of Seni himself—

"Cast my power at the blocks," Soren instructed.

Aidric immediately obeyed, shaping this newly acquired divine energy into a dagger of power as he had done with the energy of his anger. This time, there was no blast within his mind when the power Soren had loaned him slammed into the blocks. The power simply plowed on through as if the blocks of concentrated dark energy were made of fine sand.

When he released Soren's hand and the stream of divine power instantly ceased to flow into his body, a powerful wave of weakness washed over him and he collapsed to his knees.

"It's the price you must pay for wielding power that was not meant for mortals to wield," Soren explained in answer to Aidric's bewildered expression. *"Summon every breath of courage within you, my friend, for you will need it all for the trials ahead of you. I've given all the aid I am allowed. Go to Allison, and remember that the eyes of Seni will forever be on you."*

Then before Aidric could stammer out a reply, Soren's ghostly form vanished, leaving only a draft of cool air in his wake as the only evidence that Aidric hadn't hallucinated the whole episode.

"I guess—it all lies in my hands now," Aidric whispered hoarsely into the gloom as he struggled to climb to his feet again. "I just pray to Seni that I have the strength to reach her before Roderick does."

With those grim words hanging in the air, Aidric attempted to thought-speak Allison, but his thoughts immediately rammed up against the same barrier he had encountered in Na'ar.

"Damn!" he raged and immediately regretted it when a rush of weakness flooded his body and he swayed precariously.

Roderick had thought of everything. Rather than risk the chance that Aidric would somehow get past his blocks, the bastard must have placed the same type of barrier around his cell as a secondary precaution.

I'll just have to build a portal out of here, Aidric thought determinably.

Roderick had mentioned earlier that Allison had been spotted along the Telek River. If he could just transport himself along its banks, he could then pin-point her exact location by sending out a Probe of In-quiry.

Without hesitation, Aidric reached for Lamia's Mage-field, thankful that it existed on another plane and Roderick's barrier couldn't affect its flows. His muscles began to ache once the flow of energy entered his channels, and his knees were dangerously close to collapsing out from under him once again. Even so, he channeled the energy until he had collected a suffi-cient amount within him. Only then did he cast it forth and begin the construction of the portal.

When the portal was at last complete what felt like an eternity later, Aidric had only enough strength left to stumble towards the portal and literally fall through, all the while praying to Seni that he would have enough wits left to make it to his destination.

CHAPTER ELEVEN

"*W*e're *being pursued,*" Selwyn thought-spoke Allison, careful not to show his anxiety on his face. From the way Raya's shoulders suddenly tensed, Selwyn had also sent the same warning to her. "*I sense only one presence, a male, at least a hundred handspans behind us and to the left within the forest. He's guarding his mind so well that he can only be a mage.*"

"*Just one?*" Allison asked uneasily. "*Are you sure? Do you think it might be Mordant?*"

She shivered involuntarily at that thought. Her first and only encounter with Mordant was still fresh in her mind, as though it had happened mere sand-marks earlier and not moons.

"*You may be right, Allie,*" Raya chimed in. "*It*

wouldn't be Roderick since he seldom places himself in any situations that could become too dangerous ever since Aidric severally wounded him years ago. We may be riding into an ambush. Allie, I think you should construct us a portal back into Na'ar."

"I'd love to, Raya," Allison sent to the couple, "but I'm afraid I can't."

Both Selwyn and Raya turned astonished eyes on her.

"What do you mean you can't?" Selwyn demanded. "Or is it that you won't? Allison, I understand how badly you wish to rescue Aidric from Roderick's dungeons. Hellsfire, he's my best friend! I want him safe, too, but what good shall we be to him if we're all captured and become permanent neighbors to him in those dungeons?"

"No! You don't understand!" Allison sent in exasperation. "It isn't that I'm being stubborn. I simply can't cast the spell! I've never attempted it before." She heard them both groan in her mind. "Can't you cast the portal spell, Raya?" she asked, eyeing her friend hopefully.

"I don't have the control nor the channeling ability for such a major spell," Raya replied regretfully. "You know my mage talents are only average. Damn. So much for that plan. Any ideas?"

"We could retreat back into the forest," Allison offered, "and with Selwyn's help, I think that I can successfully hide our tracks."

"Gladly," Selwyn sent, *"but Mordant is a powerful mage. Could he not sniff us out since he already knows our general location?"*

"Supposing that it is Mordant, and not someone else," Allison said pointedly. *"In either case, I'm going to be using bardic magic, and from your experiences with Keldan and Aren, you know no one other than another bardic-mage can sense a bardic spell."*

"Then for what do you need my assistance?" Selwyn asked.

"I need you to plant decoy emotions in several different directions, even the direction we'll be heading. Both of you ride at least a couple of dozen handspans ahead of me. Leave the rest to me."

Selwyn and Raya nodded, urging their horses to pick up their speed until they were a sufficient distance ahead of Allison. She then dropped them completely from thought as she concentrated on the spell she was about to sing. Her singing voice was still nowhere near the phenomenal level of either of the twins, but at least she no longer sounded like a frog with a cold when she sang.

However, before she could sing her first note, Allison felt a mental "hand" touch the edge of her mind. Without thinking, she whirled around in her saddle and began to scan the terrain for any signs of movement. When she saw none and nothing tried to touch her mind again after a few minutes, Allison sent out a tentative Probe of Inquiry, ready to draw it back at the drop of a hat should it suddenly be seized. Allison received the shock of her life when her probe was indeed seized, but not by an alien mind but one that was as familiar as her own.

"Alli—son," she heard Aidric's unmistakable voice gasp weakly into her mind.

Then a figure that was little more than a dot in the distance stumbled out from within the trees. The brief flash of blue that caught her eye before the figure collapsed onto the ground was all the proof she needed to convince her of what her heart wanted to believe.

"Aidric!" she cried, no longer caring if the world heard her as she turned Destiny around and began to gallop full speed towards Aidric's crumbled form.

"Allison! Don't go! Wait!" Raya cried into her mind, but she hardly heard the frantic voice as she raced towards Aidric.

Allison didn't even bother to wait for Destiny to come to a complete stop before she slid from the saddle and landed on uncertain feet. She stumbled over to Aidric and fell to her knees beside his crumbled body with a sob of both relief and horror.

His uniform, once immaculately clean and wrinkle-free, hardly resembled that once-majestic garment. His shirt was torn in several places, wrinkled and caked with dirt. He no longer had his boots or hose, and his breeches were slashed to ribbons. It looked as if he had picked a fight with a tree with unusually sharp branches and had lost miserably.

Hesitantly, Allison pushed his hair away from his face, afraid that even that loving gesture would give him pain. Aidric had several, angry looking scratches on his cheek and forehead. As she had feared, he groaned under her touch, and she hastily pulled her hand back from his face.

Dammit! Why did I have to be so stubborn against learning the portal spell? she thought darkly as she sent urgently to her friends, *"Raya! Sel! Come quickly! It's Aidric, and he's hurt really bad! We've got to get him out of here before we're all discovered!"*

Allison was so wrapped up in searching for other injuries on his body that she didn't see the dagger he thrust up at her until it was too late. As it had been that night when Galen had tried to murder her, there was a blinding flash of light when the spelled dagger destroyed her shields. Allison had been caught so totally off guard that she didn't even have time to scream before the sharp blade was driven into her lower abdomen. She doubled over and collapsed onto her side without so much as a whimper, her head striking the ground hard.

She had just enough time to witness Aidric's features begin to blur from the, she now realized, impostor's face and replaced by the face that had haunted her nightmares since that fateful night on her journey to the Temple before darkness began to eat away her vision. She heard a voice whisper the name Mordant, and had just enough wits left to realize that it was her own before everything went completely black.

***

Flicking her ears in alarm, a doe stared intently into the forest, her body rigid and tense while her two fawns happily grazed near her legs unaware of the danger their mother sensed. For a while, nothing happened. Cautiously, the doe slowly lowered her head to continue grazing, one eye still on the terrain before her.

Then suddenly, she and the fawns bounded into the forest as a flash of golden light appeared a handspan away from where they had been grazing. When the flash cleared, Aidric's crumbled form lay in its place, his hands clenched into tight fists and his face twisted in a rictus of unbearable agony. With his abrupt arrival, the natural sounds of the forest had ceased, and a preternatural silence fell over the forest. In the silence, Aidric's groans of pain sounded excruciatingly loud to his ears.

He groaned even louder when he tentatively opened his eyes and saw that he wasn't where he had woven the portal to transport him. Above him, in the rapidly approaching dusk, the trees seemed to loom over him menacingly, their branches waving violently in the wind that made them appears as though they were reaching down to take him into the depths of the third hell as one ancient Jadwigan myth claimed they had once done.

Aidric struggled to roll onto his back, something he instantly regretted when the world around him began to darken in a way that had nothing to do with the last sun disappearing below the horizon. He closed his eyes again and willed himself to stay conscious with the last of his strength.

Sandwoods, he thought dimly. *I must be somewhere within the Evrei Forest. At least I'm still in Mihr.* He sighed. *I had thought that I at least had strength enough to transport myself to the proper destination—*

Aidric attempted to rise, an action that he quickly realized was futile when he found he couldn't even struggle into a sitting position. He let his body fall back to the ground with a harsh oath, cursing his weakness at a time when Allison needed him the most.

I must reach her before that bastard does! Aidric thought determinably, flipping over onto his stomach with considerable effort.

Then with his mind set on his goal, he began to slowly crawl towards the direction his senses were telling him was south with a single-mindedness that bordered on obsession, determined to reach the Telek River and Allison even if he had to crawl all night to do it.

A torturous sand-mark later, Aidric's body lost the battle with his mind, and he fell into a deep unconsciousness still trying to reach a hand just a little bit farther.

CHAPTER TWELVE

What in the six hells of Ter-ob did I drink last night?
was Selwyn's first thought as he stirred from
a world of darkness with the worst headache he had
ever had the bad luck to suffer. He raised his eyelids
tentatively and cursed when what felt like a half dozen
invisible daggers suddenly stabbed simultaneously into
his head.

"About time you woke," Raya said acidly somewhere in the darkness.

Selwyn merely groaned in response, suddenly re-
membering why his head hurt something fierce and
wishing that he was still in that peaceful, painless
oblivion as he shifted his body away from the sharp
stone that was digging into his side. He bit back a curse

at the pain that exploded throughout his entire body that simple gesture caused him. He felt as though he had been used as the attack dummy in arms practice.

"Sel, are you all right? Are you in pain?" he said dryly, feeling his wife draw near. "It's so kind of you to worry, love, but I'll be fine. Are *you* all right?"

Raya merely grumbled to herself about being left alone in the dark for so long. Selwyn couldn't help smiling. That was just Raya. Her arms gently encircled his shoulders, and she helped him more or less sit up.

"*You* were merely spelled to sleep," Selwyn was quick to point out. "I would be surprised to find even a tiny bruise on you, whereas *I* was struck in the back of the head with the flat of a blade, then kicked senseless. Why is it that I'm always the only one who has to suffer such torments?"

Neither he nor Raya had seen the attack coming from behind. They had been intent upon reaching Allison and Aidric at her cry for help. Selwyn had seen the man posing as Aidric draw a dagger before his wife had, but before he could cry out a warning, a blow to his head had knocked him from his horse.

Stunned, he had been trying to make sense of what had just happened when he had sensed the chaotic, emotion-like patterns of magic. A moment later, Raya had slumped over on her horse, spelled unconscious. Luckily for her, she had not fallen from her mount. Then the blows to his torso had started. That was the last thing he remembered.

"Lord Seni above, Sel!" Raya said, ignoring his last comment. "We're Roderick's prisoners, and the bastard has gotten his filthy hands on Allison! We should've tried harder to stop her. Oh! We are both such fools!"

Selwyn groped blindly for her hand and gave it a squeeze. "Do you really believe that we would've been able to stop her? Allison, perhaps yes, but back there when she destroyed your barrier, she wasn't Allison but the Golden Mage."

"But we were fools to have followed her instead of returning to Lamia to inform the king of what she was doing," Raya insisted stubbornly, refusing to be comforted. "Dammit Sel! He of all people had the right to know what she was doing! We allowed our personal feelings to cloud our judgment. Now we are all prisoners with no one the wiser, and Roderick now holds *two* keys to our Shield!"

"Then we must make certain he isn't allotted the time to use it," Selwyn replied determinably, though inside, he felt a quiver of fear. "Have you tried to thought-speak anyone? His Majesty's Spymaster dwells in this palace, still. Perhaps he can find a way to help us escape."

"I can't," Raya answered, her voice flat with defeat. Her tone unnerved him. As long as he had known her, Raya had never given up on anything. "Roderick has placed a barrier around this cell much like the one he placed around Na'ar and Kemos. I've even tried to blast the door, but no luck there. I'm surprised even *that* didn't wake you earlier."

Selwyn felt her arms tighten around him. "You had me worried there for a depth, love," she said softly. "I've never wished harder to have been fated to be a healer instead of a mage."

"Nor I, believe me," Sel replied with a grimace. "I could use a cup of Lamia's strongest *mitis* wine right about now—or perhaps two or three! At any rate, the inside of my mouth feels as if I just swallowed a pail of dirt. Just how long was I out?"

"I'm not certain," she said. He could feel her frowning in the darkness. "I don't know how long I lay unconscious, myself, but judging from how stiff my body feels, it was at least several sand-marks. You were unconscious about four sand-marks longer than I."

"So long!" he exclaimed. "Then we don't have a moment to spare! With Allison in Roderick's hands, I would bet my life that he'll waste no time in corrupting her mind with his bloody dark magic until she's completely his to command!"

Selwyn attempted to stand, determined to ignore the screaming of all his bruises that possibly included a couple of cracked ribs and the insistent throbbing of his head, but Raya refused to release him.

"You're in no condition to do anything," she scolded, a bit of her usual fire returning. "Besides, I've already tried everything I could think of to find a way out of this pit of hell. Roderick's just spelled this place too thoroughly."

"I refuse to believe that we can do nothing but sit here on our asses and wait for that bastard to decide how and when he will kill us!" Sel said darkly, but he didn't try to rise again. "Roderick has no Empathy to speak of. Perhaps my gift will succeed where plain old magecraft has failed."

"I would hardly call his dark magecraft plain," Raya said dryly, "but it's worth a shot. At this point, I would be prepared to stand on my head and sing gaudy drinking songs at the top of my lungs until I was hoarse if I thought it would help."

"Please! Leave the singing to the twins!" Selwyn pleaded in mock horror.

"Sel, how can you joke at a time like this?" Raya said in exasperation.

Selwyn grinned. "Easily. At the moment, I'm scared witless, and it's better than pounding on the walls with my fists and howling at the top of my lungs like a madman."

"Seni, give me patience!" Raya muttered under her breath, then continued more clearly, "Aidius, Sel, you could be in the darkest pit of the sixth hell, and still you would find something to joke about!"

"A man has to stay sane—" he said just as they both caught the sound of footsteps somewhere outside their cell.

Selwyn felt Raya's hands involuntarily tense on his shoulders as the footsteps grew louder, and he wondered if she could hear the pounding of his heart that was suddenly deafening to his ears.

"Is it Roderick?" Raya sent anxiously.

Selwyn could feel her breath increasing against his neck as he opened up his senses and reached for the emotions of the unknown person approaching their cell. To his utter dismay, the same barrier that prevented thought-speech from penetrating beyond the cell also prevented his empathic senses from penetrating.

"My senses can't pass beyond that damned barrier," he thought-spoke, frustrated and resisting the urge to barbarically growl and gnash his teeth. *"Shall we pretend to still be unconscious? Perhaps then, if our visitor is indeed Roderick, he'll just ignore us for the time being. It would buy us more time to attempt an escape."*

"No, it won't work," she replied. *"He'll easily see*

through our ruse. Unfortunately for us all, he's no fool. Besides, I refuse to cower before that poor excuse of a man or do anything that would please him. If dying today is inevitable, then I'll be damned three times over before I simply grovel before him like a starved dog begging for a soiled dinner napkin while he decides just how horrible he will make my death!"

"And I'll go to my grave before I allow him to lay a single finger on you!" Sel sent fervently, though deep down he knew that was exactly what was going to happen. He despaired at the thought of failing to protect Raya, but that despair quickly turned to anger as a dim glow began to filter in through the cracks of the cell door. Before Selwyn could even blink, a sudden, brilliant flash of light cut through the gloom, causing tears of pain to rise in his eyes.

No—he couldn't allow Roderick to touch Raya. Selwyn could literally feel the terror that his wife was trying to hide from him. He had power still, a special power that he loathed to use. Roderick had not yet stolen that. He would not fail her now.

Allowing his sudden rage to rule his actions, Selwyn threw a full empathic attack at the mind of the dark figure entering their cell, a concentration of every emotion he had ever experienced, intended to drive their visitor's emotions into total chaos while leaving the person as helpless as a newborn babe. More often than not, this particular attack drove its victims mad or even to their deaths if their emotions were left long in such a state of chaos. Selwyn had yet to see any enemy throw off that particular attack. He wasn't a representative for Lamia's empaths in the Circle without good cause.

Too late, as he saw the person's face for the space of a beat, Selwyn realized that he wasn't Roderick after all, but a man he knew quite well as only a member of the Circle or Council could know him. His power had already been released. The figure collapsed without so much as a cry of surprised. With his emotions in chaos, the man wasn't able to focus on one emotion long enough to scream, sob, or simply groan.

"Sel, what did you do?" Raya whispered urgently near his ear.

"The worst thing possible," Sel replied miserably. "I just felled what was perhaps our only ally in this forsaken place."

"The Spymaster?" she asked in disbelief. He could sense her gazing over her shoulder. "Did you kill him?"

Raya produced a small ball of light into her palm and peered over at the fallen figure. In that sudden illumination, the Spymaster, Valin, unnervingly did look like a corpse. His face had been drained of all color, his eyes fixed and pupils dilated. The only sign that the man was still alive was the stream of perspiration that flowed down his forehead and cheeks.

"None other," Selwyn said distractedly as he carefully crawled over to the downed man, groaning a little as his abused body protested even that movement. He breathed a sigh of extreme relief when he detected a strong, though overly accelerated pulse. "He's still alive, Seni be blessed!"

Wasting no time, Selwyn reached into the chaos that was Valin's emotions with his own and began to repair the damage he had caused, a task even more tedious then trying to tamper with a person's emotions without their knowledge. Separating his attack from Valin's own emotions was like trying to untangle an enormous wad of string infested with knots and burs. Raya wisely remained silent as he worked.

A few depths later, Selwyn withdrew his emotional "hand" from Valin's mind at the same moment that Valin released the shriek he had no doubt been aching to release from the moment Selwyn had hit his emotions with his attack. Selwyn frantically stifled his cry with his hand before he alerted the jailer. He quickly stretched out his own emotions in search of the jailer. Oddly, he felt nothing other than the distant emotions of the palace's inhabitants.

Selwyn frowned down at Valin as he withdrew his probe. Surely Roderick would have posted at least one guard at their cell. Yet his senses plainly told him that the only people in the general area were Raya, Valin, and himself. Something just didn't fit.

Only when Sel was confident that the poor man had gotten himself under control again did he remove his hand from over the Spymaster's mouth.

"Forgive me, Lord Valin, but I thought you were Roderick," Selwyn apologized as he helped the Spymaster to a sitting position despite his own screaming joints and muscles. "As you can imagine, we were desperate, and all I had was the hope of surprise. Are you going to be all right?"

"I'll live," Valin said curtly, brushing Sel aside as he rose unsteadily to his feet. "Think no more of it. I would've done the same were I in your position."

Selwyn wasn't in the least fooled by his nonchalance. He suspected that Valin was humiliated that he had been caught completely off-guard. Valin was an extremely proud man. As King Diryan's Spymaster in Mihr, Selwyn supposed that he could be nothing else but proud.

As if to prove that he hadn't been as affected by the attack as he should have been, Valin reached down and hauled Selwyn back to his feet, then lending his support as Selwyn cursed out of pain and swayed. It was then that Selwyn noticed the black and gold uniform Valin was wearing and the ring of keys belted at his side.

"*You* are Roderick's jailer?" Selwyn asked incredulously. No wonder the passages beyond had been silent!

Valin nodded, a slight smile on his lips. "What better position, other than being Roderick's own chieftain, to hear all of the palace gossip? I sleep in the barracks with all the troops. I also often share cups with the other two jailers, and they are men who are not loath to tell every bit of gossip they hear. If I didn't know better, I would swear that they were courtiers with how often their tongues are wagging. It's appalling, really. *I* would've preferred to be chieftain, but there you have it. My position also allows me to deliver mercy where I can to any Lamians who have the ill fortune of becoming Roderick's 'guests.'"

Selwyn swallowed thickly and nodded, knowing very well that Valin didn't mean that he dealt out good treatment to the wretched of this place.

The point of what Valin had not quite said had also not been missed on Raya. "Have you come to offer us that same mercy?" she asked evenly, and Sel marveled how she had succeeded in keeping her voice so steady.

"No," Valin replied, approval shining clearly in his eyes. Selwyn would have danced around joyously in relief if it weren't for Valin, who certainly would have thought him a fool. "Seni help us all now that the

Golden Mage has been taken prisoner. King Diryan must be informed of this newest calamity, and Roderick's barriers prevent thought-speech from traveling any farther than the room one stands in as you most assuredly know. I, of course, cannot leave the palace without causing a few raised eyebrows. You both are my last hope of reaching the king before Roderick is once again at our borders with his new weapon."

"And what will become of you when it's discovered that we have escaped?" Selwyn asked, gazing intently into Valin's eyes.

"Nothing," the Spymaster replied with a grin. "I'm not on duty at the moment. A man who would do every soul on this world a great favor by choking on his food will carry the blame. The fool's mind was overwhelmed easily enough. I'm ashamed to even acknowledge him as a mind-mage, weakling as he is. When he wakes, he'll wish that he hadn't once Roderick finishes with him."

"And what of the Mage-general?" Raya demanded. "Can you help him escape as well?"

"Unfortunately, no. He isn't being held in this dungeon. Roderick has hidden him well, and I'm not even certain that he still lives. Of the Mage-general, neither Roderick nor Mordant speaks openly of him. Dead or alive, he's somewhere within these palace walls, of that much, I'm certain."

"Then Allison's quest was doomed before she had even set out," Raya said flatly. "Is there greater fools that live than we?"

Valin surprised them both by saying, "You're only fools if you really believe you had any control over what's to come to pass. The Golden Mage was fated to decide Lamia's fate according to the words of the Ancients. Now we'll see if her will is strong enough to save us all. We wait, and we defend ourselves as well as possible from the cataclysm that's soon to be born.

"I can help you both escape from the palace, but once beyond its grounds, you're on your own. If you cast an invisibility spell over yourselves, then you'll be safe enough. From what I understand, it was the whinnying of your horses that revealed your location. Wretched animals never know when to be silent! Traveling on foot, though obviously longer, would be preferable unless you wish to find yourselves back in these charming accommodations."

"Seni forbid!" Sel muttered, already feeling his brow dampen with sweat.

Valin nodded then walked out of the cell. Selwyn and Raya started to follow, but Valin appeared again in the door, holding a couple of uniforms—gold and black, the colors of Mihr—a couple of golden helms, and a couple of long swords. He handed them all to Selwyn.

"Both of you put these on," he commanded. "Guards are less likely to attract attention in the corridors or on the grounds. With helm on, you can legitimately mask your identities. With all luck, we shall not run into Roderick or any man of high rank that may question your presence in the palace."

"Where did you get these?" Sel asked as he handed Raya a uniform.

"From the two guards positioned just outside the entrance to the dungeon," Valin replied absently without further elaboration as his eyes took on the faraway look that signaled he was either probing or thought-speaking.

Selwyn shed the tattered remains of his clothing and struggled to pull on the gold and black tunic and breeches with as minimal of pain as he could manage, which wasn't much.

"Quickly now!" Valin said suddenly, nearly causing Selwyn to jump out of his skin. "The corridors above us we need to take are virtually empty. Perhaps we can escape the palace without any trouble, after all."

Selwyn glanced at Raya, who was sheathing her sword, then said, "Just lead the way."

The half sand-mark it took them to thread their way out of the dungeons and through the endless corridors of the Mihran palace was the longest of

Selwyn's life. At every turn of the corner, he was certain that Roderick, Mordant, or even Roderick's chieftain waited. Although she tried to hide it, he was certain that Raya thought the same from the way her shoulders would tense whenever they approached a corner and her expression became a bit stonier.

A few moments after Valin had thought-spoken them to say the exit was near, they spotted a group of soldiers rounding the far corner, laughing and cursing, obviously headed to their various duties. Before he could began to panic, Valin thought-spoke him to begin mimicking the soldiers' behavior.

Though his heart was now somewhere in his nose, Selwyn began to laugh rowdily and slap both Raya and Valin on their backs, speaking of the wenching they would be doing once they reached the barracks and were given leave. Selwyn was certain that both Valin and Raya could literally hear his relief when the group of soldiers passed them by without more than a cursory glance. Just to be safe, Selwyn continued his crude antics until they had rounded two more corridors and they still didn't meet up with another soul.

Valin continued to accompany them as far as the barracks. Selwyn wished that the Spymaster could accompany them on their trek across Mihr as well. No one in Lamia knew Mihr better than he, but Sel knew that Valin's position in the palace was more important.

If the Domnae that the Temple was to send to Na'ar and Kemos to deal with Roderick's barriers managed to bring them down, then Valin's position would once again become invaluable.

Valin left them for a few moments while he went inside to fetch them two packs he had prepared for them. Not so much as an insect breathed without Selwyn being aware of it during that duration of time. He tensed every time someone passed them, but to his surprise, no one attempted to approach or to speak to them. It was as if they weren't even there. Selwyn began to wonder if Valin really was just the king's Spymaster.

It seemed an eternity before Valin appeared again, materializing as if from thin air, carrying one pack on his back and a second in his hand. A couple of soldiers passed him by without even acknowledging him. He didn't speak but gestured for them to follow him.

"I wish you both all the luck of Seni," Valin said sincerely when they were at a safe distance from the barracks. "If all goes well, then you should reach the Mihran border within four days, three if you travel at least one full night. I'll release two horses under the invisibility spell towards the south to confuse your trail."

"But how?" Raya asked. "You aren't a mage."

Then at his slight smile, she raised an eyebrow and demanded, "Or are you?"

"I have my ways," he said stoically, but a bright gleam in his eyes said that he was anything but. Apparently he wasn't going to indulge their curiosity, and he was enjoying the fact that he was not. "I hope one day to meet again," he continued, ignoring their glares. "I should enjoy hearing of all your adventures on your journey back to Lamia—and my children even more so."

"He has children?" Raya whispered in bewilderment as Valin saluted them and headed back into the barracks without another word.

"With a spy, who can say?" Selwyn replied, shaking his head. "Well, my dear, shall we inspect the forest like good little soldiers?"

"Just you lead the way, love."

***

Voices—they were ones she thought she should know very well, but the memory of them frustratingly stayed beyond her grasp. If her memories had been a sheet of paper and her mind a hand, her fingertips would have just barely brushed against the paper's edge. In truth, the owners of those voices were not the only things she could no longer recall.

The oldest memory she could remember was the pain, one she most certainly could've lived without. It was a pain that felt as if first, her mind was being ripped to shreds within her head and wrenched out through her ears, and then as if her soul was being devoured by a demonic being with razor sharp fangs coated with acid. Mercifully, she had fallen into a dark oblivion soon after the unbearable pain had begun.

But along with the pain, there had been the dark man enveloped in shadow, hovering over her like a demon from her worst nightmare, his eyes glowing an eerie, incandescent gold. His presence had invaded her mind completely, leaving behind a trail of vileness in his wake. Somehow she had known that it was the man who had caused her excruciating pain. She knew that she should know him, but even that memory evaded the desperate grasp of her mental hands.

Now, as she recalled the memory, it was as though she was reliving that horrible moment of unimaginable agony, and somewhere in the darkness of her mind, she could hear herself screaming, not only because of the memory of that pain and fear of the dire figure in shadow, but because she could no longer remember who she was.

CHAPTER THIRTEEN

"Aidius, does this wretched forest ever end?" Selwyn said irritably as he once again found himself kissing the ground after tripping over yet another root hidden beneath the dead leaves.

It had been too many sand-marks since they had parted ways with Valin for Selwyn to keep track. Dusk now crept over the forest, which made their footing unsure at best. Nevertheless, despite the peril the growing darkness brought with it, Selwyn couldn't help feeling a sense of relief that now they wouldn't be easily seen among the many shadows should the invisibility spell over them suddenly be disrupted.

"It does remind me a bit of the forest of the damned," Raya agreed, offering her husband her hand.

"You sure do know how to make a man feel better, dearheart," Selwyn shot back dryly as he accepted her outstretched hand. As he hoisted himself back onto his feet, a flash of blue on the ground caught his eye. "What's that?" he asked, crouching down and squinting at the ground next to the root he had tripped over. "It looks like a—"

His voice trailed off once he got his first good look at the "root" and the patch of unmistakable *sholkie* material that was half concealed by a mound of rotting leaves. Ever since Roderick had forsaken the Temple, trade had ceased between Mihr and her neighbors. Thus, it had been several years since anyone in Mihr had seen so much as a thread of *sholkie* material since the Amhar tree from which the material was derived could only be found in Lamia. This still-lustrous piece of material, untouched by the weather or time, was conspicuously out of place.

Selwyn brushed away the leaves around the exposed material, and as he expected, the material proved to be part of a sleeve that was still filled by its owner. More importantly, on the shoulder was the embroidered silver teardrop of Lamia.

By the Thrones, can it be? "Raya, come look at this," Sel said excitedly as he began to brush off more of the leaves. "Lamia's seal, and this is the robe of a mage. Could this possibly be—" They both gasped as white hair, caked with dirt but with a hint of its previous luster, was suddenly revealed beneath Selwyn's hands. "It *is* him!"

"Get back!" Raya shouted as she pulled him away from the body. Selwyn could feel her throwing up extra shields around those that already existed about him, doubling his sense of protection that having the shields caused him to feel. "It could be another trap!"

Even as those words were leaving her lips, Sel was already reaching for the emotions of the fallen man. Almost immediately, he felt the nothingness, the absolute void of any emotion associated with true and deep unconsciousness that so far no empath or mage had been successful in duplicating during consciousness.

"It *is* Aidric," Selwyn insisted stubbornly, shucking off her restraining hand from his arm, "and he's unconscious. You know that unconsciousness can't be feigned to withstand an empath's scrutiny."

"Yes, but what about the Dark Powers?" Raya demanded, but Selwyn was no longer listening to her.

He was intent on brushing away all of the leaves from the white-haired man's face, and sure enough, Aidric's face was revealed. His skin had a pasty, unhealthy look, almost the drab color of a corpse's skin. The comparison was too similar for Selwyn's peace of mind.

With a sense of dread, he lifted two fingers to

Aidric's neck, the skin feeling cold and clammy beneath his trembling fingers. Sel let out a loud sigh of relief when he detected a faint, but nevertheless, steady heartbeat.

"He lives still," Sel murmured. He felt Raya dropping to her knees beside him. "I'm not a healer, but I think he's magically damaged."

Only now did he glance over at his wife, her face scrunched up as though she was beats away from crying. Raya *never* cried.

"Of course," he said quietly, "you would know that better than me."

Raya took a deep, steadying breath, and nodded. Her eyes unfocused as she probed Aidric with her mage senses. It seemed she studied him for an eternity. When sense once again returned to her eyes, she shuddered, suddenly looking forty and not her true age of twenty summers.

"You're right. He *is* magically damaged, but most of it bears his own magical signature. Once again, the beast tried more than he could handle, but that's not the worst of it." Her mouth stretched into a grim line. "There's a spell about him, one that I'm certain reeks of the Dark Powers. I nearly lost my stomach when I touched it, it was so vile. I've never touched anything like it. I'm not certain of its exact purpose, but that doesn't matter. I don't need to be a Domnae to know its intentions. Maybe it's even causing his unconsciousness, but Seni knows I'm no healer, either."

"Then we must get him to one immediately," Selwyn said determinably

"But how?" Raya demanded wearily. "We have neither horses nor wagon to carry him in. We're both exhausted, and you're hurt. Between us, we could only manage to carry him a few spans at best, and Seni knows how much farther it is to the border!" She shook her head, looking stricken. "I can't even use a levitation spell. I would have to draw from the Magefield to maintain it. It would be like a beacon to every mage within the kingdom pointing directly to us!"

"We can't just leave him here for Roderick's lackeys to find!" Selwyn despaired. "If carrying him between us is the only option, then carry him we shall! Besides, we still wear the uniforms of Roderick's guard. If we can find a village, then perhaps we could coax a couple of horses out of them."

"If you're willing to take the risk, I can send a Probe of Inquiry to locate the nearest village," Raya said, a flash of hope lighting up her eyes for the first time since they had fallen into Roderick's trap.

Selwyn nodded. "At this point, what choice do we have? It's either that or wander around as we have been, hoping that we're lucky enough to stumble upon a village before we collapse." He gazed up towards the eastern sky and warily eyed the rapidly building clouds that had been making him nervous for the past several sand-marks. "Let's just hope that you can locate one that's near, or judging from those clouds, we'll soon be wet and frozen rather than just weary and on edge!"

While Raya probed the terrain, Selwyn tended to Aidric, turning him over so that his head lay across his lap, making it easier for his friend to breathe. Aidric didn't stir even once. Only the steady rising and falling of his chest signaled that he was even alive. No matter how hard he tried, Selwyn couldn't coax even the tiniest flicker of awareness from Aidric's mind. It was as though Aidric was no longer there, and all that remained was a soulless body barely living.

He had once read about mages who had channeled more Mage-field energy than their bodies could physically handle. In some cases, the mage had simply been vaporized without leaving behind so much as ash, but there were also those who had not seared away their bodies but a part of their *souls*. As Selwyn stared at the limp body of his friend, he felt a sudden chill that wasn't caused by the winter air.

"I've found one!" Raya's excited voice suddenly broke into his mind.

"Where?" he asked anxiously. *Please Seni, let it be near!*

"It's about a half day's trek to the northwest," she

reported. Selwyn suppressed a groan. "I believe we could make it."

That was still quite a distance away. A thousand things could go wrong between here and there, one of which was the very real possibility of Aidric dying before they could get him help.

Which would be a mercy if he has done to himself what I fear he has done, Sel thought, then instantly felt guilty. *I haven't given up on you, my friend*, he promised the silent form as he rose and waved Raya over to help him swing Aidric over his shoulder.

Selwyn winced as the added weight sent ripples of pain into his abused chest, but he said nothing. Now wasn't the time to worry about his own discomfort. With luck, there would be more than enough time for that when they reached Lamia.

With Aidric balanced securely over his shoulder, they set out in the direction Raya pointed. The first rumbles of thunder sounded out in the distance, proving his earlier observations correct. They would have to hurry if they wanted to beat the storm. Selwyn didn't particularly care to be drenched at the moment, especially in such a chill. It wouldn't do Lamia any good if they all died of lung fever before they could deliver their warning.

However, he knew that the rising storm was the

least of their worries when a larger and more dangerous storm was brewing elsewhere, and no matter how
hard they all tried to outrun it, there was no escaping
the torrents that soon would be unleashed above, not
just them, but all of Lamia as well.

**

Allison woke with a slight headache, enveloped in several quilted blankets. She slowly raised a hand to rub
her right temple where a good portion of the pain was
centered.

It had been too many sand-marks since they had
parted ways with Valin for Selwyn to keep track. Dusk
now crept over the forest, which made their footing
unsure at best. Nevertheless, despite the peril the
growing darkness brought with it, Selwyn couldn't
help feeling a sense of relief that now they wouldn't be
easily seen among the many shadows should the invisibility spell over them suddenly be disrupted.

"It does remind me a bit of the forest of the
damned," Raya agreed, offering her husband her hand.

"You sure do know how to make a man feel better, dearheart," Selwyn shot back dryly as he accepted
her outstretched hand. As he hoisted himself back
onto his feet, a flash of blue on the ground caught his
eye. "What's that?" he asked, crouching down and

squinting at the ground next to the root he had tripped over. "It looks like a—"

His voice trailed off once he got his first good look at the "root" and the patch of unmistakable *sholkie* material that was half concealed by a mound of rotting leaves. Ever since Roderick had forsaken the Temple, trade had ceased between Mihr and her neighbors. Thus, it had been several years since anyone in Mihr had seen so much as a thread of *sholkie* material since the Amhar tree from which the material was derived could only be found in Lamia. This still-lustrous piece of material, untouched by the weather or time, was conspicuously out of place.

Selwyn brushed away the leaves around the exposed material, and as he expected, the material proved to be part of a sleeve that was still filled by its owner. More importantly, on the shoulder was the embroidered silver teardrop of Lamia.

By the Thrones, can it be? "Raya, come look at this," Sel said excitedly as he began to brush off more of the leaves. "Lamia's seal, and this is the robe of a mage. Could this possibly be—" They both gasped as white hair, caked with dirt but with a hint of its previous luster, was suddenly revealed beneath Selwyn's hands. "It *is* him!"

"Get back!" Raya shouted as she pulled him away

from the body. Selwyn could feel her throwing up extra shields around those that already existed about him, doubling his sense of protection that having the shields caused him to feel. "It could be another trap!"

Even as those words were leaving her lips, Sel was already reaching for the emotions of the fallen man. Almost immediately, he felt the nothingness, the absolute void of any emotion associated with true and deep unconsciousness that so far no empath or mage had been successful in duplicating during consciousness.

"It *is* Aidric," Selwyn insisted stubbornly, shucking off her restraining hand from his arm, "and he's unconscious. You know that unconsciousness can't be feigned to withstand an empath's scrutiny."

"Yes, but what about the Dark Powers?" Raya demanded, but Selwyn was no longer listening to her.

He was intent on brushing away all of the leaves from the white-haired man's face, and sure enough, Aidric's face was revealed. His skin had a pasty, unhealthy look, almost the drab color of a corpse's skin. The comparison was too similar for Selwyn's peace of mind.

With a sense of dread, he lifted two fingers to Aidric's neck, the skin feeling cold and clammy beneath his trembling fingers. Sel let out a loud sigh of relief when he detected a faint, but nevertheless, steady heartbeat.

"He lives still," Sel murmured. He felt Raya dropping to her knees beside him. "I'm not a healer, but I think he's magically damaged."

Only now did he glance over at his wife, her face scrunched up as though she was beats away from crying. Raya *never* cried.

"Of course," he said quietly, "you would know that better than me."

Raya took a deep, steadying breath, and nodded. Her eyes unfocused as she probed Aidric with her mage senses. It seemed she studied him for an eternity. When sense once again returned to her eyes, she shuddered, suddenly looking forty and not her true age of twenty summers.

"You're right. He *is* magically damaged, but most of it bears his own magical signature. Once again, the beast tried more than he could handle, but that's not the worst of it." Her mouth stretched into a grim line. "There's a spell about him, one that I'm certain reeks of the Dark Powers. I nearly lost my stomach when I touched it, it was so vile. I've never touched anything like it. I'm not certain of its exact purpose, but that doesn't matter. I don't need to be a Domnae to know its intentions. Maybe it's even causing his unconsciousness, but Seni knows I'm no healer, either."

"Then we must get him to one immediately,"

Selwyn said determinably

"But how?" Raya demanded wearily. "We have neither horses nor wagon to carry him in. We're both exhausted, and you're hurt. Between us, we could only manage to carry him a few spans at best, and Seni knows how much farther it is to the border!" She shook her head, looking stricken. "I can't even use a levitation spell. I would have to draw from the Mage-field to maintain it. It would be like a beacon to every mage within the kingdom pointing directly to us!"

"We can't just leave him here for Roderick's lack-eys to find!" Selwyn despaired. "If carrying him between us is the only option, then carry him we shall! Besides, we still wear the uniforms of Roderick's guard. If we can find a village, then perhaps we could coax a couple of horses out of them."

"If you're willing to take the risk, I can send a Probe of Inquiry to locate the nearest village," Raya said, a flash of hope lighting up her eyes for the first time since they had fallen into Roderick's trap.

Selwyn nodded. "At this point, what choice do we have? It's either that or wander around as we have been, hoping that we're lucky enough to stumble upon a village before we collapse." He gazed up towards the eastern sky and warily eyed the rapidly building clouds that had been making him nervous for the past several sand-marks. "Let's just hope that you can locate one that's near, or judging from those clouds, we'll soon be wet and frozen rather than just weary and on edge!"

While Raya probed the terrain, Selwyn tended to Aidric, turning him over so that his head lay across his lap, making it easier for his friend to breathe. Aidric didn't stir even once. Only the steady rising and falling of his chest signaled that he was even alive. No matter how hard he tried, Selwyn couldn't coax even the tiniest flicker of awareness from Aidric's mind. It was as though Aidric was no longer there, and all that remained was a soulless body barely living.

He had once read about mages who had channeled more Mage-field energy than their bodies could physically handle. In some cases, the mage had simply been vaporized without leaving behind so much as ash, but there were also those who had not seared away their bodies but a part of their *souls*. As Selwyn stared at the limp body of his friend, he felt a sudden chill that wasn't caused by the winter air.

"I've found one!" Raya's excited voice suddenly broke into his mind.

"Where?" he asked anxiously. *Please Seni, let it be near!*

"It's about a half day's trek to the northwest," she reported. Selwyn suppressed a groan. "I believe we could make it."

That was still quite a distance away. A thousand

things could go wrong between here and there, one of which was the very real possibility of Aidric dying before they could get him help.

Which would be a mercy if he has done to himself what I fear he has done, Sel thought, then instantly felt guilty. *I haven't given up on you, my friend,* he promised the silent form as he rose and waved Raya over to help him swing Aidric over his shoulder.

Selwyn winced as the added weight sent ripples of pain into his abused chest, but he said nothing. Now wasn't the time to worry about his own discomfort. With luck, there would be more than enough time for that when they reached Lamia.

With Aidric balanced securely over his shoulder, they set out in the direction Raya pointed. The first rumbles of thunder sounded out in the distance, proving his earlier observations correct. They would have to hurry if they wanted to beat the storm. Selwyn didn't particularly care to be drenched at the moment, especially in such a chill. It wouldn't do Lamia any good if they all died of lung fever before they could deliver their warning.

However, he knew that the rising storm was the least of their worries when a larger and more dangerous storm was brewing elsewhere, and no matter how hard they all tried to outrun it, there was no escaping the torrents that soon would be unleashed above, not just them, but all of Lamia as well.

***

Allison woke with a slight headache, enveloped in several quilted blankets. She slowly raised a hand to rub her right temple where a good portion of the pain was centered.

What a night, she thought with a slight shudder at the memory of all the horrible dreams her drunken mind had conjured last night. *I never should have had so much wine. I should have listened to him.*

With that thought, she realized that she was quite alone in the huge bed, and the place beside her was cold, signaling that he had risen a good while earlier. Feeling somewhat guilty, Allison rose from the bed and reached for the robe she had shed before she had retired for the night. She wondered why he hadn't awakened her. As she was belting the robe, the door opened behind her, and she turned to smile brightly at her visitor.

"Ah, at last you have risen, my dear," Roderick said, strolling over to her and pulling her close against his body. She kissed him lightly on the lips in response, causing him to chuckle softly. "Is that all you have for me this morning?" he asked in mock astonishment.

"Of course not," she said, blushing a bright crimson.

Then she melted into his embrace as his mouth devoured her own, and his hands hungrily began to explore her body. As he began tugging at the knot in her robe strings, she pulled back a bit.

"But my mage lessons—" she protested breathlessly.

"—can wait," Roderick finished, successfully untying her robe and wasting no time in ridding her of it. He bent to roughly nuzzle her neck. "We have all day to worry about our duties," he murmured, his voice muffled against her skin.

Allison needed no more prodding as her hands sought the laces of his tunic. Soon she found herself once again enveloped in the soft blankets, but this time she shared the warmth with another. Before long, the memory of those terrible dreams of pain and fear was lost in the throes of pleasure.

Somewhere in the distance, far from the ears of any at the Mihran palace, a cry sounded out at the moment Allison and Roderick were joined—the cry of one whose soul was shattered.

CHAPTER FOURTEEN

"What's wrong with him?" Raya cried, staring down at Aidric as though he was a creature she had never seen before.

Only moments earlier, he had suddenly let out a bone-chilling wail that would haunt her nightmares for the rest of her days. Now, he had returned to his earlier comatose state, with the exception of the steady stream of tears that spilled from beneath his closed lids. Selwyn had been trying futilely for the past half sand-mark to determine what had caused Aidric to cry out so horribly.

Kneeling beside Aidric, Selwyn shook his head, his forehead creased with worry. "I don't know. All I'm certain of is that something *has* happened, something vital, to have produced such a change in him.

Before, there was nothing—no awareness, no emotion—but now, although he's still not aware, he's experiencing a single emotion, an incredible level of despair bordering on madness." He gazed up at his wife soberly. "At least now my fears of him having seared his soul away are put to rest. Aidric is still in there somewhere, but he's fading fast! How much farther is the village?"

Raya sent out her mind-probe and instantly pulled it back when it immediately encountered a cacophony of voices.

"At least a couple of spans," she said, her eyes falling back down to Aidric. Tears still leaked from his eyes, but other than that, he looked like a corpse. "Should we carry him to the village or hide him here among the trees?" she asked.

"His face is well-known among the Mihrans," Selwyn pointed out. "Roderick has made certain of that. Plus, we aren't certain if it's common knowledge that the Mage-general of Lamia was taken prisoner by Roderick. If we were to suddenly appear in a village with Aidric slung over my back, it would raise too many questions that we couldn't possibly answer. In fact, by now every soldier in Mihr will be searching for *us*."

Sel stood abruptly and looked over at her with that oh-so-familiar expression of his that said she wouldn't like what he had to say next, and she had a pretty good idea of what he had in mind.

"No, you most definitely will not," Raya said firmly before he could open his mouth.

"They'll be searching for a young man and woman, not a man alone," he argued. "It would be less conspicuous if I go on alone while you stay with Aidric."

"To the six hells it would!" she growled. "Your hair would stand out in the largest of crowds! My features are more common here, and besides, if the uniform doesn't fool anyone, I'm more equipped to get out of a scrape than you are!"

"Your being a mage is exactly why I do *not* want you to go!" he shot back in exasperation. "No mage would dress in the uniform of a soldier, especially here in Mihr. The village most assuredly has several mages in residence, if for nothing more than to keep the people from rebelling. They would sniff you out before you came within distance of the first farmhouse. Besides, have you forgotten that you're a woman? I certainly haven't. When was the last time you saw a *female* Mihran soldier?"

Raya opened her mouth to retort, but annoyingly, she could find no fault in his logic.

"All right," she grumbled in resignation. "You win. I'll stay here with Aidric, but dammit, Selwyn!

Don't let your mouth get you into trouble! And don't you dare hesitate to thought-speak me if you do manage to find trouble! I didn't bind my soul to yours for all eternity only to lose you before either of us has really begun to live!"

Sel pulled her close and planted a kiss firmly on her trembling lips. "I'll be careful," he promised, "and hopefully I'll have at least one horse with me when I return. I'll send you the usual burst of emotion to let you know it's me."

For once in all the time Raya had known her husband, Selwyn's parting words were not a jest.

Without another word, Raya dismissed the invisibility spell around her husband and stood silently watching him as he waved farewell and disappeared into the thick foliage. With a sigh that bordered on tears, Raya sank down beside Aidric, adjusting the thick cloak she wore more closely against her body in preparation for what could very well be a very long wait. She did the same for Aidric, though the fine *sholkie* material of his robe hardly provided any protection against the biting, winter air.

Luckily, the approaching storm had shifted in its course before it reached them and had continued on its way to the southwest. In that, at least, Seni had been watching over them and had heeded their prayers.

"Well, beast, it's just you and me," Raya said to

the silent figure beside her while she gazed out into the forest where Selwyn had disappeared into, already wishing that she could see his forever cheerful face and the shock of red hair that reminded her of the fierce fire that burned in their hearth on the days he insisted that they have a *normal* fire.

Please, Seni, keep him safe, she prayed, and closed her eyes tightly before any of the tears welling in her eyes could fall.

∗∗∗

Selwyn swallowed against the knot of fear in his throat as he approached the outskirts of the Mihran village and heard the first signs of civilization in over a day. Before he had reached the village, he had stopped and rubbed some of the dark soil into his hair to try to dull the redness of it. Without a mirror or a pool of water to gaze in, all he could do was hope that the dirt achieved the effect he desired. The dirt also helped to fuel the lie he had come up with to tell the villagers of how his horse had been spooked by a deer that had suddenly darting into his path, resulting in him being thrown from his mount and his horse disappearing into the forest in blind fear.

As it turned out, he had worried over his appearance for nothing. When he had reached the first of a series of farmhouses, the few peasants who had been tilling their fields or herding livestock had either ignored him completely or had taken one look at him and turned away in insolence.

Well, well, it seems as if the peasants here hate Roderick's soldiers more passionately than I had first anticipated. That may prove to be a bit of a problem. What if I stir up more trouble than I need? Should I go on?

However, before he could worry himself into a headache with those troubling thoughts, Selwyn reached the main road of the village and found himself immediately face-to-face with a soldier, a rather large, brown-haired man who frowned in disgust at the state of his torn and dirty uniform.

The man was tall even for a Mihran, who all tended to reach at least the six handspan mark. He easily topped Selwyn's a little under six-handspan frame by at least a handspan. He was a man of rank, a captain judging from the arrangement of golden rings on the left sleeve of his uniform. Selwyn saluted curtly to him, feeling rather like a five-summers-old boy facing his intimidating father for punishment, and waited for the man to speak first as was custom among Mihran soldiers.

"Hail, soldier, what brings you to Decia in such a state?" he demanded, eyeing Selwyn with scrutiny.

"Rotten luck, would ye believe it," Selwyn replied

flawlessly in the speech of the Mihran peasantry, doing his best to appear disgusted as well as cowed. "Me horse got spooked by a damned deer and threw me. By the time I'd picked meself up, the horse'd already disappeared into the forest. Ran off with me supplies too! I was just damned lucky that it happened so close t' Decia. If I'm not at the palace barracks by the noon mark t'morrow, then Roderick'll have me ass for sure!"

"And you want to borrow a horse, is that it?" the soldier sneered. "I should just send you on your way with my boot, is what I should do. But I'm in relatively good spirits today, so I'll lend you one of my mounts. Come on."

"And don't look so outwardly nervous, Lord Selwyn Phelannik," a voice suddenly said into his mind in Lamian, a voice that matched that of the soldier. *"Would you have the whole of the village infantry breathing down your neck?"*

Selwyn froze in his tracks. He had once seen one of the stableboys kicked in the teeth by a horse that was famous for its placidity. Now as he stared at the soldier in mute astonishment, he was certain that his expression topped that of that stableboy. Somehow he managed to pull himself together before he could follow his urge to suddenly dart down the nearest alleyway.

"You know who I am," Selwyn said evenly in Lamian, proud that his voice didn't tremble.

The soldier shot him a hard look.

"Aye, and if you aren't careful, everyone else in the village will too, empath," he sent impatiently. *"At first, I didn't recognize you because of all the grime smeared on your face and in your hair, but I've seen your face many times among those of the Circle. Only when you spoke was I certain of your identity."*

"The Circle?" Selwyn repeated dumbly. He was careful not to look at the soldier, but inside he was aching to get a good look at this unexpected ally. *"If you've seen me at court with the Circle, then that means you are—"*

"—one of King Diryan's many spies," he finished rather smugly. *"You may call me Yuric. Point in fact, I'm the spy who relays all information gathered by all the others to Lamia since I'm stationed closest to the border. I'm also captain of the infantry positioned here in Decia."*

Yuric turned and gazed at Selwyn with piercing black eyes. *"Word has already reached us of you and your wife's escape. Roderick has issued the order to execute you upon capture. It was wise of you to dull the hue of your hair as that's the one description of you that stands out in one's mind. I take it the Lady Raya hides within the forest?"*

"She stayed behind to watch over the Mage-general while I came here to try my luck at filching a couple of horses for us."

"So it's true," Yuric sent. *"Roderick did manage to capture the Mage-general. We had only heard rumors of it here, and as Roderick had not sent us official word of it, I had dismissed it as such. I would've thought Roderick would've been more cautious with him considering his power, and yet you have freed him."*

"Not us," Selwyn corrected. *"I don't know how he came to be free, but it was under his own hand. We luckily came upon him deep within the forest hidden beneath a blanket of leaves and quite unconscious, apparently from the exhaustive use of his own magic. I tripped over him."*

"Everyone always said that man has Seni's own luck," Yuric remarked.

"He's in dire need of a healer," Selwyn said anxiously. *"Raya has detected a spell about him, a spell that reeks of the Dark Powers, the purpose of which she was unable to decipher, but the worst is what Aidric, himself, has done to himself by taking on considerably more Mage-field energy than he could safely channel."*

Yuric fell silent as they continued on their way. Although his expression didn't change, Selwyn sensed a certain indecisiveness in him, strange for a spy.

"I believe I can help you with that," he sent finally, *"as well as give you a couple of horses and supplies. I have a healer friend who has secretly been on Lamia's side for years."*

"You revealed yourself to him?" Selwyn asked incredulously.

215

"Of course not, empath," Yuric sent tartly. *"It wasn't like that at all. In a sense, he revealed his own hatred for Roderick to me first. I wanted to marry his daughter, and he had made it clear to me that he didn't want any 'latrine scum soldier of Roderick's' to lay so much as a fingernail on his only daughter. Thus, I told him the truth about my duality, and even then it took me a couple of moons to convince him that I spoke the truth. He is completely trustworthy, as well as a powerful healer. If anyone can help the Mage-general, it's him. His farm lies on the outskirts of the village. I'm certain you passed it on your way into the village, but first, let's see about getting you a couple of sturdy mounts."*

As they reached the stables that housed the horses used by the infantry, Yuric said aloud, "My men'll have a good laugh over this one. Damned as if we'll have to glue you lads to your saddles to keep you from losing 'em!"

Several of the stableboys snickered, then froze when Yuric cast a stern eye upon them. "Find something funny, do you?" Yuric sneered. "There won't be nothing to be laughing about when you get an ass full of my boot!"

After that, none of the stableboys uttered so much as a sound, each keeping a wary eye on Captain Yuric as he walked back and forth among them while he barked out orders, likely expecting him to carry out his threat despite their cooperative silence.

Selwyn silently stood off to the side at stiff attention, acting the role of a soldier cowed under his superior. Although it seemed to Selwyn to take the stable-boys centuries to ready the horses and supplies, Yuric and Selwyn were soon on their way to the spy's father-in-law's farm.

Yuric stopped long enough to bark out several instructions to his men that were posted at various points around the village. None seemed to find it strange that their captain was leaving the village with a strange, rather scruffy looking soldier and two extra horses. In fact, they hardly seemed to notice Selwyn at all, as if he was not worthy of their notice.

They said little on the way to the old man's farm, Yuric breaking the silence only to ask of the state of affairs in Lamia. With the barrier still up, it was impossible to learn anything of Lamia without leaving Mihr. Selwyn was more than willing to fill the silence with conversation. It left his mind less idle to dream up all the horrible things that could be happening to Raya at the moment and all the infinite reasons of why she wasn't able to mind-call him for help.

Yuric's father-in-law was out working his fields with several men, some, by their authoritative postures, clearly his sons. He turned at the sound of their approach, the smile on his face instantly melting into a frown of suspicion as he saw that his son-in-law was not alone.

"Hail, Aeson, a fine morning, isn't it?" Yuric called out.

"Aye," Aeson replied steadily, fixing Selwyn with a measuring look. "I don't believe I've met your friend, Yuric."

"Name's Sedric," Yuric said promptly, but even as the lie rolled off his tongue, the sudden change of expression on Aeson's face and the blankness of Yuric's told Selwyn that this man also shared the ability of thought-speech and was being informed the real story away from prying ears and wagging tongues. "He and his partner had a stroke of bad luck in the forest. His companion has need of a healer."

Aeson nodded and swiftly mounted the riderless horse without a word. Selwyn marveled at Aeson's agility when he mounted, an agility that would be the envy of men half his age.

"Now, you hear me, lads," Aeson said sternly to the men watching them curiously. "I want no slacking while I'm gone. Cadin, you're in charge until I return."

The tallest and presumably oldest of the dozen men surrounding them, a younger copy of Aeson, himself, nodded reluctantly as if he would have preferred to accompany his father than stay to supervise his brothers and the hired help. By the barely suppressed groans of the rest, it appeared that they too wished that Cadin was going along.

"Remember, laziness never feeds bellies in the dead of winter, lads," Aeson said as Yuric signaled them on their way.

When they were out of earshot, Aeson urged his horse up until it was even with Selwyn's. "So, you're the lad who has Roderick foaming at the mouth like a rabid beast," he said pointedly, his eyes lighting up with what seemed like glee. "A member of the infamous Circle of Lamia. Strange, I'd have thought you to be older."

"In Lamia, power and wits are held in higher esteem than age," Selwyn retorted more sharply than he had intended, a little ruffled by Aeson's offhanded remark. "Any fool can reach old age by sheer luck, but not every fool can reach it with wisdom."

This only seemed to amuse Aeson even more. Yuric only shot Selwyn a warning look. After all, this man was Aidric's only hope in surviving the night, so Selwyn just bit his tongue and allowed the old man to chatter on without much interruption no matter how insulting the comment—and there were several—as Selwyn led them to the spot where he had left Raya and Aidric. Selwyn wondered how Aeson had managed to keep himself from being hauled to Roderick's dungeons in chains with such a mouth. The old man was feisty. Selwyn gave him that.

They soon reached their destination. Raya sat where he had left her, her chin resting loosely on her chest as she dozed. Selwyn reigned in his horse and dismounted. He purposely made a lot of noise as he walked over to the two sleeping figures as to not catch her by surprise. Selwyn didn't fancy a bolt of lightning through his body, and he didn't think his companions would, either. An earlier such unpleasant experience taught him well. It had taken half a year for the hair singed away to begin growing back.

"Where are you going, empath?" Yuric hissed in Lamian. "Why have we stopped here?"

They, of course, didn't see Raya and Aidric because of the spell of invisibility. "This is the place," Selwyn called back to them. "They lie just beneath that tree under an invisibility spell."

Sel was surprised that with all the noise the leaves were making crunching beneath his boots and their talking that Raya didn't even stir. She must have been more exhausted then she had admitted earlier. Not surprising, really. When most husbands were forever trying to protect their wives from harm, Raya was forever trying to protect *him*. It was rather deflating to his male ego.

Before he reached her, Selwyn sent out a tiny thread of emotion that was his personal signature between them. He had meant to send it earlier, but had forgotten due to the rather large distraction of Aeson's blunt commentary. Raya's eyes flew open immediately, her body instinctively ready for magical battle, but she instantly relaxed when she saw that it was indeed him.

"Selwyn!" she squealed, jumping up into his arms.

It was a few moments before Raya finally noticed Yuric and Aeson. She colored and pulled away from Selwyn. She never liked to show such an emotional vulnerability, especially to strangers.

"Sel, who are they?" she asked, casting a nervous glance at them. *"Do they know—"*

"Captain Yuric and his father-in-law, Aeson, are allies," he assured her. *"Yuric is one of King Diryan's spies. As for Aeson, he's quite a character. It seems he hates Roderick's guts more than even we!"*

Aloud he said, "Aeson is a healer and has come to see if he can help Aidric. Seni was indeed watching over me by leading me to these two." Selwyn glanced down at Aidric and frowned. Although the tears had stopped, his friend looked even worse than before if such a thing was possible. "Has he stirred?" he asked anxiously.

Raya shook her head. "He only seems to be fading even farther away. I think that whatever it was that made him cry out so horribly earlier is what's causing him to lose his grasp on life. But—the strange thing is, as I dozed, I had a dream that a man's voice was telling me that we mustn't give up on Aidric because that would leave him to a fate worse than death. Then I jerked awake, and I swear to the Thrones that I saw the image of a man dressed in the gray robes of the Domni standing over Aidric. He was brushing the hair back from Aidric's brow. I gasped, and he turned, disappearing in the same instant. But his face was visible to me long enough to get a good look, and I swear that the figure was Domnae Soren."

"Allison's friend who was murdered?" Sel asked in disbelief. "Surely you were still dreaming—"

"I was *not!*" Raya insisted testily. "You know that the Senini teach that such encounters are possible. Besides, Allison claimed to have spoken with him after he died. It was him, and I think he was trying to tell me what's wrong with Aidric."

"The lady's right, empath," Yuric suddenly said behind him, startling Selwyn badly. He hadn't even heard the spy approach. "Spirits can prove to be powerful allies. You should never question, just accept."

Selwyn just grunted and shook his head. "I stand rebuked, but none of this philosophical nonsense is helping the Mage-general any."

"I'm already one step ahead of you, M'lord Selwyn," Aeson said.

The healer was already kneeling beside Aidric's limp body with his hands pressing gently on either side of Aidric's temples. His eyes were squeezed tightly shut and his forehead creased in concentration.

"This man *should* be dead," Aeson announced a few depths later.

"Is that all you can say?" Selwyn snapped back before he could stop himself. "I know he should be dead, but that man has always had Seni's own luck!"

"No, no, you misunderstand me," Aeson said impatiently. "What I mean is that it's physically impossible to survive the magical damage his body has suffered, and yet, he still lives." The look in the healer's eyes was odd—haunted and at the same time full of a smoldering anger. "However, I've got a pretty good idea of *why* he still lives.

"You know he has a spell attached to him, M'lord Selwyn, one cast using the Dark Powers attributed to Arioch. You say that you don't know its purpose, but I know its purpose only too well. I've seen the likes of it a few times while I served in the Mihran palace back when Roderick first took his throne. One of the first things he did was rid himself of all those nobles who didn't support him. But death was too good for them. Roderick condemned them to the bowels of his deepest dungeons to rot in a kind of living death, a powerful spell of immortality cast over them that condemned his victims to suffer eternal hunger and thirst."

"Come again?" Selwyn asked in bewilderment, sure that he had heard the old man wrong.

"Lamia's Mage-general can't die, lad," Aeson said plainly. "This dark spell will keep him alive no matter the trauma to his body. You could slit his throat until all his lifeblood flowed out and still he'd live. Roderick surely meant for him to rot in the dungeons for all time with the rest of the wretched. It's no secret how much he hated the Lamian Mage-general."

Selwyn fell to one knee beside the old healer and looked at Aidric's face. Now he understood the gray, corpse-like pallor of Aidric's skin. In a sense, Aidric *was* dead but through the darkest of magicks, denied the freedom of the Thrones. Roderick couldn't have condemned Aidric to a crueler, more horrible fate. Hesitantly, Selwyn touched the back of Aidric's hand and willed a sense of comfort and wellbeing into him, hoping that there was enough of Aidric left in his mortal shell to be soothed.

Slowly, Selwyn turned to Aeson. "Can the spell be broken?" he asked quietly.

"Any spell can be broken, m'lord," Aeson answered, "but as an answer to the question you didn't speak, *I* can't break it. I am, after all, a mere healer. It would take a mage of considerable power to break it, but the attempt, itself, is very dangerous. If not done properly, breaking the spell could not only finish him, but also permanently damage his soul."

"We'll concern ourselves with the consequences when the time comes," Selwyn said. "As for now, what I'm most concerned with is the question of whether or not *you* can do anything at all to ease his suffering?"

"That's what you've brought me for, isn't it?" Aeson replied hotly. "I can heal all the damage he's caused himself easily, but in order for my healing to do him any good, he must be taken to a warm, dry bed as soon as possible."

"You just leave that to us," Selwyn said firmly, "and do what you can for him. If you can ease his suffering, healer, than all of Lamia will forever be in your debt."

"I'll remember that," the old healer muttered under his breath and set to work on Aidric.

Selwyn rose from the ground and turned in search of Raya. He wasn't surprised to find her and Yuric deep in discussion.

"...many days travel until we can reach the border?" Raya was asking as he came within earshot.

Yuric turned his eyes to Selwyn, nodded, and then answered, "The normal border station to the east lies a full day's journey on horseback, but as is true in Lamia, it's heavily guarded to prevent any illegal crossings. I would be sending you to your deaths if I allowed you to attempt a crossing there. My best bet is for you to cross in the exact place you and the Golden Mage crossed before since your presence in the kingdom wasn't discovered until you were well within the border."

"We crossed through the Telek River," Raya informed him.

"Through the rapids?" Yuric interrupted, raising an eyebrow in disbelief.

Raya nodded. "It wasn't difficult. Allison cast a bridge spell in order for us to walk above the water. Our horses didn't even get their hooves wet. We kept to the center of the river until we were several spans into Mihr before resorting to the cover of the forest a few dozen handspans away from the banks of the river, but it won't be so simple this time. My mage abilities are average at best, and I can't safely channel the amount of Mage-field energy the bridge spell requires."

"Hmm," Yuric said thoughtfully, "then we'll just have to find another route. You'll do Lamia no good by drowning."

Yuric gazed off into the distance, his eyes becoming vacant. For several beats, he didn't move or blink. However, before Selwyn could become impatient, sense came back into his eyes, and apparently, he found whatever it was he had been probing for because his lips curved up into a faint smile.

"I have your route, the only route possible at this point," he stated. "It lies to the southwest and will take you the better part of two days to reach, but it's better to go a bit out of your way than to be staring down the end of a blade or taking a lightning bolt to the chest. You must first cross the river and travel at least a couple of spans before you'll come to an old deer trail that's been long forgotten. Even Roderick doesn't know of its existence. It's the trail that none but Lord Valin and we who are under his command ever travel. I'll give you a map to guide you along the way. When you've crossed the border into Na'ar, go to the village of Raidon. There, talk to a man named Bruin. He'll lead you to a mage who has the ability to cast the portal spell. I'm afraid that's all the aid I'm able to give."

"It'll be enough, Lord Yuric," Selwyn assured him. "You have given us more help than we ever had any right or hope to expect." His eyes flickered over at Aeson, who was intent on his healing of Aidric, and then back to meet the startling blackness of Yuric's hard eyes. "I only hope that we can reach the Lamian palace in time to warn the king of the rising storm."

***

"Ye must be bloody mad if ye think I'm gonna go in

there first, Arlon," Yulin said stubbornly to his companion "That bloody demon'll fry me for sure!"

Arlon swore and gave Yulin a rough shove towards the cell door. "If ye don't get your sorry ass in there, then King Roderick'll fry ye instead! There's something funny happenin' in there, I tell ye."

"Ye heard it, so how come I have t' go first?" Yulin complained.

"Because I said so, that's why, so stop whining. Blazing tits, ye sound worse than me two-summers-old brat!"

"I don't!" Yulin growled, insulted.

Arlon didn't even bother to honor him with a reply. With an oath, he pushed past Yulin and touched the spell-lock of the door in the right sequence in order to banish the shield around the door. A brilliant light flashed for a beat and was gone before he could even blink. Then, still muttering, he flung the door open and peered into the gloom within—and let out a sharp gasp.

"What, what?" Yulin demanded, pushing Arlon aside to peer inside.

The cell was empty.

CHAPTER FIFTEEN

"Nothing short of Lamian troops at the palace gates had better be occurring to justify this interruption, Toryn, or else you'll soon know what it feels like to hold your own skin," Roderick growled as he untangled himself from Allison and the mass of blankets.

He stood and reached for the hose and breeches he had shed earlier, his nakedness not seeming to bother him in the least. Allison, on the other hand, held the blankets even closer to her nude body and blushed furiously. In her worst nightmares, she had envisioned herself being caught in such an embarrassing position. She didn't know whether to cry or to be furious at this deliberate violation of her privacy.

"I assure you, My Liege, that I wouldn't have intruded without a sound reason," Toryn insisted, his face betraying none of the fear he must be feeling at the thought of facing Roderick's wrath.

If it was one thing Allison knew about her lover, it was not to ever cross him.

"So what is it?" Roderick demanded impatiently.

"The two recently captured Lamians have escaped from the dungeons, My Liege," Toryn reported. "Two guards were found dead at the entrance and several others were spelled to sleep."

"Insufferable fools!" Roderick spat out angrily. "Can I not trust *any* of my men to perform even a task as simple as that? I want them found and brought to me immediately—or better yet, I want their corpses brought to me. A dead Lamian is always better than a live Lamian, at any rate."

"Several battalions have already been assigned to scour the forest in search of them, My Liege," Toryn said. "Messages are already being sent out to the infantries in every village in the kingdom and to the border guard. Rest assure, we'll find them if they are to be found. However, that isn't the whole of it, My Liege."

"I had hoped for your sake that the news of two rodents escaping wasn't the ground shattering news you felt I had need to hear," Roderick said flatly.

"The Lamian Mage-general has also escaped."

"*What!*" Roderick boomed so loudly and fiercely that even Allison cringed under the heat of it. Before

Toryn knew what was happening, Roderick's hands were tightly around his neck, and the Chieftain's eyeballs were in danger of popping out of their sockets. "Why didn't you tell me sooner, you little bastard! He could already be sitting snugly in the Lamian palace by now!"

"Roderick, please! It's not his fault!" Allison cried, torn between wanting to pull Roderick off his Chieftain and her modesty.

Thankfully, the sound of her voice seemed to snap him out of his killing rage, and Roderick flung Toryn away from him as if the mere touch of him was disgusting. He stalked over to the chair beside his bed and snatched up the shirt he had carelessly thrown onto it earlier.

"Toryn, get up from there and go fetch Mordant," Roderick barked. "I want him in my study now!"

Toryn scrambled up onto his feet faster than Allison thought would have been possible after such rough treatment and bowed calmly to Roderick as though he hadn't just been nearly strangled to death by his king. Before Allison could blink, the Chieftain was already closing the bedroom door behind him.

Muttering angrily under his breath, Roderick turned to her and said rather harshly, "As for you, I think we have postponed your mage lessoning long enough. Get up and get dressed. In the library there are countless volumes of spells that I want you to study. I shall not wait much longer to lay siege to Lamia, and I want you prepared. It will be your duty to destroy the Shield of Lamia and pray that you don't disappoint me! That's where I had better find you when I return!"

Then before Allison could get over her shock to utter a single word, he was gone. Suddenly, Roderick wasn't the man she thought she knew. No, the memory of the man she held in her mind was of one who was kind and gentle, not only to her, but to those he ruled.

Roderick, what's happened to you? she thought, near tears. *This coming war with Lamia is all you can think about these days. You used to be so loving, and now it seems if you aren't screaming at your people, then you're screaming at me.*

What made matters worse was that Allison knew he expected her to fight alongside him in the war, and that eventuality frightened her to no end. She had never taken another life, and she knew that she was expected to do just that with her magic. Now, as she rose from within the sheets and blankets and fumbled for a robe, reminded of her future duty, she didn't think that she would ever be capable of killing anybody, enemy or no enemy.

After dressing, Allison slowly made her way to the library, resigned to studying her magecraft for the rest of the day. Roderick's library was impressively large and the rare titles within his collection of books even more impressive. The room easily housed at least a half-million volumes along its walls, a quarter of which were various spellbooks from every religious sect of Seni's World, even a few that had once belonged to Roderick's Domnae teacher. Allison had fond memories of spending various days seated in the library reading over the seemingly endless volumes.

Today, she headed directly to the late Domnae Nelek's collection, intending to plow through at least one of them before the day's end. She reached for the first volume and instantly pulled her hand back with a startled cry as a burst of power unexpectedly shot through her hand the moment she touched the book. It felt like something akin to an electrical shock, though the feeling it left behind was somewhat like the headiness of wine. Rubbing her hand vigorously, Allison carefully peered down at the book, wondering if she had accidentally touched a book that had been spell-locked. She nearly choked when she realized that the words written on the spine were in English.

"But—how can that be?" she whispered perplexedly, shaking her head and peering at the book again, convinced that she had been mistaken of what she had seen.

Nevertheless, upon the second glance, the letters

hadn't changed. They were indeed English, and the subject matter conveyed by the title was ridiculously straightforward:

Spells of the Golden Mage

Allison swallowed nervously, feeling a sudden chill that had nothing to do with the draftiness of the enormous room. If ever she had doubted that she was the Golden Mage, this book diminished the last of them. She wondered why Roderick had never mentioned the book before as it was obviously meant for her alone.

Unless—

"He doesn't know he has this," she whispered to herself.

How could he possibly know? She was probably the only person in all of Seni's world that knew the English Language, and didn't she read somewhere that the legendary spellbook of the Golden Mage had been lost in time along with that mad Seer? Did Domnae Nelek even realize what it was that he had held in his possession?

Almost on its own accord, her hand hesitantly reached out to the book again. This time there was no flash of power when her fingertips brushed the spine, no sudden shock. With more confidence, Allison pulled the volume from the shelf and promptly sneezed when at least fifteen years of dust followed, proving that the book had likely not been disturbed since the day Roderick had placed it onto the shelf. Allison listened carefully for any approaching footsteps in the hall outside the library, and only when she detected none did she take the spellbook to her favorite chair next to the fireplace.

The book, itself, didn't appear any more special then all the countless volumes she had previously studied. Bound in a linen-like cloth, its external lettering inked by hand, it could have easily passed for a history or work of fiction. Many of Roderick's spellbooks that contained the most basic of spells easily outclassed it with their leather bindings, jeweled borders and golden-etched lettering. If the book was indeed authentic, it was in remarkably good shape for a book that was several millennia old, the result of a spell, no doubt.

Maybe its simplicity was the reason for its neglect. Roderick was a man of extravagant taste, so why would he interest himself with a book that appeared as though it had been written and bound by someone of modest means?

Curiosity now overpowering caution, Allison eagerly opened the book—and a power greater than any she had ever encountered immediately seized her mind, a power that was infinitely greater than hers and Roderick's powers combined. She didn't even have time to cry out in alarm.

Distantly, she was aware that the book had fallen out of her hands and onto her lap. The pages began to turn rapidly, as if a sudden gust of wind had swept across them. Then, like her previous encounters with portals, Allison suddenly felt a brilliant light fill her entire being, but instead of the light forcing every molecule in her body apart, it became one with her, filling her essence with words and images too rapid for her overwhelmed mind to grasp.

Then as quickly as it had begun, the mysterious power released her mind. Although only a few moments had passed, it seemed to Allison that her mind had been seized for sand-marks. She slumped over onto the book, too weak and shaken to catch herself. Darkness was also beginning to invade her mind, but no matter how much she fought it, in the end, it was the darkness that won.

***

"I think we're in trouble," Raya sent to her husband, pausing amidst a thick clump of trees and motioning him to join her.

Selwyn winced inwardly as he led his mount to

her. He had hoped that Raya hadn't noticed their pursuers.

"I know," he replied soberly. *"Mages?"*

"Naturally," she said sardonically. *"We aren't exactly two lovers out for a romantic stroll in the forest. Can you tell how far away they are? I can sense only their magic and even that just vaguely. There's no sense of direction. I would've missed it had I not been looking specifically for it."*

Sel shook his head and glanced uneasily to the west. *"They have an empath with them. He's confusing their trail. He would have us think that they are both near and far, to the north and east of us. For all I know, they could be coming from the sky or beneath the ground. I can't in good conscious rule out either. At any rate, whether near or far, you can bet your ass they know we're here. It seems Yuric's secret path is not as secret as he thought."*

"Figures. Do you think we can outrun them?"

"Probably not."

"How comforting," Raya snarked. *"Well, I guess now would be a good time to prove that you deserve your position, love. I'll see what I can do about hiding our appearance."*

Dismounting, Selwyn walked over to the horse he had bound Aidric to and began to loosen the ropes that prevented his still unconscious friend from falling out of the saddle. After gathering Aidric into his arms, Selwyn carefully sat him down onto the frost-covered ground and arranged him as comfortably as he could against the trunk of one of the larger trees. Even against the light bark, Aidric's face appeared ghastly pale.

Frowning, Sel straightened and began his search, joining his emotions with the natural energies of the forest, expanding them several dozen spans to the very edge of his limitations.

However, it wasn't really necessary. He had failed to mention to Raya that although he couldn't pinpoint the location of the mages, he did, however, know exactly where every one of the two thousand plus Mihran soldiers stood. Not even their empath, a man near to Sel's equal, could have masked the emotions of everyone.

Sel glanced over at Raya, her eyes closed and her hands moving in fluid patterns as she cast her spells. He knew he should feel guilty for deceiving his wife, especially about something so serious, but he knew Raya too well to trust her sense in their current situation. Sel was forever accusing Aidric of being reckless, but his friend was nothing compared to Raya's recklessness when she thought she was trapped.

And he was no fool. They *were* trapped. For perhaps the last few sand-marks, the Mihrans had been unknowingly closing in on them, and Sel hadn't sensed them until only a few depths ago. There was no longer any time to run. The only option left to them was to cloak their appearance and hope that neither their empath nor mages were cunning enough to see through their ruse.

"Whatever you're going to do, dearheart, you had better do it quickly because they're almost right under our noses!" Sel warned.

"I thought you couldn't sense them!" Raya sent accusingly.

"I can now," Sel replied, refusing to feel guilty.

He was positive he had done the right thing, more so now that he could easily sense Raya's rising panic. If they were to escape, he needed her thinking as rationally as she could. If he didn't do something quick, then her panic would betray them both. He would die first before he allowed that to happen.

Selwyn reached deep into himself, gathering the memory of every comforting emotion he had ever experienced. Using the bond through his life-ring, he sent those emotions to Raya. Instantly, the panic swelling within her was stilled as she welcomed this new sense of comfort, of security. He could feel her whole being sigh with the relief it brought her.

They didn't have much time. Selwyn could already feel the slight vibration in the earth of the army's approach. Not even an empath could mask that inevitable tremble. Calmed, Raya set about her tasks of masking their appearance while he began to trigger all the false trails of emotion that he had set periodically since their departure from the Decia area. Selwyn was weak with relief that he'd had the foresight to set them up. Aidric would be proud.

Selwyn hoped that this newest distraction would confuse the Mihran empath from their trail, though he knew better than to put much faith in it. At the very least, it would buy them a little more time. Aidius, how he wished for Aidric's council! He was certain that Aidric would've known what to do, but Aidric was far from them, lost to whatever demons he had found in the darkness of a death that was not death.

A flood of warning interrupted Selwyn's thoughts as it struck his senses. One of his warning traps had been triggered, one of the nearer traps. His false trails had failed him. The enemy had found them.

"Raya, they come," Selwyn sent carefully. *"Despite our efforts, they know exactly where we stand."* His eyes found and met hers. *"Now you listen to me. One of us must escape. There's no if ands or buts about it. The king must be told what's happened to Allison."*

"Selwyn—"

"No! Let me finish Raya. You know it has to be you. You're a mage. I'm only an empath. It's as simple as that. You have a greater chance of reaching the border than I do. You know as well as I that an empath is virtually useless when the numbers of the enemy are this high."

"I won't go without you, Selwyn," Raya insisted stubbornly. *"I refuse to willingly leave you behind to the enemy! If it's your fate that you'll die today, then it's a fate I'll share, as well. If I go, then you go with me, or have you forgotten our bond?"*

"Have you *forgotten our sworn duty?"* Selwyn countered angrily, hating that he was forced to throw their sacred oaths to Lamia back in her face. *"Our duty is to Lamia first. Lamia! Not ourselves. Don't you understand? By going with you, I would have to leave Aidric here to be captured again. You know damned well that I can't condemn him to that fate if there's even the slightest of chances that I can save him!"*

His voice softened. *"Beloved, please understand that we* must *do this. One of us must escape, and we can't allow anything else to be. King Diryan must be told, and Lamia's Mage-general mustn't be allowed to die in Roderick's dungeons or a cataclysm greater than anything you can imagine will thunder across not only Lamia, but all of Seni's world!"*

Selwyn had no idea where those words had come from, but he instantly knew them to be true. For a moment, it had seemed as though someone else had been speaking through him—but that was crazy. He didn't have the Foresight ability. It was just the stress finally taking its toll on him. He was just allowing his imagination to run wild. But still, where had the words come from?

The look in Raya's eyes was unreadable, but his

senses knew the truth of her emotions without having to read them in her eyes—she had just seen something in his eyes that terrified her. What in the name of Seni was happening?

"Stay then," she sent, her mind-voice so faint that Selwyn had to strain to understand her words. *"It's out of our hands."*

"If there's a way for us to escape, I promise on the oath I have sworn to you that I'll find it. Wait for me, Raya, when you reach Na'ar. Wait for me near the Southeastern Road. If I haven't come within half a day, go on to see Bruin as we planned. Swear to me that you won't make the same mistake as Allison."

Raya tore her eyes from him, as though the mere sight of him was unbearable. Through the Bond they shared, Selwyn could feel her love, her hurt, and just how frightened for him she was.

As he watched her hurrying into the forest, Selwyn belatedly realized that she had not given her promise. However, the sight of the first Mihran solder quickly banished any further thoughts of his wife.

It had begun.

Selwyn eased himself between a couple of trees, pressing his back as closely to one of them as he could, the bark rough and feeling utterly alien against his skin. He longed to be able to melt into the tree. He knew with utter certainty, despite what he had told Raya, that he would never leave Mihr again.

His eyes shifted from the advancing soldiers to the still form of his friend, barely visible in the gloom of night. What a cruel twist of fate had led them both to this end. Aidric had given his life in escaping, despite the life Roderick's dark spell had condemned him to, only to be caught again because he, Selwyn, had failed them all.

Silently, Selwyn watched the enemy draw nearer. He could feel beads of perspiration beginning to fall down his cheeks despite the cold. He angrily clenched his hands into tight fists at his sides as they began to shake. How had he let it come to this?

The Mihran soldiers were now so close that Sel could begin to distinguish voices. A few agonizing moments later, he began to pick out words.

"...felt...definitely three...Mage-general...senses don't deceive me."

Selwyn started. Riding within the first battalion of solders was a man who was unmistakably the empath he had sensed earlier. The whirlwind of emotions that surrounded the man was unnerving, as if he drained them from the surrounding men in order to strengthen his own power. Selwyn had thought the Mihran empath his equal at the most, so he wasn't prepared for the power this man truly wielded. Compared to this man, Sel's power was the morning dew on the palace lawns, thinking to overpower a raging waterfall.

It was no wonder that the Mihrans had found them so swiftly. Against an empath of that power, they had never stood a chance. The empath had been playing with them since the beginning, lifting their spirits with a false hope of escape, all the while knowing exactly where they had been all along.

Dear Seni, did the empath know that Raya had left them behind? Had she already been captured? Sel nearly wept with the knowledge that he dared not probe the forest for her. Might as well summon a bolt of lightning to strike where he now stood. The results would be the same.

Please Seni, let her be safe!

To his further horror, the first battalion of men stopped a mere thirty to thirty-five handspans from him. Distantly, Sel could sense two more battalions approaching, casually as if they were simply out for a pleasant stroll. He thought that his heart would soon burst with fear.

The enemy empath slowly dismounted. In the gloom, Selwyn couldn't make out his features, which made him all the more ominous. Willing himself to swallow his rising panic, Sel watched the empath whisper something to one of the soldiers. Then the empath slowly turned his head, and Sel almost cried out when he saw that the empath was looking directly at him. His skin began to crawl. He was certain Raya's spell of invisibility had failed.

Even so, Selwyn couldn't make himself run, nor could he tear his eyes away from the empath. He was a field mouse caught in the deadly gaze of a viper. Then the moment was gone as the empath shifted his gaze to the right, his entire manner searching.

He still doesn't see us, Sel realized in disbelief. *He knows we're here, but he can't pinpoint our location exactly.*

Perhaps Seni had heeded his prayers after all. Selwyn wasn't about to throw this small chance away by doing something stupid. As much as he itched to use his power, Sel knew that silence was his best weapon at the moment.

Glancing down at Aidric, he prayed that his friend wouldn't moan or cry out as he did before. He dared not even send Aidric a sense of security and warmth, something that would've assured his silence. Selwyn was terrified that even his own fear would be detected by the Mihran empath, no matter how tightly he had shielded his emotions.

To his alarm, Sel saw the empath coming right for him. The sweat began to fall more rapidly down his face as he helplessly watched the empath's approach. So, he had been discovered after all. He despaired of going back to Roderick's dungeons after all they had been through to escape them.

Selwyn wasn't sure when the extra chill had

started, but suddenly he was freezing, as if the already cold temperature had instantly taken a drastic nose-dive below the freezing mark. It penetrated him, freezing the sweat on his face until it felt like frozen beads sliding down his skin. His entire body also stiffened until he literally couldn't move even a pinky.

It had to be the empath. There was no other explanation. Not even a mage could make someone feel this cold without channeling a great deal of energy, and he sensed none of that in the area around them. What unholy power did this empath wield?

Selwyn was now face-to-face with the empath, so close that he could feel the other's warm breath on his frozen lips. The other's lips were stretched in a mocking smile as Sel stared into his eyes. There was no mistaking it. It was over. Sel could only manage to tremble in his helpless immobility.

Quite casually, the empath lifted his hand and reached out to touch Selwyn's chest, a gesture that would instantly banish the invisibility spell. His smile was cruel.

Selwyn almost cursed, but he clenched his jaw to prevent it. He would go down with dignity if nothing else. It was all he had left.

Curiously, as he felt the empath's hand on his chest, the man's expression changed from smug to puzzled. He began to frantically touch Selwyn all over his body, his frown becoming more and more prominent and his hands more and more frantic. In the next instant, Selwyn felt a violent blow to his abdomen, followed by a second and third, before he realized that the empath had begun to kick him as though he was kicking the tree behind him.

"Where is he? Where *is* he!" the empath raged as Selwyn crumbled to the ground, gasping painfully.

Even after he fell, the empath continued to kick the unfortunate tree. Sel couldn't believe it, but it was indeed the tree, not him, that was the object of the empath's wrath.

"My senses *never* fail me! Where is he!"

But—*he* touched *me*, Selwyn thought, utterly confused as he struggled to climb back onto his feet as his newest injuries screamed. *He touched me, and the spell was broken. Yet, he didn't see me. He didn't feel me. What in Seni's name is going on?*

Only when he saw the faint figure walking within the trees a few dozen handspans from them did he have his answer.

It was Domnae Soren.

CHAPTER SIXTEEN

S itting in his study impatiently waiting for Mordant's arrival, Roderick couldn't decide whether to strangle the insolent man the moment he stepped across the threshold or to continue with his earlier plan of discussing this latest outrage. He was certain that Mordant was taking his time to answer his summons out of spite and the sheer pleasure it gave the bastard to annoy him. What Mordant didn't realize was that Roderick's forced idleness only gave him the time to stew over losing Aidric and his friends, which only endangered the Silver Mage's own neck that much sooner.

"Damned if his new throne is making him entirely too bold," Roderick growled to his closed door. He itched to stand up and pace, but he didn't want to allow Mordant to see how much his tardiness was irritating him. "I should've rid myself of him long ago! After all, there's only room for one great emperor in these lands, and I have the Golden Mage on a leash to boot! What does he possess but a tiny thread of Lord Arioch's power? Perhaps I'll make it her first task to relieve him of his life."

But no—Roderick had been aching to squeeze the life out of Mordant since the moment of their first meeting. He almost hated the dark-mage as much as he hated Aidric. Why should he deny himself such an extreme pleasure? Especially since Aidric had miraculously escaped his judgment. A man had to have some pleasure in his life, didn't he?

The thought of pleasure brought up an image of Allison into his head, and the sneer on his lips widened. How delicious it would be when he captured Aidric again—of that he had no doubt of—and he forced the bastard to listen to him recount all their amorous liaisons. Perhaps he and Allison would even perform before him. Roderick licked his lips at the thought.

Unfortunately, Mordant picked that moment to come gliding into the study without knocking or waiting to be announced, his demeanor full of self-assurance, shattering Roderick's sense of triumph into a sense of barely controlled rage.

"What is it now?" Mordant demanded irritably. "I would think that you were still tumbling the golden-haired wench. What's the matter? Your sword not as sharpened as you would like?"

"I would ask you the same thing," Roderick replied coolly, refusing to show him how much that insult stuck in his craw. "According to several of *your* wenches, yours has the edge of a child's wooden practice blade."

Roderick felt a measure of triumph seeing a flash of anger in the Silver Mage's eyes before he could conceal it.

"You forget, Roderick, that I'm now a king," Mordant retorted. "I don't have the time to play a part in your schemes anymore. I have my own pursuits to attend to."

"Yes a king," Roderick echoed sarcastically, "a king who has secured his throne through usurpation. A king who was placed on his throne by *me* and a kingdom with twice the power as his. A king who can be *relieved* of his throne with just the wave of my hand." Roderick narrowed his eyes. "Now, you were saying?" he asked, a hint of menace replacing the casualness of his voice.

"You insufferable bastard!" Mordant spat out.

"Come now, is that the best you can do?" Roderick taunted.

He only had a couple of beats to react as Mordant attacked, not the magical one he had half expected but in the form of a spelled dagger. Roderick, however, had a faster reaction time than the Silver Mage. In a brilliant red flash, he shot a burst of dark energy at the dagger. The dagger exploded on impact into a multitude of pieces a mere quarter handspan away from his chest, the shockwave sending Mordant's body slamming into the door a beat after.

Roderick slapped a paralysis spell over the Silver Mage before his body hit the floor. Then, as casually as though he was going over to shake his hand, Roderick strolled over to Mordant's crumbled form, grabbed the mage by the neck, and lifted him up until he was on his knees.

"You must tire of smashing into my walls whenever we meet, *Your Highness*," Roderick purred, "and I tire of wasting energy on you." He squeezed Mordant's neck until the man's eyes began to bulge and his face began turning an interesting shade of purple. He bent low until his mouth was nearly touching the mage's ear and said, "Remember this, Mordant. I shall *not* tolerate another incident like this, and the next time you so much as think to cross me, only your head will be gracing my wall."

Roderick released his hold on the mage and grinned with immense satisfaction as he watched the undignified way Mordant crumbled to the floor. He released him from the spell and once again took his seat behind his desk. Mordant picked himself off the ground, his eyes full of poison-tipped daggers as he glared down at Roderick. However, he made no more attempts to attack.

"Now that we're finished with this petty nonsense, we must address the business I summoned you for in the first place. By that fool's own luck, it seems that the Mage-general of Lamia has escaped, as have his two friends."

"I'm not surprised," Mordant said with disgust, "with all the fools in your guard. A babe still in the cradle could escape from your dungeons."

"For once, mage, I agree," Roderick said just as disgustedly. "I'm surrounded by nothing but fools, it seems." His eyes looked pointedly at Mordant. "I want all of them found immediately. The mage, Raya, and her weakling of a husband must be killed on sight, but I want Aidric brought back to me uninjured. If anyone is to kill the Mage-general, it will be *me*. Send out the entirety of your army if needs be, but *I want them found!*"

A slight inclination of his head was all the acknowledgment Mordant gave him, but instead of taking his leave he asked, "And what of the Golden Mage? Are you certain that she's entirely under your control? If the Mage-general can escape so easily, magically shackled and damaged, then I imagine it would be no challenge for one with such power to do the same."

"Rest assure, she is entirely mine—mind, soul, *and* body," Roderick replied smugly. "She remembers nothing of Aidric. In fact, in her memories of the bastard, it's my face she sees not his. In her eyes, Lamia *is* the enemy and always has been. Her memories of Lamia are completely gone, replaced by those which I have constructed. She believes that the Prophecy of the Golden Mage is a Mihran prophecy. Within the quarter-moon, she will prove how much she belongs to me when she shatters Lamia's Shield and the throne and Mage-field is at last mine!"

"The problem with you, braggart," Mordant said mockingly, "is your overconfidence. The day *will* come when your confidence will become your greatest enemy." Then before Roderick could do more than frown, the Silver Mage was gone.

***

It was at least a dozen sand-marks past the evening-mark when Diryan finally managed to drag his weary body up to his chambers to grab what little sleep he could before he had to rise to face the many problems that would be awaiting him in the morning. He sighed. At least he could escape them for a few precious sandmarks if he couldn't escape them altogether. There were many who couldn't do even that.

As he expected, Ileanna was waiting for him, still dressed in the gown she had worn that day. She sat with her back to him at the small desk in their bedroom that was hers and hers alone, scribbling furiously in the little gray book that she never allowed him a single glance. She kept it in the top drawer of her desk, neither book nor drawer locked with magic or key.

Although curiosity often burned within him regarding the contents of that book, he never once thought about violating her trust, and the servants would've rather burned for all eternity in the second hell than violate the queen's privacy. It seemed to Diryan that the gray book would remain a mystery to him forever.

As she heard him approach, Ileanna quickly slammed the book shut and slid it into its drawer. Diryan had often caught her unawares when she was writing in that book, but never since the first time he had seen her writing in the mysterious gray book did he even acknowledge its existence.

"My dear, you shouldn't have waited," Diryan said softly as she turned to meet his gaze.

Though obviously stressed and fatigued, she still

looked as beautiful and radiant to his eyes as the first day he had seen her walking amongst the merchant shops of Peri.

"I wouldn't have been able to sleep without you beside me, you know that," Ileanna replied, her lips stretching in a wry grin. "Besides, there was much I needed to catch up on. But never mind about me. How did the Council meeting go?"

"Need you even ask?" Diryan replied with a groan.

"That bad, huh?"

"Worse," he said as he collapsed onto their huge feather bed. Wouldn't it be nice if he could lie there enveloped in warmth and softness for the rest of his days and not have to ever deal with the pressing problems facing his kingdom! "Pyrs and Claudium were at each other's throats again. Ion could not make up his mind whether to cry or shout angrily—in either case his tongue never ceased wagging—and to top everything off, Gaelle came barging into the room to demand her position back scarcely a sand-mark after she had been dismissed!

"I swear to Seni, Ileanna, if I'd had a knife in my hand, I would've slit every single one of their throats just to silence them! We are at war with Mihr, Aidric is in Roderick's hands, and the Golden Mage, along with a mage and a powerful empath, have disappeared into the night—one can only presume to rescue Aidric against my wishes—and the whole of my council is squabbling about petty nonsense like children! I believe at this point that I'm ready to slit my *own* throat, so I suggest that you keep any sharp objects away from my sight and temptation!"

Ileanna sighed and sat on the edge of the bed. "Word has already reached the ears of the kingdom of Allison's disappearance. One can only guess how that was possible, but that's not important right now. They're *terrified*, Diryan. Whispers of what they feel is our imminent downfall are already spreading from village to village with the swiftness of a wildfire during the dry season."

"The blame is solely mine," Diryan murmured. "I saw the look in Allison's eyes when I bluntly informed her that nothing would be done to deliver Aidric from Roderick's hands. I *knew* what she was capable of where Aidric was concerned. Damn it, Ileanna, I warned Aidric of the danger of becoming involved with a woman such as she! I knew nothing but ill would come of their union in the end, but who am I to deny him happiness no matter that I thought their love unwise? He's had so little of it in his life."

"Who indeed?" Ileanna said softly. "But Diryan, you must realize that the fate of Lamia ceased to be in our hands from the moment Seni brought the Lady

Allison to this world. The Providencen priests knew it, Allison and Aidric knew it, and deep down we knew it, as well. The Prophecy of the Golden Mage must be fulfilled. Nothing short of Seni's decree can prevent that from coming to pass. It's all in Allison's hands now, and we can only pray to Seni that the choice she makes, or *can* make will be the right one."

"That's what I'm afraid of," he whispered.

As it turned out, Diryan didn't get a wink of sleep that night.

***

Crouched within the tall brush, Raya peered into the darkness at the lone horseman that approached, not daring to hope that it was her husband coming as he had promised. Her Probe of Inquiry had only met up with the blankness that signaled that his mind was heavily shielded. It was still too dark and the horseman too far away to see anything useful, the first sunrise still a couple of sand-marks away.

Silently, Raya watched the horse slowly trot down the road as if its master didn't have a care in the world. *It can't be Selwyn*, Raya reasoned, closing her eyes against the tears that threatened. *There's only one man on that horse, and he wouldn't have left Aidric behind. I'm just dreaming. He isn't going to come. I need to face it. Sel wouldn't have sent me on ahead if he had thought we would all make it across the border.*

Yet, despite the certainty of her thoughts, Raya knew that she would wait the allotted time Selwyn had given himself. She wouldn't give up on him until she had to. He still had a few sand-marks left to reach her.

When she opened her eyes again, the horseman had vanished as though he had never been there at all, a ghost of her desperate hope. Raya sighed and sat down onto the dry grass. A few more sand-marks—it was going to take an eternity.

A few depths later, a slight sound behind her caused her to stiffen and whip her head around in alarm, reaching for the Lamian Mage-field even as she turned. Out of the gloom stepped a figure, cautiously edging his way towards the spot where she sat concealed in the brush. As the figure moved forward, a sliver of moonlight illuminated his face for the slightest moment, but it was enough for Raya to see all she needed to see.

"Selwyn—" she whispered, suddenly frozen in the grips of an emotion she had never experienced.

"Raya, is that you?" came her husband's unmistakable voice.

It couldn't be. No. But it was. It was her Selwyn.

The next thing she knew, Raya was falling into Selwyn's arms. She didn't even remember standing up.

"You're in big trouble, you know that, right?" Raya scolded as the tears she had refused to shed since she had left Selwyn began to stream from beneath her tightly-closed lids.

"Aidius, for once in your life, Raya, can't you at least say that you're glad to see me?" Selwyn said in mock exasperation, then silenced anything she would have said with his lips.

It was a long time after before Raya learned of her husband's adventure.

CHAPTER SEVENTEEN

"Hold!"

Selwyn froze at the harsh command, suddenly finding himself staring down the points of two swords. His horse danced slightly in reaction to his sudden agitation. He pulled on the reigns a bit to settle the horse, hoping that the owners of the swords wouldn't decide to use him as a human pincushion simply because he had moved.

His first thought was that bandits had ambushed them, but he quickly discarded that thought, knowing that had their unexpected visitors been bandits, he would now be dead. His empathic senses detected at least a half-dozen more human presences hiding within the trees on either side of them. Behind him,

Selwyn could hear another voice give the same command to Raya. He breathed a silent sigh of relief when his wife wisely held her tongue and obeyed.

Border guards, Selwyn thought with relief, noting the green and silver uniforms and the two battling snowcats on their breasts. *Seni be praised, at last we've made it into Na'ar!*

After spending two nights within Mihr either riding or dozing among the shadows of the trees, jumping at every sound and dealing with Mihran soldiers waiting in ambush, the sight of allies was a gift sent straight from Seni. Never again did Selwyn want to spend a night as hellish as the last one had been when he had thought for sure it was all over for Aidric and him.

"Let me handle this, dearheart," Selwyn sent urgently to his wife, knowing very well how much trouble his wife's freely-speaking tongue could bring for them if she wasn't careful.

"What business have you in these parts, stranger?" demanded the soldier holding his blade to Selwyn's chest, suspicion showing clearly in his narrowed eyes and the tautness of his body. "Only one place you could have come from—Mihr."

The soldier's eyes flashed dangerously, and Selwyn could feel the point of the second soldier's sword pressing more insistently into his side as keenly

as he could feel the agitation of the rest of the guardsmen now emerging from the forest. Selwyn was at
once infinitely relieved that they'd had the foresight to
remove the black and gold tunics they had worn over
their own shirts before venturing any farther within
Na'ar. He didn't think that they would have lived long
enough to even know the faces of their murderers had
they still sported the Mihran uniforms.

"I don't know how you've managed to make it
this far into the kingdom from the border," the soldier
continued stonily, "but if you would like to live to ride
another day, then I suggest that you and the girl turn
around and ride back to that pit of vipers from whence
you've emerged!"

"Yes, we've come from Mihr," Selwyn said carefully, using the Na'aran tongue, "but we aren't Mihran.
My name is Selwyn Phelannik, empathic representative in the Circle of Lamia." He gestured towards
Raya, watching the swords warily as he did so. "She is
Raya Phelannike, adept-mage of Lamia. We are en
route to Lamia, and—"

"Captain! They have Lamia's Mage-general!" one
of the guards suddenly exclaimed.

After that abrupt declaration, everything was
chaos. Selwyn suddenly found himself flung to the
ground, the breath wrenched from his lungs on impact. Bright, white lights flashed before his eyes, and

the world began to spin, momentarily giving him the frightening vision of several boots readying themselves to bury themselves in his side and at least a dozen blades rising to strike. Spans away, he could hear Raya shouting.

No, not the boots again— Selwyn pleaded silently to Seni. Aloud, he could only groan and instinctually curl into a more protective position. The scores of bruises he had obtained from the last kicking he had received were still very tender.

Then like the voice of Aidius, himself, through the shouts, the curses, and the screaming of frightened horses, a weak, but powerful voice commanded, "*Stop!*"

Time suddenly came to a standstill. Several boots stopped a mere half finger-span away from Selwyn's body, and the advancing swords froze and then were slowly drawn away. Not believing what his own ears were telling him, Selwyn slowly turned his head and fixed his eyes on the horse that carried Aidric. Sure enough, pale-violet eyes caught and held his gaze. A flood of immense relief washed through his soul so that Sel forgot the burning of his lungs.

"Don't harm them," Aidric whispered, so low that had the world not fallen into an instant silence, he wouldn't have been heard. "They are my friends—and my saviors."

Then Aidric closed his eyes and fell still once again, apparently slipping back into unconsciousness.

If Seni, Himself, with Aidius in tow, had suddenly appeared in their midst, Selwyn didn't think that a single soul there would have noticed, least of all him.

"We must speak with Bruin of Raidon at once!" Selwyn heard himself say before he even realized that he was going to speak, his voice sounding appallingly breathy and strained. He carefully pulled himself up into a more dignified sitting position and declared, "The life of the Mage-general and the fate of Lamia and her surrounding kingdoms depend upon the swiftness of our arrival to Lamia!"

Without asking, a couple of soldiers reached down to lend their hands to Selwyn. Wordlessly, he accepted their aid and rose stiffly to his feet, proud that his knees didn't buckle or his legs wobble. Though sore in several places, Selwyn didn't think anything had been broken, a blessing that he silently thanked Seni for.

His eyes immediately searched for Raya, who, Seni be praised, didn't appear to have been hurt at all. Naturally. She was, however, glaring menacingly at all the guards surrounding her. Selwyn wondered if any of them knew just how lucky they were that Raya hadn't sent any offensive spells their way. Her eyes immediately softened when she turned them to him, and her forehead suddenly creased with worry.

"Are you hurt, Sel?" she sent anxiously.

"No, love," he assured her. *"I just had the breath knocked from me. Luckily Aidric spoke up when he did or things could've gotten a great deal worse than they were."*

"Bastards—I should've blasted them while I had the chance—and the excuse!"

Selwyn could almost see the anger flowing from her as well as his heightened senses felt it.

"Don't hold it against them, Raya. Aidric is well respected in Na'ar, especially after all he did for Idona, and word must've reached them of his mysterious disappearance courtesy of Lamia's gossips. When they saw him trussed up like so much game on his horse, they thought the worst. I admit, they never should've reacted as they did, but with everyone still on edge from the war, do you blame them?"

"I suppose not," Raya said grudgingly. *"At least they seem embarrassed over the whole mess. An apology or two would be nice, though."*

"I agree," he sent, rubbing his backside irritably. *"I don't think I'll be able to sit comfortably for at least a quarter-moon!"*

"Only you, lover, could joke at a time like this!" she retorted.

"Who's joking?" Sel grumbled.

The soldiers did indeed appear deeply embarrassed over the whole situation. Many of them wouldn't meet his eyes. The captain, however, looked as stoic as ever, even in his apology, but Selwyn didn't doubt for a moment that it was sincere. The captain explained that many Mihran spies crept across the border every day, claiming that they were people of some import. This close to Mihr, one really couldn't be too cautious.

"I know of this Bruin you spoke of earlier," the captain said. "He's a blacksmith in Raidon of some reputation. His goods are rivaled by no other in this kingdom. I'll send a half-dozen of my men with you so that this unfortunate episode won't be repeated. Again, I express my humble apologies, Lord Selwyn and Lady Raya and bid you a good journey. If you would be so kind to send us word of how the Mage-general fares once you reach Lamia, we would be much obliged."

"I'll do that, Captain," Selwyn promised as he mounted his horse, wincing when he was seated.

Raya glanced expressionlessly at her husband before she added, "And Captain, a word to the wise. In the future, ask questions before you act. Next time you may have the misfortune to meet with those who aren't of such even temper as we—or so forgiving."

Selwyn was sure that his face burned brighter than his hair as they rode off into the forest towards Raidon.

***

With a moan, Allison opened heavy eyelids and attempted to lift up her head from its unnatural position on the arm of the chair, which immediately began to protest the sudden movement by throbbing rather insistently. Rather than fighting it, she closed her eyes again and allowed the pounding in her head to die down a bit. God—she hadn't felt this bad since the time when she—

What? For some odd reason, she couldn't recall the time her memory had tried to bring forth. *What does it matter?* she thought irritably. *I still feel like crap!*

Then the weight in her lap suddenly caused her to bolt upright in alarm, instantly regretting her harsh reaction when the throbbing in her head sharpened until she thought her head would explode. Allison pressed her hands against her temples and began to moan again, but not just in response to the pain.

She remembered the spellbook.

What had happened? One minute she was opening the book, the next, her mind had been overwhelmed with words swirling around like the thundering waters of the Telek River and after that, visions of terrible spells that she was sure no mortal had ever cast. Allison looked down at the thick book still

267

opened in her lap with a little fear. She didn't know whether it was wise to touch it or to wait until Roderick came for her and have *him* remove it from her lap.

However, the moment that she thought of Roderick discovering her with the book, she felt an overwhelming sense of secrecy, and she realized that she didn't want Roderick, lover or no, to discover that she had such a legendary spellbook in her hands.

He can't find me with this! Allison thought frantically, her ears immediately straining for any sounds of approaching footsteps. *If he finds out what this book contains, then he'll ask me to use those awful spells against Lamia, and I don't know if I could refuse him anything.*

Cautiously, she touched a fingertip to the book, and when nothing happened, she breathed a sigh of relief and closed the book with a loud bang that seemed to echo ominously throughout the library. Then, with a few whispered words, she banished the book into her magical storage plane, a place not even Roderick had access to.

Rubbing her temples vigorously, Allison attempted to stand, knowing that she had better produce some evidence that she had been studying as instructed before Roderick found her. She had faced his temper once. She didn't want to have to face it again, especially since he had been in such a bad mood when he had left her.

He's been under so much pressure lately, especially with Lamia declaring war on us, but I wish he wouldn't take his frustrations out on me! Unfortunately, standing up only seemed to make her headache worse. *Damn it all! Why did I have to find that stupid spellbook?* she thought irritably as she forced her wobbly legs to walk over to the bookshelves.

As she reached for a book at random, Allison abruptly heard the sound of insistent footsteps in the hallway and as she feared, coming to a stop just outside the door. She knew it was Roderick. Only his footsteps would be so solid and confident. Frantically, she yanked the book from the shelf and all but flew to her chair, nearly falling on her face when the pain in her head threatened to blind her. She was just opening what was luckily a spellbook when Roderick came barging into the room.

Allison immediately looked up, a ready smile on her face despite the fact that she wanted to howl with pain, but the smile instantly melted away when she saw Roderick's expression.

"Bad news?" she ventured timidly.

"That, my dear, is an understatement," Roderick said roughly. "I hope you've been studying hard as the time to invade Lamia is nearly upon us. Lamian prisoners have somehow escaped our clutches, prisoners that possess vital information that could damage our cause severely. Mordant has sent out several battalions in pursuit. All the infantries in the villages have been alerted, as well, but as cunning as these Lamians are, they have thus far eluded my forces. We mustn't allow King Diryan to win the upper hand in this war. His evil tyranny must stop once and for all!"

"I'll do what I can, Roderick, but—"

"But what?" he demanded sharply.

Allison swallowed hard, refusing to be hurt by his tone. "I-I'm afraid."

"Afraid?" he echoed, bewilderment showing clearly in his expression. "You, who has the power of a hundred mages combined—*afraid?*"

"I've never been to war, Roderick," she said, struggling to explain the chaos of her emotions. "And I've never taken—taken a l-life before. A lot of innocent people will die in this war."

Roderick shook his head as if he didn't quite believe what he was hearing. "But surely you realize that if we don't fight this war, many innocents will die anyway under Diryan's boot. We do what we must, my dear, and in the end, all will be as it should be."

Allison nodded reluctantly and gave herself over to his waiting embrace. "I guess you know what's best," she whispered against his chest.

"That, I do," he replied firmly.

A pity she didn't see the look of triumphant cruelty that flashed in his eyes—one full of greed and a blood lust that would have revolted her down to her very soul.

CHAPTER EIGHTEEN

As he stared at the shimmering portal before him, Selwyn asked worriedly, "Iaen, are you certain that traveling through a portal won't harm Aidric in his condition?"

Iaen, the mage Bruin had directed them to, glanced down at the unconscious Aidric before answering, "I'm certain, Lord Selwyn. In all honesty, he won't even be aware that he has traveled through one in his present condition. I urge you all to hurry. I can't channel this amount of energy for much longer!"

Selwyn nodded. He was more than ready to see the familiar walls of the palace after the hell they had experienced over the last few days. At times he had truly feared that he would never see his own hearth again.

"Words can't express how grateful we are for your

help, friend," Raya said sincerely, squeezing Iaen's shoulder in gratitude. "You're the golden key to the gates of the Thrones at the end of a hellish journey."

"I don't know about that," Iaen said offhandedly, but he was smiling.

"My sincere thanks as well," Selwyn added as he carefully lifted Aidric into his arms.

Aidric didn't bat so much as an eyelash. He hadn't stirred once since the time he had saved them from a beating by the Na'aran border guards, which worried Sel a great deal more than he had confided to Raya.

He turned to his wife. "Let's go."

With one final nod to Iaen, Selwyn closed his eyes and stepped through the portal. The weight of Aidric in his arms suddenly disappeared, and he found himself traveling swiftly on the journey through that realm of light that always seemed to sicken him. Behind him, he could sense Raya's presence and feel her excitement. He envied her ability to see traveling through a portal as an adventure and not a nuisance that must be endured.

Soon, in a bright flash of light, his feet were once again touching substantial ground, and he wavered a bit under the sudden weight of Aidric's body before he was able to regain his bearings. Blinking his eyes to clear away all the flashing colors, he looked up—right into the astonished eyes of King Diryan. With a start, he realized that he was in the Throne Room, and Iaen had sent them right smack into the middle of Court.

Immediately, Selwyn fell down to one knee, carefully cradling Aidric in his arms, and bowed his head. Behind him, he could feel Raya following his example. The only sounds in the Throne Room were their steady breathing and the rapid beating of his heart.

King Diryan, however, was quick to recover from his initial astonishment and began shouting for healers. Several men and women immediately began to swarm over to him like ants. Healer Dallan was the first to reach them just as, to Selwyn's incredulity, King Diryan dismissed all dignity and propriety and kneeled down before *him*.

"Aidius, he looks dead!" Dallan exclaimed to no one in particular as he dropped to his knees beside them. "I can do nothing for him here. We must get him to the Healer's Hall immediately!"

Several healers relieved Selwyn of his friend, and before he could even bat an eye, they had whisked Aidric out of the room, leaving him, Raya, and the king still on their knees looking foolish. As if reading his mind, Diryan seemed to realize his undignified position and quickly rose to his feet, gesturing for Selwyn and Raya to do the same.

Selwyn rose slowly, never taking his eyes off the king. He had seen something in the eyes of the king that disturbed him. The turmoil of emotions his empathic senses were picking up from him only seemed to confuse him further. Had he not known better, Sel would have sworn that King Diryan had been on the verge of tears. He knew that the king and queen were very fond of Aidric, but now he wasn't sure if that was all there was to it.

However, before he could examine Diryan's emotions further, the king unconsciously erected a barrier, preventing any more emotions from leaking through, and the expression on his face became curiously blank.

"We must speak in private," King Diryan said quietly.

Selwyn nodded. He expected as much. Now that the initial excitement was over, it was time to face the consequences of their rash actions.

Diryan turned to address those gathered for Court. "Forgive me, lords, ladies," Diryan said, "but I must attend to this unexpected matter. Circumstances allowing, we shall resume Court tomorrow as we have left it today."

Then he turned back to the couple and said, "Come."

Silently, they both followed his lead to his study. The king seated himself behind his desk, and for a long, uncomfortable moment, he said nothing. He merely stared at them both through narrowed eyes.

Selwyn could practically see the wheels turning in his head. He began to fidget nervously under that hard scrutiny.

When at last King Diryan did speak, it was so abruptly that they both jumped.

"Where is Allison McNeal?" he asked pointedly.

Selwyn swallowed hard as a knot formed in his throat. He opened his mouth to speak, but no sound emerged. Raya, however, rescued him from his awkwardness by answering for them.

"In Roderick's hands," she admitted softly, which was uncharacteristic of her.

Diryan nodded as if he had expected as much. Selwyn was instantly alarmed. This silence, this quick acceptance of the greatest calamity Lamia would endure wasn't the furious reaction he had been anticipating.

"Your Majesty," Selwyn ventured almost diffidently, "I can explain—"

"Explain?" Diryan cut him off harshly, his eyes finally flashing with anger. "*Explain*? What is there that you can possibly explain? What excuse can possible condone what you have allowed to happen?"

"We tried to stop her!" Raya snapped back. Selwyn winced at her tone and shot her a warning look, but she wouldn't be silenced. "It was *she* who rode to Aidric's aid initially! Selwyn and I tried to stop her when we discovered that she was missing from her room. Even without speaking to Master Ahern, we knew where she had gone. I tried to reason with her, but there's no reasoning with love! I even imprisoned her within a barrier of magic and threatened to not release her until she saw reason, but she shattered my barrier as if it was merely a breath of air! She wasn't to be diverted, Majesty! I swear it!"

"Why then did you not ride back for help?" King Diryan demanded. "Golden Mage, or no, several mages would have been enough to prevent her where one could not."

"Believe me, Your Majesty, they wouldn't have succeeded," Selwyn insisted, hating the defensive note in his voice. "I felt the turmoil of her emotions. I saw the look of obsession and extreme determination in her eyes. No soul short of Seni would've been able to keep her from her task. However foolish we now believe we acted, nevertheless, at that moment, we thought it better to give her our aid rather than allow her to ride alone into that nest of vipers. Not even the Shield gave her a moment's pause from her journey."

"Yes, the Shield," Diryan said sharply. "I had wondered how you had managed to cross the border without detection. I want you to speak the truth. Did she or either of you tamper with the minds of the border guards?"

Selwyn bit his lip and looked at Raya worriedly before he met his king's eyes again. "I swear on all I hold sacred that we used no such means to cross. I'm not certain whether you are aware of this or not, Your Majesty, but the four mages assigned to each border station are not the only ones who know how to open the Shield."

"What!" King Diryan boomed. Selwyn imagined he saw the walls shrink back under the heat of the king's anger.

Apparently Aidric hadn't seen fit to enlighten his king either. Surprising, since it seemed to Selwyn that neither Diryan nor Aidric hid any secrets from one another.

"Allison revealed to us that Aidric had the knowhow, and he had passed it on to her."

"That still doesn't explain how you were not detected," Diryan persisted. "I want a straight answer, Selwyn Phelannik."

"She mentioned that Aidric had devised an alternate spell," Selwyn explained a bit uncomfortably, "similar to the one that allows someone to pass through the Shield but without having to open it. I'm no mage, so I really didn't understand her explanation of how the spell works, but it had something to do with melding our life energies to the Mage-field energy that fueled the spell. I was skeptical at first, but she

278

accomplished just what she said she would."

"Wonderful!" Diryan growled as he raised a hand to rub his temple. "What you are saying is that Roderick now holds the key to our Shield in his hands."

They both nodded grimly.

King Diryan rose from his seat and began to pace the length of the room. "How much longer before his forces will overrun our lands?" he demanded, though it seemed he was speaking more to himself than to them. "And all for the mistake of a headstrong maiden!"

"All wasn't for naught, Your Majesty," Raya said quietly. Her uncharacteristic reticence was beginning to unnerve Selwyn. "We've brought the Mage-general back when we had all thought him lost."

"Indeed you have," Diryan said, his voice softening a bit, "but now, what is to prevent Aidric from making the same foolish mistake as his lover?"

For that, neither Selwyn nor Raya had an answer.

***

"I'm sorry, Roderick, but I have to do this," Allison whispered to the sleeping form that held her possessively in his arms.

Carefully, she lightly touched his forehead, and

with a slight exertion of her power, she placed him under a sleep spell. With any hope, Roderick wouldn't wake up until the morning, and when he did, he wouldn't suspect what she had done.

Allison then immediately disentangled herself from him and rose from the bed, hastily throwing on her robe. She crept over to a lone chair in the far corner of the huge bedroom and slipped into it. For a moment, she just simply sat there, listening to all the night sounds of the palace. In the silence, Roderick's steady breathing was almost deafening. Somewhere in the distance, she also thought she heard a faint scream. She shivered involuntarily.

Earlier, she had eavesdropped on the conversation of a couple of servants as they attended to the bedroom. She had heard them coming, and in no mood to face anyone after everything Roderick had revealed about his expectations of her in the coming war, she had quickly cast the invisibility spell over herself.

Believing that they were alone, the young women had spoken freely of some very disturbing things concerning Roderick and the treatment and punishment of the prisoners he kept deep in the bowels of the palace. They spoke of cruelties and tortures so horrifying that Allison refused to believe that they were true. The man she knew, the man who had thrilled her with such gentle caresses, couldn't possibly have committed the kinds of atrocities those two women had whispered between them with fear in their eyes.

Yes, but lately he hasn't exactly been so tender, has he? a little voice whispered in the back of her mind. *Where was that tenderness tonight when he took you so roughly? Or in the library when he looked at you with scorn because you were scared? Where is that sweet tenderness now?*

"Shut up," she whispered weakly into the darkness, but the voice wouldn't be quieted.

Something about their whole relationship just didn't feel right at all these days. Something crucial had changed, but not even that mocking voice in her head could give her an explanation for her sudden misgivings. It was as if Roderick wasn't at all the man she had loved before. It was almost as though she now shared a bed with a stranger.

"It's just the war," Allison insisted stubbornly to herself, though her voice lacked any real conviction. "It has him on edge, and when it's finished, he won't be so angry all the time anymore."

Will he? That mocking voice again.

I won't think about it any longer! I have more important things to worry about than my personal problems!

That, in fact, was what had driven her out of bed in the first place, why she had risked Roderick's wrath to spell him to sleep so that she might have a few, undisturbed sand-marks to inspect the Golden Mage Spellbook. Nervously, Allison retrieved it from her magical storage plane, holding it tentatively in her lap as if it would crumble into dust at the slightest touch. Her stomach was tied in knots as she slowly opened it, half-fearing that her mind would be seized a second time by that unknown power.

However, for all her worry, nothing unusual happened. The book appeared as ordinary as any other, and she released the breath she hadn't realized she had been holding.

As she suspected—or feared—the words were still English, but that wasn't what had her mind racing in disbelief. When she read one of the pages and deduced that it was indeed a spell that wasn't known to even Roderick, she also realized that she knew it already, in its translation of Ti'ar, in fact. It was then that she understood exactly what had happened in the library.

Through the magic contained in the book, every page, every horrible spell in that cursed book had been infused into her mind, just as Roderick had infused the entire Mihran language into her mind the day the portal had brought her to this world. That spellbook was now no more useful to her than a beginner's reference volume of magecraft. And still the unbidden thought came.

Roderick can't know.

She glanced at the unmoving figure in the bed anxiously. Sleep spell or no, Allison didn't want to risk Roderick finding her with the book. Silently, as she returned the book to her magical storage plane, she vowed never to lay hands on the book again. It was power that was never meant for mortal hands to wield, and with any luck, she would take its contents to her grave.

As Allison shifted in her chair, she detected movement to the left out of the corner of her eye. Her eyes instantly searched the shadows of the room, brushed across the far corner, and then did a double-take when they spotted the faint outline of a man. Her breath instantly froze in her lungs, and the beating of her suddenly racing heart became almost deafening as she scrutinized the shadows in the corner and saw— only the normal shadows cast by the bedroom furniture.

Only when her chest began to burn did Allison realize that she still hadn't breathed, and she slowly drew in a breath. Her heart, however, refused to calm down. What exactly, if anything, had she seen? A trick of the moonlight? Fatigued eyes? Maybe it was something as simple as her expectation of seeing something within the darkness.

Whatever it was, whether a trick of her mind or something else entirely, the corner was now empty. She supposed she would never know either way. No, she didn't *want* to know.

It was probably way past time to go back to bed, but the thought of the dreams that were sure to come made her hesitate. Allison had never found the right moment to confide the disturbing dreams she had been having to Roderick. Each time she had tried, his foul mood or hungry lips had silenced her. Imagining that she saw shapes in the corners didn't necessarily make her eager to embrace those dreams so soon, either.

Even as she stared out into the darkness of the bedroom, Allison could still see the same scenes of war, hear the screaming, the cursing, and see the rivers of blood flowing over an infinite land of corpses. However, those ghastly images were not the main reason why she dreaded sleep. It was a dream of a different nature altogether, a dream of a world of darkness, that she feared, and in that darkness was the figure of a man with a distinct familiarity that she couldn't quite reason.

However, it wasn't the man, himself, that had her waking up in a cold sweat. It was the eyes, a preternatural shade of pale-violet that seemed to stare at her from everywhere with an accusation that reached out to crush the light within her soul.

Would those eyes be waiting for her tonight?

Would *he*?

***

The first thing that greeted Aidric's eyes as he groggily opened them was Diryan. For a moment, Aidric was utterly confused. He instinctively knew that the bed he was lying in wasn't his own. Where in the six hells was he? Why was Diryan sitting at his bedside looking exhausted and rumpled as though he had spent the night there? He stared perplexedly at the older man for a few more beats and then, as if the curtains had been flung open within his mind, he remembered everything.

Everything...

He closed his eyes tightly so that he could no longer see the love, the pity, and the fear in Diryan's eyes.

Seni, why oh why didn't you let me die?

"Lad?" Diryan inquired softly.

Fuzzily, as if in a dream, Aidric could hear the scrape of the king's chair as he rose. Then hands firmly grasped his own between them. Slowly, Aidric opened his eyes again, but he refused to meet Diryan's gaze. Instead, he fixed his eyes on a tiny imperfection on the far wall. Before he could prevent it, a single tear escaped down his check.

"I've failed her," Aidric said quietly.

"You have danced the line between life and death, and still all you can think about is her," Diryan said just as quietly. Aidric said nothing. "Can you not look at your king even now?" he asked. "Because I fail to see why you think this current mess is your personal failure."

"It's because of my weakness, my foolish pride, that she was even put into the position to choose to leave the safety of our kingdom in the first place, and now, for her love of me, I've sent her and our kingdom to their dooms! Seni help me, I tried to reach her before it was too late. *I tried*! But in the end, I was *weak*!"

"All is not lost just yet, Aidric," Diryan said gently. "All is not lost."

"But it is!" Aidric cried brokenly. Only then did his eyes finally fix on Diryan. "Don't you see? You were right in your warnings! Nothing but grief has come of our union!"

He sneered in disgust. "How vain I was to think that I could love one touched by Seni as she was without consequence!"

Diryan's eyes darkened. "Always, you think the worst of yourself," he said angrily. "Why must there always be pain, always fault in everything that you do?

Aidius, Aidric! Why should you be denied any happiness? I've never seen you more alive, your step quicker and your spirit lighter, than in these last few moons when you held that maiden in your arms! Nor did her heart lack for any happiness. She glowed with it!"

"Happiness!" Aidric spat out bitterly. "What *is* happiness? It's a mockery, the elegant hand that conceals a dagger behind a beloved's back, ready to shatter all your hopes, your dreams, only to show you the harsh reality that's called life! Well, I'm through with life! I'm tired of having its glittering dagger plunged into my heart time and time again!"

"You would give up just like that, Aidric?" Diryan demanded. "The mighty Mage-general of Lamia, the man who puts fear into the hearts of his enemies at the bare mention of his name. The man who has inspired such hope for the people of many kingdoms? Would you have Alina triumph so easily?"

He struck Diryan.

For an eternal moment, they simply stared at one another, Aidric frozen with a look of utter astonishment and Diryan with a peculiar glint in his eyes. He couldn't tear his eyes away from the large welt his fist had imprinted onto Diryan jaw that was beginning to swell with seemingly every breath he took. Then to Aidric's further bewilderment, the king began to laugh softly.

"No, I didn't think so," Diryan said between chuckles.

"Diryan, I—" Aidric stammered, but the king waved him to silence.

"There's nothing to apologize for, lad," he assured him. "I provoked you intentionally. The look in your eyes—it was too similar to the last tragedy you suffered for my peace of mind. I had to show you that there was still a spark of spirit left in you." He rubbed his jaw and then winced. "Although, had I realized just how *much* spark you did have left, I would have thought better about provoking you!"

Aidric found his lips curving up slightly despite himself, and it was in that moment that he knew Diryan had won—again.

"And now, I'll leave you to your rest," Diryan said. "I do believe I've earned a coddling from Ileanna, but when I return, I expect to see the Mage-general, Aidric, lying in this bed and *not* the wretched man that awakened in it."

"Don't worry," Aidric replied, a weak grin slowly stretching across his lips. "I do believe that you have lain that man to rest."

Only when the king had left did Aidric's smile falter and wilt. Yes, Diryan had won, but it was only the first battle.

CHAPTER NINETEEN

A idric wasn't in the least bit sorry to leave his small room in the Healer's Hall. After being confined in the darkness of Roderick's dungeons for so long, it seemed as if the walls of the tiny room were closing in on him. That night, he had awakened several times in a cold sweat, certain that he was still a prisoner in that cold blackness.

Therefore, the first thing he had requested of Healer Dallan in the morning was to be moved to his own bedroom. Surprisingly, Dallan had relented without too much prodding or comment. Aidric's only irritation had been the fact that he was still too weak to stand, much less walk, so he had to endure the humiliation of being carried throughout the palace corridors on a stretcher for everyone to see.

However, Aidric immediately perked up when he

saw that both Raya and Selwyn were waiting for him in his quarters. Though they appeared a bit tired and sported a number of cuts and bruises, they didn't look as bad as he had feared. He vaguely remembered his attempt to prevent Selwyn from being beaten, but he had passed out before he knew whether his efforts had been successful.

"How are you feeling?" Selwyn asked anxiously as he dragged a chair to Aidric's bedside.

"Oh Sel," Raya chided as she did the same. "I'm certain that he's tired of everyone asking him that question."

Aidric managed a weak smile. "Yes, it did seem as if every healer in Lamia asked it from the moment my eyes opened, but from you, my friend, I don't mind it as much. I feel like hell, thank you, but given the circumstances, that's to be expected."

"At least you no longer look like a day-old corpse," Raya observed while Selwyn shot her a warning look that she, of course, ignored.

"Charming as always," Aidric said wryly.

"Well, it's true," she said defensively, folding her arms against her chest.

Aidric just shook his head. *It's good that she hasn't been assigned to the Healer's Hall to boost the morale of the patients. She would have them all at Aidius's Gates within several depths with that tongue!*

"Seriously though, you're better?" Selwyn persisted.

This seriousness—it wasn't like his friend at all who could always find something to joke about, even in the face of death.

"I'm out of danger, Sel, I assure you," Aidric replied. "I'm just weak, and there's still the matter of that curse of a spell. The healers, of course, can't possibly break it, but they tell me that Diryan has already requested the aid of the Temple. A Domnae has already left for the palace."

"A relief," Diryan said suddenly from the doorway.

All eyes turned to him as he strode into the room, looking as worried and careworn as he had the night before. For the first time, Aidric noticed that there was more gray in his hair. Selwyn rose from his seat beside the bed and bowed, offering the seat to Diryan who accepted it with a grateful smile. Judging from the dark circles beneath his eyes, the king had probably not slept a wink last night, which only made Aidric feel guilty. Some of the king's insomnia was on his behalf, he was sure.

Once again, my selfish insensitivity has caused another pain, Aidric thought bitterly. *Shall I never learn?*

"I take it the Mage-general has survived the

night?" Diryan asked casually, though his eyes betrayed his true concern.

Selwyn and Raya glanced at one another blankly before turning questioning eyes on Aidric. This sudden formality between the king and Aidric was new to them. Both of them rarely addressed one another by their titles when not in public. It was all Aidric could do to keep a straight face.

"He has," Aidric replied, then sent to both his friends, *"A private joke between us, my friends. Let's just leave it at that."*

Aidric had no intentions of ever speaking about what had happened between Diryan and him the previous night. Such things were better left buried in the past to be forgotten. At least *he* thought so, but as he looked into those smoky-blue eyes, he knew that Diryan wouldn't be as quick to dismiss the matter. Aidric's chest tightened with trepidation. He did *not* want to have that conversation.

"Perhaps we should take our leave—" Selwyn began but Diryan silenced him with a quick shake of his head.

"No, I wish you both to stay," Diryan said. "There is much that hasn't been said about your adventures of the past quarter-moon, and I believe now is as good a time as any to begin. I'm certain that everyone in this room has many unanswered questions to pose to one another." He turned his eyes to Aidric. "My first question is for you, Aidric, about the mystery that has plagued us for over a quarter-moon—"

"—which is the circumstances of my capture," Aidric finished for him with a sigh.

He knew he would've had to speak of it sooner or later. Might as well get it over with. Aidric shifted a bit in his bed until he was in a more comfortable position and then closed his eyes. Maybe if he didn't have to see their faces, then speaking of one of the worst screwups of his life would become a little easier.

After a moment of tense silence, he began, "It happened at the Na'aran palace." He could sense them jolting in surprise, but he still didn't open his eyes. "I followed whom I thought was Mordant into a portal he had constructed on the battle site. Perhaps I was foolish to do so. No, I *know* I was foolish, but after all the grief that damned bastard has caused us, I just couldn't stand idly by and allow him to escape so easily.

"I had hoped to force him into a confrontation. However, as I exited the portal, you can well imagine my shock when I discovered that the Na'aran king and queen had been taken prisoner, and the man whom I had followed into that portal wasn't Mordant after all but Roderick."

"A trap," Diryan said flatly.

Aidric grimaced. "He tricked me into believing that he had taken Allison prisoner, and in my—rage, I allowed myself to be distracted long enough to be stabbed by a spelled dagger from behind. The dagger was dipped in *Tangel*. I never saw the face of the one who stabbed me."

"You're lucky you were more valuable to him alive than dead," Diryan said pointedly.

"I don't think his true goal was information. When I awoke, I lay in Roderick's dungeons, my legs and arms shackled together. They were spelled, of course. When Roderick appeared, it was then that I learned the bastard had placed blocks in my channels that reeked of the Dark Powers. No matter what I tried, I couldn't even scratch them."

"And he cast a spell of immortality onto you," Selwyn added quietly.

Aidric finally opened his eyes and looked deep within his friend's eyes before he nodded. "As I said, he wasn't really after information. It was his thought to leave me to rot in eternal agony in that cell."

"But you escaped," Diryan said, "and according to Selwyn and Raya, it was done without their aid. It was Seni's own luck for them to have stumbled upon you when they did."

"I could make it no farther," Aidric whispered, but he really wasn't speaking to them. "I tried to portal over to her, but I was too weak, too damaged. I couldn't make it. Pain—Seni help me, the pain—

I must go on—no energy—

I can't fail—

"Aidric…"

Why didn't you give me more strength?

"Aidric!"

With a start, Aidric abruptly came back to himself, realizing that he had allowed himself to be swept up into reliving his nightmarish memories.

"Perhaps we should leave you to your rest and continue at another time," Diryan suggested, his forehead crinkled with worry.

"No," Aidric insisted, "I merely—lost myself for a moment. I'm fine. Please. I have questions of my own. Of the last battles, how did we fare in the end?"

"We lost many in the Na'aran battle—at least half of our army," Diryan recounted gravely. "Had it not been for the timely arrival of the Sononese forces, then Roderick surely would have been victorious. As for the battle in Kemos, we lost only a couple hundred soldiers. Roderick's army was almost entirely annihilated."

"And the Na'aran king and queen?"

Diryan sighed and shook his head sadly. "Still in Roderick's hands. We aren't even certain if they still live."

"How is Prince Ashur taking the news?" Aidric inquired.

"As well as can be expected," Diryan replied. "He blames himself for his absence, but he understands why we cannot aid his parents. For a lad of only ten summers, he is incredibly learned in the ways of the world."

"With Mihr as a neighbor, he must be," Raya said pointedly.

"If only I hadn't allowed myself to be so blindsided, then perhaps I could've saved everyone much grief by taking Roderick's head," Aidric said bitterly.

"You cannot blame yourself for that demon's every atrocity," Diryan chided. "You have enough burdens in your heart to add another."

A faint knock at Aidric's front door interrupted the king from saying more. Selwyn dashed off to answer it and returned a depth later with a page at his heels. The boy, barely five or six summers old, fidgeted nervously as he bowed clumsily to the king and presented a sealed parchment to him. Diryan accepted the parchment with a slight nod, and the boy wasted no time in darting out of the room.

Diryan unrolled the parchment and scanned its contents. Good news apparently. The lines of worry smoothed out on his forehead and his lips stretched into an unconscious smile.

"Seni be praised! Domnae Kasen has at last succeeded in destroying the barriers Roderick erected! I must take my leave for the moment, but I shall return shortly with any news."

In the blink of an eye he was gone.

"And we should be going, too," Raya seconded as she jumped to her feet. "You need your rest, beast."

"You go on ahead, love," Selwyn said quietly, his eyes still fixed on Aidric. "I'll follow shortly."

"But—" she began to protest, thought better of it, and then nodded.

Only when the sound of the front door closing after her reached their ears did Selwyn speak.

"Ask me," he said pointedly.

Aidric blinked at him, then sighed heavily.

"Is it that obvious?" Aidric asked.

"No," Sel replied, "but I know you, my friend. Remember that you also can't hide anything from an empath."

"How could I forget?" Aidric said dryly, but he was smiling. "You know my question then. Tell me."

"Believe me when I say we didn't abandon her, Aidric," Selwyn began heatedly.

Aidric closed his eyes. "The thought never crossed my mind, Sel."

Selwyn was silent for a couple of depths before he continued, "As with you, we were captured by deceit.

A man wearing a glamour of you was planted in our path. Before we could stop her, Allison was already racing to 'your' side. She never saw the dagger coming, and we, too late. By then, I was falling from my horse with a blow to the head. The last I remember was the kicks."

He shuddered involuntarily. It was a moment before he was able to continue.

"When I became aware again, Raya and I were locked in one of Roderick's dungeon cells. We never set eyes upon her again."

"The man who wore the glamour," Aidric said sharply, "did you see his face at all once the illusion shattered?"

"No," Selwyn replied a bit uneasily.

"Just as well," Aidric muttered darkly. "I'm in no condition now to avenge her."

"Aidric…I know what you're thinking, and I beg you not to do it," Selwyn said fervently, eyeing Aidric with blatant alarm. "I'll demand that you be spelled to sleep if I even begin to *suspect* that you plan to go to her rescue. It's what we should have done to *her*. Perhaps then we wouldn't be in this mess right now."

"It's my decision to make and mine alone," Aidric spat back angrily, and for once, Selwyn didn't flinch at his tone.

"You forget, *Mage-general*, that your decisions

ceased to be entirely your own from the moment you spoke your oaths to the Horae!" Sel replied hotly. "Would you have us mourn the loss of yet another loved one?"

"She *must* be saved," Aidric insisted darkly.

"At the price of what?" Selwyn demanded. "Your life? My life? Or how about the life of the king and queen? The life of the entire bloody kingdom? You of all people should know that desperation doesn't solve problems, it only digs early graves. I'm your friend, Aidric, and I'll not stand idly by again and watch you destroy yourself as you so nearly did those few years ago!"

"You can't possibly understand my pain!" Aidric cried. "You, who has been happily wed to his soulmate these two years past! What do you know of pain? Of despair? I lost half of my heart to that whore, Alina, and all of my soul when that bastard took Allison to his bed! Yes, you heard me correctly! Roderick has had her as only I have had her before. I felt the desecration as keenly as if I had given her my life-ring! You and Raya should have just left me to die in that forest!"

Aidius, it hurt. Aidric had been trying to not think about what Roderick had done to Allison, to *both* of them, suppressing the memory in a vain attempt to somehow make it not true. Now the memory was only too real.

"I remember you cried out," Selwyn whispered, his eyes haunted, "a cry uttered by one denied the Thrones. I never realized—"

"No, you didn't!" Aidric snapped, and then he began to laugh maniacally. "Of course, had you left me, I couldn't have died. Roderick's thrice-damned spell curses me with immortality! Even as he's stolen the heart of my very soul, he's won the ultimate triumph of denying me the peace of death!"

"Aidric, please—"

"Dammit! Let me be!" Aidric roared with such rage that Selwyn actually took several steps back from the bed. "Leave me!"

Then Aidric turned his head sharply away from Selwyn, his fists clenching his blankets so savagely that they began to hurt.

After a moment of dead silence, Aidric heard Selwyn sigh followed by the sound of his footsteps walking towards the door. Then they stopped abruptly.

"You say I don't know pain," Selwyn said quietly. "If that's so, then today you have given me a bitter lesson in it."

Then without another word, his footsteps echoed loudly as he left the suite, and every one was like a dagger in Aidric's heart.

CHAPTER TWENTY

With a feeling of dread, Allison stood silently off to the side, watching Roderick bark out last minute orders to his men of rank before she was to transport them all via portal to the Lamian border. Before her eyes, the ranks of men seemed to stretch on forever. Never in all her life had she imagined seeing an army of this magnitude in person, men ready to kill and to die for their monarch all because of one man's tyrannical ambitions.

She had never hated a man more in her life than she now hated King Diryan Lasha of Lamia. Despite her misgivings on killing, had Diryan suddenly been presented before her, Allison knew she wouldn't so much as bat an eye while she blasted him into oblivion. Today was the day her worst nightmare was about to be realized.

By the time Roderick strode over to her side, Allison was a breath away from puking up the little breakfast she had forced herself to swallow. Apparently, her face must have still appeared a little green since Roderick gave her a reproachful look as he stepped up to her.

"Roderick, I don't think I can do this," she said in a small voice when he was within earshot.

"Of course you can," Roderick said sternly. "I'm confident that you have the power to—"

"That's not what I meant," she interrupted hastily. "I know that I can build a portal large enough to transport all of us to Lamia's border. That's not the problem. I just don't think that I can fight as you want me to in this war."

"Nonsense!" he growled. "What need you fear the soldiers of Lamia? It's *they* who should fear *you*! You have the power to destroy their entire army with one burst of energy, and that's exactly what I expect you to do!"

"But—" she protested weakly.

"Not another word!" Roderick boomed. "You *are* going to fight in Lamia today, and that's the end of it! Even though you share my bed, I am still your king, and you will do as I command!"

Suddenly his golden eyes didn't look as beautiful to her as they had before. Now, they only reminded her of a tiger ready to pounce on his prey. However, before tears could threaten, Roderick pulled her into a tight embrace, and his mouth bit hungrily into her own.

"We are fated to be together," he said curtly, "you with the golden hair and I with the golden eyes. When all this war nonsense is done and Lamia is under my control, then we'll have more time to indulge ourselves."

He licked his lips, a gesture that reminded Allison too much of a cat with a feather sticking out of his mouth for her comfort. How could she have ever thought this man gentle? He was obviously an alpha predator. It was almost as if the loving man she remembered had never existed except in her dreams.

Roderick released her and headed over to where the mage-king, Mordant, was instructing his own troops. Hastily, Allison turned away when her eyes met the Silver Mage's, but not before she saw the sneer he directed at her. There were times when she felt that had Roderick not been holding his leash, then Mordant would have done all the violent things to her that his eyes promised. The mere thought of that vile man touching her left her feeling sick to her stomach.

But then Roderick was calling to her, and Allison had no more time for her troubling thoughts as all her concentration went into the construction of a portal, the likes of which had never been seen by anyone in all of Seni's lands. It was the first portal she had ever attempted to erect, and she hoped with all her heart that she would never find occasion to do it again. Channeling the amount of energy required for such a major spellcasting left her feeling uncomfortably transparent, as if the energy that she wove into her spell was not only from the Mage-field, but also eating away at her physically.

It was almost like creating a large tunnel, weaving the entrance and exit with the threads of power leaving her hands, the words from her lips her giant loom, and in a sense she *was* creating a tunnel, one which burrowed through a higher dimension. Then, as she shouted the final word of the incantation, a brilliant burst of blinding, white light flashed before them.

When her vision cleared, a great monstrosity of a portal stood before her, seeming to stretch right to the heavens as well as to touch the ends of the southern and northern horizons. Although she had seen portals built on numerous occasions, Allison still gawked at this, her own creation, in amazement.

This is really happening, Allison thought with a sickening feeling as she watched line after line of foot soldiers disappear into the shimmering light, followed by an endless amount of cavalry. *I'm really going to war!*

But then her thoughts were interrupted by the

strong tug on her mind that reminded her of her still-unfinished duty. The portal still required an unholy amount of energy to maintain its stability until it was no longer needed. She immediately lost herself to this endless channeling, relieved to have something to take her mind off the horrors she was no doubt about to face.

Only when she felt a hand shake her shoulder roughly did Allison come back to herself and realize that the entire army had already gone through, and only she and Roderick remained. He pulled her up into the saddle behind him without a word and then plunged into the shimmering brightness she had come to hate.

By the time their journey ended, she barely had enough wits left to cry out the sole word that would unravel the portal into nothingness. Allison was immediately grateful for Roderick's presence since only his body prevented her from falling out of the saddle. However, to her dismay, he didn't ask if she was all right. He merely galloped to the front of his army positioned at the base of the Lamian Shield and impatiently urged her to dismount.

"The Shield!" Roderick called down to her. "Bring it down now!"

For one wild moment, she had the urge to tell him that she couldn't do it, that even her magic wouldn't be enough. She could still prevent this insane war from happening. She could still save thousands of innocent lives, but then she found herself gathering energy from both the Mihran and Lamian Mage-fields into her mind almost automatically, knowing that she would go through with it despite her misgivings.

Allison wove the energy into the Shield until the two energies merged, chanting the words at the top of her lungs that would cause her energy to destabilize that of the Shield, thus causing it to explode up into the air. At least, that was what she hoped would happen. One wrong gesture, one slip of the tongue, and she would blast their entire army straight to their Aidius's gates!

Then suddenly, an explosion sounded, the sound of Seni's hands tearing open the very earth. The world instantly filled with a blinding, white light a split-second before a tremendous backlash of power slammed into her shields. Although Allison was tightly shielded, the sheer power of its momentum shattered several of them as if they were fragile eggshells. Before she knew what was happening, her back slammed into the hard earth, the breath wrenched from her lungs.

As Allison lay gasping, chaos had erupted all around her. It seemed as if a million shouts and curses rose up all at once, causing her to throw her hands over her ears with a cry of her own. She could see nothing. That blinding light still filled her vision no matter how rapidly she blinked her eyes.

Behind her, Allison could hear the sounds of horses rearing amidst the deafening roar of human voices. She didn't know which was worse, the screaming of the horses or the frightened curses of the men. However, one cry out of thousands reached her ears despite the chaos behind her, and she knew at once that it was Roderick's. It was a voice that left her feeling cold inside.

"The Shield is down! At long last, the bloody Shield of Lamia is *down!*"

***

Aidric wasn't sure how long his tears flowed, but judging from the horrible ache in his head, it must have been for sand-marks. He had cried for both himself, and for the coming calamity his mistake had condemned Lamia to suffer. Never had the name of his kingdom seemed more fitting than it did at that moment.

A slight sound to his right caused him to clamp down on his remaining sobs. He knew that it was Diryan before he even turned his head. He hadn't even heard him enter the room.

"Selwyn thought I should come," the king said

simply. "He thought that I might succeed where he feels he has failed."

"Let me be," Aidric whispered hoarsely.

Diryan shook his head. He seated himself on the side of the bed and firmly grasped Aidric's face in his hands before he could turn away. "You can't rid yourself of me quite as easily as he, I'm afraid."

"Then Selwyn's told you," Aidric said bitterly.

"He has told me nothing," Diryan said. "Do you think he would betray your confidence so easily? Whatever dire secret you have confided to him will remain secret unless you choose it to be otherwise. I'm here not as your confessor, but as a shoulder that I think you desperately need."

"I don't—" Aidric started to say curtly, but the rest of his words were muffled when his mouth was suddenly pressed into Diryan's shoulder.

"I don't care what you believe you do or don't need right now," Diryan said heatedly, his voice roughened with the threat of tears. "My only concern is with what I *know* you need."

Aidric made a halfhearted attempt to pull away from Diryan, but when the king's arms merely tightened around him, all of Aidric's carefully built walls suddenly crumbled. He collapsed against Diryan's shoulder, sobbing with what seemed like the grief of an entire lifetime. The king said nothing. He simply held him tightly, stroking his hair as if Aidric was a child of two and he, the father that could comfort him as no other could.

It was enough. Seni help him, it was enough.

"What a sight we two must be," Diryan said with a chuckle into the silence that followed after Aidric's sobs had stopped and he no longer trembled. "The Mage-general and the king weeping in each others arms! What would the kingdom think?"

"I suppose they would breathe a sigh of relief to know that their leaders are not so stone-hearted after all," Aidric replied with a weak grin. "A pity that they don't know that their Mage-general is also a fool."

"A fool that is no more foolish than the fool sitting next to him," Diryan added firmly. "You are only a mortal man, Aidric. We aren't perfect, but when we do fall on our faces, we always find the strength to pick ourselves up."

"Good, because I do believe that there's a certain empath down the hall that's itching to pound my face into the ground!"

"Well, that's not exactly the image I wished to inspire," Diryan said wryly, "but at least your humor is back."

"For the moment, at least," Aidric promised him. "Thank you, Diryan."

He shook his head. "No thanks needed. Seeing

you smile again is all the thanks I could ever ask for."

"How high we set our sights," Aidric remarked, shaking his head.

But then the room abruptly began to spin, and he had to sink back down into his pillows and shut his eyes tightly before the spinning stopped.

"You have overly wearied yourself," Diryan scolded.

"It's nothing that a few sand-marks worth of sleep won't remedy," Aidric insisted. Then bitterly, "At least I'm in no danger of dying. Roderick has seen to that."

"You mustn't dwell on it, Aidric. It will only depress you, and I believe you have had enough depression to last you several hundred lifetimes. Besides, Domnae Lordan will be here within a day, and you will be rid of that wretched spell forever."

"The Domni..." Aidric said thoughtfully, the bitterness easing from his expression. "Since the barrier is down, have you had news from Valin?"

"I'm sorry, lad, but no," Diryan replied reluctantly. "It seems as though Roderick has erected a barrier around the majority of Mihr as well, and the Domni's methods of removal require physical contact with the barrier. You know as well as I that any of the Brothers in Divinity would rather skin themselves alive than set foot on Mihran soil."

Aidric nodded. Given the way his luck had been

lately, it didn't surprise him in the least that another problem had presented itself.

"Do you believe that it's possible to—"

"Your Majesty!" an excited voice abruptly called from within the sitting room, followed immediately by its owner, who practically flew into the bedroom without waiting for an invitation.

It was one of Diryan's messengers, but strangely he didn't carry the expected sealed parchment.

"The Lord Seneschal sent me to find you," he panted. "The *Shield* is down, and—"

"I know Roderick's barrier has been broken, lad," Diryan began patiently.

But the boy shook his head fervently and exclaimed, "But, Your Majesty, you don't understand! I speak of *Lamia's* Shield. A section of it is down, and as we speak, Mihran soldiers are marching towards Avidon!"

CHAPTER TWENTY-ONE

T he scene Diryan walked into as he burst into the Council Room was one of chaos. All members of the Council and Circle had been summoned. However, none were in their proper seats, and everyone was speaking simultaneously so that all that could be heard was a cacophony of agitation. Most didn't even notice his presence as Diryan quickly made his way to his seat.

Then, in his most commanding voice, Diryan boomed, "*Silence!*"

The effect was as though everyone in the room had suddenly been spell-silenced, most cut off in mid-syllable and some still with their mouths open. The scene would have been comical had the situation not been so dire.

"Everyone please take your proper seats," Diryan

commanded in a lower voice. "Nothing will be gained if we proceed with such chaos! Ion, would you please relay to me all intelligence you have received."

"The Shield is down along the eastern border, 'Highness," the Seneschal reported, his voice high with agitation. "We received a warning from the border guards that a monstrous army of at least one hundred thousand had suddenly appeared only several hundred handspans from the border, all wearing the uniform of Mihr."

He paused and swallowed hard—against fear? Diryan stiffened as a sense of foreboding washed through him.

"'Highness, the Golden Mage was among them. It was *she* who destroyed the Shield! In less than a depth, she destroyed what no other has been able to destroy throughout a dozen centuries! The army now marches towards Avidon. That was all the information given us before our communication was cut off. We assume that everyone stationed in the area are either dead or prisoners."

"And what of Avidon?" Diryan demanded.

"Our thought-speakers can't reach them!" Galen spoke up, his tone both frustrated and anxious. "Nor can we reach Biros. I fear the bloody bastard has erected one of those cursed barriers around both villages."

The news was already worse than he had imagined. By cutting off communications from the very beginning, Roderick had dealt them a severe blow they could little afford, especially with such a volatile variable as the Golden Mage added to the mix. Diryan ran his hand agitatedly through his hair and tried to calm his racing heart and mind.

"Lord Pyrs, how many troops do we have stationed at the palace?" Diryan asked as calmly as he could manage.

"Scarcely sixty thousand, Your Highness," the Lord Commander replied without bothering to try to hide his worry, "and at least ten thousand injured still recovering in the Healer's Hall."

"Only sixty thousand able-bodied soldiers!" Diryan exclaimed in disbelief. "Surely that is not all!"

"Our losses were heavy at the Battle of Na'ar, Your Highness," Lord Pyrs said bitterly. "Only half out of fifty thousand survived that slaughter. We are also down to only three-quarters of our original magical force. The infantries scattered among the four villages and our borders besides the eastern section would only make up another two thousand soldiers."

"Sixty-two thousand altogether," Diryan figured aloud, "plus approximately fifty mages, one hundred mind-mages, and thirty empaths, against an army of at least one hundred thousand non magical troops and

Seni-only-knows how many magical troops."

"*And*, the Golden Mage," Galen added quietly.

Instantly, everyone began murmuring at once. Diryan fixed his eyes sharply on Galen. As he suspected, Galen wore an I-told-you-so expression. Diryan silently cursed the man for ever mentioning Allison.

"Yes, Your Highness," Lord Claudium demanded. "What of the Golden Mage? What shall we do about her?"

"How can we possibly go against a force such as her?" Galen wailed before Diryan could even open his mouth. "She'll kill us all with a single wave of her hand! We must focus our efforts to destroy her once and for all!"

"Are you mad?" Keldan barked in disbelief. "She's as much a victim of Roderick's evil as we!"

"That's all and well, spoken by a man who has befriended—perhaps even bedded—that spawn of demons!" Galen spat back.

His eyes smoldering, Keldan sprang from his seat and had to be restrained by both his brother and Healer Dallan.

"Galen, Keldan, that's enough!" Diryan shouted angrily. "We have enough to worry about with the war beyond our walls without another occurring within!"

Keldan ceased his struggles and then slowly, he peeled his eyes away from Galen and fixed them on the king.

"Forgive me, Your Majesty," he said, bowing his head, though the anger didn't leave his eyes.

Galen, however, remained silent, his sullen expression completely unrepentant for the rash words he believed to be nothing but truth.

Diryan nodded his acceptance to Keldan, and the bard wordlessly took his seat. He chose to ignore Galen's insolence.

"The Golden Mage will be dealt with when the time comes," Diryan said, addressing not only Galen but also the entire Council. "Although Roderick has stolen her mind, let us pray to Seni that he has not stolen her humanity, as well. While capable of tampering with her memories, he cannot alter her personality in such a short amount of time. The prophecy has not been fulfilled. She may still save us from this calamity."

"A calamity *she* has caused!" Galen cried. It seemed he wouldn't be silenced.

"Galen, I said that was enough!" Diryan snapped. "What is there to be gained by your hatred? It does *not* change the fact that we have been forced to face an army against terrible odds with scarcely any time for preparation. It does *not* change the fact that the Mage-general now lies severally damaged in his bed. I don't want to hear another word about the Golden Mage!"

Galen jumped to his feet and announced angrily,

"If you won't do anything to protect my family from that demon then I'll have to take matters into my own hands!"

"You will *not*!" Diryan roared. "I forbid it!"

"I hereby renounce my position in the Circle!" Galen continued, completely ignoring him.

Was the man mad?

Before anyone could recover from their shock, Galen had already stalked out of the room. Ion was the first to shake himself and rise from his seat, intending to run after Galen, but a sharp look from Diryan made him hesitate.

"Let him go, Ion," Diryan commanded and then sighed. "He spoke out of fear and not reason. Galen will be dealt with in time. We cannot waste any more time on this nonsense." He turned to Lord Commander Pyrs. "I want you to recall every soldier you can still reach through thought-speech from the borders to the palace. Transport them in by portal where possible. It's too late to stop the Mihran army's approach, but damned if we can't still give that bastard a battle he'll ultimately regret! General Caith, have them assembled into formation as quickly as possible."

His eyes focused on the twin bardic-mages. "Keldan, you must serve as Mage-general in Aidric's absence. You have proven yourself more than worthy in Kemos. It will be you and your brother's tasks to recall to the palace every adept-mage, mind-mage, empath, and weather-mage in the kingdom from their assigned posts. The eastern border station is lost to us, but I wish for the three remaining border mages and a maximum of two mind-mages at each border station to remain at their posts. Make certain that the mind-mages left behind are the strongest thought-speakers of those assigned to the border. It's essential that messages get to and from the palace as swiftly as possible."

Both Keldan and Aren bowed their heads to him.

"We are no longer assured of the palace's safety," Diryan said gravely, fixing his eyes on each member of his Council in turn. "It's been decades since the palace has been threatened directly, and I realize now that I, if not my father and grandfather before me, should have taken steps towards making certain that the palace was as impenetrable as the Temple of Seni. I fear that the Shield has allowed us to unwisely feel a false sense of security. Now, the skill and determination of our army will have to suffice."

Diryan's face suddenly hardened. "While the danger is ours to face head-on, the queen need not face the same danger, nor should the families that live within these walls—or the injured Mage-general, for that matter." The king turned to Keldan once again. "Keldan, I also charge you and your magical troops with this task. Assign the most powerful of your mages to magically seal every possible entrance to the palace. It's too late to coordinate an evacuation of everyone, so let us hope that there will be no need to test the strength of those seals. Find Maldon Felan and assign him the task of seeing both the queen and Lord Aidric safely to her father's farm in Peri by portal, and from there, to the Sersian palace."

Before Keldan could even nod, Diryan was already issuing orders to the Seneschal. "Ion, I need you to begin conveying messages to our ambassadors in every surrounding kingdom as quickly as possible and explain the situation. There is no time for foot messengers and official documents. I shall not delude myself, nor should any of you. We need their aid badly! Our army is simply not enough. Perhaps it would be if we faced an adversary that respected the laws of the Horae, but I wouldn't even bet the life of the lowest scum in my dungeons against Roderick's sense of honor. Without the help of our allies, we shall need Seni's own luck and then some to prevail.

"Now go. There isn't a moment to spare! Lord Pyrs, I shall keep you current on the situation with our allies. The remaining Council will remain here with me for the time being. May the hand of Seni touch us all today and lead us to victory!"

As he watched the Lord Commander, General Caith, the twins, and those of the Circle who would fight file out of the room, Diryan couldn't help feeling that this was the last time he would set eyes on any of them. A bad omen, especially for a king.

***

Allison wanted nothing more than to wake up from the nightmare she was now living. As she had seen in her dreams for the past several nights, a good portion of the village of Avidon lay in ruins. Several buildings in the merchant's district were slowly being consumed by mage-flames—flames that she had reluctantly helped to set. As she stared at the otherworldly, green fire spreading down the thatched roof of a gem merchant's shop, Allison didn't know whether she was going to burst into tears or start retching—or both, for that matter.

Over and over in her mind, she heard Roderick's insistent voice telling her that what they did here in the village was necessary. He had spoken of examples, of martyrs, but Allison had closed her ears and refused to hear more. What justification was there in burning the shops and houses of an innocent village? Why must these villagers pay for the atrocities of their monarch? What choice did they have other than to bow down to him?

All of those questions whirled around in her mind

until she thought she would go mad with them, but still, somehow through her fear and uncertainties, she had managed to fight on along with the army. Roderick had commanded her to kill as many mages as possible, but in the end, she found she didn't have the stomach for it—or the justification. Therefore, she had secretly spelled as many mages as she could to sleep.

Now, as Allison stood half-mesmerized by the flames, she realized with a start that it had been some time since anyone, whether mage or swordsman, had attacked her. She tore her eyes away from the fire and quickly scanned the area. Bodies of both Lamian and Mihran soldiers alike lay in heaps all around her, some deep in slumber due to her magic, but most a ghastly display of twisted bodies and faces eternally frozen in their last death throes.

This time, she did fall to her knees retching. Even in the worst of her dreams had the carnage not been as horrible as this reality. At least in her dreams she hadn't been able to really smell the stench of death, the metallic stench of blood and burnt flesh, or to feel the heat of the fires all around her, the black smoke stinging her eyes until they watered and scorching the breath from her lungs. Only when nothing remained in her stomach for her to vomit did she hastily wipe her mouth with the sleeve of her dress and slowly rise back onto unsteady legs.

It was then that Allison made a decision, and to hell with Roderick if he raged against her for it. She lifted her arms into the air and cried out the incantation that would snuff out the flames instantly. Only when she was sure that not even a spark was left did she begin to search for Roderick.

Roderick was nowhere to be seen.

Allison instantly felt a strong desire to know exactly where he was and what he was doing. She closed her eyes and began to softly chant one of the new incantations she had assimilated from the Golden Mage Spellbook, one with a purpose very similar to that of a portal but on a *much* smaller scale and a million times more convenient. She only had to think of where she wanted to go, encase herself in a bubble of mage-field energy, say the incantation, and *poof!* She was there in a matter of seconds, whereas, with a portal, a mage had to have actually seen the location before a portal could be built and the two points connected.

It was like a spell within a spell, her brief incantation triggering a spell that already existed, one that lay dormant until the right "key" unlocked it. For all she knew, maybe even Seni, Himself, had been the spell's caster. This spell also required considerably less Mage-field energy, therefore making it easier on the caster.

At the completion of the spell, Allison felt a slight

disorientation, as though she had spun around in a circle a few times and then had stopped in place. Although she knew what the spell was supposed to do in theory, when she opened her eyes, she couldn't help gasping in astonishment when she saw several stone houses before her instead of the smoldering shops. Then she quickly forgot her astonishment when she caught sight of Roderick and realized exactly what he was doing.

Several families had been herded out of their homes by his soldiers and now stood in huddled groups before Roderick and Mordant. The women and children were crying, and many of the men were cursing Roderick blatantly. One even dared to spit at Roderick.

"I have no use for the women and their daughters," Roderick was saying to the soldiers. "Do with them as you please, but in the end, I want them dead!"

"*No!*" Allison shouted in horror.

Both Roderick and Mordant turned as one to face her, the former with a look of irritation and the latter with his ever-present sneer of amusement. Before she could lose her courage, Allison rushed over to them and placed herself between the two kings and the trembling families.

"What are you doing?" she demanded furiously, feeling the heat rising to her cheeks.

"This is no concern of yours," Roderick barked angrily. "Your only concern is getting us into the Lamian palace!"

"Are these the poor souls whom you plan to make martyrs?" Allison demanded. "Do you think that they *want* to be martyrs? Will they thank you for it? My God, Roderick, why are you doing this? I thought this war was about saving these people from tyranny, not in order for you to become a tyrant yourself!"

"That's quite enough!" Roderick boomed and for one frightening moment, Allison was sure that he was going to hit her.

But he didn't. He merely grabbed her roughly by the arm, his fingers digging painfully into her flesh, and dragged her off a distance until everyone was out of earshot, and all the while, she could only think that this wasn't happening.

"You're hurting me!" Allison cried, struggling to wrench her arm from his grasp, but it only caused him to tighten his iron grip.

"How dare you dress me down as if I was a child!" Roderick boomed, squeezing her arm even more until she cried out sharply in pain. "What do you know of war? You, the portrait of innocence from a world unknown! *I* decide what can or can't be done!"

"Then you are no different from Diryan," Allison whispered.

Roderick struck her then. His open-handed blow caught her on the cheek with enough force to send her sprawling to the ground. For a moment, Allison could only lie where she had fallen, her hand pressed against the throbbing pain exploding from her cheek, not quite able to believe what had just happened. Then the tears came, slowly creeping down her face at first, but then coming down in steady streams as if the floodgates had been ripped open within her eyes.

"I am *worlds* different than he!" Roderick shouted down at her, his eyes blazing with fury. "Never again compare me to that fool who has been like a thorn in my side since the day I took my throne! Now get up, and cease your blubbering! We waste precious time here with this foolish whining."

"You aren't the man I loved," she whispered, more to himself than to him, which was just as well since Roderick ignored her comment completely.

"It's time that I unleash my forces on the Lamian palace, and you damn well better have a portal ready to transport my troops by the time I settle the unfinished business you so rudely interrupted."

"You ask the impossible!" Allison said coldly as she raised herself to a more dignified sitting position. She could already feel her cheek swelling, and by the tightness and throbbing pain around her eye, she knew that she was going to develop a black eye. "I've never been to the Lamian palace. How do you expect me to build a portal to a place I've never seen? Assuming I would do anything at all for you after the way you've treated me and these poor people!"

"Oh, rest assure you've lain eyes on the Lamian palace on numerous occasions. You just don't remember them," Roderick said smugly.

"What the hell does that mean?" she demanded, jumping to her feet.

"When you build the portal, you will know," he said with amusement as he turned to leave.

"If you so much as *breathe* on those families," Allison warned, her voice low and dangerous, "then your troops will just have to walk to the palace, *leaderless*, because I swear to you, Roderick, that I'll kill you myself!"

Roderick stopped dead in his tracks.

"You *dare* to threaten me?" he snarled as he turned to face her.

His eyes seemed to literally glow with a cold fury, but Allison swallowed hard against the knot of fear that had formed in her throat and refused to allow him to intimidate her. No, not anymore.

"Yes," she said coldly. "I'll do it if you force me to."

How could she have ever shared a bed with this man? How could she have ever loved him? Was the man she remembered, loving and gentle, merely a dream? Suddenly, just the thought of him touching her left her feeling sick.

Shockingly, instead of roaring in fury as she had expected, Roderick simply began to laugh, a laugh that instantly sent every mental alarm within her screaming.

"Do you really believe that I would allow you to harm me even the slightest bit?" he sneered. "After all I have striven for? Do you think me a fool?"

Then, before Allison could even open her mouth to retort, a consuming darkness filled her mind, like a black storm cloud swallowing up the sun, followed by an all-consuming pain so excruciating that she couldn't even find her voice to scream—a pain that was somehow familiar. She sensed more than felt her body collapse to the ground, but after that, her world consisted of the smoldering darkness, the unbearable pain, and Roderick's booming voice.

"You will *construct that portal,"* Roderick's voice commanded firmly within her mind, lodging into every corner like a burr, *"and you* will *obey my every command henceforth without question."*

And to her horror, Allison heard her own voice answer clearly, "Yes."

CHAPTER TWENTY-TWO

Although there were no windows in his room, Aidric immediately knew that the Lamian troops were assembling on the palace's vast lawns for battle. His Empathy served as his eyes and ears, his own feelings stretched out like a thousand fingers throughout the entire palace to touch the emotions of the unsuspecting residents. He was greeted with an odd mixture of emotions that could only signal a battle—anticipation, fear, excitement, anger, resignation, and determination. With the Shield down after centuries of protection, Aidric expected no less.

He wasn't surprised that Diryan had not sent word to him of his plans. It was the king's way of expressing his worry for him. It was clear that Diryan didn't want him to take part in the upcoming battle at all. Aidric was still tremendously weak from his ordeal, and the dark spell he carried was a constant weight on his soul, sinking its fangs deeper and deeper as the sand-marks rolled by.

Even so, Aidric knew that his role in this battle wouldn't go unplayed. Whether he or Diryan would have it so or not, it made no difference. He was now merely a child's puppet, and it was Fate who was master of his strings.

It was with that thought that Maldon found him, slipping so soundlessly into Aidric's room that had Aidric not been invoking his Empathy, he wouldn't have even known the older man was there. Still, he didn't turn his head to acknowledge the mage's presence. Maldon's emotions spoke to him as clearly as though his friend had spoken aloud, his trepidation all Aidric needed to discern the reason for his sudden visit.

The silence between them seemed to stretch on to infinity's end. Maldon, of course, knew his presence had been noted, and had simply chosen to await comment.

"My place is here, Maldon," Aidric said finally, his voice so low as to almost be inaudible.

"I'll have to remember to shield my thoughts more closely in the future," Maldon quipped.

Only then did Aidric turn his head to lock eyes with his friend. "We both know that I had no need to pluck from your mind the reason for this visit."

"I guess we do." The look in Maldon's eyes was indecipherable. "However, the king has given me his command, and I must carry it out. The queen is ready to depart. I can ask her to come here if you feel you can't rise from your bed."

"Maldon," Aidric said quietly, "you know I can't leave."

"It's the king's *order*," Maldon insisted just as quietly.

"The king will understand."

"Will he?" Maldon challenged, stepping forward.

"This is how it has to be. Diryan knows this to be true, the queen knows, and deep down you know it, as well. The path my life has followed ceased to be the one I initially paved for myself the moment I first saw Allison lying in that forest clearing and realized that she was the Golden Mage. I'll remain here to witness the outcome of this calamity as I'm meant to do, and you'll carry out the rest of Diryan's order and take the queen to safety."

Before Maldon could argue, Aidric calmly turned his head back to the wall that had grown so familiar within the last day and refused to say any more.

In the end, his arguments falling on deaf ears, Maldon could only do as Aidric wished. Even weakened, everyone knew not to cross Lamia's Mage-general.

***

"They come!" Ion announced, his voice tinged with fear. "Seni help us all, but can this be true? Lord Keldan sends that the *entire* Mihran army suddenly appeared along the outside of the palace wall!"

Allison, Diryan thought gravely, but he didn't voice his musings aloud. Although from the looks of extreme terror on the faces of his remaining Council, it looked as though he didn't have to say a word.

He didn't think that matters could get any worse. Although the kings of Kemos, Sonon, and Sersia had been willing to send immediate aid to Lamia without further negotiation and debate, it remained to be seen whether they could reach the Lamian palace in time. Diryan had at least one mage who could cast the portal spell stationed in each of the treatied-kingdoms, two in Kemos, but none came even close to wielding the power or control necessary to build the large portals Aidric, the twins, or Maldon were capable of. Nor were they capable of transporting an army great distances through one portal. Unfortunately, none of the four who could were available at the moment.

The armies would just have to be transported little

by little, requiring travel through at least two different portals to reach their destination. Diryan held little hope that his weakened army could hold the enemy at bay for the sand-marks it would take for the entirety of the three armies to arrive. With Allison as his weapon, Roderick would soon be storming the palace, perhaps even within the sand-mark. Aidius, how could he have allowed his kingdom to be backed into such a hopeless corner?

"They use the Golden Mage," Lord Claudium proclaimed, echoing Diryan's thoughts. "Only she would have the power to build a portal large enough to move an army of that magnitude. Aidius! She will be our destroyer, yet!"

"All is not finished," Diryan said sternly even though he was no longer sure of the certainty of his words. "I don't wish to hear a word from any of you that says otherwise."

"Majesty, the danger here grows more swiftly with every passing depth! We must evacuate you at once!" Lord Ambrus insisted.

Diryan was appalled at the thought. "Would you have me abandon my own people?" he demanded hotly, staring at his councilor as though he was a stranger.

"Of course not, Majesty," Ambrus stammered. "What I meant was—"

"I understand clearly what it is you meant," Diryan interrupted. "I shall *not* abandon the palace to Roderick without a fight! What would my life be worth if I flee like a coward and condemn my people to that heathen's boot? I would be dead, whether or not it's Roderick's sword that has done the deed! It's enough that the queen is safe. As long as one from the House of Lasha still lives, then Roderick can never ultimately hold the Lamian throne. I shall remain here until either I or Roderick lies dead!"

"Seni willing, it *will* be Roderick who lies dead at the end!" Lord Osrik said fervently.

"Indeed," Diryan said quietly, the hope in his eyes saying more than words could ever convey. "Indeed, Seni help us all."

***

Everywhere, as far as the eye could see and seemingly stretching from horizon-to-horizon, line after line of silver uniformed and black- and gold-uniformed soldiers marched closer in a wave of darkness that swallowed the land surrounding the palace like a horde of insects devouring an entire crop. They marched literally from within a hole torn into the very fabric of the world, a monstrous portal that no one had ever conceived to be possible spitting them forth onto the land.

It was a demon of brilliant light giving birth to its seemingly infinite army of hellspawn.

From her vantage point in the first watchtower above the main gates to the palace wall, Raya watched the impossible scene unfold before her, feeling more helpless and exhausted than she had ever felt in her life. Her time within Roderick's dungeons was a pleasant memory compared to both the physical and emotional horrors she now experienced. Even her flight with Selwyn and an unconscious Aidric within the Evrei Forest seemed a delightful afternoon excursion in light of what she now faced.

They had been surrounded even before the initial charge, the Lord Commander's hasty plans crumbled to dust and scattered to the four winds even before they could be carried out. Now any chance for surprise was nonexistent. All they had left to them was their skill in arms and magery, the skill of their generals' tactics. Even so, Raya knew in her heart that this time skill wouldn't be enough. This was *the* Battle, the confrontation prophesized within the lines of the Prophecy of the Golden Mage, and she knew without a doubt that the outcome of this battle would change the many kingdoms of Seni's World forever.

Aidius, how Raya wished for Selwyn's presence now! But her husband was currently far from her, lost somewhere below within the fray of battle as he led his squad of empaths in the desperate attempt to keep the Mihran army from breaching the palace wall.

At first she had been furious with Keldan for sending Sel directly into the viper's nest, but her anger surprisingly didn't burn long. Seemingly before she could even blink, she had found herself pelting fireballs into the center of the Mihran army with her comrades at Keldan's order in an attempt to create chaos within the enemy ranks and then frantically defending herself against the enemy mages' counter-attacks of lightning and flames. Now, her anger was no longer even a memory.

Raya could feel the waves of Mage-field energy swirling through the air all around her, bending to the wills of the mages behind the walls who now worked feverishly to strengthen the magical shield they had built to encase the palace. Although no one said a word, it was clear in the eyes of all the soldiers that it was no longer a matter of *if* the Mihran army would reach the wall but *when*.

Their only real hope lay with this newly-constructed shield, and that, only until Allison appeared onto the battlefield. If Allison had shattered in one blast of power as was rumored a shield legendary for its apparent indestructiveness, then the shield they now constructed was laughable at best, an annoying spider web to be brushed away.

Luckily, Allison had yet to make an appearance. They still had time—time enough for a miracle, for Raya knew with an instinctual foresight greater than any Seer could boast that a miracle was what it would take in the end. Word was that help was at least on the way, but from the grim looks of the mind-mages who spread this information through the ranks, it was clear that neither the Lord Commander nor Keldan believed that the additional troops would reach them in time.

With a grim determination, Raya focused the onslaught of her attack on the circle of mages positioned in the forefront of the enemy's left flank where the attacks to the new shield were the strongest. Within moments, she and three other mages had managed to dispose of a quarter of their number, but it wasn't nearly enough to make a major difference. It seemed that where one mage fell, there were two more ready to fill his place. It was maddening!

She was so intent on her battle with the mages that Allison's appearance escaped her notice until the first notes of an eerie melody reached her ears. Raya's attention shifted in enough time to spy the woman who had been her friend calmly edging towards an unsuspecting Keldan before a sudden darkness reached into her mind and ripped her consciousness away before Raya could even suspect what was happening.

CHAPTER TWENTY-THREE

K eldan could scarcely believe it.

All around him, his magical troops were dropping like flies, some seared away until only ash remained. Others had collapsed where they stood with no visible wounds and an incantation unfinished on their tongues, as if they had been destroyed from an attack within their bodies. But that wasn't the main reason behind what had him staring in a sort of dumb shock at the scene unfolding around him. It was the sight of Allison, her form surrounded by an eerie, green incandescence that made her appear inhuman, and the knowledge that it was she—his student, his friend—who had felled these men.

It was the very scene he had seen played out on numerous occasions in his nightmares.

From Allison's hands rose fiery streams of mage-flames, writhing towards the palace gates and the newly constructed shield.

Reflexively, Keldan began to sing softly, a melody that flowed as strong and sure as the wind. He sensed more than saw her falter amidst his magical song, and the flames disappeared from her hands. He used that moment of distraction to douse the flames that were already devouring a portion of the shield.

Then slowly, as if he was in a dream, she turned to him, and green eyes that glowed with an inner light met his own. It was then that Keldan knew that the creature before him was not Allison, because never, from the moment he had first lain eyes on her on the Eve of the Birth of the World a year ago, had he seen the coldness that now deadened her eyes like the cruelest of winters.

With a start, as the battle around them began to fade into the distance and his perception of her heightened, Keldan realized that what he had first taken to be a shadow across her face was in fact an ugly, darkening welt that appeared fresh. That injury only served to make her appear more menacing, more alien than the cheerful woman he had known and cared for.

And now this woman meant to kill him.

Keldan opened his mouth to sing, but to his shocked dismay, no sound emerged. It was then that he heard the underlying melody beneath the harsh cacophony of the battle around them that was neither his nor his brother's, and he could have kicked himself for not noticing it at once for what it was.

A mute spell, he thought in astonishment. *It's no wonder why our mages are failing. She's slowly silencing us all!*

And from the menacing gleam in her eyes, it looked as though Allison was about to silence *him* for good if he didn't do something quick! But what could he do? She had stolen from him the sole weapon he had carried into battle. It was as though he had engaged himself in a sword fight and had realized too late that the urchin beside him had stolen his sword.

Desperately, as Keldan felt the prickling on his arms that signaled that she was drawing from the Mage-field, he used the only resource left to him— speech without spoken words.

"Allison! Hear me!" he thought-spoke her just as she raised her hands to begin her spell.

She froze instantly, and the dark expression on her face melted into something unreadable. Keldan didn't know whether that was a good sign or not. At least she had paused in her spellcasting.

"Who are you?" she asked abruptly, her mind-voice sounding curiously strained for someone who held all the cards.

"Don't you remember me, Allison?" Keldan asked,

thinking quickly. *"It's me, Keldan—your teacher, your friend. I know that Roderick hasn't destroyed you completely. Let me help you. It's still not too late to free yourself from his control!"*

He could now blatantly see the conflict in her eyes. Hesitantly, Keldan took a step forward and held out his hand to her. In that same instant, he realized that he had made a huge mistake. The moment she saw him move, the spell of uncertainty he had created was broken, and her eyes hardened from uncertainty to suspicion.

"You're lying!" the Golden Mage accused angrily, her body suddenly glowing more brilliantly than before. *"I've never been to Lamia before today! I couldn't possibly know you!"*

"Retreat to the wall! Protect the shield! The Golden Mage comes!" Keldan managed to broadsent his magical troops before a mental hand squeezed all sense from his mind and he was falling, plunging into a terrifying darkness that he feared he would never emerge from again.

***

General Caith watched in numbed disbelief as the Golden Mage felled Keldan, the bardic-mage's body crumbling to the ground without any visible proof that she had done anything to him. The very woman Keldan had been viciously ready to defend with his fists earlier. However, the General's face remained as stoic as ever.

In all his years as a soldier of high rank, Caith had refused to show his men any emotion, whether it be fear, joy, or sorrow, lest that emotion caused those who trusted him with their lives to lose their lives on account of it. One sign that their general was anything but confident, professional, and his men would fall apart.

This was one such occasion. This battle was something out of his worst nightmare, worse than even the hopeless situation Second Gwidon had faced in Na'ar before the Sononese army had swept in like avenging warriors sent straight from Seni.

This time, there had been almost no warning, no time to prepare any strategic course of action, no Sononese army waiting to come to their rescue. General Caith and the newly-promoted Mage-general had barely had enough time to position the units of their army before the seemingly infinite stream of Mihran soldiers were upon them, pouring out of what had appeared to be the very bowels of Ter-ob.

Their abrupt appearance had shattered any of his hopes for the upper hand. He, the Lord Commander, and Mage-general Keldan had planned to charge them from three different directions the moment they marched into view. The left and right flanks had been cloaked in the spell of invisibility much as they had done in Kemos with several hundred lines of cavalry, pikes and swords ready to impale any enemy soldier that was unfortunate to be in the path of their on-slaught.

Keldan had scattered a couple dozen mages to several strategic positions along the ground and in the watchtower, ready to cast lightning bolts into the cen-ter of the enemy ranks in hopes of splitting the army before the initial charge. Surprise, the Lord Com-mander had insisted, was the best chance they had un-matched as they were.

Instead, Roderick had once again blindsided them. Bad enough that, but to make matters worse—much worse—the Mihran ranks had borne down on them from not one, but all directions, spilling out of four monstrous portals a mere couple hundred hand-spans from where the Lamian army waited. Hopelessly surrounded, their initial plan shattered, and no real strategy to improvise on, General Caith had ordered them to carry out the simplest of orders, to concen-trate on driving the enemy away from the wall, away from the gates, in the desperate hope that the prom-ised help would reach them in time. Brute force was all they had left.

The stone wall surrounding the palace, rising a scant twenty handspans, was no real defense against invasion, built only a few centuries earlier as mostly a structure of ornament, intended for the barest of defenses against internal scuffles within the kingdom. The wall had barely managed to keep the angered mob of several thousand peasants at bay whose intentions were to besiege the palace to remove King Diryan's grandfather from the throne. Although King Balasi, along with King Diryan's father, had managed to restore order to the kingdom, the threat of a second revolt had been ever-present in the air throughout Balasi's reign.

Nevertheless, King Balasi never thought to strengthen the wall against another such internal threat. Nor did any other king give a moment's thought to strengthening the wall against any *external* threats. The Lamian Shield had always been protection enough from would-be conquerors, and past Lamian kings had foolishly believed the Shield to be impenetrable. Until the Golden Mage had appeared, even Diryan had believed the Shield indestructible. Now, it seemed as if Lamia was about to pay the highest price for her overconfidence.

General Caith noticed that several groups of both mages and mind-mages had disappeared while he had been distracted by the Golden Mage, in all likelihood retreating closer to the palace gates under cloaks of invisibility with the fall of their Mage-general to join their comrades positioned within the watchtower.

"General, they are breaking through our ranks!" he heard Second Gwidon suddenly shout behind him.

With a start, General Caith turned his eyes from the fallen bardic-mage to what remained of his army. He bit back a curse as he saw hundreds of soldiers that had escaped the swords, pikes, and arrows of his men barreling towards them, shouting at the top of their lungs like madmen. General Caith suddenly had a disconcerting vision of a herd of spooked *antar* bearing down onto him and his Second.

Shaking his head to shatter the vision, he turned to Second Gwidon and commanded, "Take the right flank of cavalry and position them directly in front of the palace gates. At my signal, have them charge the bastards directly!"

"But General, the cavalry has been weakened tremendously!" Gwidon protested.

"Just do it!" General Caith barked. "No soldier of Mihr must be allowed to set foot in the palace! *None!*"

Gwidon needed no more urging. Soon the Second was lost in the chaos of the clanging swords, flying arrows, and the occasional bolts of lightning and fireballs. Caith could hear Gwidon's voice rise distinctly above the clamor of swords and cries of agony, anger, and hatred.

General Caith then turned to the mind-mage assigned to him by Keldan and commanded, "Larres, thought-speak as many of the magical troops positioned within the watchtowers and the base of the wall as possible and instruct them to focus all further efforts in strengthening and defending the shield they have constructed around the palace. We can't hold them at bay for much longer, and the best hope we now have is to use that shield once our initial line of defense is broken to stall the bastards long enough for the reinforcements from the surrounding kingdoms to reach us."

Then with a shout, General Caith raised his sword into the air and kneed his horse forward straight into the thick of the charging men, cutting down enemy soldiers left and right with wide slashes of his sword as they recklessly charged his horse. Blood splattered onto his uniform and across his face with each slash, but the blood might as well have been drops of rain for all the notice he took of it.

He was a soldier. He couldn't afford to allow what he saw to affect him lest he began to notice that the soldier he now ran through was only a boy barely into his teens, began to see the fear and the agony in the next. Seni help him, to see the blood of a generation staining his hands. No, General Caith didn't see any of that. His sanity didn't allow him to really *see* those scenes of hell that had become his world.

Yet—somewhere deep inside him, deep in the darkest recesses of his soul, a man wept for all the lives taken by his hand.

What felt like a small eternity later, the general caught sight of the first of his goals.

"Captain Casnar!" he shouted, drawing the man out of the confusion. He rode up alongside the other along the edges of the fighting and while the men under the Captain's command kept the enemy at bay, Caith leaned close so that only Casnar could hear. "The enemy breaks through! Fall back! Towards the palace gates! Let them think that you are retreating. Second Gwidon and the right flank of cavalry will be waiting. At the last possible moment, split your ranks and allow the cavalry through. Then circle back and attack them from both sides. They must *not* be allowed to reach the wall!"

Before Captain Casnar could react, General Caith was already gone, in search of Captain Janus and Captain Kasen to deliver similar orders for their ranks. However, before he could ride more than a few paces, an unseen object struck him violently in the chest, and he tumbled to the ground. Though he was prepared for it, Caith nevertheless landed hard, rolling uncontrollably a few paces before he could stop himself. He lay curled in a fetal position, clutching his chest and gasping after the breath that had been wrenched from his lungs.

Then hands roughly grabbed him, and through the tears of pain that blurred his eyes, General Caith saw several soldiers in black and gold towering over him like the moonlit dark trees of the Forest of Illusions that had intimidated him as a child. Strange, that now he recalled that particular childhood phobia. They hauled him to his feet, and he could feel the sharp points of their swords pressing painfully into his body, leaving scarcely any room for movement.

It was then as he stood on unsteady legs wheezing that he saw *her*, golden hair blowing wildly in the wind and her body glowing a powerful green incandescence, and he understood what it was that had struck him. It had likely been a milder version of the offensive attack that the Mage-general had often referred to as a "dagger of power."

Standing beside the Golden Mage was the vile man himself, the mage-king of Mihr who had been the cause of so much grief throughout the lands. At that moment, General Caith felt his emotional walls crumble to dust, leaving behind in their wake a hatred so keen that he shook with the intensity of it. The sounds of the battle all around him became a distant resonance, as though they were no longer real. General

Caith fixed burning eyes on the dark-mage, daring him to speak.

Roderick's expression changed from smug to something indecipherable. Could it be that he had made the bloody bastard uncomfortable? Him, a general with no powers except the skill of his blade, his intelligence and honor that made men willing to follow him? Perhaps it was the hatred in his eyes, a hatred that Roderick saw everyday when he looked into the eyes of his kingdom.

And it became abundantly clear that none of them intended to strike the death blow. Their manner was threatening, not murderous. At that moment, General Caith knew that it was over, and there was only one thing left to do. Long ago, he swore to himself and to his family that he would never allow himself to be taken prisoner and forced through torturous or magical coercion to reveal any secrets, and now, as he stared straight into the eyes of Death, himself, Lamia's Arms-general was equally determined.

"You have lost," Roderick said evenly, his eyes glittering with barely suppressed mad glee. "Yield to me, and you'll not suffer the same fate as your comrades."

"Lamia will never bend knee to you!" General Caith shouted, every syllable saturated with his hate.

"Not to lick the filth from your boot as your own people have done for decades!" For a moment, his eyes fell on Allison, the diffident woman he had known, the mage who now held Lamia in the palm of her hand—the woman whose soul Roderick had desecrated. "And I shall not suffer the same fate as she!" he cried fervently.

Then before astonished eyes, General Caith calmly stepped into the swords.

CHAPTER TWENTY-FOUR

The palace shook violently again, and Galen's curse was lost in the noise of the blast that followed. Milyn and Sandria shrieked and pressed themselves closer to him. The boys, however, wanting to prove their bravery, remained silent and at a distance though their eyes betrayed their terror. As he led his family down the Mage Hall, the same unbidden thought came over and over.

We should have left long ago.

It had taken Galen far longer than he had anticipated to get his family packed up and ready to depart. The first wall he had come across was his wife. Milyn had been shocked when Galen had told her about his resignation from the Circle. Then she had been equally shocked when he had declared his plans for them to flee.

At first she had adamantly refused. As a healer of Lamia, Milyn had felt that it was her duty to stay behind to treat the wounded and that it was his duty as well. Galen had been forced to confess his Foresight dreams in the end, telling her of the dreadful end he feared they would suffer should they stay any longer at the palace. Finally convinced, Milyn had agreed that taking their children to her family's home in Ell was the best thing they could do.

Then there had been the matter of locating the children. It had taken him quite a while to find everyone as they had all been at different friends' suites scattered throughout the palace. Thus, a sand-mark had passed before they finally were able to head for the stables.

"Perhaps we shouldn't leave, after all," Milyn said nervously.

"And remain here to be butchered by that golden demon!" Galen demanded. "Would you see our children murdered before your eyes?"

"No!" she said fiercely. "But Galen, the battle sounds so near! What will become of us if the Mihran soldiers have already broken through the main gates? Would you have our children in the midst of a battle?"

"I would rather us attempt to flee and die in the

process, knowing I did everything under the Thrones to save you and the children, than die here like cornered rats as I have Foreseen!"

An image of their burning bodies flashed through his mind, piercing his heart like a dagger. Seni save them all from such a fate!

"Surely they have more chance of survival here than stumbling across a battlefield!" Milyn insisted stubbornly. The palace shook again and her eyes grew desperate. "Galen please! Listen to reason!"

"Stay if you want!" Galen snarled. "However, the children are coming with me! I will save them at least!"

"Galen, please—" she pleaded again, but he ignored her, ordering his children to follow his lead.

Looking stricken, she followed.

However, when Galen tried to thrust the doors open, they wouldn't budge. Cursing under his breath, he grasped the handle more firmly and tugged more forcefully. The doors might as well have been painted there in jest for all they opened. With an oath, Galen whirled around and headed back down the hall, his family quickening their step to keep up with his angry strides.

"We'll *not* be kept here!" he growled, speaking more to himself than to his wife. "They can't have blocked all the exits. We'll jump from the king's bedroom window if needs be, but we *shall* escape!"

They reached the door connecting the Mage Hall to the indoor garden, but as Galen pulled it open, a hand reached over and promptly shoved it closed again.

"Would you listen to yourself?" Milyn demanded, placing herself between him and the door and reaching a hand to his shoulder to keep him back. "You're obsessed, Galen! You'll have us all jumping to our deaths if you don't see reason soon!"

"Obsession!" Galen roared. "*Obsession*! Don't speak to me of obsession!" He roughly shoved her hand away from his shoulder. Vaguely, he was aware that Sandria had begun to cry. "This is the thanks you give me for my concern! Accusations!"

"Galen, *please*, you're frightening the children!" she hissed. "Is that what you wish?"

He didn't even bother to answer. He flung the door open, grabbed the hands of his daughter and his sons and pulled them through. He then proceeded to drag them down the garden path. He didn't know if his wife followed or not.

At the arch into the main courtyard, Galen suddenly froze, and the white-hot anger in his eyes was instantly replaced by a cold fear.

The Golden Mage.

As it had happened in his worst nightmare, she

stood there, alone, an incandescent, green-glowing demon with the ethereal beauty of an angel. Her green eyes stared into his own with no hint of recognition.

Seni help me, just like my dream—

But no—something was different. It took Galen's panicking mind a few beats to realize that it was her eyes. Instead of them swirling with cruelty as they had in every one of his Foresight dreams, they were oddly vacant, soulless, as if he stared into the eyes of an animated corpse. They were infinitely worse.

Galen could hear Milyn and his children sobbing in terror as they cringed behind him. In some distant part of his mind, he realized that he had unconsciously placed himself between the Golden Mage and them.

This can't be happening—dear Seni, let this be another dream!

But it wasn't a dream, he knew. He could hear her heavy breathing, smell the sweat of his own fear and feel the slight warmth emanating from the magic engulfing her body.

Slowly, Galen fell to his knees before her, shamelessly prepared to beg for the life of his family. The Golden Mage raised her hands as though she was preparing to spellcast.

"No!" Galen cried with anguish. "It's *me* who has wronged you, not they! Kill me if you must, but for

Seni's sake, spare my wife, my children! They're innocents in this!"

Her hands paused in the midst of gesturing, and the expression in her eyes changed, the emptiness suddenly filling with a flicker of warmth, horror, and finally a faint glimmer of something like recognition. Slowly, miraculously, she began to lower her hands, and Galen's hope surged.

Then without warning, a loud crash boomed throughout the palace, and the sounds of battle reached his ears. In the same instant, the warmth in the Golden Mage's eyes iced over.

The spell had been broken.

Galen didn't even have time to cry out a warning to his family before her first attack came.

There was no pain. There were no flames licking at his skin.

He was then falling into darkness, the terrified cries of his children rapidly fading from his ears. *It wasn't supposed to be like this!* Galen thought in anguish. *I was supposed to save them!*

Then his mind knew no more.

***

Diryan whipped his head sharply towards the door when he heard the commotion outside, but before he could say anything, the door exploded open and crashed against the wall. His eyes widened in horror as first, the bodies of his two personal guards fell across the threshold with swords imbedded deeply into their hearts, followed by a stream of countless Mihran soldiers. His councilors began to shout alarmingly in unison.

He started to stand up, but the end of a sword prevented him from rising more than half a handspan. He sat back down slowly, with dignity, his eyes fixed on the doorway where Roderick stood smirking with all the arrogance of the world.

"Ah, *King* Diryan, at last we see each other face-to-face," Roderick said casually as he—slithered into the room. That was the only word that could describe it. "It was inevitable, really," the bastard continued with that same infuriating tone. "Did you really believe that you could hide beneath your throne forever?"

Diryan said nothing.

"Your infamous army has been defeated, your generals dead. My men have secured all the exits of the palace, and the Golden Mage is mine. I have won. Surrender to me, and I may allow you to live—in the dungeons, of course."

The king began to laugh, taking pleasure in seeing the bastard's eyes fill with rage.

"How vain you are!" he said with a shake of his

head. "All is not lost yet, demon. I still live. The queen is safely beyond your reach. What need do I have to surrender?"

"Bring him," Roderick said darkly to his men. "We'll show *His Majesty* how much he will regret his words.

Diryan was roughly pulled to his feet and shoved towards the door. For a brief moment, he was face-to-face with Roderick. Black rage instantly filled his being, and the urge to squeeze the life out of the dark-mage who was the cause of all this madness and grief was almost overwhelming. However, before Diryan could act, Roderick stepped aside, and what he saw beyond the threshold of the door caused the fight to instantly melt from his limbs.

"Ileanna," he whispered brokenly.

Bound by the invisible bonds of magic and guarded by a half-dozen Mihran soldiers, the queen met her husband's stricken gaze, her eyes haunted and infinitely sad.

"I'm sorry," she said before Diryan felt the first of many blows to his head and body.

CHAPTER TWENTY-FIVE

Allison opened the massive doors of the Lamian Throne Room with a single thought, unsure of what she was walking into. Roderick had summoned her here a few moments after she had taken care of the dark-haired man who had begged so fiercely for the lives of his family. Strange, that for a moment, she had almost known him—but no. More than likely, he had attempted to tamper with her mind just like the mage who said his name was Keldan had tried.

However, all thoughts of him and his family immediately melted from her mind when she fixed her eyes on the scene before her. Along the sides of the blue and silver carpeted aisle that stretched to the dais, at least a dozen prisoners, all richly dressed and likely members of the Lamian aristocracy, were being held at sword point by several Mihran soldiers.

With a jolt, Allison realized that the prisoner everyone was currently focused on was a middle-aged, brown-haired man that was rooted to one of the throne seats both magically and physically by a paralysis spell and a series of thick, leather straps. He was glaring at Roderick with blatant hatred. A dark bruise at his temple seemed to cry out for attention.

On the second throne seat sat a silver-haired woman of considerable beauty, equally helpless. Her eyes blazed with the same level of hatred.

So, this is the infamous King Diryan Lasha of Lamia, Allison thought darkly, *the man who has shattered my happiness with Roderick and the man who turned him into the monster he's become!* As if to mockingly remind her, the cheek where Roderick had hit her earlier began to throb insistently again.

She longed to gather energy into her body, to lash out at the son of a bitch before her whose tyranny had destroyed not only her life but the lives of all his people, but the power Roderick held over her mind prevented her from acting outside the orders he had given her.

Roderick stood at the foot of the dais, looking as if he was paying homage to the royal couple. Maybe that was his intention, a mockery that had become characteristic of his personality lately.

Mordant was nowhere to be seen. Where had the insufferable man run off to? Allison's heart twisted with dread as her mind was suddenly flooded with visions of him committing all sort of atrocities to the people who lived in the palace. She feared that they were only too true and desperately wished she could go find him, but her feet refused to turn around.

As she walked down the sapphire carpet, Allison had the strangest feeling that this wasn't the first time she had walked this particular path. A little voice in her head instantly instructed her to forget about it, that it wasn't important.

Roderick turned as she approached, the maniacal glint she had seen ever since she had destroyed a portion of Lamia's Shield still glowing as strongly as ever within his golden eyes. Inside, she shivered under that gaze, while on the outside, she felt herself smile. It was as if she had been possessed by another person, forced to watch in silence from the prison of her own mind while the stranger who had become her bowed to Roderick's every whim. In a sense, she *had* been possessed, her mind invaded by a man she now felt nothing but contempt for.

"Ah, my dear," Roderick purred, holding out a hand to her which, to her disgust, she eagerly accepted. *Just like a dog.* "You must see this glorious sight. The king of Lamia, after all these long years, is completely at my mercy, powerless in the face of his own death."

Allison stepped forward and fixed eyes cold with fury on Diryan. There was no need for Roderick's coercive power over her to force her to show him her rage. *Because of you, I've lost the man I love forever!*

Diryan matched her gaze for gaze, although instead of rage, his eyes held a deep sorrow that confused her. It didn't mesh with the ruthless tyrant Roderick had described him as.

"Why do you glare at me with such hatred, child?" the Lamian king asked abruptly, his tone unnervingly calm.

She said nothing. Yes, she could hear the sorrow in his voice, feel it with her empathic senses, but it didn't make any sense! He had to be trying to play her.

It makes perfect sense, a voice whispered, unbidden, in the back of her mind.

"What lies has he fed you that you would look at us so?" Diryan demanded. "What memories has he stolen or twisted? Do you not recall the night you wept on my shoulder, we both wept, for one we had thought lost?"

"It's *you* who's lying!" Allison spat at him furiously. "I don't know you. I don't know anyone here who has talked to me as if I did! Lies! It's all lies!"

God, she itched to strike out at him, to end the

pain and confusion he caused in her.

"The fate of my kingdom rests in your hands, Allison," Diryan continued seriously as if he hadn't heard her outburst at all. "It's for you, and you alone, to decide. You have the power to stop this madness, to free the lands of decades of bloodshed and pain all for the greed of the man who now holds you chained beneath his soiled boot! You are the *Golden Mage*! And only the Golden Mage can set us free!"

"Shut up!" Allison cried, flinging her hands up to press tightly over her ears. *He's lying. He's lying! God, help me, let him be lying!* "Just shut up! I don't want to hear any more of your lies!"

She felt Roderick's arms embrace her from behind, but she summoned all the willpower left to her to pull away. She didn't want to be comforted, least of all by him whose sudden greed and bloodlust had betrayed her more than he would ever realize.

Roderick's eyes flashed dangerously for a moment, but rather than blow up at her as she had expected, the angry fire within them died down a bit. His wounded pride was the least of his concerns now, and he knew it. However, Allison knew that a time would come when she would have to pay, and the price would probably leave her with more than a bruised cheek.

"Yes, my dear," Roderick said casually, stepping

up onto the dais until he was face-to-face with Diryan. "I do believe we have heard quite enough out of Lamia's former king and none of it the words I wished to hear."

From the confines of his robes, Roderick drew from a jeweled scabbard a magnificent black sword, gleaming with a glass-like luster which reminded Allison of obsidian. Her arms began to prickle the instant he had unsheathed the sword, and she knew that, like the daggers that the Mihran soldiers carried, this blade was also spelled. However, compared to a spelled dagger, the sword was a raging inferno and the dagger, a fleeting spark.

Also, the magic that flowed within the sword was completely alien, a power she had never touched. If the power didn't originate from the Mihran Magefield, then what was its source?

"You'll be aiding me more than you realize, old fool," Roderick sneered, making a great show of pointing his black sword at Diryan's abdomen. "With a single thrust of my blade, you'll be adding years to my life."

Roderick's odd words confused Allison. Why would Diryan's death add years to Roderick's own? Was he just speaking figuratively?

"Vile dark-mage!" Diryan spat. His face began to turn an angry shade of red, and the strain was clear in his eyes as he raged against his paralysis. "Demon from the lowest of the six hells! You would desecrate the laws of Seni even more by stealing my life-energy with your filthy Dark Powers?"

"What fear have I for Seni?" Roderick said with a laugh. "Didn't I drive him out of my kingdom? Didn't I hang one of his precious servants without consequence? Tell me this, Diryan. If your Seni is so powerful, why hasn't he reached his mighty hand down from the Thrones and crushed me within his fist? Your god has no power, and in the end, it's Lord Arioch who will rule the souls of mankind!"

Allison felt as though she had been hit in the face with a sledgehammer. *Roderick* can't *be a dark-mage! Not the man that I—!* Yet, how could she deny it? The admission had come from his own lips!

Without warning, a blast from behind sent her sprawling hard onto her hands and knees. Stunned, Allison looked up wildly in enough time to see Roderick take the full force of a lightning bolt. The incredibly brilliant white flash had her squeezing her eyes shut with a cry of pain a split-second before the sound of several of Roderick's shields shattering reached her ears followed immediately by an inhuman roar of rage and fear. She sensed rather than saw Roderick crumble to the ground.

Allison forced her eyes open, blinking furiously in

an attempt to clear both the tears and the spots of light flashing across her vision. She *had* to see, wondering if Seni's hand had indeed come down for judgment. Roderick was on his knees a few feet away, cursing up a storm and shaking his head violently.

The entire Throne Room had erupted into chaos. Soldiers began to shout in alarm, several of them rushing to the aid of their king, who shoved them aside angrily as he staggered onto feet again, a bit unbalanced, but otherwise unscathed. Allison could already feel him drawing energy from the Mihran Mage-field and a second, unknown source identical to the magic within his black blade in order to rebuild his bodily shields.

Then, through tear-blurred eyes, she saw *him*.

A lone, white-haired man stumbled across the threshold of the large doors into the Throne Room, wobbling badly as if he was extremely drunk, but Allison knew that he wasn't. His body was completely saturated with power, his hands visibly glowed with it. She had found the source of the lightning bolt.

The stranger managed to stumble a few paces before he collapsed onto his knees. His sweat-streaked face was nearly as pale as his hair. He looked sick, sick but determined as he gritted his teeth and immediately forced himself to his feet again.

For a moment, Allison bemusedly wondered why

no one had heard him enter, and then with a start, remembered that *she* had left the doors wide open. Her carelessness had given him the perfect opportunity. Had this man not been so ill, so physically weak, Allison was sure that Roderick would now be dead.

Then his eyes fell on her, *pale-violet* eyes.

This can't be—

It was *him*. She was sure of it, the man cloaked in shadows in her dream—the man with the accusing eyes standing only a few feet away as solid and real as the pain in her cheek. Only now, those eyes weren't in the least bit accusatory. They held a pain that was so soul-sick that she inadvertently felt tears threatening behind her eyes.

He's the enemy, whispered the unbidden voice of before.

Hastily, Allison jumped to her feet, never once taking her eyes off the man who had taken them all so completely by surprise. She would be damned first before she faced him on her knees! Her sudden movement caught Roderick's eye, and as he turned to her, his eyes fell on their unexpected visitor.

"*You!*" Roderick raged. Allison had never seen him so livid. "By Lord Arioch, shall I *never* be rid of you, Mage-general?"

She scarcely had time to blink before a ball of green fire was streaking towards the white-haired man.

Aidric.

However, before it could reach him, the Mage-general gestured slightly, effortlessly, and the fireball vanished as though it had only been an illusion. However, Allison was close enough to him to see how his body had tensed and wavered slightly after that gesture. His defensive spell had probably cost him a great deal more than he was letting on.

"Attack him you fools!" Roderick barely had time to shout to his mages before a circle of power only those with Inner-sight could see enclosed him and slowly began to contract inward. Roderick gestured and shouted words frantically, destroying the solidified mage-field energy a scant few seconds before the circle could crush him.

At the opposite end of the room, the Lamian Mage-general had sent the half-dozen mages who had advanced on him flying hard into a wall covered with tapestries with a burst of sheer energy as easily as if he was swatting away a swarm of annoying insects. They landed in a tangled heap of limbs at the base of the wall. None of them rose for a second attempt.

Roderick grabbed that precious few seconds of distraction his mages had created and flung a dagger of power at the Mage-general, one which he had no chance to deflect. The Mage-general made no sound as the blast flattened him, shattering all of his bodily shields. Roderick flung a paralysis spell at him before the shock of the blast could wear off.

The Mage-general had been defeated.

Roderick stalked over to the fallen man and gave him a sound kick in the ribs. Allison winced inwardly as she heard the unmistakable snap of bones cracking. Not a single whimper emerged from the Mage-general's lips, but she could see the agony in his eyes, the hatred. She quickly averted her eyes. Enemy or not, she couldn't bear to see any more, couldn't bear the bitter truth that she was now powerless to stop Roderick because of her own stupidity.

"Insolent bastard!" Roderick roared as he delivered another brutal kick. Only Roderick's spell over her prevented Allison from crying out her distress. "Did you really believe you could best me? Now you'll watch your precious king and queen die at my hands before I deliver the same fate to you in a way that'll have you begging for it. Lamia is mine! Her power is mine! Every army in the world will now quake before me!"

Roderick turned away from the Mage-general and sauntered over to where his black sword lay. With a single thought, it rose into his hands.

"Now, I finish this," he said smugly and advanced towards the dais, every pore in his body practically radiating his glee.

"Allison!" an unfamiliar male voice shouted urgently in her mind.

Startled, she scanned the area around her until her eyes fell on the fallen Mage-general. Sure enough, his eyes were fixed on her, and she could see the pleading, the panic and the pain swirling in them.

"For the love of Seni, fight him!" he pleaded. *"Fight his control over your mind! You can still stop him! I know what he's done to you. He's stolen your memories of Lamia, your memories of friends and trials, your memories of us! I know that somewhere deep within the farthest depths of your soul you remember who I am, remember our love and all that we shared. You must remember, little cat. For Seni's sake, you must!"*

Little cat... Those words stirred something deep within her subconscious—was it an emotion? However, before Allison could grasp it, it was gone as though she had only imagined it, some trick of her empathic gift or his.

"I don't know you!" she felt her mind send to him coldly.

But I do know you! the part of her that was still fully Allison screamed in her mind in the same instant. *You're the man in my dreams! God help me, who are you?*

"But you do!" the Mage-general insisted, echoing her thoughts. *"I am the first man you took into your bed. Our souls are bound together! You can't deny that! Even down, deep within myself, I can still feel your presence. Roderick didn't*

destroy our bond completely!"

    "No!" Allison's mind-voice screamed. *"No!"*

Aidric. His name is Aidric.

CHAPTER TWENTY-SIX

Only two sand-marks after the battle had begun, the palace lawns were littered with an unholy amount of bodies that were scorched, mangled, and twisted in the last throes of death, their life-blood seeping into the earth until it was dark with reddish-black mud. Over fifty thousand men wearing the colors of three kingdoms, most fighting for a land they held dear, some fighting out of fear, subversion, or hate, had seen their last sunrise. They had felt the pleasure of a cool breeze brush across their face for the last time and had died fearing that their life had been given in vain.

The stench of death and the wounded was sharp in the air, a foul taint that left those still breathing with a greater sense of their own fragile mortality. Cries of pain, both physical and emotional sounded out across the palace lawns. Felled men and women begged for healers that would never come. Others begged for the release of death and the promise of the peace of the Thrones.

Watching the writhing, moaning bodies of his soldiers that still clung to life buried amongst the bodies of the dead, his eyes hard and his expression fixed in defiance as if they had been cast in stone, Second Gwidon genuinely envied the dead. Bound with magical bonds he couldn't see, surrounded by a dozen hard-eyed Mihran and Bar'tain soldiers ready to beat him senseless if he dared to move, the Second's fate was already sealed.

Gwidon knew without a doubt that they wouldn't kill him. No, death was too easy for him, a high-ranking officer of the enemy army—of *Lamia's* army. It was Roderick's dungeons for him where things would be done to him that he didn't dare allow himself to contemplate. It was why he understood better than anyone why General Caith had calmly chosen to step into his death. Still, understanding and accepting were two very different things, and the Second knew that if by some miracle Seni delivered them from this hell, it would be a very long time before he could come to terms with his mentor's death.

Around him, the sounds of cursing and laughter floated through the air amidst the cries and moans of the dying. The smells of cook fires wafted all around them, nauseating within the stench of blood and gore. After taking the wall and imprisoning what was left of the pathetically reduced Lamian army, only a portion of Roderick's troops had stormed the palace along with the Mage-king and the Golden Mage.

The rest had remained beyond the wall and had immediately begun to set up camp, clearing away a portion of the bodies, both enemy and comrade, as nonchalantly as though they were merely clearing away brush and dumping them in piles along the edges of their camp. For the life of him, Gwidon couldn't fathom how the Mihran and Bar'tain armies managed to ignore the death all around them. Their behavior was appalling!

A little ways in front of him, Gwidon could see the huddled forms of the bardic-twins, Aren cradling the body of his brother as best as his bound hands allowed as the latter lay deep in unconsciousness, mercifully oblivious to anything that had befallen them. Considerably more than the amount of soldiers that watched him were assigned to guard the bardic-mages, along with several mages, though Gwidon knew from the whispers of their captors that both men had been spelled mute. Without the use of their voices, any musical instruments at hand, or even mobility of their limbs, the twins were as helpless as a swordsman without his sword.

However, no matter how diligently they had tried, no enemy mage had been able to bind either man with the paralysis spell as they had immediately done to all those who remained of the Lamian army. There had been a lot of grumbling about impenetrable personal shields. Thus, the twins had been trussed up with ordinary rope.

Earlier, several Mihran soldiers had attempted to separate the two men, but Aren had held firm, refusing to relinquish his hold on Keldan no matter how badly the Mihran soldiers had beat him. In the end, they had tired of the sport and had allowed Aren his small victory.

His grief was renewed as Gwidon thought of the only man who would have fought as fiercely for him as Aren had for his brother and the fact that his mentor was now lost forever to him. Roderick hadn't even left a body. The Mihran king had been so enraged when General Caith had escaped his judgment that the bastard had reduced his mentor's body to ash. General Caith had been one of the greatest Lamian generals to ever live, and his remains wouldn't even receive a proper burial.

Gwidon unconsciously attempted to shift his body before the effects of the paralysis spell cast over him reminded him of the futility of it, denied even that small release for comfort. His eyes were also beginning to burn horribly with his natural need to blink, his vision beginning to blur. The spell allowed him to breathe on his own; that was about it.

His shoddy eyesight was why Gwidon failed to realize the significance of the dark line that had suddenly appeared and then almost in the same instance disappeared against the eastern horizon, dismissing it as nothing more than shadow or a trick of light caused by his blurred vision. Only when he felt the first vague tremors in the earth did he understand that what he had seen hadn't been a trick of his eye or the desperate hallucination of a battle-fatigued mind.

Fortunately, the enemy failed to notice that anything was amiss at all. Even the mages didn't show any sudden alarm.

The first ranks of black-uniformed soldiers abruptly appeared at the foot of the enemy camp like dark wraiths summoned by the hand of Seni to avenge the deaths of those on the battlefield, and the small bands of soldiers who had apathetically kept watch along the edges of the camp were cut down within the blink of an eye, some with their swords still halfway in their scabbards. Mihran and Bar'tain soldiers sitting and eating their meals were also decimated before they could even do more than look up in shock.

The Sononese had come.

What followed was what the Lamian army had attempted and failed to create—chaos.

In the arrogance of their triumph against one of the most formidable armies throughout Seni's World, Roderick's troops had foolishly failed to properly guard against the appearance, however unlikely, of reinforcements from any of Lamia's allies. That the few scouts sent out to keep watch had failed to see the advance of King Govannon's army was unforgivably careless.

Lamian soldiers stirred to life in droves from the bounds of paralysis by the efforts of the still unseen mage or mages that had so cleverly managed to keep the Sononese army concealed. Stripped of their weapons earlier, they rose with howls of renewed determination and ferocity, grappling with their captors for possession of their weapons while the enemy was still frozen in shock and confusion.

By the time the Mihran and Bar'tain soldiers recovered from their initial surprise, around a fourth of their ranks had been cut down. Nevertheless, the Sononese army was still outnumbered three to one by the larger force, and despite their initial success, it would take both every bit of skill they possessed and Seni's own luck to prevail. Were other armies on their way? Had His Majesty only managed to convince King Govannon of their desperate need? What of the Kemosian, Olerian, and Na'aran armies?

Gwidon, still trapped within the confines of the paralysis spell, could only sit helplessly and watch the fierce struggle all around him, his mind racing with a thousand questions that no one but King Diryan and the kings of their allies could answer. He itched for freedom, for a sword, wanting desperately to join his men in battle.

He was so intent on the raging battle, that he never saw the blade coming. Gwidon grunted with surprise when he abruptly felt fire lance into his side. As the momentum of the brutal stab knocked him over onto his side and he felt the blade being torn from his body, all he could think was that he couldn't die now, not when there was still hope of victory. Still bound by magic, he couldn't even scream his rage as out the corner of his eye, he saw the blade covered with his own blood rise and swing down for its final stroke.

***

He couldn't reach her.

Seni help him, but Roderick's fangs had latched

onto her mind too firmly. His venom ran too deeply. Aidric could still hear Allison's mind-scream of denial echoing throughout his mind. His empathic senses could keenly feel the turmoil within her. Her subconscious was likely fighting against the damage Roderick had inflicted, but he knew that it was a losing battle. She was still too new to magic to understand how to fight the enemy within.

Seni help him, he couldn't reach her!

Roderick was now at the foot of the dais, sword quivering with malicious anticipation. Seni help him! The bloody bastard was going to do it! He was going to do it!

"Father! Mother! *No!*" Aidric wailed like a man dying as Roderick raised the glittering black sword for his first strike.

The paralysis spell binding Aidric shattered under his fury, his desperation. He sprang to his feet in an instant and charged Roderick like a man possessed despite his injuries, his eyes wild with panic and a spell already spewing from his lips. However, before he could voice the last words, a force he couldn't see seized him, flinging him backwards at a breakneck speed. His back crashed into a couple of the Circle's chairs before he slammed into an unforgiving wall.

The energy that he had already gathered scattered out wildly into the air on impact, inadvertently taking some of his life-energy with it before his connection to the failed spell was severed. He couldn't breathe. He couldn't see as a creeping darkness consumed his vision, and a terrible pain inundated his body. But with the last ounce of strength left in him, Aidric hung onto consciousness by the skin of his teeth.

Roderick was laughing. The bloody bastard was *laughing*!

"The surprises just keep coming today!" Roderick said gleefully, his voice echoing mockingly throughout the room. "The deceased prince of Lamia is not so deceased after all. The *mageborn* prince! And under those fools of the Brothers in Divinity's noses all along!"

Aidric couldn't move. There was no strength left in his body, no strength in which to fight. In his mind's eye, he saw the sandwoods of the Evrei Forest, and the sharp smell of decaying leaves invaded his senses, ghosts from his most recent failure come to cruelly taunt him.

Seni help me, not again! his mind raged in anguish.

Roderick stepped up to Ileanna and raised her chin roughly. "How fitting a punishment for all the years of irritation he's given me that your *son* will watch you both die, but don't despair! He'll be quick to follow you to your pitiful Gates and god who couldn't even save you from my blade."

"*No!*" Aidric screamed, desperately trying to pull

energy from the Mage-field but failing miserably. "Allison, for Seni's sake, *stop him!*"

But he knew she was beyond hearing him. He could see her now, knees drawn up to her chest, her face buried within them. She was trapped deep within her mind, and only the shell that Roderick had created remained behind.

Aidric helplessly watched in horror as Roderick slowly and deeply ran his blade across Ileanna's throat, a sickly yellow light appearing along the edges of the blade where it had sliced into the delicate flesh of her throat. Her body immediately began to glow a brilliant gold, the black sword seeming to absorb it hungrily as the light emerged.

In the end, the queen couldn't even scream as her life-blood gushed out of the ghastly wound, the golden light about her fading with the flow of her blood. Yet, even in the face of death, Ileanna's eyes glared out at her murderer in defiance, denying him the satisfaction of seeing her pain, her fear, until her eyes saw no more and the golden light was completely snuffed out.

The cry that was wrenched from Diryan's throat was unearthly, as though it had been his own throat that was slashed and not his wife's. Roderick looked back at Aidric with a smirk before he turned to the grief-stricken king. Then just as slowly as he had done to Ileanna, Roderick pressed the point of the disgusting sword to Diryan's heart and began to run him through, abruptly ending the king's chilling cry in a gush of blood and flash of golden light, which his sword immediately devoured.

—and the bastard *laughed!*

With that final stab, a part of Aidric was destroyed, murdered forever along with his parents. He heard someone screaming, and it was a long while before he realized that it was him.

***

Selwyn turned in enough time to see Second Gwidon impaled by a Bar'tain soldier. *No!* his mind shouted fiercely. He knew that with General Caith gone and Keldan lost to unconsciousness, this man was their last hope of taking advantage of the second chance the Sononese army had provided and leading the Lamian army once again against the still-sizeable remnants of the monstrous army that had invaded their land.

The Lamians, free of their magical bonds, had instantly reacted out of rage and not reason. They had begun to attack the enemy with their bare hands like men and women possessed. The result was that a good many of them, even those who were seasoned veterans that had seen and lived through more battles then they could count, had been slaughtered. These were soldiers that they should have never lost. If left to their own maddened whims, it wouldn't be long until the Lamian army was annihilated, and the lives already lost and the lives of the Sononese army who had already fallen would have been lost in vain.

Selwyn had been searching for Raya among those that had been captured before catching sight of the Second. He *knew* that his wife was still alive. The soul-bond they shared through the life-rings they wore had still pulsed with life. Every bonding with the life-rings was unique, every couple reacting to the magic of the merging with different results. Sel had refused to even think about the possibility that Raya and he were among that small minority of married couples who had bonded so deeply that the part of their soul they had given to their life-mate remained connected with them even after the death of their spouse. She was *alive*, dammit, and that was the end of it.

Now, all thoughts of Raya were reluctantly shoved aside. A furtive glance around proved what Selwyn already knew. Only he had been near enough to witness the attack on Gwidon, so it was up to him to come to the Second's aid—him, an empath, a virtual nobody whom some had whispered at his induction to the Circle was not strong enough to hold his position and forever in the shadow of his powerful best friend.

Although he would have it no other way, it still hurt when others measured his worth to his friendship with Aidric. A man, Selwyn thought bitterly, who had, as Aidric had once said in jest, "fainted at the sight of a beautiful maiden."

Though his energy had been stretched to its very limits in the first battle, Sel managed to banish all his misgivings and find a small reservoir of strength within him. He didn't hesitate to use every last ounce of it in a brutal attack against the emotions of the soldier who was now posed to deliver the death stroke to the Lamian army's last hope.

A mere handspan away from its target, the sword suddenly jerked away and slipped from nerveless fingers as Selwyn's assault hit the soldier's emotions, twisting them until they drove the man to the brink of madness. Unlike Spymaster Valin's response when Selwyn had hit him with the same attack, the Bar'tain soldier shrieked and began to claw at his face, scratching deep furrows into his flesh and howling like an enraged demon as he then proceeded to claw his own eyes out. Finally, the soldier managed to end his madness by grabbing the sword he had dropped and running himself through the heart.

Though horror reflected within Sel's eyes, and the sight of the man—enemy or no—destroying his own face left him sickened, Gwidon's expression didn't once change. Selwyn would never forget that stoic face as the Second watched his would-be murderer destroy himself through the mask of paralysis and a burst of satisfaction that hit is Empathy with all the subtlety of an ax.

Then Selwyn had no more room for thought as he reached the fallen Second and saw just how badly the other was injured. Had the sword been imbedded just an inch or two higher or lower, then perhaps things would have been different, but as fate would have it, it was not to be.

Second Gwidon was dying.

Even so an inborn stubbornness in Sel refused to accept what was inevitable, a stubbornness that his mother liked to say had been there since the time of his birth when the healers attending his mother had told her that he wouldn't live past the first sand-mark. Yet with a ferocity that matched his flame-colored hair, he had taken on death and won. Hellsfire, didn't Aidric always tell him that the future wasn't etched into the magical parchment of the Horae, that the future was written based on the choices you made?

The fury of the battle still hadn't reached them, a blessing Selwyn was quick to thank Seni for. He could *not* allow the Second to die! Lamia *would* have its second chance at victory!

With a grunt, Sel heaved Gwidon onto his shoulder, bringing on a horrible sense of *déjà vu* of the time when he had carried an injured Aidric towards an uncertain fate. He swayed under the sudden weight, his body fatigued and mentally drained from his empathic battles, and for a few depths, a wave of exhaustion threatened to send them both pitching to the ground.

Gritting his teeth and willing his exhaustion away, Selwyn surreptitiously began to make his way towards the wall where he had last seen the healer, Dallan, held captive. If Gwidon was to be saved, then Dallan was the sole man who had the power and skill to do it.

Sel could feel Gwidon's raspy breath against his ear, becoming more and more labored with every step he took. Death was near. Selwyn glanced through weary eyes towards the wall. He could see it in the distance, perhaps only half a span away, but it might as well have been a thousand spans.

Over his shoulder, the Second's life-blood continued to flow at an alarming rate. Now, Selwyn's enemy was no longer Roderick but time, and it looked as though time was winning.

CHAPTER TWENTY-SEVEN

A llison wished that she could melt into the floor. She denied to herself that she had just witnessed the atrocities Roderick had committed, but no matter how hard she tried to bury them, those ghastly images insisted on flashing through her mind, images that would haunt her nightmares for the rest of her life.

Then that horrible scream had filled the Throne Room, sounding too uncannily like what she imagined the screams of the damned would sound like. It had been even more terrible than Diryan's scream when Roderick had murdered the queen. Allison had known without looking that the inhuman cry had been torn from the Mage-general's throat. His obviously genuine pain only confused her more than his presence had done earlier. How could anyone care so deeply for a man as evil as Diryan as to cause such unbearable grief at his death?

How could a man as evil as Diryan have ever loved someone as he obviously loved his wife? How could you *have ever loved a man as evil and sadistic as Roderick?* a voice suspiciously sounding like her own whispered mockingly at the back of her mind.

Then, with horror, Allison realized that Roderick was walking towards her, the sword he had used to kill Lamia's monarchs, still wet with their blood, gripped tightly in his hand. A faint, yellowish glow radiated from him that hadn't been present earlier, and she instantly knew that it was the result of the life-energy he had stolen from the king and queen.

She fixed sickened eyes on him, hands raised in readiness to fling him away with a burst of power from her palms if he tried to touch her even though she knew deep down that the leash he held on her mind wouldn't allow her to harm him. But no—the monster had a different target in mind. Roderick passed her without a glance, striding over to where the Mage-general lay weeping.

Leave him alone! came the unbidden thought, suddenly, angrily. The fury of emotions that came with that thought shocked her. Without understanding why, Allison's heart began to bleed for the young man with hair the color of the purest snow who wept so brokenly.

Haven't you caused him enough pain? Enemy or no, he doesn't deserve to suffer like this!

"You see? It's *this*, this disgusting vulnerability to emotion that's led to your kingdom's downfall!" Roderick sneered, giving the Mage-general a rough shove with the toe of his boot. The Mage-general didn't even raise his head. "The weak never prevail! It's a pity, *Prince* Aidric, that your true heritage has been revealed today. I had thought to reinstate you to my dungeons again. However, that's no longer an option I can afford. I can't risk having an heir of the House Lasha still living no matter how amusing. The royal house of Lamia *must* die out today! Even so, I'll at least still have the joy of watching you slowly die as it'll take at *least* a few sand-marks after I've split your gut open and lodged my blade into your heart for it to absorb the dark spell of immortality that you carry. Perhaps by then, the agony will have driven you mad."

Roderick pointed the tip of the blade in the center of Aidric's abdomen, the hilt grasped tightly in both hands and ready to strike at will. Blood from the tip began to drip down onto the Mage-general's white shirt, the crimson liquid standing out in shocking contrast to the brilliant, lustrous white. Only then did

Aidric raise his head, but it wasn't Roderick, nor the dripping sword that claimed his attention. Allison once again found herself staring into his haunting eyes.

"Allison," she heard him whisper into her mind, more steadily than she would have thought possible. *"Don't let me die like this."* Then more angrily, *"Would you deny me vengeance for the cold-blooded slaughter of my parents?"* When she didn't reply, she heard his heavy sigh echoing throughout the regions of her mind. *"Forgive me."*

Before Allison could even began to wonder what those last words meant, his attack came, though not through any physical or magical means. There were no fiery balls of green death, no bolts of lightning, no daggers of power, or spelled steel. The attack was purely empathic and aimed at the deepest cores of her mind and soul.

An onslaught both images and emotions invaded her mind and body, filling them, saturating and possessing them, images of Lamia and people that were at first as alien as this world had seemed when she had first arrived. Allison felt herself cry out, was distantly aware that she was falling, and then the blocks to her true memories that Roderick had painstakingly created were painfully shattered, the fragments of dark energy seemingly slicing and imbedding themselves within her head under the sheer weight of the truth—and

Aidric's unmistakable love for her.

Through the pain, she remembered *everything*. Aidric, the king and queen, Raya, Selwyn, the twins, God help her, even Galen. She remembered that day within the Evrei Forest when Mordant had stabbed her in the guise of Aidric. She remembered the million-nails-jamming-in-her-head level of pain as Roderick ripped through her mind, the same excruciating pain she now felt as Aidric brutally did the same.

Gasping, Allison could only lie shell-shocked and helpless on the floor as the blinding pain became her whole world. She distinctly felt tears running down her face, but she couldn't even get enough air into her lungs to scream, denied even that release by the magic that imprisoned her mind and body.

As she lay there for what could have equally been seconds to days and the pain began to gradually fade, only one thought ran through her mind over and over as though stuck on infinate loop.

God, they were his real parents!

As though to further torment her, all the pieces abruptly began to fall into place—the story Aidric had spun her of his supposed family in Sersia, the story of the ill-fated prince of Lamia who had also lived in Sersia and had supposedly died. His unusual closeness to the king and queen. Even Diryan and Aidric themselves, though their hair and eyes were of different colors, bore strikingly similar features.

The shape of their faces, the same shape of the eyes and the same timbre of voice—the similarities were plain for any idiot who bothered to look closely enough to see them. She now knew why King Diryan's eyes had seemed so familiar when they had first met. They were Aidric's eyes! Everything fit so closely together that she, herself, must have been blind not to have made the connection earlier.

His parents, she thought with horror, *and I let Roderick kill them! I stood by and watched while Aidric pleaded with me to stop him! Aidric... Dear God, what have I done?*

But then, the menacing, mocking tones of Roderick's voice jolted her out of the pain and past images to the present, and in a panic, Allison remembered what Roderick intended to do—to end the House of Lasha. She opened eyes that suddenly seemed to weigh a ton in enough time to see him raise the sword slightly in readiness to either jab or slice it across his belly.

"I have waited a lifetime for this moment," Roderick purred, a smile of pure maniacal glee stretching his lips. "The throne and Mage-field of Lamia are mine!"

Ignoring the pain and disorientation within her mind, Allison frantically threw the strongest shield she could think of between Aidric and the blade, one which she had learned from the pages of the Golden Mage Spellbook that would deflect spelled weapons. More importantly, it was one that Roderick wouldn't expect because to his knowledge, if it was something mage-related and he didn't know about it, it wasn't possible.

There was a horrible screech when Roderick's sword impacted with the shield, almost like the sound of fingernails scraping across a chalkboard but amplified at least a hundred times. Sparks flew in every direction, but those effects paled in comparison to the howl of rage coming from Roderick's throat. Before she could lose the advantage of surprise, Allison sprang unsteadily to her feet and bowled Roderick over with a burst of power from her outstretched palms, sending him crashing into the far wall.

"You bastard!" Allison cried with rage as she hit him with yet another burst of power before the flash of the first was gone. Her body began to tremble with her wrath. There would be no sleep spell for Roderick. This man, she meant to kill.

All but one of Roderick's shields shattered under the impact, but before she could fling another spell at him, he called down lightning to stike her. The impact against her shields threw her off balance, but from the look of disgust on his face, it didn't have nearly the effect he had expected. She was already pelting him with a dozen fireballs even as as a boom that sounded as though the entire earth was cracking open nearly burst her eardrums. Unfortunately, the bastard had already reinforced his shields and they repelled her attacks instead of reducing him into a pile of ash.

Then several blasts from behind did succeed in knocking her to her knees. From the corner of her eye, Allison could see at least a dozen black-robed men advancing towards her. Roderick's mages had at last decided to join into the battle at the worst possible moment. Using that distraction, Roderick began an attack not on her, but on Aidric, who, in his weakness, was still as helpless as a newborn babe.

Without hesitation, Allison cast a deflection spell over Aidric's new shields while at the same time she encircled the mages in a wall of flames, the intertwined incantations of the two spells sounding like garbled nonsense but worked as intended, nonetheless. Double spellcasting, another gift from her spellbook. She would never forget the expression on Roderick's face before his own reflected spell slammed into his personal shields.

As Roderick staggered back into the wall, momentarily stunned, she abandoned her attack and sprinted over to where Aidric lay. He couldn't go on in such a helpless state and survive much longer. He needed strength and fast! Allison hastily fell onto her knees and placed her hands onto his head and gifted him with a portion of her own life-energy. She sensed that he wanted to protest, but wisely, he kept silent. This wasn't the time for them to get into an argument over her well-being!

Another series of blasts rocked them as she lifted her hands away, sent by the few mages who had miraculously managed to survive her fire assault. Yet her deflection spell remained soundly intact, the deflected spells of raw power, fire, and lightning destroying all but five of the remaining mages who realized the capabilities of the spell cast over their targets in enough time to prepare the proper defenses.

Then, as if a voice whispered it into her mind, Allison knew exactly what she had to do. Roderick had caused enough damage. It was time that she did a little damage of her own, damage only she had the power to create.

"Aidric, I need you to help me!" she cried urgently into his mind, her eyes fixed determinably on his own. *"I'm about to cast a spell that hasn't been seen since the creation of the Mage-fields. I need you to shield Diryan's councilors, yourself, and me with the strongest of your shields!"*

"But what do you plan to do?" Aidric asked anxiously, gripping her arms tightly.

"There's no time for explanations! Please Aidric, just do as I ask!"

Then without waiting to see if he would or not, Allison pulled out of his grip and rose to her feet again. Immediately, her eyes found and met Roderick's boldly. He must have sensed that something big was stirring as a wariness that was uncharacteristic of him lay within that golden stare. She was vaguely aware that Aidric had risen to stand beside her, but she didn't dare look away. Even so, his mere presence lent her a strength that no one else could have provided.

Please God, whether your name is Yahweh or Seni or both, don't let me make a mistake!

She had seen the spell she was about to attempt only once—when it had been magically imprinted into her mind during her initial encounter with the Golden Mage Spellbook. She only prayed that her grasp of Ti'ar was advanced enough to put to voice the translation of the English-worded spell.

Roderick had his hands on either side of his head, cursing her loudly and still trying to pull himself together after her last attack.

Allison quickly raised her hands into the air, closed her eyes, and shouted until her words echoed loudly throughout the Throne Room, "*Aeon Seni'ae mawn, lansanai ta marekanai dius allon!*" —By Seni's hand, light and magic we become!

There was no need to channel energy this time. For this particular spell, the incantation was all the guidance the energy of the Mage-field needed, the key that turned one particular law of magic on its head and opened the gates that usually kept a Mage-field's energy contained.

For a moment, there was only silence, her words heavy in the air like the foreboding echo throughout the courtroom of a judge's final, condemning words, but then a faint roar reached her ears, rapidly gaining in volume. At first, it sounded like a tornado bearing down on them from a distance, its roar swiftly crescendoing by the second as it neared. Allison shivered at the terrible roar and prayed that Aidric had accomplished the task she had set him.

Then there was no more time for thought as the room was suddenly—alive with light. That was the only way Allison could describe it. It was a light that didn't blind, a light full of warmth and a sense of power—*life*. She felt it all around her, felt it pressing insistently against her bodily shields, then against the shields on her mind, hungry for the entrance to her channels, but she knew it couldn't enter no matter how long it prodded at them. Despite his weakness, Aidric had done his job well.

"Allison, what have you done?" Aidric cried anxiously into her mind. His mind-voice dripped with fear.

"Vengeance," she answered simply, reaching over and grasping his hand tightly. She was surprised to find

that her hand was trembling.

Allison knew that Aidric would require no explanation when he witnessed what happened next.

At the appearance of the light, both Roderick and his mages had frozen in their spellcasting, each staring into the light as if seeing some terror only they could see. The light descended upon Roderick and his men and surrounded them. For a split-second, their shields became visible to the normal eye as the energy of the Mage-field began to tear into the shields that glowed with an eerie purple-yellow taint that reminded Allison immediately of sickness. If evil had a color, then it most certainly matched that of Roderick's and his dark-mages' shields. Effortlessly, the golden light shattered their shields that had undoubtedly been constructed with the Dark Powers, as fragile as soap bubbles when confronted by Seni's power.

Then the screams came, first Roderick's men, then Roderick himself, screams filled with unimaginable terror and pain as the light fell upon their unprotected bodies, seizing them like Seni's great hand of judgment. The light penetrated their bodies until they were merely a human silhouette of light, transforming them into a pure energy state much like what happens when traveling through a portal.

In a sense, what Allison had done was open a portal that swallowed everything in its path, but with this portal, there was no exit after the journey or reconstruction of the separated molecules. In this portal, the only destination was obliteration. In several brilliant flashes of light that forced her to briefly close her eyes, their life-forces were consumed and distributed throughout the light all around them, their souls destroyed.

Then, as abruptly as it had come, the light disappeared. Roderick and his men were gone, his black sword and the carnage he had wrought the only evidence that he had been there at all.

The proceeding silence was unnerving, suffocating, but thankfully it was shattered almost at once when first one sword, then several clattered to the floor. The dropping of the swords was followed a few seconds later by several Mihran soldiers who had miraculously been spared by the light dashing towards the doors as if Arioch, himself, was at their heels ready to steal them away into Ter-ob.

Upon seeing the soldiers, Allison eyes flitted around the room, suddenly worried that a few of Aidric's shields had been misguided. She caught sight of several men and women she recognized as Diryan's councilors and members of the Circle huddled together in little groups, and she breathed a sigh of relief when she saw that the magic had destroyed none that she hadn't intended. As to why the mage-field had spared these particular Mihrans, Allison had a feeling that it would forever remain a mystery.

As she turned her eyes to Aidric, who was still staring at the place where Roderick had stood mere seconds earlier as if he couldn't quite believe what his eyes had just seen, the elation she felt for Roderick's destruction vanished. It wasn't over—at least for her. Several more tasks still remained.

Allison stared at Aidric for a moment, tears beginning to well up in her eyes before she could stop them. However, before she allowed them to fall, she muttered a few Ti'ar words softly to herself and disappeared while Aidric was still distracted by his disbelief, heading for a confrontation that was long overdue.

CHAPTER TWENTY-EIGHT

About a couple hundred handspans from the wall, Selwyn's strength left him, and he and the Second went pitching to the ground, determination alone not enough to reach his destination. Gwidon was no longer conscious, his breathing slow and ragged. Selwyn knew that the man's will alone was what kept him alive. Tears of anger and defeat began to flow down his cheeks. He was so close! Only now did Selwyn truly understand Aidric's pain when his friend had realized that he didn't have the strength to reach Allison.

Suddenly, a shadow fell across him, and Selwyn turned startled eyes towards its source, frantically reaching for energy he no longer possessed. But the figure crouching down beside him wasn't the Mihran soldier he had expected. Dressed in robes of the blackest pitch, dark blue eyes stared down into his own from the darkness within the folds of the figure's hood.

For a heart-stopping moment, Selwyn forgot to breathe, thinking wildly that Death had come as a man to claim him. Slowly, gloved hands reached up and pulled the hood away. A face and hair equally as dark as his robes was revealed. Selwyn finally remembered to breathe. The man was Sononese, but more importantly, Sel realized that the cut of his robes was that of a healer.

"Please help him," Selwyn whispered hoarsely, unable to muster up enough strength to say more.

The man stared at him a moment longer, as if appraising him. Then without a word, he laid his hands onto Sel's forehead before he could flinch away, flooding his mind and body with a warm flow of healing energy that drove away his weariness and left in its wake a burst of renewed energy. The healer nodded with satisfaction as he removed his hands and quickly turned to Gwidon. Selwyn watched as the Sononese turned the Second over until he was resting on his back. He then tore the fabric of Gwidon's uniform away from the wound, and laid his hands onto the damaged flesh.

"The wound is deep and has damaged vital organs," he said abruptly a moment later in heavily accented Lamian. Again he fixed Selwyn with those eyes of blue flame. "I promise you nothing."

Selwyn nodded, unable to find his voice. What was it about this man that made him feel so overwhelmed?

He was so intent on the healer and patient that at first, Sel didn't notice the faint roar that had begun to fill the air above the distant sounds of battle, his subconscious most likely dismissing the sound as just another of the battle. Only when a flash of light appeared at the edges of his vision did he tear his eyes from the pair and look towards the wall and the palace beyond. With a start, he realized that the roar he heard wasn't coming from the battle below but from the palace.

Selwyn gasped as he saw a bright, golden light envelope the palace, pouring into its every crevice until nothing of its outer walls remained revealed. Something huge was happening within the palace, maybe the very thing that would finally bring the Prophecy of the Golden Mage to a close.

Sel tuned back to the pair, intending to point out to the healer what he saw, but his words froze on his lips, instantly forgotten. His breath caught sharply. Second Gwidon sat where only moments before he had lain a breath away from death, staring at him with eyes and a stony expression that were so like General Caith's.

Although his uniform was torn and still stained with his blood, the wound was gone—there wasn't even the slightest hint of a scar—and the Second looked as fresh and ready for battle as he had when they had first set out beyond the palace walls. There was no sign of the mysterious Sononese healer.

"My thanks, Lord Selwyn Phelannik," Gwidon said sincerely, his eyes softening a bit. "You have a greater courage than I think even you realize, and I'll not be quick to forget what you've done for me and Lamia today."

Sel thought to ask Gwidon what had become of the Sononese healer, but a little voice inside told him sternly to let it be, that it was a place he didn't wish to go.

Gwidon glanced over to the now illuminated palace. Sel thought that he saw a faint smile touch the Second's lips, but he wouldn't have staked his life on it.

"I believe that the battle within has been fought and won," the new Arms-general of Lamia said curtly. He rose to his feet and held out a hand to an astonished Selwyn. "Come, my friend. One last battle remains, and this time, we shall be victorious!"

***

Aidric could scarcely believe what Allison had done. Roderick was gone. The filthy bastard that had tormented them for so long was gone within the blink of an eye, converted into Mage-field energy like the legendary Natian twins, Rhan and Reznik, had been converted by the Natian Six centuries ago. How was it possible? How in Seni's name had she gained that kind of knowledge in such a short time? From what source?

Then all thoughts were erased from his mind when his eyes fell on the slumped figures of Diryan and Ileanna—his parents—still bound to their throne seats, as lifeless as a grisly set of ragdolls. With a choked sob, Aidric stumbled up to the dais and frantically began to tug at the leather straps around his father's abdomen. Diryan's smoky-blue eyes, now filmed over with death, seemed to stare at him accusingly, as if even in death his body demanded to understand why this tragedy had been allowed to happen. Hastily, Aidric ran his hand over Diryan's eyes to close them.

"For the love of Seni, please help me get them down!" Aidric cried to no one in particular, but all of Diryan's councilors, even Horae Adorjan, rushed forward to oblige him, none of them uttering a single word.

The king and queen were carried down from the dais and laid out side-by-side onto the silver and blue carpet. Except for the ghastly wound on Ileanna's neck—which Ion immediately covered with his own *sholkie* handkerchief—and the blood staining their clothing, it appeared as if the royal couple were merely sleeping peacefully.

The sight of them that way was too much for Aidric. He collapsed onto his knees beside Ileanna with a moan that sounded as if it had been wrenched from his throat and threw himself over both their bodies, sobbing with all the grief of the world. He couldn't believe it. They were dead—dead! He would never visit Diryan's study again and see him look up with annoyance at the interruption, never hear Diryan's voice scolding him for yet another bout of foolishness. He would never hear the sweet sound of Ileanna's laugh, hear her gentle voice comforting him.

Aidius, Aidius—he killed them! He killed them! And I was powerless to stop him. My Lord Seni—why did this have to happen—

Aidric didn't know how long Lord Ion had been calling his name, but it was the sound of the Seneschal's voice that finally brought him back to the Throne Room from his world of grief. Wearily, he raised his head from Diryan's chest and fixed his eyes on the Seneschal. He saw his own grief mirrored in

Ion's eyes. Diryan had meant a great deal to Ion, but unlike Aidric, propriety didn't allow him his tears, at least not in public. The Seneschal had to be strong in the face of tragedy. The Seneschal did not cry.

"Milord—Mage-general?" Ion said, the latter title with enough hesitation to show his uncertainty.

Then it suddenly dawned on him.

Aidius, they know! They know!

Feeling as if he had been slapped, Aidric abruptly realized that all his father's councilors had circled him, gazing down at him with the same uncertainty, the same bewildered questioning in their eyes. *Seni help me, I am the king now!*

Reading his expression, or maybe even his thoughts, Horae Adorjan nodded once, slowly.

"Yes, young Mage-general, young *prince*," the stress on the word prince not missed by Aidric or anyone else, "you are now indeed the new king of Lamia."

Aidric shook his head in denial. No, he couldn't be king. He wasn't *ever* supposed to be king. He was a mage. He was the son that should never have been.

"My dear child, did you honestly believe the Brothers in Divinity ignorant of your true heritage?" Horae Adorjan asked gently, placing a comforting hand on Aidric's shoulder. "Did you believe it possible for a mageborn son of the monarchs of Lamia to have undoubtedly escaped the notice of the Order of the

Providence? Of his Eminence, the High Priest?"

"But—all this while—you said nothing—hinted *nothing*—" Aidric stammered.

"Yes," Horae Adorjan said solemnly. "Though by our own divine laws, your very existence is a crime, but as Seni willed it, it was meant to be—the mageborn prince of parents whose blood was completely devoid of any magical potential. With you, with this new revelation, today the law that has governed Lamia's royal offspring for centuries has come to an end, and I'm proud to say that you have proven yourself more than worthy to wear the crown of the kingdom of eternal sorrow."

"But why were the king and queen never told?" Aidric demanded angrily. "My parents suffered every day from the moment I first entered this world and it was discovered that I bore the mark of the mageborn, wanting to show their affections for their son but denied that pleasure that so many others take for granted for fear of discovery! Now they have gone to their g-graves," his voiced cracked, "without ever having experienced the freedom of naming me son where my ears and others could hear!"

"The kingdom wasn't ready to accept, Aidric," Horae Adorjan replied patiently, unaffected by the anger in Aidric's voice. "The public announcement of the Temple's acceptance of your birth would have caused shock in the kingdom, perhaps even unrest. Some would have even thought 'if one divine law has been broken without consequence, why then can we not break another?' It was a dangerous situation during dangerous times. Thus, it had to be handled delicately, and I'm proud to say that Diryan and Ileanna couldn't have done a better job of it. You are the rightful heir to the throne, Aidric, and now, through all you have done for this kingdom, the people will not be loath to accept you as such."

The Horae's words made too much damned sense for Aidric's peace of mind. People did tend to dislike change and were slow to adjust if they didn't outright rebel against it as had almost happened during his great-grandfather's time. But Seni help him, this wasn't the time for him to deal with his sudden elevation in stature, the sudden burden lifted onto his shoulders. Not now. Maybe in a few days, but not now.

Then, with a start as his mind frantically rebelled against the Horae's words, Aidric realized that he hadn't seen Allison for some time now. In his grief for his parents, he had forgotten all about her—and all that she had been through while in that bastard's hands. A quick glance around the room proved what he already suspected. She was gone.

The Council looked down at him expectedly, as if

they waited for him to make a proclamation. He couldn't bear it—their questions, their demands. No, he couldn't deal with any of it now, not when all he could think about at the moment was Allison. Where in all of Seni's World was she?

Aidric suddenly sprung to his feet with more vitality than he thought he was capable of, and he grabbed the front of the Seneschal's tunic, causing him to squawk in the most undignified manner. His injured ribs instantly blazed with pain, but he ignored them.

"Allison has disappeared! Did you see her leave, Ion? Where has she gone?"

"I don't know!" Ion cried. "The Golden Mage was one moment standing next to you, the next, she just—vanished."

"What do you mean, she 'vanished'?" Aidric demanded.

"As I said, Your M-Majesty," Ion replied nervously, stumbling over the formality while Aidric winced inwardly upon hearing it.

Not now—I cannot bear this right now.

"She vanished as though she had cast an invisibility spell over herself, but Milord Aidric, I was staring right at her—we all were!" Several heads bobbed in agreement. "I *knew* she was there, and she just vanished!"

Aidric had heard enough. It seemed as if Allison

had learned more than he had imagined, and with a sinking feeling that bordered on Foresight, he understood only too well what it was she planned to do.

"I must find her," he said. "I've already lost two people whom I loved dearly. I'll be damned first to the six hells before I'll willingly lose another!"

Then amidst their protests, Aidric began to construct a portal.

CHAPTER TWENTY-NINE

At first, Allison saw nothing but darkness when she appeared at her destination. Yet, she instantly knew she had arrived in the right place and that *he* was there. Her empathic senses registered surprise and a little fear within the room even before her eyes found the faint illumination behind her, before she turned and saw Master Kiryl sitting in the center of the room exactly where she and Aidric had left him with more questions than answers a little over a year ago, his features illuminated by a single blue mage-flame-lit candle before him.

Strange, that now as she looked down at him, the Seer no longer seemed so powerful, so intimidating, but maybe even a bit frail. This time, the alienness of the place didn't cloud her mind, and she now saw what had always been there to see.

Kiryl rose slowly to his feet, his eyes locked warily on hers. He still said nothing. She could only stare at him, rising fury muting the accusations on her lips. The Providencen priest must have then seen something disturbing in her eyes because he suddenly took a couple of involuntary steps back, his eyes now betraying his rising fear.

That was his first mistake. His movement was like the catalyst before the storm, shattering the fragile intensity between them. With a cry of rage, Allison charged him, snatching a handful of his silver robe in both her fists—and not so incidentally managing to grab a good chunk of his long hair—before the Seer knew what was happening.

She could feel his fear, hear it in the rapid beating of his heart, the harshness of his breathing. She even imagined she could taste it in the thickness of the air around them. His fear only served to infuriate her more.

"You bastard!" Allison cried. "You knew didn't you? You *knew*!"

Kiryl could only stare at her with widening eyes, helpless as a fly caught in a spider's web. He opened his mouth, but no sound emerged. Where was his confidence now? Where was his smug arrogance? His amusement?

Beyond the room, Allison could hear the distant sounds of men shouting, of pounding footsteps. So, *Master* Kiryl had called on his Brothers for help after all. That could be remedied easily enough. Her confrontation with Master Kiryl left no room for interruption.

With a low, melodious hum and a series of elaborate gestures that would've made Keldan proud, Allison constructed a barrier of music that would allow no soul to enter the room other than another bardic-mage who had the power to break it. Within seconds, she could hear several men banging on the door, followed by numerous mage blasts. Their efforts were futile.

"Child, in the name of Seni, release me!" Kiryl commanded sternly, though he made no physical effort to free himself from her death-grip.

"I won't!" Allison replied heatedly. "I saw it in your eyes, in your secretive manner, that you were hiding something vital from me, but back then, I was too timid and overwhelmed by the alienness of this place and you, too scared to demand answers. You *knew* this, playing with my frustrations by allowing me to see that you had the knowledge of this secret! You *enjoyed* my discomfort!"

"I could not—it was Seni's will—" he stammered.

"Seni's will my ass!" Allison raged. "It was *your*

will that refused to tell me everything that you knew would happen. Dammit, back then you knew that I would fall into Roderick's hands! You knew he would corrupt my mind, steal the memories that I cherished and turn me against those I loved!"

She was suddenly crying, and for once, she didn't care that another, a stranger, saw her tears.

"You *knew*, you bastard, and you said *nothing*!" she sobbed. "And because of you, I allowed innocent people to be murdered in cold blood. Oh God help me, I stood by and *watched* Roderick slaughter the king and queen—Aidric's *parents*. His parents! They loved me, cared for me as if I was their own daughter, and in the end, I betrayed their love, their trust! I could've stopped Roderick, but I did nothing! Dear God, it's all my fault they're dead!"

Allison flung the Seer from her in disgust, as if touching even his robe would contaminate her. Master Kiryl stumbled back and then fell, rather undignified, onto his backside. Wisely, he didn't try to rise or speak.

She slowly lowered her hands until they dangled lifelessly at her sides. Then just as methodically, she collapsed onto her knees and buried her face into her hands. "Dear God, I even went willingly to Roderick's bed!" she cried. "You knew I would, *Gashae*!"

He winced at the name as if hearing it had caused him actual physical pain. There was something akin to shock in his eyes. Allison didn't know why she had called him such a strange name, but instinctually knew that it was appropriate without his negative reaction. The word's meaning lay at the edges of her memory, just beyond her grasp.

"You let him defile me as he willed," Allison continued to rage, "let him destroy everything that I had held sacred with Aidric! You let him destroy our love!" Slowly, she lowered her hands from her face and glared at him with accusing eyes. "You knew, and you didn't even warn me," she whispered brokenly.

For a few moments, silence fell over the room, only interrupted now and again by the sounds of the Seers trying to break her spell and her silent crying. When Kiryl finally spoke, at first, Allison thought she had imagined hearing the sound of his voice because it was so low.

"Yes, I knew," Master Kiryl admitted softly, his voice flat and emotionless, "but it's not that simple, Allison McNeal. There is much that you do not comprehend. The path you have taken was the destiny you were born to live. It is unchangeable, lest Seni wills it so. There is reason even in this tragedy, although we do not yet understand it. We Seers Foresee what Seni wills, are burdened with visions of the future, and we give aid when given leave. Remember, this world was given to us to do with as we may, and in it, it is for us to strive to prove our worth so that we are rewarded with entrance beyond Aidius's Gates into the Thrones.

"A cataclysm larger than any before it awaits us, Allison McNeal, and this is but a small piece you have played. The larger whole is yet to come. You have become stronger in this tragedy, stronger than the diffident, frightened child that Aidric Stanisnik *Lasha* first brought before me those many moons ago. Remember, there is reason even in tragedy."

"I don't want to hear any more of that crap!" Allison cried, covering her ears as she had when Diryan had forced her to face the truth of what Roderick had done to her. "Prophecies, the end of the world—none of that matters now because my world has already ended! It ended the moment I betrayed Aidric! It ended the moment I betrayed Diryan and Ileanna! It ended the moment I betrayed myself!"

The last image she carried with her as she magicked herself to her final destination was the look of utter confusion on Master Kiryl's face. Someone who had been cut off from emotion and life for most of his existence would never understand her pain. Maybe in the end, it was better that way.

***

Selwyn could scarcely believe it.

Standing beside Second Gwidon and the So-nonese general, he watched in bewilderment as more than a dozen Mihran soldiers cautiously approached them side-by-side in a single line, helmless, weapons sheathed and intertwined hands held forward in the Natian sign of truce. At his back, Sel could feel the tension of the Lamian soldiers assigned to protect their new Arms-general as the enemy approached, his empathic senses easily reading their anticipation, suspicion, and underneath, a vague sense of hope.

The soldiers stopped a respectable distance away from them, but it was close enough for Sel to see their eyes, some haunted, others terror-stricken, and a couple seemingly struggling at the brink of madness.

At their appearance, the battle had slowly come to an uncertain halt as more and more Mihran and Bar'tain soldiers had witnessed their comrades' shocking display. These soldiers, Selwyn knew, were Roderick's personal guard by the stylized golden eyes on their left breast that everyone knew to be the insignia of Roderick's House. Sel had watched these very men enter the palace with Roderick and Allison as he lay paralyzed beneath the eyes of his captors. He was certain that he wasn't the only one that had taken note of the golden eyes.

For a few breathless depths, Lamian Arms-general and Mihran soldiers stared at one another,

Gwidon's face, as always, betraying no emotion. It was impossible to determine what he was thinking. Then abruptly, the entire line of enemy soldiers reached for their swords. The Lamian soldiers at Sel's back instantly stepped forward to defend their general, but Gwidon immediately held up a staying hand.

Only then did Selwyn realize that the Mihran soldiers were relinquishing their weapons, one by one tossing them into a pile a few handspans before the Lamian Arms-general. The clanging of steel echoed preternaturally loud in the stillness all around them. Then even more shockingly, the sixteen men proceeded to kneel before them in deference, heads bowed, all but the center-most man.

"The Light has sent us," the soldier said in Mihran in a voice that didn't sound quite sane, "sparing our lives in order that we may bring word of King Roderick's defeat by the Golden Mage."

He reached into his tunic and pulled something from within, stretching it above his head where all could see. The air was instantly filled with numerous gasps and curses. It was the Natian silver cloth of surrender. Then calmly, the soldier tossed it before the two Arms-generals, and proceeded to kneel in capitulation.

Total mayhem erupted at the silent proclamation.

Every Bar'tain soldier immediately regrouped and began their retreat. Many bands of Mihran soldiers simply broke and ran. Yet Gwidon didn't give the command to follow.

Selwyn, nevertheless, was surprised at the sheer number of Mihran soldiers who had thrown down their weapons and had sunk to their knees in surrender. Without Roderick's threats to drive them, the will to fight had abruptly left these men. Several cheers rang out among the Lamians—what remained of them. The battle had finally come to an end.

As the two generals began to oversee the handling of their newly acquired prisoners, Selwyn finally allowed himself to think of his wife again. Where in all of Seni's lands was she? He had last seen Raya in the watchtower near the palace gates, but that had been in the first few sand-marks of the battle. Plus, everyone had seemingly disappeared from them sometime before the Mihrans had stormed the palace.

He could still feel her presence strongly within himself, but no matter how hard he looked among those who had fought, she had not appeared among them. He decided that the watchtowers were as good of place as any to begin his search.

The going was slow. He had to force his way across the bodies of Lamians and enemies alike who had fallen. Sel gritted his teeth and refused to let himself really see the carnage all around him beyond a glimpse as he carefully avoided tripping or stepping on them. He was dangerously close to losing not only the contents of his stomach but what remained of his sanity as well. Still, he forced himself to glance at every twisted face, knowing that Raya's could be one of them.

Praise Seni that he finally reached the wall without finding Raya among those who had fallen. He circled around the palace to the watchtower next to the gates. Twisted and scorched where Roderick's mages had finally succeeded in blasting them open, the still smoking gates lay open and unguarded in invitation. He seemed to be the only living soul around.

To his horror, Selwyn immediately spotted Raya within the tower, lying unmoving amidst a pile of bodies, her face pale and blank. With an anguished cry, Selwyn raced to her side and roughly shoved the bodies of fallen mages aside.

Aidius, Aidius, she can't be dead! Seni help me, she can't be dead! I feel her, *dammit! I feel her! We aren't like those others!*

Sel was sobbing as he cradled her limp body in his arms. Her skin was as cold as ice. He couldn't find a pulse. Desperately, he reached for her emotions, any emotion that might prove to him that she was still alive.

Nothing.

"Raya, dear Seni, *no!*" he wailed like a man dying.

Suddenly the world had turned dark. He could no longer breathe. He could no longer feel anything save grief. His life, his other half of his soul, was gone from him forever.

So lost in his grief, it was a long time before he noticed that golden eyes were staring up at him in confusion. He could only stare back at her, not daring to believe that his eyes weren't deceiving him.

"Whatever are you crying for?" Raya chided softly, her voice weak, but nonetheless, *alive*.

Selwyn let out a choked cry and immediately bombarded her face and lips with kisses.

"Seni help me, I thought you were lost," Sel whispered between kisses. "You were so cold, and your heart was still—what in Seni's name happened to you?"

Raya frowned, pulling back from him. "I'm not certain. The last I remember was seeing Allison edging towards Keldan, and then nothing."

Allison—

Suddenly, the answer was clear. Blinded by grief, Selwyn had ignored the obvious. "You were spelled to sleep," he declared. "There's no other logical explanation. Only a strong sleep spell could so thoroughly mask your vital signs. It looks as if Roderick wasn't able to steal her humanity after all."

"Then—we've won?" she asked, her voice filled with both uncertainty and cautious hope.

Sel hugged her closer. "We have. Roderick is dead, and what remains of his army have all surrendered. Of Allison, and the king and queen, I know no more than you. After over a decade of Roderick's tyrannies, it's at last finished. The lands have been set free."

For a long while, neither one spoke, content to hold each other in their arms and allow their presence and emotions to speak for them. Selwyn gazed out into the western horizon, his eyes far above the horrors left behind in the aftermath of the battle. A faint gray line stood against the horizon, and he instantly knew that it was the Sersian army, come belatedly of course to fight a battle already won.

"Would you look at that," he murmured into her hair.

"Hmm?" Raya turned her head towards where he pointed, and her eyes hardened. "*Now* they come," she said dryly.

And for some reason, Selwyn thought that was the funniest thing he had ever heard.

CHAPTER THIRTY

Everything was still when Allison appeared along the eastern border of Lamia, a few feet away from where the Lamian Shield had once stood. Without hesitation, she invoked Inner-sight and forced herself to stare at the gaping hole that stretched for several miles on either side of her—the hole that she had created.

The hole she must now mend.

For a moment, she closed her eyes, wanting to savor the feel of the cool breeze blowing against her face one last time with the sounds of nature around her, singing Her song despite the death and destruction that had occurred that day. Strange, that even in the shadow of tragedy, nature always seemed to sing itself back into the sunlight, its song always full of hope, never despairing.

When she sighed, it was a half-sob. The time had come. She could stall no longer. She had to repair the damage she had done, and there was only one way to do it.

Aidric, I'm sorry.

Allison opened her eyes and stared at the enormous hole for a moment before she raised her arms to begin the required spell. Her only regret was that her sacrifice wasn't near as noble as the sacrifice that ancient king of Jadwiga had taken in order for his people to live safe from the tyrannies of the outside world. The safety *she* had shattered because she hadn't been strong enough to face the truth of what Roderick had done to her.

Calmly, Allison opened her channels as wide as was possible and allowed the fiery fire of the Mage-field to fill her mind, her body, her very soul until she was nothing more than a shimmering being of light. Then, before she could feel afraid, she merged the Mage-field energy flowing within her to her own life-force until they became one.

She could feel her mind drifting, feel herself being lost to the personality of the light. Desperately, she fought the urge to surrender, to allow the power to consume her until nothing of herself remained. The

Golden Mage Spellbook had warned her that this would happen, so she was prepared to fight it. If she allowed herself to be consumed, then all she strove for to atone for her sins would be for nothing.

She forced her mind to concentrate on the English words of the incantation, to then begin the tedious task of translating them into the Ti'ar language. With the last of her willpower, she forced the words to her lips, forced herself to scream them aloud. There was no turning back now.

"Dine akanai ta lansou—"

Without warning, her mind exploded with light, her incantation frozen, unfinished, on her lips. Something had gone wrong. The magic was no longer controlled, had somehow gone rogue.

Frantically, Allison separated her life-energy from this rogue energy before it could consume her. She tried to fling it from her body, but it wouldn't obey. It wouldn't flow back into the Mage-field. Blocked—her channels had somehow been blocked with a shield that wasn't of her own making.

It was at that moment that she knew she was about to die, not in the aid of Lamia as she had planned, but because of a foolish mistake. Is this where Mordant had disappeared to?

Then she felt him, a presence so achingly familiar that had she been able, she would have wept. It was a presence that filled her mind with power, patiently taming the rogue magic to his will and pulling it into his own channels.

Allison must have been floating for a while because the next thing she knew, she lay limply in his arms, and he was on his knees in the soft grass. She had thought she would never again see his face or feel his arms around her.

And he was crying.

"Ah, foolish girl!" Aidric cried, hugging her body so fiercely against his own that for a moment, she couldn't breathe. "What you have almost done—Seni help me, what you must have been thinking!"

"You can't be here!" Allison cried despairingly, struggling to release herself from his iron-like hold. "Don't touch me! Don't look at me! You shouldn't have stopped me! You should have let me die!"

"No! *Never!*" Aidric said viciously. "If you attempt something so foolishly rash again, then you'll just have to take me with you! I've already lost two that I love, and I'll *not* lose you now!"

"But don't you see?" she cried. "I *killed* them! I did! It doesn't matter that it wasn't my hand that did it! You pleaded with me to stop Roderick, and yet I did nothing! *Nothing!* How can you bear to look at me? How can you bear to touch me after what I allowed *him* to do to me?"

Aidric kissed her then, so fiercely that his entire body quivered with reaction. At first Allison struggled, but the more she fought him, the more firmly he held her body to his, the more insistent his lips became. Finally, with a moan of anguish, she fell limp in his arms and surrendered herself to him, his passion, his grief, his desperation, until she was no longer certain where her own emotions ended and his began.

She began to cry, her tears intermingling with his own, her lips trembling against his. Aidric pulled back and lovingly brushed his lips against her eyes, forcing her to close them as he kissed her tears away.

"Nothing in the past matters now," he whispered tremulously into her ear. "I won't let it. Now that I have you in my arms again, my grief is no longer so unbearable. I feel that I can face the future instead of dread it. Somehow, little cat, you and I shall pick up the pieces and go on."

"Can w-we?" Allison asked quietly against his cheek. "I'm not sure I deserve to after—after everything that has—happened. The Lamians will hate me after everything I've done, and rightfully so!"

"Don't say that! It's *Roderick* whom they'll curse to the darkest pits of the six hells. It's *he* who has brought this misery upon us. *You* were as much a victim of this as we were. Remember that it was you who saved us all in the end, *you* who destroyed Roderick forever. Do you believe that they wouldn't acknowledge that? You are the savior of our land as the prophecy foretold. It was that bloody bastard who—murdered my parents. Not you. Believe it to be true as I believe it."

"But I could've saved them," she said brokenly, refusing to look at him.

"It wasn't Seni's will," Aidric said gently, unknowingly echoing Kiryl's earlier words.

"How can you say that?" Allison demanded raising her head to look at him incredulously. Immediately, she regretted her hasty words when she saw the amount of grief his eyes held, the pain he still endured—the pain he would always endure.

"Because I must," he answered with a sigh. Suddenly, he looked twice as old as his twenty-four years. "Throughout my life, I've endured more heartache than any ten mortal men should ever have to suffer, and yet, in the end, each time I accepted what fate had dealt me because it was what Seni willed. Each time I wanted to give up, and I longed for the release of death. However, each time I was given an excuse to live and endure. This time, it's *you* who is my best excuse to endure."

It was she who kissed him then, slowly, without any of their earlier urgency but with all the tenderness and passion. It felt good to savor the taste of his lips when she had thought she never would again.

His face brushed against the bruise on her cheek and she winced involuntarily. Until then, Allison had completely forgotten about the injury. Aidric felt her flinch away, and he pulled back. His eyes widened when, for the first time, he really looked at her and saw the darkening bruise on the side of her face. Having no mirrors handy, Allison could only imagine how ghastly she looked.

"Aidius!" Aidric exclaimed in more horror than she thought he should as he hesitantly touched her bruise. "Little cat, what happened to you?"

"Roderick hit me," she answered quietly.

Aidric snarled an oath in a language she didn't recognize, but the sentiment was quite clear. Allison suddenly thought that Roderick was one lucky bastard that he was dead, and Aidric could no longer get his hands on him. The rage in his eyes was more than murderous.

"Stay still," he commanded, his voice rough with angry. "I have enough energy to spare."

Before she could protest, he placed his hand gently onto her injury. She felt the familiar warmth of the healing energies seep into her cheek. Then her eyes suddenly watered as she felt the muscles of her cheek spasm with a sharp pain that quickly traveled up into her eye, feeling as if her cheek was being torn off and her eye plucked out of its socket. She let out a small cry, but she knew better than to move during a healing.

Almost immediately following the pain, the soothing warmth returned, numbing the pain away until she couldn't even feel the pressure of Aidric's hand against the tender flesh. A moment later, he removed his hand and smiled with satisfaction. The throbbing and tightness were gone from her face.

Allison raised her hand to her cheek and gingerly touched the skin. The huge knot was gone, along with the soreness. She was sure that if she had a mirror, she would see no trace of the disfiguring bruise.

"Thank you," she said softly. Then without hesitation, she placed her hands on his chest and said, "Now let me repay the favor."

Aidric smiled slightly and patiently suffered her healing in silence. He only winced a couple of times as she knitted the delicate bones of his ribs and healed the torn internal tissues around them. The entire process took only a few depths, but to her, it seemed as if she had been under her healing trance for sand-marks.

Allison sighed shakily as she removed her hands, still trembling with the aftershocks of rapture from the healing. She caught his gaze and said quietly, "I wish I could heal you of the dark spell that's still within you as easily."

His eyes widened slightly. "You know about

that?"

She nodded. "It may take some time, but I think I can break it."

"But *how* have you come about this sudden knowledge?" Aidric asked, his expression suddenly deathly serious. "Today, I've seen you perform magical feats that haven't been seen for centuries. How?"

Without hesitation, Allison said a few Ti'ar words, gestured accordingly, and the Golden Mage Spellbook appeared in her hands. "From this," she said simply and handed it to him.

He took the book, frowning down at the words on the front that were entirely alien to him. He opened the book and began to flip through the pages, his frown becoming more and more prominent by the moment.

"Obviously this is a spellbook," he said. "It resonates with magical energy, but it's written in neither Ti'ar nor Natian. The lettering is like none I've ever seen. What language is this?"

"My language," Allison replied, watching his expression closely. "English."

Aidric dropped the book as if it had suddenly burned him. "Seni be blessed," he breathed in an awed voice. "Are you saying that this is the Golden Mage Spellbook?"

"Yes."

"But—but, *where* under the Thrones did you find this?"

"Can you believe, in Roderick's library?" she said. "It was covered in at least twenty years of dust, so I think it's safe to say that he had no idea what it was."

"Roderick's library?" Aidric echoed in disbelief. "All this time, centuries of mystery and speculation, and it was in the Mihran palace all along!"

Allison shook her head. "I found it along with some of Domnae Nelek's books, so I'm pretty sure he brought it to Mihr. Lord knows where he found it."

"And now you have possession of it."

"No, *we* have possession," she corrected firmly. "I know the prophecy says that this book was meant for my eyes only, but why should I keep this to myself?" She sighed suddenly as Kiryl's warnings whispered within her mind. "This is, after all, only the beginning of what lies ahead. Your Prophecy of the Golden Mage came true. That means that there's a damned good chance that other prophecies will come true, too. It won't hurt to prepare for them now."

"You're right," he said gravely. "Today has been but a tiny rainstorm before the hurricane, and this war's casualties have depleted our army down to almost nonexistence. The lawns of the palace were nothing but a sea of corpses as far as the eye could see."

Suddenly Allison laughed gleefully. Aidric gripped her hand, a look of alarm flashing across his features.

She took both his hands in hers and said, "No, I haven't gone mad. I'm just happy, and maybe even a little smug." At his blank expression, she explained, "Most of the soldiers lying on the lawn, those along this border, and those in Avidon aren't dead. I merely spelled them asleep!"

"Asleep?" Aidric echoed dumbly.

"Asleep," she confirmed happily. "Roderick wanted them dead, but I couldn't bear to hurt anyone. He may have stolen my memories and changed them to suit his fancy, put a leash on my mind, but he didn't steal my sense of morality. So, I spelled them asleep. He never stopped in his cruelties to realize what I had done."

Aidric suddenly jumped to his feet, bringing her with him. He began to twirl her around, laughing ecstatically. "Thank Seni for your heart!" he said then hugged her close to him. "Because of you, there can be a little happiness for everyone in the face of this tragedy."

He then silenced any remark she would have made with a passionate kiss.

"Aidric, I have a question for you now," Allison murmured a moment later as she laid her head against his chest.

"Hmm?"

"How *did* you find me here?"

He pulled back a little and regarded her thoughtfully. "I just *knew*. Perhaps it was a touch of Foresight—Seni nudging me in the right direction—or something else entirely. I just knew I had to get here. Somehow, I found the strength to portal here." He suddenly grinned weakly. "Although I don't yet feel the consequences of what I did, I suspect you'll know when I do when it's you who will be carrying me back to the palace instead of the other way around. Perhaps Seni's good will will save me from such a humiliating fate. Imagine how tongues will wag when they see the new king of Lamia being carried in the arms of his chosen queen!"

"Queen? What—" *Did he mean—*

"Yes, queen," he said, suddenly looking serious again.

Aidric gently pulled away from her. He said a few Ti'ar words, gestured, and a ring suddenly appeared in his hand, a beautiful golden ring that held a breathtaking stone that was almost the color of blood. At the sight of it, Allison was sure that her heart had stopped.

"I am the sole remaining blood offspring of Diryan and Ileanna," Aidric explained matter-of-factly, "and because of my words before their—assassination, now those of the Council, including members of the Brothers in Divinity, know the truth. It seems as if the Temple knew of my true heritage all along, and Horae Adorjan has named me the rightful king of Lamia with High Priest Casimer's total blessings. It was Seni's will, they said, that the throne of Lamia be mine, and I can't possibly rule a kingdom without somebody at my side for support."

His eyes stared down at hers intently, lit with a fire—a blazing inferno—she had never seen in them before. She was certain that her legs were about to crumble beneath her.

"Do you recall the time I said so offhandedly that I believed you had been brought to this world for a reason other than to fulfill a prophecy?" he asked abruptly.

Allison could only nod, not trusting her voice. Surprisingly, she did remember such a time ages ago when they'd had their first conversation and that proclamation had been one of many of his assurances to a frightened, timid girl facing an unknown future for the second time.

"Well, I do believe that I've found that reason," Aidric said quietly, his eyes glistening as if with unshed tears. "Allison McNeal, I offer you my life-ring, half of my soul, for all eternity. Will you accept and become my wife, my queen, the other half of my soul to fill what I have gifted you?"

Aidric held out the ring to her, his hand trembling slightly in nervous anticipation.

She didn't hesitate. With fingers that equally shook, Allison accepted the proffered ring and clumsily slipped it onto her middle finger as Raya wore hers. The instant she released it, she felt a tightness and warmth around her finger as the ring magically melded to her flesh, and a slight wave of disorientation washed over her.

Then she felt *him*—a presence that filled a void she hadn't known existed within her, a void in which she would fill for him when her own life-ring was made and slipped onto his finger. Allison didn't need to feel the joy that instantly swelled within him. Aidric's feelings were quite clear when she gazed into his eyes and saw not only the flames, but once again, the burst of radiant light she had often seen in them before this tragedy had begun—a light she had never thought to see again.

Allison threw her arms around him, and embraced him with more feeling than she ever thought she could feel for another. "Yes!" she cried, the sum of her feelings, her love, and her joy, expressed in that single word. "Yes, for now and for all eternity!"

At last she had found her true place, a place where she was wanted, a place where she was no longer the outsider, but more importantly, she had found a place where she would never be alone again.

As if on cue, somewhere in the distance, a single bird began to sing.

***

In the silence of the Chamber of Worship, Ans-domnae Eban watched his legions of Domni, along with the Senini, the Seers, and Horae, bowed in prayer before the High Priest. He could feel the energy they emitted while they prayed for the souls of Lamia and Mihr in the aftermath of such a devastating war. Such power—and soon it would be at his fingertips to use as he pleased. The first hurdle had been cleared. Now elevated to Ans-domnae and the only living witnesses of what he truly sought bound by silence or madness, Eban was well on his way to accomplishing his ultimate goal.

Only one obstacle now remained, one that would take all the cunning he had. When he was at last acknowledged as High Priest, then all of Seni's lands would be under his boot.

Eban needed only to bide his time.

EPILOGUE

The stranger in the hooded cloak of darkness watched the happy couple from the shadows of the forest and shook his head in disgust. How could he have misjudged things so badly? The pattern he had woven so carefully should not have unraveled so easily.

His mistake had been in not realizing the extent of the emotional bond the Mage-general of Lamia and the Golden Mage shared, a bond he knew was now virtually impossible to break. That fool mage-king of Mihr had tried and failed. One empathic sending and Aidric had shattered what had taken Roderick sandmarks of intricate spells and mind-magic to accomplish.

He had emerged too early, he realized. The time

of alignment was still too distant, Seni's power too great. He must be patient now. He must remain hidden within the shadows and be content to be the unseen observer. There was still one last thread of his web intact within Seni's World and one other who would soon be woven together with that thread to begin the pattern anew.

What was time to him?

ABOUT THE AUTHOR

C.G. Garcia lives in a small West Texas town whose claim to fame is having the world's largest Rattlesnake Round-Up. She has a degree in computer science, but due to life's twisted sense of humor, ended up working in a pharmacy. A lifelong lover of all things fantasy, science fiction, paranormal and romance, she is also the author of the *Fractured Multiverse* urban fantasy/science fantasy series and the *Old Souls* epic fantasy series.

THE PROPHECY OF THE SIX
BOOK ONE
Coming Fall 2016

www.ingramcontent.com/pod-product-compliance
Lightning Source LLC
Chambersburg PA
CBHW031413240626
47154CB00001B/13